I0664210

Published by Bru E-books

Word Count: 96,283

This is a work of fiction. Names, characters, places and incidents are either the product of the author's imagination or used fictitiously. Any resemblance to actual persons, living or dead, business establishments, locales, or events is entirely coincidental.

ISBN: 978-1-926467-25-2

Cover Art by Trifle Ink Design

trifleinkdesign@gmail.com

Published works up to August 2020:

Escape Through Time Series:

Timeless Knights

Her Place in Time

Time For Magic

Winsome Regency Romances:

The Black Duke

That Wicked Earl

The Melancholy Marquess

Untamed

The Villager's Conspiracy

Christmas Cracker Romances (Time Travel Romances):

The Christmas Cracker

A Viking Christmas

Stand alone books:

An Angel for Julian

(Formerly Julian's Chance)

(A contemporary angel romance.)

Jessica L. Jackson

Pemberley Haunted

(A Pride and Prejudice Continuation.)

A Witch For Mr. Darcy

(A Pride and Prejudice Variation)

Look Behind You Series:

Dance With Me

(Formerly Come Dance With Me)

Watch Your Step

Remember to Breathe

Summer Starter Set

(includes the first book in each of my three series.)

A compilation of short stories written as Jessica Lund:

Waiting for the Master

Lizzy's Curious Talent

By

Jessica L. Jackson

Jessica L. Jackson

Something magical happens every time Miss Elizabeth Bennet paints or sketches an image. However, she cannot control how her talent is revealed in her art. Lizzy is determined to live as an independent lady and needs her talent to provide the income for her dream. But, she has to be so very, very careful that no one discovers her secret.

Mr. Fitzwilliam Darcy wants Miss Bennet, a notable artiste, to paint a portrait of his beloved sister, Georgiana, and he is willing to pay handsomely. She, however, refuses to paint adults. He does not understand her reluctance. Darcy is determined to discover whatever it is that Miss Bennet is hiding.

Dedication

I must thank my family for their support in my writing. Also, I have drawn upon memories of playing cards with many of them over the years: Norwegian whist with any three other family members who would join in, as well as crib, and Chinese crib, with my grandmother, my mother, and my siblings.

I spent many hours playing cards with my best friend, Susan Lunn. I taught her Chinese crib and she taught me how to play crib-to-lose. She died in a car accident while I was writing this book and I have honored her with a place in my story for her game. She was a great friend and a wonderful supporter of my writing. She was the type of friend who always told the truth but was never unkind about it. Everyone needs a friend like that. I miss her immensely. God bless her and keep her eternally. Until we meet again…

I would also like to thank the staff of the National Trust in England for assisting me in the dimensions of the nave window of Fountains Abbey in Yorkshire. I asked the question and they scrambled all hands to discover it. Well done.

Jessica L. Jackson

Jessica L. Jackson

Chapter One

London...

Mr. Fitzwilliam Darcy waited in a small parlor while Lady Smith-Roy fetched the painting of her spaniels. The butler entered with a glass of sherry and a plate of ratafia biscuits for his refreshment. Darcy thanked him and the servant left him alone once more.

Darcy sipped his sherry and frowned, thinking. He had come to London specifically to view the painting, for he wanted his sister, Georgiana, to sit for a portrait. On no account was she to sit for a male artist.

Unfortunately, professional female painters could not be found. His only hope was Miss Elizabeth Bennet, a lady from Hertfordshire, who lived with her brother-in-law and sister. Her name could be heard bandied about select London drawing rooms as a true artiste.

"She has talent," one matron had praised, her nose stuck in the air. "I knew it the moment I saw her painting of my two little ones. They never looked so angelic. I do not know how she managed to get them to sit still for her."

"True, true," another said. "And so much the lady, too."

This had sounded promising to Darcy. He would not abide a vulgar person around his sister. He had been greatly disappointed in Mrs. Younge, Georgiana's former companion, who had permitted his sister—nay, encouraged her—to meet his former friend, George Wickham, on the sly. Fortunately, his sweet sister, who had very little guile, had told him of her love for that despicable man, who had been pressuring her to run away and marry him. Darcy recalled with grim satisfaction his scotching of that affair.

"Here it is, Mr. Darcy," Lady Smith-Roy said, entering the parlor. She was a deep-bosomed woman of middle years, fond of wearing a preponderance of ostrich feathers. A footman followed, carrying a framed painting, its back to the room. They both stopped short. "Why, sir, what can be the matter? You look positively furious."

Darcy straightened and smoothed out his expression. "Do I?" He bowed his shoulders. "I beg your pardon. Are these your spaniels?"

She raised an eyebrow. "Indeed. Peter, please hold it so my darlings are illuminated by the light from the windows."

"Yes, m'lady," the footman murmured.

The afternoon light fell upon a truly remarkable image of two black-and-tan spaniels sitting on a vast wine-colored velvet cushion, staring adoringly upward and to the right.

"Heavens," Darcy murmured, blinking rapidly in his surprise. He had never seen their like. So animated. Their eyes…the lift of one ear. Every brushstroke spoke volumes.

"I know precisely what you mean, sir," Lady Smith-Roy said, smiling broadly. "Somehow, Miss Bennet has managed to capture them at their absolute best. Scruff still has his torn ear, but instead of looking, well, scruffy, he looks noble, does he not? And Dandelion's personality, which is sunny and easygoing, seems to shine forth from her image." She shook her head. "I *know* they are not perfect in reality, but…"

"…they look perfectly innocent," Darcy finished for her.

She turned from the painting and stared at him. "Yes, that is it precisely. They look perfectly innocent. But such scamps, they are, every day. They get into so much trouble, I promise you."

He realized he had to force himself to look away from the dogs. If Miss Bennet could capture his Georgiana just as well, then he would pay a small fortune for the result.

"Pray, are Miss Bennet's portraits just as fascinating?" Darcy asked.

"I must warn you, Mr. Darcy, that Miss Bennet only paints children." Lady Smith-Roy waved the footman away and he left the parlor. "She is quite particular about it. I believe the oldest child who has sat for her was twelve. Dear Georgiana must be seven and ten, is she not?"

"You are correct," Mr. Darcy replied, frowning at her caution. "Perhaps, Lady Smith-Roy, if you were to write me a letter of introduction, I may be able to persuade Miss Bennet to make an exception. I am willing to pay handsomely for her efforts. She does take payment, does she not?"

His hostess tilted her head and keenly examined his expression. She cleared her throat before she spoke. "Yes, she does. I do not scruple to tell you that though she lives comfortably with her elder sister, she was not left well situated after her parents' death. Now that you have seen her work, you must perceive the monetary value of her talent. If you mean to…to lord it over her that she earns an income from her painting, then I will not give you an introduction."

Darcy stiffened, suddenly furious that anyone would think his honor depended on belittling others. He glared at Lady Smith-Roy. She did not flinch. She merely raised an eyebrow.

"You forget, Mr. Darcy, that I was acquainted with your father. He could put one out of countenance with only a glance. Your heavy brow will not intimidate *me*," she stated tartly.

Darcy bowed and relaxed his expression into a slight smile. "I beg your pardon, my lady. I am insufferable, as anyone can tell you. I swear, however, that I will not give Miss Bennet any reason to regret accepting a commission from me."

Lady Smith-Roy sniffed and relented. "Luckily for you, you have your mother's smile. Very well, I will write you the letter. Miss Bennet is away from Hertfordshire for a few months. She told me that she means to travel into Yorkshire with her sister and brother-in-law. I do not know her itinerary, except that they mean to visit the great houses and some of the more impressive ruins of the county. You may have to wait until she returns home before you contact her."

Darcy bowed his shoulders in gratitude for her information. "You are too kind. Thank you."

"You may have to find a little more charm if you expect to convince Miss Bennet to paint Georgiana," she said, and left him alone again to write the introductory letter.

∞

North Riding, Yorkshire…

"Lizzy, you promised," Jane Bingley said reproachfully. "I can see already that you have not constrained yourself."

Lizzy set her new painting on the display easel in the private parlor of the Yorkshire inn that enjoyed their patronage. She stepped back to survey it, still wearing the all-encompassing beige smock that covered her pretty blue and white striped day dress from her neck to the floor. Her brother-in-law, Charles Bingley, rose from the chair beneath a window and joined them.

"Oh, dear," he said, shaking his head and clasping his hands behind his back. He rocked on his heels. "Hmm."

"You swore you would confine your efforts to painting birds," Jane reminded her.

Lizzy pointed at the small gray and black bird in the corner. "There is a jackdaw."

Her sister sighed. "It is not even a quarter of an inch tall."

"She is correct," Bingley said, leaning over to inspect the bird. "I can hardly tell it is a jackdaw. It is the scale, of course. The main subject is impressively huge."

"I could not help myself," Lizzy admitted, sinking onto a padded bench and studying the painting. "The remains of Fountains Abby are magnificent, are they not?"

"Indeed," Bingley said, staring at the ruins painted in vivid, watercolor detail. "You have caught one of those awe-inspiring windows perfectly." He looked conscious. "I cannot remember which part of the Abby contains that window. I am sorry."

"It is of no consequence, my dear," Jane said, patting his arm. "The ruins are vast."

In softly spoken wonder, Lizzy observed, "Imagine what that window must have looked like before it was destroyed."

"There is no need for us to *imagine* anything," Jane replied in an almost tart voice. "You have painted it there for all to see."

Lizzy cocked her head to one side and tore her gaze away from the image on the paper. She blinked at her elder sister. Jane sounded put-out. And, Lizzy had to confess, she had reason to be.

Placatingly, she said, "Jane, dearest, there is nothing to fear here. Anyone who sees this painting will merely think I have indulged in a flight of fancy. No one alive can say what the window actually looked like before it was destroyed."

Bingley pinched his bottom lip and glanced between his wife and his sister-in-law. "She is correct, my dear. The image is quite unexceptionable. Beautiful, as always."

"Thank you, Charles," Lizzy murmured, keeping her focus on her beloved sister.

Jane's shoulders slumped. "Of course, it is beautiful. Your paintings are always exceptional."

Lizzy lips twisted into a crooked smile and she looked down at her folded hands where flecks of paint indicated the nature of her occupation all morning.

"The painting is not finished," she admitted softly, steeling herself for Jane's remarks.

"Are you certain?" Bingley asked, frowning. "It appears to be finished, though I am no judge."

"I saw more," Lizzy confessed and she watched Jane's eyes widen. Wistfully, she continued. "The abbey really was quite magnificent. I wish you could have seen it. But I knew you would object, dearest, and I stopped myself from continuing."

"Thank the good Lord for that," Jane said on a sigh. "We will hang it with the others when we get home."

"I think we can display this one," Bingley protested, swinging to his wife. "It is really beautiful and what a shame to hang it behind a locked door in the private gallery. The dinning room at Netherfield will be the better for it."

Jane gazed at her husband for a moment and relented. "The breakfast parlor, I think. The light is better in there."

Bingley beamed. "Yes, certainly. The perfect spot."

"I…I think I could sell this one," Lizzy suggested, giving Jane a grimacing sort of grin. "Framed. Twenty pounds? What say you?"

"Sold," Bingley said gaily before his wife could open her mouth.

Lizzy frowned at him, brushing a lock of her rich brown hair back behind her ear. "I was thinking of offering it to Lady Smith-Roy. She adored the painting I did of her spaniels. And she told me her family is from Yorkshire. The North Riding, too."

Jane's hand closed into a fist and she pressed it to her heart. "Let Charles purchase it, if you mean to sell it. You have no need to earn money," she said earnestly. "You know we live quietly. Your fifty pounds a year is more than adequate as long as you continue to live with us." She rushed over to the bench and sat beside her sister, folding both her hands around Lizzy's arm. "If you keep painting portraits of dogs and children and…and horses and…so many things, then ultimately your gift will be revealed."

Lizzy covered her sister's hands with her own. "I mean to become independent. I am saving my earnings for a nice cottage. Somewhere near the sea, I think," she said, gazing up at nothing, her vision unfocused. "Maybe here in Yorkshire, though that would be too far from my family. Perhaps Great Yarmouth would be better. I already have a nice tidy sum saved."

"What?" Jane demanded, leaning away in alarm, her blonde curls bouncing. "You mean to leave us? When? Not soon?"

"No, you pea-goose," Lizzy said, reaching out instinctively to embrace her favorite sister. "I think, if I am careful, I shall have enough money to live independently by the time I am thirty. You will be heartily sick of me by then."

She laughed softly. "What an old maid I shall be."

"This is nonsense talk, as you know full well," Jane said, scolding a little in her obvious relief. "You are only two and twenty. There is time and enough for us to find you a husband."

Lizzy's eyebrow twitched. "As I have said, often and often, I will only marry for love."

"And, so you shall," Bingley said, grinning. "What man could not love you? Indeed, I thought Wickham was—" He faltered under his wife's gentle glower. "Uh, yes. Well."

Lizzy grimaced. "He and Lydia will fare well together, I think, for he is as reckless as she."

Their father and mother, rushing to the side of their youngest daughter in her distress—for Lieutenant Wickham had *not* married Lydia when he had run away with her—had died when their carriage overturned. Their cousin, Mr. Collins, had inherited Longbourn House. As a clergyman he had been outraged at Mr. Wickham's careless treatment of his young cousin. Between his, Bingley's, and their uncles' efforts, the feckless officer had been forced to marry Lydia. She, being a foolish girl of sixteen years, had been ecstatic. They lived in the north, now.

Their middle sister, Mary, lived with their Aunt Phillips in Meryton. Kitty had gone to live with their aunt and uncle in Cheapside. Mr. Collins, who had married Charlotte Lucas, Lizzy's best friend in the world, next to her dearest Jane, months before the accident, had been an easy cross to bear in order to have Charlotte nearby again.

"I cannot think of Lydia and Wickham without a pang of alarm squeezing my heart," Jane admitted. She frowned and bit her lip in contemplation.

"Then we shall not think of them," Bingley asserted, taking his wife's hand. "Instead, we shall look at dear Lizzy's painting and feel happy. All her paintings please me greatly."

Their gazes returned to the watercolor. Lizzy blinked at it in surprise and Bingley leaned forward, frowning. The jackdaw, formed from only a few strokes, shook out its feathers and hopped toward the edge of the painting and disappeared. Jane covered her eyes with her hand and sighed.

Bingley straightened. "There, there, my love. It is gone." He scratched the back of his head. "I suppose…I suppose it cannot be hung in the breakfast room either—not if that little fella continues to hop in and out of the painting." He tore his gaze away from the image and focused on Lizzy. "Um, will it?"

She shrugged helplessly.

"We shall watch it and see," Jane said, smiling softly. "If he rarely returns, we will hang it in the breakfast room, for it is a wonderful painting. And when we have guests, we will eat in the dining room." She sighed and rose. "I think I shall lie down for a while before our tea. I am tired."

"A sound idea," Lizzy said.

Lizzy slipped into her own room after tea and closed the door behind her with the sigh that comes after escaping from well-meaning relatives. She walked across the generous room to where her painting chest sat at the end of the four-poster bed. The box was the size of a large trunk and featured a stout lock. She set the painting of Fountains Abbey on the floor, unlocked the lid, and laid the new painting on the empty tray, covered it with a sheet of tissue paper, and closed it away where no one could see it.

She stood and folded her arms, making her way across the carpet to the window. Lizzy leaned her head against the mullion and stared out at the backyard where chickens pecked at grain the landlady had thrown out. Beyond the yard, the village, the farmland and then the great gardens of Studley Royal met her gaze. She meant to go to the Water Gardens there as soon as she received permission from the owner to paint on the premises. How would that painting be different? Perhaps nothing would happen to it. Perhaps she could paint without worry.

Perhaps.

Lizzy wished she could be more confident. The jackdaw

had surprised her. She had thought the window revealed her talent. Such randomness in her gift caused her a good deal of consternation. If only she could predict or control what happened.

If I could, I would make certain that nothing ever happened again. But, then, would the wonder of my work disappear? If I reject this aspect of my talent, will my ability to paint evaporate? I just do not understand, still, why I have been given a gift like this. What is its purpose?

She wondered if any of the great masters had felt the same way. Of course, as far as she knew, none of those men had ever had a talent quite like hers.

Lizzy stroked an eyebrow and then rested her head on her hand. She chuckled to herself and then whispered, "How much would a client pay for one of my paintings if she knew it would 'change'?"

I would be famous. Or, rather, infamous. That thought made her shiver. *No. I must be careful. Even so, it will be my talent that will give me my independence. If only I could find a way to control what happens to the paintings.*

∞

Pemberley House, Derbyshire...

Miss Georgiana Darcy looked up from her plate and accepted the letter resting on the silver salver held by their butler, Mellor.

"From Mr. Darcy, miss," he said, smiling slightly. "I hope it is good news and we will see him home soon."

"As do I," Georgiana replied, unfolding the missive. She scanned her brother's strong scrawl. "Oh, dear," she murmured pensively. "He is travelling to Yorkshire in search of a lady-painter to do my portrait."

"Ah," Mellor sighed.

"He expects to be another week or more, though he may break his journey here for a night or two." Georgiana set aside the letter and rested her chin on her hand and her elbow on the table. "Is my aunt coming down soon?"

"I could not say, miss. Mrs. McDougall's maid said she

passed an indifferent night and awoke with a small headache."

"I expect she will feel more the thing when she has eaten," Georgiana offered.

Aunt Sophia always took a breakfast tray in her rooms in the morning, leaving her niece to eat alone. Ever since Mrs. Younge had been let go—without a reference—no other companion-governess had been hired. Fitz did not trust any of them. Hence, Aunt Sophia McDougall, their father's youngest sister—a widow—had come to live with them as proof against another debacle like that concerning George Wickham.

Fitz does not trust me either, and that is the truth of the matter. He believes I will be led astray like I was two years ago. I am seven and ten now and quite grown up. I am to be presented to society in December. By this time next year, I might be married. How much more grown up must I be before Fitz trusts me again?

Mellor cleared his throat and Georgiana looked up at him. He held out a slip of paper.

"Mr. Kearn sends his compliments and a list of those tenants who might benefit from a visit from the ladies of Pemberley."

Georgiana took the estate manager's note and opened it, revealing three names and their particulars. Two were woman who were ill and would have a hard time looking after their families. The last one was the name of a farmer who had broken his leg and so his wife and children were working their farm, making housework and cooking difficult. Mr. Kearn, an exceedingly fine and capable man, would have sent a laborer over to their farm to assist with the heavy work. She glanced out of the tall Palladian windows.

"The day appears to be a fine one for visiting," Georgiana said, frowning slightly. "Kindly have Cook and Mrs. Reynolds prepare a hamper for each family according to their needs. Be certain they include fruit."

"Yes, miss," Mellor said, bowing his shoulders. He went to the door and passed the order along to a footman. He returned to stand next to the sideboard.

"Mrs. McDougall and I have an appointment to visit Mrs. Franklin and her daughter this afternoon, so we will have tea at the vicarage with them." Georgiana held up the list. "I will pass this along to Mrs. Franklin, and thus the Parish Women's Auxiliary will know of their needs."

Mellor bowed his shoulders. "Mr. Kearn has already sent a message down to the vicarage."

"Excellent," Georgiana said. "Then we will make our report when we arrive for tea."

She picked up her coffee cup and discovered the liquid had gone cold.

"I will take that, miss," the butler said, accepting it from her. Instead of coffee, he returned to the table with a small glass of soft apple cider, cold from the ice house.

"Mellor?"

"Yes, miss?"

Georgiana took a sip and savored the wonderful taste of apple before she spoke. She blinked up at the butler and asked, "What do you think of my brother's desire to have my portrait painted?"

Mellor took a second to answer, and then carefully said, "Except for the miniature Mr. Darcy carries with him, the last proper portrait of you, miss, was painted when your parents were still alive and you were only a toddler. And the miniature was painted when you were just ten. I think, miss, that there is an excellent spot for your portrait to hang in the gallery next to your brother's. Perhaps the artist will be able to do a full-length rendering as well as one where you are seated, showing only your shoulders and head. That one would look lovely in the drawing room, over the fireplace."

Georgiana narrowed her eyes. "You have been speaking of this with my brother, have you not? Conspiring with him?"

Mellor tugged at his black waistcoat. "Conspiring, miss?"

"Very well, shall we say contriving together? It is not that I do not wish to sit for my portrait, but this nonsensical notion of his to search for a female portraitist is most annoying." She continued to glare at the butler who had been with the household since before her birth. “Surely, a male artist could have been found in a trice and the work would have been well along by now.”

“Mr. Darcy is most exacting, miss,” Mellor observed, his expression impassive.

A voice sounded from the doorway. “He is arrogant, is what he is.”

The butler stepped away from the table and bowed to Georgiana’s aunt.

Chapter Two

Aunt Sophia, a vibrant woman with masses of chestnut hair, a lithe figure, gowned in scarlet and trimmed with black piping, entered the breakfast room using sharp, staccato steps. A strained smile on her striking features testified to her unrestful sleep. Georgiana knew her aunt to be forty years of age, but except for laugh lines, one could be forgiven for thinking her five years younger.

"My nephew is arrogant and prideful," she stated again with characteristic frankness. "Good morning, my dear," she added, leaning over her niece for her customary salute.

Georgiana kissed her scented cheek. "Good morning, Aunt. I am sorry you did not sleep well."

"I mean to kill that cockerel one morning," Aunt Sophia stated, scowling. "Mellor, coffee please."

"We could move you to a different wing of the house," Georgiana offered—not for the first time.

"Thank you, my dear, but I want to be near to you," she said, accepting the cup of hot coffee from the butler. Then she hopefully suggested, "We could both move?"

Georgiana laughed and shook her head. "We belong in the family wing, Aunt. Imagine my brother's feelings if he came home and discovered we had abandoned him."

"We could move his things, too." She took a sip of coffee, sighed, and added, "Or, rather, the footmen could do it."

"I expect killing the cockerel would prove easier,"

Georgiana said, chuckling again.

Aunt Sophia pointed dramatically at her. "Did I not just say so?" She glanced around. "Where is the armory in this place? I have not found it yet. There must be one. You have every other type of room. And I am accounted a magnificent shot, you know."

The butler cleared his throat and both ladies looked at him. He took a step forward.

"I beg your pardon, miss and madam, I thought I should mention that the cockerel is a prize bird."

Georgiana bit her lip and tilted her head to one side. "I suppose Fitz would be unhappy with us if we killed it."

"But if we ate the thing, we would not be wasting it," Aunt Sophia pointed out. "I remind you, that I am also a noted cook. I prepared all my dear husband's meals when he was home from war. We could instruct Cook to throw some red wine in the pot, maybe some mushrooms, and braise the bird for hours until there can be no doubt that the dastardly loud-mouth is thoroughly dead."

Mellor's uncharacteristic gasp turned into a muffled squeak, but the two ladies chose to ignore him.

Georgiana laughed again, dabbing at the corner of her hazel-brown eyes with her napkin. "I am afraid Mr. Kearn will simply purchase another cockerel."

Momentarily stymied, her aunt simply stared at her. Then, she narrowed her gaze and said ominously, "There is something wrong with that man."

"Who? Mr. Kearn? How can you say so?" Georgiana asked, frowning now, her heart racing a little. "He is perfectly unexceptional. If he were not, Fitz would never have taken him on."

"Hmm, I wonder." Aunt Sophia sipped her coffee and stared into the distance with narrowed eyes. "You know, I never trust a man in a beard. My Joseph only ever had sideburns and a mustache."

Georgiana chuckled away her frown. "Rather magnificent military ones, as I recall. Mr. Kearn has a particularly fine, full beard. You cannot tell a man's character from his facial hair. You need to look into his eyes. And, you must allow that our estate manager's eyes are kindly, knowledgeable, and…and keen."

"Ye-es," her aunt drawled. "The three k's. Very revealing."

Georgiana tsked. She handed her the list of visitees. "Cook is making up hampers."

Aunt Sophia glanced at the names and sighed. "And, Mr. Kearn is always setting us to work."

Georgiana opened her mouth, but before she could speak, her aunt interrupted her.

"I know. I know. It is our duty." Her shoulders slumped dramatically and she poked the piece of paper at her niece. "I recognize one of the names on this list. We have visited her with a hamper four times this last six-month. Is she ever well?"

"I have never known her to be anything but sad and gloomy," Georgiana admitted. "This attitude cannot help her health. Poor woman."

Aunt Sophia eyebrows drew together. "Melancholia is a debilitating condition."

"Yes," Georgiana said on a sigh. She met her aunt's gaze. "I am thankful you are not afflicted with it."

"As am I, my dear."

∞

North Riding, Yorkshire…

Lizzy entered the Studley Royal Water Gardens the next morning after permission arrived from the owner, Mrs. Elizabeth Lawrence. A middle-aged groom and a young footman followed behind her, carrying her easel, paint box, folding chair and table, picnic basket, and an enormous umbrella to protect her from the sun and in case it came on to rain. She had decided to paint the Temple of Piety, a folly nestled next to the trees by the lake. From this vantage point she also overlooked the statue of a pair of wrestlers grappling atop a rectangular plinth, in the middle of a reflecting pond.

"Nothing living here," she whispered to herself. "Just

grass and trees. Not even a swan."

"Miss?" Jeremy, the footman asked, pausing behind her.

"This will do," Lizzy said, pointing at the lawn in front of her.

While they set up her equipment, she examined the vista before her. No breeze rippled the reflection in the ornamental pond, making the flipped temple almost as crisp as its counterpart. The green of the trees behind the temple framed the portico and columns. A blue sky graced the day.

If she had enough money to stop painting, would she? When there were such delightful landscapes in the world, the answer must be a resounding *no*. In spite of the mind-numbing vagaries of her talent—no one painted quite like her—she could not resist continuing to exercise her gift.

Once, she had spent three weeks painting a still life of pink roses, purple clematis, and trailing ivy in oils. Every petal had been perfect, every leaf glowing with life. Her parents had eyed it with misgiving and had reluctantly hung it in the drawing room—behind the door. It had taken a se'nnight for anyone to notice that all the petals had fallen off and lay scattered about the vase. The leaves had curled into tight, dried brown fists.

Her mother had fallen onto the sofa and moaned. "Why? Why?"

Lydia, only thirteen years of age at the time, had laughed with delight and clapped her hands. "Famous," she had cried. Swinging around to face Lizzy, she had demanded, "Will they keep dying until they crumble to dust?"

"And then come back again like…like some sort of Phoenix flowers?" her sister Mary had asked, tilting her head to one side.

Lizzy recalled that all she had done was shrug and say, "Maybe. We shall see."

Mrs. Bennet reared up from her semi-reclining position. "Not in this room," she stated tartly. "Take it to your room, Lizzy. Now."

"Yes, Mama," Lizzy said, moving to take the painting off

the wall.

Jane joined her and they lifted the heavily framed masterpiece down. They took it to the attic studio where no servants were allowed. The painted flowers continued to this day to age, turn to dust, and then return to its original perfection at fairly regular intervals. It hung in the 'special' gallery at Netherfield, and was one of Charles' favorites.

Lizzy wished her talent displayed itself in the same manner with each painting. Something different happened each time when she put paint to canvas, or to paper, or to wood. Only when she painted children and pets could she expect that nothing would happen to the image. *That pesky jackdaw yesterday!* She supposed the almost-divine innocence displayed when she painted children and pets comprised the metaphysical aspect of her gift.

In vain had her family begged her to abandon her gift but she could not. Sooner could she have cut off her arm than not paint. She supposed in a less enlightened time that might have been her fate. Imagine if the occupants of the ceiling of the Sistine chapel had gamboled about after Michelangelo had finished them? The Church would have burned him at the stake. And the chapel, too.

"Rain's comin', miss," Arthur, the groom said, pointing to the north.

Lizzy looked at the dark clouds hovering on the horizon. "We still have a few hours yet."

"Aye, miss," he said.

She saw him exchange a glum look with his cohort. Arthur did not like getting wet—an unfortunate affliction for a groom.

"Watercolors today, Jeremy," she said, taking her seat and adjusting her easel to the horizontal. The footman poured out a can of water from a flask and set it on the table within her reach.

∞

Hertfordshire…

Mr. Darcy climbed out of his traveling carriage the

moment it rolled to a stop. He faced the double doors of a handsome, brick country house. Netherfield Park, the home of Mr. Charles Bingley, his wife Jane, and Darcy's quarry, Miss Elizabeth Bennet, sat surrounded by acres of parkland near the village of Longbourn. The doors opened and a butler stepped out onto the landing to greet him. Darcy climbed the five steps to the porch and the butler bowed.

"Good day, sir," he said. "How may I be of assistance?"

"My name is Darcy."

"Renquist, sir."

"I have come to enquire if Mr. Charles Bingley is still at home. I understand he means to make a journey into the north soon."

"I beg your pardon, but he has already left, sir," the butler said. "A week past. The family is visiting Yorkshire first. The North Riding, sir."

"The family?"

"Yes, sir. Mr. and Mrs. Bingley, and Miss Bennet, Mrs. Bingley's sister. So, you see, no one is at home."

"I see." Darcy frowned. "I mean to visit them in Yorkshire, for my business with Mr. Bingley is quite urgent. Will you tell me where they are staying?"

The butler nodded. "At the Aldfield Inn, sir, in Aldfield. The village is part of the Fountains Hall estate. Miss Bennet is a great painter, sir. I believe they'll spend a fortnight there, or perhaps longer, before moving on. If you proceed to Yorkshire directly, I expect you'll be able to catch them up."

"I know the place," Darcy said, nodding. "I am from Derbyshire. I hope to convince your master to visit my home there. If he agrees, I shall suggest that he send you a missive with his new itinerary." He took a silver embossed card case out of his pocket and extracted a card. "Here is my card." He slipped the man a yellow-boy with it. "Thank you, kindly."

The butler cast a surreptitious glance at the gold coin peeking out from beneath the card in his hand. "Thank *you*, sir."

Darcy left Hertfordshire and proceeded north. Since he

would reach Derbyshire on Saturday, he would break his journey at Pemberley for a few days. Following social convention, he would not travel any distance on a Sunday. After sending ahead the letter of introduction to Miss Bennet, he would continue onward.

∞

London...

Edmund Bissell had no such compunction. Sunday was the best day to travel, for commercial vehicles were forbidden to venture forth, leaving the roads comfortably empty. He climbed into his chaise-and-four, carrying the precious painting of his wife under one arm. He set the wrapped portrait on the seat beside him, holding onto it carefully when the carriage swayed as his valet, Clark, joined him.

The day after his wife's untimely death during childbirth two months before, he had wandered his Islington country seat, disconsolate. He eventually entered the long gallery where ancestral portraits hung along one wall, opposite north-facing windows. He had meant to have his wife's image painted, but they had decided to wait until after the baby's birth. Because of this, the only image he had of his poor wife was a sketch done by a young lady who had attended one of his wife's garden parties. He had sent it off to be properly framed and it hung beside his portrait.

Edmund had hurried down the gallery, anxious to view the sketch.

Except, the sketch was no longer there.

In its place, a watercolor painting hung. His wife sat on a delicate chair in the midst of their rose garden. Her beloved expression had been caught in the most brilliant way. She had been laughing—just like the sketch had shown.

"Oh," he had gasped, reaching out a hand to touch the image. "But…when…?"

No one stood in the gallery with him to provide an answer. He glanced about, looking for the sketch. It was gone. Presumably, the charcoal drawing had been replaced with the watercolor. Who had painted it? He checked the bottom right-hand corner.

"LB," he whispered. "But…those were the initials on the sketch."

On impulse, he lifted down the portrait and carried the painting to his own bedchamber. He set it down, cleared the mantel, and rested the portrait on the marble slab. Now he could see his wife as he wanted to remember her. Happy. Laughing. Full of life.

Ten days later, coming to bed late after returning from dining with friends, he was met at his bedchamber door by his valet.

"Sir," the smaller man said.

His former scout from his college at Oxford, Clark had a dour disposition and seldom showed any emotion. Tonight, he appeared pale and agitated.

"What is it, Clark?" Edmund asked, closing the door behind him.

The man gestured to the painting over the fire. Except, it was no longer a painting—it was a sketch.

"What the devil?" Edmund uttered in a hoarse voice. "Who did this? Who swapped the sketch back into the frame?"

"No one, sir," Clark assured him. "When I came into yer room to turn down the bed, the paintin' was there as usual. I turned from the bed and glanced up at it—it *is* a beautiful paintin', sir—and it'd turned into the sketch."

"That is impossible!" Edmund cried. He hurried over to the mantel and lifted down the framed sketch. He turned it over, hoping to find the watercolor portrait tacked to the rear.

It was not there.

"I know it, sir," Clark said, shaking his head. "No one entered. I was alone, sir. I swear it."

"You must be mistaken. It *must* have been the sketch when you entered the room."

Clark started to wring his hands, his expression one of misery. "I'm not mistaken, sir. That portrait of Mrs. Bissell was the most beautiful paintin' I'd ever seen, sir. I look at it every time I come in here. It was the paintin'. And then it wasn't."

Edmund placed the sketch back on the mantel. Both men stood and stared at it. Waiting. Would it change again?

"Maybe, sir," Clark began. Then he licked his lips and started again in a sort of rush of sound. "Maybe, sir, the sketch changed to the paintin' because Mrs. Bissell'd just died, like. Maybe. She was an angel, sir, yer lady."

"So, you think *God* changed the sketch?" Edmund demanded, his tone scoffing. He had never had much time for the Almighty and his wife's death had not changed his mind.

"Who else, sir?" Clark replied softly.

"Well, it could not have been *Him*," Edmund snapped. "First thing in the morning, we will get to the bottom of this mystery."

"Are yer thinkin' of tellin' the staff about the change?" Clark asked dubiously. "Most of them are plenty superstitious, like."

Edmund thought for a moment and then said, "We will start with discovering who LB is. She attended one of my wife's garden parties. Surely, there will be a list of invitees amongst the party journals in her desk."

"Indeed, sir. She was a fine one fer makin' lists."

Discovering the identity of LB had taken some weeks, however, since his darling wife had only listed her as one of the Bennet sisters. No first name. Then, one fateful day, a matron had revealed her name.

"Oh, you mean Jane and Elizabeth Bennet. Or Lizzie, to her family. Miss Elizabeth is a fine artiste. She painted my baby. Charming. Absolutely charming."

He had not known how to ask her if the portrait had altered over time. How could one pose such an inquiry?

For ten days the sketch remained as it was before it changed to a watercolor again. After another ten days it reverted. Edmund wondered if the cycle had begun from the moment the sketch had been formed and no one had noticed. He could not ask the maids. They would say nothing that might jeopardize their positions. How would it look to the housekeeper if they claimed the sketch changed back and forth to a painting? The phenomenon was fantastical. No, they would stay mum.

Another examination of his wife's party journals, revealed the Bennet address. Longbourn House, near Meryton, in Hertfordshire.

"We should arrive in Longbourn village this afternoon," Edmund said as soon as the carriage began to roll down the drive. "Then, I will have my explanation."

"Yes, sir."

Edmund frowned at his valet. "Why do you look so glum? Finally, we will discover the truth. You should be ecstatic."

Clark stirred on his seat.

"Out with it," Edmund ordered.

"I missed going to church this mornin', sir" the valet said.

"That is no reason to be miserable. Your Friday face is enough to ruin my mood."

"I beg yer pardon, sir," Clark said, appearing contrite. "I know you are most lenient to give me Sunday mornin's free—usually—as well as my Wednesday half-day. Thank you, sir."

Edmund nodded once at him and turned to stare out the window, one arm resting protectively on top of his wife's portrait. It was a watercolor painting again. He did not know how he would be received at Longbourn House. He needed answers and his determination to get them would brook no arguments or denials from Miss Elizabeth Bennet.

Chapter Three

Hertfordshire...

Longbourn House, a fine, red brick building with white trim around the large windows, appeared welcoming to Edmund. Magnificent flower gardens, where white and pink hollyhocks swayed amidst blue delphinium spikes, graced either side of the drive. His coachman pulled up before the small portico that protected the front door of the early Georgian home. Clark jumped out and lowered the step for his master. Edmund exited the chaise, leaving the painting on the seat behind him. He would send for it if Miss Bennet agreed to receive him.

One of the double-doors opened, revealing a crisply dressed, middle-aged housekeeper. She bobbed him a short curtsy.

"Good afternoon, sir," she said "Me name is Hill, sir. How can I help you?"

"You may tell me if Miss Elizabeth Bennet is at home," Edmund said, drawing out a card. He handed it to her, but before she could take it, a tall man who had not yet reached his thirtieth year, dressed in a dark suit, touched her shoulder.

"I will take that, thank you, Hill," the man said, reaching for the card.

"Of course, sir," the housekeeper said stiffly. She backed up and left the men on the doorstep.

"Edmund Bissell," the man said, reading the card.

He glanced up and stared at Edmund. The reflection off his spectacles partly obscured the view of his watery gray eyes. He appeared to be a fatuous gentleman who enjoyed knowing his own worth.

"I do not believe we have met," the man said. "I am Mr. Collins, and this is my home."

Edmund frowned. "I beg your pardon, but I thought this was the home of Miss Elizabeth Bennet."

Mr. Collins' thick eyebrows, too dark for his light-brown hair, shot up. "I am her cousin. Please, come through."

His host stepped backward and waved Edmund inside.

"Follow me to my book room," he said after closing the door. Mr. Collins glanced at his housekeeper, who hovered in the background. "Tea, please, Hill."

She gave a slight curtsy. "Sir."

The book room proved to be of a comfortable size, with a desk, a dark-brown sofa, and several padded arm chairs. Many volumes lined three walls, the fourth giving way to multiple windows that overlooked the rear rose garden and park.

"Kindly be seated," Mr. Collins said, waving toward one of the chairs.

Edmund sat. "Thank you."

His host took the other chair. "Now, tell me, if you please, what business you have with my cousin."

"My business is of a private nature, sir," Edmund said, tilting his head to one side. "I assure you, there is no need for you to be concerned. Will you tell me where I might find Miss Bennet? Does she continue to reside here with you?"

Just as Mr. Collins prepared to speak, the door opened and a plain, but pleasant-looking, lady entered the room. Both men stood. She smiled at them, confidently crossed the room, and sat down on the sofa. She appeared to be a few years older than Mr. Collins.

"May I introduce my wife, Mr. Bissell?"

Edmund bowed. "Mrs. Collins. A pleasure."

"Mr. Bissell. Kindly be seated. I understand you are here to ask after my cousin-in-law?"

He sat and smiled. "Yes, indeed. However, my information seems to be woefully out-of-date. I understand she no longer resides at Longbourn House?"

Mr. Collins opened his mouth, but it was his wife who answered.

"Unfortunately, no. Lizzy now lives with her elder sister, Mrs. Charles Bingley. They live at Netherfield Park."

Trying to keep the eagerness out of his voice, Edmund asked, "And where is that, pray?"

"My dear, perhaps—"

Mrs. Collins looked at her husband and he lapsed into silence.

She focused her attention back on Edmund. "Netherfield Park lies but three miles from Meryton, which you passed through on your way here."

"Of course." Edmund eased forward in his seat. "I will trouble you no more. Thank you for your assistance."

"Tea is coming, Mr. Bissell. Do not rush off," Mrs. Collins said graciously, smiling. "I believe I recall your name. You are married to Cassandra Bissell, are you not? Lizzy mentioned her visits to your dear wife's garden parties. She enjoyed them immensely."

Edmund experienced the familiar stab of pain at the mention of his precious wife. He bowed his head and sighed. "Alas, my Cassandra has passed on. Only two and a half months ago. We were married twelve years."

He caught both of the Collins' looking down at his arm, expecting to see a black armband, no doubt. Instead of the armband, he wore a black cravat, but many men wore black cravats without being in mourning, so they had had no warning of his bereaved state.

"We are very sorry for your loss, sir," Mr. Collins said, looking suitably grave. "Before I inherited Longbourn, I was a clergyman. I have prayed over many a family who have suffered grievously. This is a sad time for you."

"Indeed," Mrs. Collins said, sighing.

They all fell silent. Then, the door opened again and Hill

entered, carrying a silver platter loaded with tea and a plate of sliced spice cake.

Edmund accepted a cup of tea from his hostess. Remembering that Lizzy was the name used for Miss Bennet by her family and friends, he hazarded a guess and asked, "You and Miss Bennet are particular friends, Mrs. Collins?"

She beamed. "Yes, indeed. We have known each other for most of our lives."

"Then," he said, pausing to take a sip of his tea. "You must know how great her gift is."

He watched Mr. Collins frown, but Mrs. Collins' eyebrows shot up.

"Her gift? Which one?"

"Her artistic gift," Edmund clarified. He smiled disarmingly. "Miss Bennet presented a lovely sketch to my wife. The sketch was of Cassandra while she sat in the garden at one of her parties. We hung it in our gallery."

"Yes, there is nothing quite like her talent in that regard," Mrs. Collins said sunnily. "Is that why you are seeking her out? Are you hoping she will turn the sketch into a painting?"

Too late.

He latched onto that explanation for his search and lied. "Yes, I am. Unfortunately, you see, I have no other image of her."

Mrs. Collins lost her smile and sadly shook her head at him. "I am sorry to be the one to tell you, sir, but my cousin-in-law does not paint adults. She paints only children, pets, still life, and landscapes."

She does.

Edmund let his shoulders slump a bit. "I cannot deny that I am disappointed. Most disappointed indeed."

"Perhaps you could take my cousin's sketch to another portraitist," Mr. Collins suggested. "And he could take a likeness from it." A movement from his wife caught his eye and he glanced at her, caught her expression, and stilled. "What is it, my dear?"

Edmund stared at Mrs. Collins' white countenance and

wondered if she knew that her friend's talents were unique. It was entirely possible that the character of his wife's image was not the only one that changed. Could there be other sketches, or paintings, that behaved in an unorthodox manner? Was it possible that they *all* had a metaphysical aspect in their make up? But, surely, if that was true, would not others have noticed the phenomena?

Mrs. Collins took a gulp of her tea and attempted a recovery. "I am perfectly well, my dear. I was startled only by your suggestion. You could not have known it, but *I* know that Lizzy would not agree to Mr. Bissell using her sketch as a template for a portrait from some other artist."

"Would she not?" Edmund asked politely. He tipped his head to one side and said, "Then there is no question that I will do so. The sketch will have to be sufficient. It is very lovely as it is."

"My cousin's art is always beautiful," Mr. Collins said. He set down his cup and stood. "Come with me into the front parlor. There is an exceptionally well-done painting of this house and grounds there that you must see. If you like it, then perhaps you will commission her to paint one of your own home. Where is your place, Mr. Bissell?" he asked, holding open the door for his guest.

"I have a country home in Islington, sir," Edmund said, rising and bowing first to Mrs. Collins, who did not rise and join them, before following his host out of the book room.

Upon entering the front parlor, Mr. Collins said, "My cousin is away from Netherfield at the moment, Mr. Bissell. It is a shame you have come from London to no purpose. Though we have been delighted to make your acquaintance, of course. Expanding one's society is always welcome."

"Thank you. I do not consider my journey wasted. Perhaps your cousin is visiting family in London? I might see her there."

"No, not London. Yorkshire."

"Oh? As far away as that?"

"Yes. They will be gone for months."

Months? No, that will not do. I cannot wait for months.

∞

Pemberley House, Derbyshire…

"I do not understand this positive fixation you have with finding a female artist to paint my portrait," Georgiana said over her shoulder as she walked to the Broadwood grand pianoforte that sat at one end of the long drawing room. "Why must you hie off to Yorkshire tomorrow? Are you not exhausted by all this travel?"

"I have explained my reasoning to you more than once," Fitz said, smiling and patient.

He is always so patient with me. Even when…

"What I think, is that you no longer trust me," she said in a pained whisper, not wishing Mr. Kearn to overhear them. He had joined them for dinner as was his custom when Fitz was at home.

"I trust you completely," her brother said, offering his hand to steady her as she sat on the piano bench. He leaned over and kissed her brow, then whispered in turn, "It is the artists I cannot trust." He straightened and smiled down at her. "If this lady does not prove skilled enough to paint you, or if I find her objectionable in any way, I will find a male portraitist and have Aunt Sophia keep you company during your sittings."

Georgiana met his gaze and nodded. "An admirable compromise."

Her brother laughed. "I think we should find a diplomat for your husband."

Georgiana shrugged and firmly kept her gaze from straying to where Mr. Kearn, the third son of an admiral, sat chatting with her aunt. He had no prospects higher than his current position and must work for a living. Not that she cared a jot for that as she was an heiress and would receive three thousand pounds per annum upon her majority, or when she married. But she knew it would be a concern to Mr. Kearn.

She was not even certain that he ever thought of her other than to give her lists of chores suitable to a lady. Only that morning he had advised that she inspect the lining on the bed drapes in the blue bed chamber and to decide if the drapes should be repaired or replaced. She had, in turn, consulted with Mrs. Reynolds, their housekeeper, before giving her answer. She had intercepted him outside by the stables where a gig sat waiting for him.

"Mr. Kearn?" She stood at the edge of the immaculate stone-paved yard.

He stopped striding toward the carriage and immediately turned in her direction. When he came within a few yards of her, he doffed his tweed flat-cap, revealing his lovely head of mahogany-colored hair. Sharp light-blue eyes twinkled at her.

"Good afternoon, Miss Darcy. How may I assist you?"

She loved his voice—so full and rich—and suppressed the shiver that ran up her spine.

"I have inspected the lining of those drapes as you requested."

"Thank you, Miss Darcy."

Heat suffused her cheeks. Georgiana so wished her fair skin did not reveal her blushes so readily.

"And what have you determined?" he asked.

She touched the curl hanging below her ear. His attention—particularly his complete attention, like now—cast her mind into confusion so that she struggled to concentrate on his question. She swallowed and dragged her composure into order.

"I consulted with Mrs. Reynolds and we have decided that the drapes are too faded to keep any longer. We shall clean them and give them to the vicar's wife. Her team of women will remake the drapes and give their results to the poor."

Mr. Kearn nodded. "And admirable scheme. I shall arrange to have some fabric samples brought to the house for you to choose from for the new drapes. Mrs. Chambers will sew them for us."

Georgiana frowned a little and took a deep breath. "Mr. Kearn, I believe the…the wisest course would be to ask Mrs. Brown to make the drapes. Mrs. Chambers is busy and the drapes may take a long time to finish."

The estate manager tilted his head and looked into the distance as he often did while thinking.

"Mr. Brown is laid up with a broken leg," he stated slowly. "Hmm."

"Yes, indeed. His wife was on the list you gave me on Wednesday morning, if you recall. Aunt Sophia and I visited her. While we talked, I discovered that she was nearing the completion of her needlework apprenticeship when she married. I admired the work she had done on the curtains and the tablecloth in her cottage. Her stitches were tiny, even, and straight."

"You are confident she will do a good job? A superior job?"

Georgiana swallowed again. "I am."

Please agree. Please.

"Very well." He nodded and smiled at her.

Georgiana's heart flipped and she found breathing difficult. He approved of her. He thought she had good ideas. It was not just that she was his employers' sister, and lady of the house. Or, was it?

"I will contact her and see if she is amenable," Mr. Kearn said. He shifted his weight from one foot to another.

"I am keeping you," Georgiana said, taking a step back.

He stroked his full beard and gave a sheepish grin. "I must see to a few matters before Mr. Darcy returns and wants my report." He bowed his shoulders.

And held out his hand.

She blinked at it.

Her stomach trembled.

His hand.

Attempting a sensible disinterest, she took it and he clasped it warmly in his. Without releasing it, he asked, "Forgive me, but is there anything else I can do for you, Miss Darcy?"

She shook her head and her mouth went dry.

When will he release my hand?

"Thank you for listening to my suggestion," she finally managed.

"Of course," he said, smiling down at her in such a way that she wondered if she would ever breathe again. He released her hand. "Have a good remainder of your day, Miss Darcy."

"Mr. Kearn."

Georgiana had waited until he climbed into the gig before she had turned her steps back toward Pemberley.

"Mrs. Miles Kearn," she whispered beneath her breath.

If only.

Georgiana shook herself mentally back to the present and reached for the new piece of music her brother had brought her from London. "Ah, an Irish air, arranged by Haydn. This should be pleasant."

∞

North Riding, Yorkshire...

Lizzy sat down to break her fast with her sister and brother-in-law. Jane nodded at Jeremy and he began serving. The inn staff had brought the food to their private parlor, but Jeremy had been taught well by their butler and knew better than to allow the inn servants to serve any of their meals.

"I know I mentioned it yesterday, but I must say again that the church service was very pleasant. I wish our good vicar back home had even half of Reverend Forsyth's dynamic presentation," Jane observed, accepting a ramekin holding a coddled egg onto her plate.

"He has asked me to paint the church," Lizzy revealed, shaking her head at Jeremy. She did not want an egg this morning. Toast, marmalade and tea would do for her.

Jane tensed, eyed Jeremy, and kept her query innocuous. "What was your reply?"

Lizzy shrugged. "I said I would be happy to. What else could I say?" Jane cast another quick glance at Jeremy. Lizzy knew better than to say anything of import in front of servants and calmly continued, "I thought I would start with a sketch. I am almost finished the piece I am doing of the Temple of Piety and I can work on that here. Shall we go for a walk today? You know how I love to walk. I shall bring my sketch book and perhaps we can pause for a quarter of an hour at the church. You and Charles can examine the cemetery and look at the headstones while I work."

Jane picked up her spoon and addressed her husband. "Does that program agree with you, my dear?"

Charles beamed. "An admirable scheme. The rain will have washed everything nice and clean. I was thinking, if you both agree, that we could take an expedition into Ripon tomorrow and view the Minster church of St. Peter and St. Wilfred. I am reliably informed that it is only four miles from here—barely a half hour carriage ride. What say you both?"

The ladies assented and they talked of the treat while they completed their meal. When they were about to leave the table, one of the inn staff brought a letter for Lizzy.

She took it, nodded her dismissal, and then frowned at the letter.

"Is it from one of our sisters?" Jane asked, her eyebrows raised and her cheeks flushed with anticipation. "We have not had a letter from Lydia this age."

"It is not from Lydia, or Mary, or Kitty," Lizzy said. "The addresser is Mr. F. Darcy."

"I do not know any Darcys," Charles mentioned, leaning forward. "Do you?"

Lizzy shook her head. "No." She broke the seal and unfolded the letter, exposing another missive. "This one is from Lady Smith-Roy." She set it to one side and read Mr. Darcy's letter.

"'Dear Miss Bennet, please permit me to call upon you at the Aldfield Inn on Tuesday, July 7th, in the afternoon. I have included a letter of introduction from Lady Smith-Roy. I have known her for many years as she was a friend of my dear mother, Lady Anne, who passed away some years ago. I will arrive before a letter from you will reach me. I hope you will forgive the impertinence of my calling upon you when you will have had no opportunity to refuse me. I also look forward to meeting your sister and Mr. Charles Bingley. Your obedient

servant, Fitzwilliam Darcy.'"

"How very odd," Jane said, accepting the letter from her sister. She examined it. "He has a nice, strong hand. And good penmanship. No blotches." She passed on the letter to her husband. "What does Lady Smith-Roy say?"

Lizzy unfolded the letter and spread it out.

"'My Dear Miss Bennet, I am writing to recommend my sweet friend's son to you. He is honest and reliable, if a little stiff in his manner. A gentleman of means, as well. He wishes to discuss the possibility of a commission for you. I will let him explain the project. He can afford to be generous, my dear, so make certain you charge what your time and talents deserve.

Please, call on me the next time you are in town. Kindest regards, Lady Smith-Roy.'"

"A possible commission?" Charles restated. "I wonder what he wants you to paint."

"He is in an awful hurry to get it done if he is willing to drive all the way to the North Riding to see you, Lizzy," Jane said, her brows drawn together.

"Perhaps he lives in the North," Lizzy suggested. "Or the Midlands."

"Is there no direction on the letter?" Charles asked. He realized he still held the paper, chuckled, and turned it over. "Oh, yes, here it is. Pemberley House, Lambton, Derbyshire. So, in the north part of the county, near the Peak District." He sucked in a breath through his teeth. "Still, that is well over a hundred miles away. He will have to have left first thing this morning and will need to break his journey—at Leeds, perhaps—if he is to make his appointment."

"This will mean a put-off of our excursion to Ripon," Jane said, taking the letter from her husband and returning it to Lizzy. "Perhaps we may go on Wednesday."

"You think I should meet him, then?" Lizzy asked, gazing into her sister's eyes. "He is a stranger."

"Not entirely," Jane reminded her. "Lady Smith-Roy has vouched for his character."

"And we shall be here to greet him with you," Charles

promised. He nodded decisively. "He may be a very pleasant fellow and we shall be happy to know him."

Lizzy folded both letters and slipped them into her reticule, saying, "Lady Smith-Roy says he has a stiff manner. Perhaps he is prideful."

Jane teasingly shook her finger at Lizzy. "Do not let your prejudice against the wealthy influence your opinion before you have even met him. Look at my Charles. Not all well-to-do men are arrogant and full of pride."

Charles looked everywhere but at them, his cheeks a little flushed.

Lizzy smiled at them both. "You have chosen the pick of the litter, dearest."

∞

London...

Edmund Bissell, back home before Sunday had ended, sat down on Monday with his collection of investors, who jointly owned several sugar cane plantations in Jamaica. He champed at the bit to be away to Yorkshire, fearing that Miss Bennet might move on from there before he could arrive to ask her about the painting of his wife. However, he was the primary in this investor group and could not leave London until the end of the week when the last of his guests would depart.

"When is Our Lady of Faith due to arrive in port?" one investor asked.

Edmund dragged his attention back to the meeting and tapped his finger on the schedule resting upon the table in front of him. "In three weeks."

"And you will go to Bristol to meet it?" another man demanded.

"Do I not always meet our ships?" Edmund asked, lifting an eyebrow. "My dear sirs, I have no intention of neglecting my duty to our collective merely because I am in mourning."

"Of course not," some of the men murmured and did not meet his gaze.

I will have only three weeks, minus the next four days, so seventeen days, to get to Yorkshire, speak with Miss Bennett and then travel to Bristol in time to meet the blasted ship. Can I do it? I cannot make the journey to the North Riding in less than six days. Seven is more likely. Will there be enough time? There must be.

Chapter Four

North Riding, Yorkshire…

Darcy arrived in Aldfield just after noon. His carriage drew up before the inn and he climbed stiffly down. He would have liked to stretch, but he did not know who might see him engaged in such an undignified activity. His valet, Booth, hurried before him, seeking the landlord. The inn, formed from gray Yorkshire stone, was a rambling building. A tap room occupied the end of one wing and a café-cum-tea room occupied the end of another.

He glanced around, hoping for a sight of his quarry. Several groups of strolling persons inhabited the lane, enjoying the sunshine, he presumed. The gentlemen touched their hats in polite salute. He nodded to them in turn. One gentleman, several years his junior, leapt forward, holding out his hand.

"Hallo," he said, grinning, the light of good-humored welcome shining in his blue eyes. "I am Bingley. Are you Darcy?"

Darcy gripped his hand and had it shaken heartily. Something like a smile twitched his lips. "I am," he admitted.

"By Jove, you made good time." Bingley glanced around. "Were you hoping to stay the night? The place is full up, I fear. Fountains Abbey is a devilishly popular place to visit."

"Indeed," Darcy replied, raising one eyebrow. "I am confident in my valet's ability to engage a suitable room."

Bingley's expressive and open face declared his

skepticism. He gestured toward the entrance to a garden path. "Should you like to take a short walk to work the fidgets out after your journey?"

Darcy nodded. No doubt the man wished to ascertain if he was a proper person to introduce to his wife and sister-in-law.

"So, Pemberley House, eh?" Bingley said. "What sort of estate is it? Or, is it just a house and garden?"

Darcy gazed at him for a moment, hoping to stare him out of countenance, but Bingley simply looked back inquiringly. There appeared to be no guile in the man.

"It is an estate," Darcy finally revealed.

"Ah. Has it been in your family for ages?" In response to Darcy's nod, Bingley continued, "I am merely leasing Netherfield Park, in Hertfordshire, trying to decide if I should buy a tidy estate of my own. Do you recommend it?"

Darcy could not resist his earnest request and they spent a pleasant half hour discussing the pros and cons of owning a large estate.

"We had best turn our feet back," Bingley said with some reluctance. They entered a path that led them toward the inn.

"It seems to me," Darcy said, "that you have little interest in farming on any scale. So, I suggest you look out for a small estate that benefits from rents and has a home farm where you can learn and leave the running of it to your farm manager."

"You may have the right of it," Bingley said, nodding. He coughed, and said, as though he thought he might be revealing more than he should, "My dear wife grew up on such an estate. It was entailed, however, and her cousin took up residence when my father-in-law died."

"Unfortunate," Darcy said. "Your wife is the eldest, I understand?"

"Yes. The eldest of five sisters. I can see your astonishment and it is understandable, sir. Only one other sister has married. The youngest. Lydia. Or Mrs. George Wickham as she is now.

Darcy stopped in his tracks and Bingley took several steps before he noticed. He returned to Darcy's side.

"I acknowledge that it is a strange thing to have the youngest married before three of her older sisters. But so it is," Bingley offered with a shrug.

In a strangled voice, Darcy asked, "George Wickham, did you say?"

"Yes." Bingley frowned and stared at him, wide-eyed. "Come, sir, is it that you know my brother-in-law? Lieutenant George Wickham of the militia?"

Darcy nodded curtly, feeling his features hardening and his stomach churning. *Wickham. Dear Lord.* He started walking again—stalking, actually. Bingley fell into step beside him.

"Forgive me, but was your wife's youngest sister an heiress?" Darcy bit out.

Bingley shook his head. "Not at all. Quite the contrary, I assure you." He sighed. "In fact, sir, Mr. Wickham is a—"

"A scoundrel," Darcy finished. His hands opened and closed in tight fists.

"Yes. I see you know him well," Bingley said quietly. He looked up at the sky. "Yes, by God."

"I beg your pardon," Darcy said through clenched teeth, "But, how did Miss Lydia fall into the blaggard's hands? Was her father not watching out for her?" He experienced the guilt of not watching Georgiana well enough most keenly.

Bingley stopped walking and stared at him. Darcy felt an embarrassed flush suffuse his countenance.

"Excuse me," Darcy said stiffly. "Pray forgive me for speaking out of turn."

Bingley relaxed and smiled. "Of course. Let us not give that cursed fellow any more of our time and energy. Let us see, instead, if your good valet, the miracle worker, has found you a room for the night."

Darcy took several deep breaths, ordered his thoughts, and nodded. "To be sure. You will be made to eat your scepticism, mark my words."

Booth did not disappoint and his reputation remained

intact. He broke the mould of self-effacing diminutive, gentleman's gentleman. Instead, Booth was a towering, spare man, of middle years. He bowed correctly when he approached Darcy, whom he topped by several inches, at the entrance to the gardens.

"Sir," he said, then bowed deferentially to Bingley as well.

"What have you, Booth?" Darcy asked. "A room in the stables, perhaps? Or the barn?"

"The *barn*, sir?" the valet asked in his soft baritone, clearly shocked. "I've done much better than the barn, or the stables, as I hope you know." He added a belated, "Sir."

"I knew it, but my new friend here, Mr. Bingley, doubted the veracity of my expectations."

Darcy threw a glance at the younger man and found him smiling widely. He had the air of a man always happy with his place in the world, easily amused, and not above being pleased.

"I am ready to be convinced," Bingley assured them.

"The landlord, sir," Booth said, addressing Darcy, "always keeps the best set of rooms back in the event a personage *ton* should need it. He has discerning tastes, if I may say so. He'll not let it to a mill owner or a coal baron. No, sir. Only one such as yourself could induce him to part with it. And only after I revealed that your grandfather was an Earl."

"Well, how do you like that?" Bingley asked rhetorically, shaking his head and displaying a false moue. "I thought *we* had the best rooms." He dropped his feigned pout and added, "They are very nice, though."

Darcy found himself chuckling—not an activity he indulged in often, not since the death of his father and his sudden increase in responsibility. Wickham's recent insults had not helped his temper, either. The son of his father's steward, Wickham and he had played together as children. Darcy's father had paid for Wickham's education so that he could act the part of a gentleman. His true character eventually betrayed himself and showed him to be a bounder. However, his former friend had charm in spades and could easily wheedle himself into whichever society that took his notice. He knew how to make himself likable—a trait Darcy occasionally envied.

"This way, sir, if you please?" Booth asked him.

Darcy flicked a finger and his valet smoothly moved ahead of them into the side entrance of the inn.

"I have got to see these famous rooms," Bingley said, falling into step beside him. "If you have no objections, of course."

"None," Darcy said.

"Good. My dear wife and her sister are awaiting our company in approximately one-half hour," Bingley said. "Plenty of time, then, for you to wash the dust off your person and allow your valet to make you more presentable."

Darcy agreed and kept himself from glancing down at his pantaloons, waistcoat, and coat to see if they were dirty. They would not be. Creased, perhaps, but not dirty.

"Your letter came as quite a surprise to us," Bingley said, standing to one side so Darcy could fit through a corridor doorway alone. "Is it true that you are looking to commission a painting from my sister-in-law?"

Darcy frowned. "Do forgive me, but I prefer to discuss my business with Miss Bennet directly."

"Oh, of course, of course." Bingley touched him on the shoulder and Darcy turned his head to look at him. Bingley pointed to a door as they passed. "This is us—our private lounge, I mean. Jeremy is the name of our footman. I shall have him be on the look-out for you, shall I?"

"Thank you."

They climbed another set of stairs, crossed two more corridors, and finally arrived at a lovely set of doors. Booth pointed to an opening a little further along.

"That, sir, is the stairway that will take you to a foyer and the tea café. We've come the long way around."

Booth threw open both doors and Darcy and Bingley entered a comfortably appointed lounge decorated in browns, blues, and cream. The room contained a table large enough to sit six, a fireplace, excellent draperies, several deeply tufted leather couches and floral armchairs. Three doors led off the room. Two were plain—servant rooms—and the other was of nicely carved oak—the master's room.

"Very nice," Darcy said, nodding once to his manservant.

Booth withdrew a step to permit the gentlemen to fully enter the room. He waved at the table where a platter of tea, pies, and cakes awaited their pleasure.

"Refreshments, sir."

"Thank you," Darcy murmured again.

"A can of hot water should arrive soon," Booth said. "I'll await the menial in the corridor."

Once the valet closed the door, Bingley exclaimed softly, "By Jove, Darcy. What a gem you have in him. These rooms are superior to ours. It is as though you have captured a djinn and he has magicked this place into existence."

Darcy chuckled. Again.

Bingley approached the table. "Tea?" He began to pour out. "I thought my *ton* was reflected in my financial status, but I must be wrong."

Darcy, who had been listening carefully to his tone of voice, heard no distress in it. Bingley appeared to care not a whit about his level in society. He knew, since the man had told him, that his father had earned his fortune, not inherited it. He had gone to good schools, as had his sisters, and they had attained a ranking that was not unfavorable. However, they had no connections. If he had married higher, instead of to the eldest daughter of a member of the landed gentry, then his position would have risen to hers. But he had not and Darcy could not be sorry for one who seemed completely content with his lot.

"I have often found that the greatest elitists are found in the lower classes," Darcy replied. He moved across the room and accepted a cup of tea. "Booth, for instance, is a notable elitist. He is more aware of what is due my dignity than I."

Bingley chuckled and swallowed his grin when Booth opened the door, admitting a member of the inn staff who carried a large can of steaming water. Bingley set down his cup.

"My wife and sister-in-law are awaiting my report," he said, grinning. He waved at the platter of fancy cakes and pies. "You should bring your left-overs. I cannot assure you that the landlord will send up as fine a platter of cakes as these for *our* refreshments. I shall not know where to look."

Darcy surprised himself with a shout of laughter. "Booth shall bring them there while I wash and we can all enjoy them together."

"An excellent scheme," Bingley said, then bowed his shoulders and left him.

I do *like that man. A new friend would be an unexpected dividend of this journey,* he thought, following his valet into the bedchamber.

∞

Lizzy and Jane leapt up from their seats in their private lounge when the door opened and Charles entered.

"Well, Charles?" Jane asked, her eyes wide.

"Yes, yes. What is Mr. Darcy like?" Lizzy demanded. "Do tell us."

"I knew you would be anxious," Charles said, closing the door behind him. "I left the fellow in his rooms—and fine rooms they are, too."

"Oh, Charles," his wife cried softly. "Do not be so exasperating, I pray. We care nothing for his rooms."

"Do you not? They are nicer than ours, I must say. Or, at least, his lounge is bigger and more finely appointed than ours. I did not see his bedchamber."

"*Charles Bingley*," Lizzy said, lowering her voice ominously, "if you do not answer our most pressing question immediately, I shall paint your portrait."

Charles stopped abruptly and stared at her. "Do you promise? You know how I have longed to have you paint me."

Jane lost the color in her cheeks. "She is only jesting, my dear. Only jesting."

"But, my darling, I yearn to know what metaphysical

effect would occur to my portrait," he argued. "Possibly it would be like that painting I love best. Perhaps my image would age until I withered away to dust. And then, *voila,* I would be my young, handsome self again. Would not that be something to behold."

"Something, perhaps," Jane said weakly. She sat back down. "Would you really like to know the age you will be when you die?"

Charles, who had been about to press the issue, closed his mouth with a snap. He considered for a moment and then said, "No, perhaps not. However, it may not be like that. I might only stand up and then sit down again, over and over again. That sounds exhausting. Or maybe, my portrait nose will itch and my image will scratch it, and then go back to his original pose."

Jane gave a reluctant, soft laugh. "And only when Caroline is visiting. Your sister would run screaming from the room."

"I would give much to see that," Charles admitted.

"Oh, no," Jane said, her tender heart betraying her. "She is so kind."

"Hmm, to you, perhaps."

Lizzy glanced between them. She lifted her sister's limp hand and pressed it between both of hers. "I was only jesting, as you say. I have promised never to paint Charles and I mean to keep my promise."

"It is too late for you, however, dear heart," Charles said, grinning widely. He tapped his chest. "I keep your miniature close to my heart. Every time I open the locket your image smiles at me. It is magical."

Lizzy smiled, pleased with how much Charles loved her sister. "Dear sir, kindly tell us your opinion of Mr. Darcy. We have been on tenterhooks."

Charles relented and pulled forward a chair. After he sat, he put on a solemn expression.

"I met him outside as soon as he stepped down from his carriage. His person is well-formed and attractive, I believe.

He is a few years older than I, but I do not think he is yet thirty years of age. Certainly not older."

"Younger than we thought," Lizzy said, frowning. "Is he married? Does he want me to paint one of his children?"

Charles shook his head. "He would not discuss his business with me. And he said nothing of a wife. After we greeted each other, he graciously assented to my suggestion that we take a walk. We discussed our idea of possibly buying a small estate. His estate is vast, as I understand it. Twenty thousand acres, or thereabouts. I can hardly fathom such a number. Pemberley must be one of these great houses, like Harewood House here in Yorkshire."

Jane breathed, "Harewood House. Goodness. I read about it in our guide to places to visit in the North. It is a grand house. 'Capability' Brown has done the landscaping for the gardens."

"Mr. Darcy's estate must be something indeed," Lizzy commented, her eyes wide.

"Yes." Charles crossed his legs and waited for them to ask him another question about their soon-to-be guest.

"What else did you speak of?" Jane asked.

"Oh, this and that. Manly pursuits," he confessed. "He likes prize fighting."

Lizzy and her sister wrinkled their noses. Having had no brothers, no one had explained to them why men liked to watch other men beat each other. Their father never went to prize fights, or cock fights, or even to horse races. He had been a quiet, scholarly gentleman.

"And horse racing, I suppose?" Lizzy asked, her eyebrows furrowed.

Charles nodded. "He was at the August meeting last year in York. As was I. I am surprised our paths did not cross," he mused. "He had two horses running."

"As fascinating as this account is," Jane said in her gentle way, "I still have no idea of the man's character."

"How much can a person learn in such a short time?" Charles protested.

"Your first impression, then—did you like him?" Lizzy asked.

"Oh, yes," he said immediately and then pursed his lips. "But then, I liked Wickham at first, too. I am uncertain as to whether I should trust my first impressions." He rested his elbow on the arm of the chair, rested his chin on his palm, and strummed his cheek. "If I cannot, how can you? What a conundrum."

The sisters looked at each other and then at Charles. His report had been of very little help.

"Oh, and he knows Wickham."

"Does he *like* him?" Lizzy demanded.

"Oh, no. Not a bit."

"Well, that is something," Jane wryly commented.

∞

Mr. Darcy's valet arrived a few minutes before him, carrying a tray of superior refreshments. Charles had told them of his mild jest and he had been pleased to see the food arrive

"Ah, a man of his word," Charles said.

Lizzy found the action a little odd, but she knew men often did things she found entirely perplexing. After all, Jane was perfectly capable of ordering tea and suitable refreshments so why should they be accepting Mr. Darcy's leavings?

Then the man himself arrived.

Tall and imposing with his London-tailored coat, pantaloons, and Hessian boots that shone so brightly that he might use them as a tolerable mirror, Mr. Darcy stalked into their lounge as though he counted himself as the King of Sheba or something equally royal. She detected a subtle curl of his lip. She doubted that Jane or Charles would discern it. Her hands curled into tight fists in her lap.

Too rich and powerful for his company, is he? Stiff in his manner, Lady Fitz-Roy had said. I can easily see that.

What Mr. Darcy found to disgust himself she could not tell. Their private lounge was pleasant, light, and not at all shabby. Was it her provincial fashions? She wore a blue and white striped day gown for the occasion. Their local seamstress had designed it with a blue sailor's collar and a broad dark-blue band beneath her bust. Jane had blessed the day by wearing one of her London dresses of apricot silk and looked exceedingly lovely in it. They were both unexceptionally gowned.

Lizzy straightened in her chair even more and relaxed her hands. Mr. Darcy had requested this interview. What right did he have to look so haughty?

Charles hastened across the chamber to greet their guest. "Darcy, here you are," he said, holding out his hand. When their guest took it, Charles used their clasped hands to draw Mr. Darcy further into the room. "Come, I would like to introduce you to my wife. Jane, dear, this is Mr. Darcy."

"Sir," Jane said, bowing her head slightly, and, without rising, offered her hand.

Is that it? Does he think we should have risen when he comes in?

Mr. Darcy bowed over Jane's hand. "Charmed, Mrs. Bingley."

"You are too kind," Jane murmured. She indicated her sister with a graceful sweep of her hand.

"Lizzy, this is Mr. D—" Her voice faltered when she met Lizzy' narrowed gaze. "Uh, Mr. Darcy, this is my sister, Miss Elizabeth Bennet, whom you have come specifically to meet."

Was that a reminder to me, that this man has come some distance to see me? Lizzy wondered. *Or to him, that I have kindly consented to meet a stranger?*

"Miss Bennet," Mr. Darcy said, bowing. "The Talented Miss Bennet, as they call you in London."

"La!" Lizzy said, affecting an excitement at meeting him that she did not feel. "Imagine that. My name is being bandied about in the capital. In drawings rooms, I hope? Not in gentlemen's clubs?"

"*Lizzy,*" Jane whispered faintly.

Heat rose in Lizzy's cheeks. *What is the matter with me? Why does Mr. Darcy affect me this way? It is my prejudice, only, I fear. Perhaps he is merely shy and uses his arrogance to cover it. Oh, dear, I must recover the tone of my mind.*

Darcy found Miss Bennet's barbed comment entirely inappropriate. However, he responded by saying, "In drawing rooms. I meant nothing untoward by my comment, I promise you."

The woman actually sniffed at him and refused to meet his gaze. She was not nearly as beautiful as her sister. Miss Bennet's dark hair shone, however, and her skin seemed particularly smooth. Finally, she glanced up at him, revealing a pair of fine brown eyes. Direct and intelligent. Something flickered in their depths. *The veriest hint of an apology?*

Mrs. Bingley rose. "Shall we sit around the table to partake of this lovely tea? So much easier than holding a cup and saucer on our laps, is it not?

"Yes, indeed," Bingley said, his expression cautious after he scanned his sister-in-law's face.

Darcy wondered if Miss Bennet had the type of temperament that thrived best outside of company. Like himself. He held out his arm to her.

"May I escort you?" he asked.

She set her hand on his arm and stood. "Thank you."

Have I already put her off me? How? What have I done so that she has taken me in dislike?

Chapter Five

Lizzy observed him while they ate their tea. She could not be certain, of course, but it seemed to her that he was making his best effort to be polite and accommodating. He spoke of his home in glowing terms. Evidently, he loved it dearly.

"My sister, Georgiana, and my aunt, Mrs. Sophia McDougall—whose husband, a Captain of the Scots Guards, died during the Peninsular War—keep Pemberley running smoothly while I am away," Mr. Darcy said. He patted his mouth with his serviette. "I have an estate manager, as you would expect, but the ladies run the heart of the estate. Do you not find it so, Miss Bennet? That the ladies of an estate are its heart?"

Lizzy blinked. "Uh, I hardly know. My father's estate was a small one. So there was little for my mother to do. She directed the gardener in a rather haphazard fashion and looked after the servants, though I shall say that Jane took care of that duty most of the time."

"And you managed the gardens as soon as Mama realized you had a turn for it," Jane pointed out, smiling at her.

"I am not surprised to hear that garden design is one of your talents," Mr. Darcy commented.

Lizzy's eyebrows lifted. He took a sip of his tea and then glanced her way.

"And your meaning, sir?" she asked in as sweet a voice as she could manage—not terribly sweet. So, she added a smile that felt tight.

What is it about this man that pricks at me so?

"You are naturally attuned to the artistic, I think. You are well known as an excellent portraitist," he said, setting his cup down.

"Our Lizzy also paints astounding landscapes," Charles praised, ignorant of the glare his wife cast his way.

Lizzy saw that Mr. Darcy noticed it, however. A nerve by his eyebrow twitched.

"Why, since we have arrived, Lizzy has painted an absolutely charming scene of Fountains Abbey. She imagined what one of the great stained-glass windows might have looked like before the building's destruction."

Jane broke in, "Pray, how old is your sister, Mr. Darcy?"

His eyebrow twitched once more—at the interruption, Lizzy must suppose, since her question had been innocuous and not one that he should object to answering.

"Almost nineteen," he answered. "Her birthday is only a few months off."

"That is young, is it not, to expect her to be the 'heart' of your estate?" Jane asked, ignoring her husband's goggling stare. Jane, in an attempt to redirect the subject of their conversation, had been betrayed into being more forward than was her wont. "She must be…uh…highly accomplished."

Mr. Darcy nodded. "Indeed. Georgiana plays the pianoforte with great skill. She draws and paints as well. She speaks some Italian, too, besides French, of course. And, oh, yes, her needle work is superior in every way."

"She sounds like a paragon," Lizzy said dryly, only half-beneath her breath. Then, she silently kicked herself.

My accursed tongue. Why do I keep baiting him? His presence is…imposing. Perhaps that is why I am on my guard. I like men who are more open. But, then, Wickham was open, or so we thought. I shall strive to give Mr. Darcy the benefit of my good opinion until he does something that destroys it.

Mr. Darcy frowned. "Please, forgive the doting fondness of an elder brother. I suppose she is no paragon—not in the negative sense, I mean. Besides her physical accomplishments, she has a lively wit and she is kind to a fault, perhaps."

Lizzy held up a hand, palm forward. "You have no need to explain her character to us. Forgive my remark, I beg of you. She sounds like a delightful young woman. You have every right to be proud of her. Is she whom you would like me to paint?"

His frown disappeared. "Yes. I am exceedingly proud of her, and I would like to have her painted before she goes to London to be presented."

Lizzy and her sister exchanged glances, then Lizzy said, "I am truly sorry you did not know before you travelled all this way." She spread her hands wide. "I do not paint adults."

He blinked at her.

"It is true," Jane said. "My sister never paints adults. Children and pets only. If you had explained more in your letter and then waited for a reply, you need not have inconvenienced yourself."

"Georgiana *is* a child," Mr. Darcy claimed. His hand clenched around his serviette. "She is not yet out. She *is* a child."

"So she may seem to you, sir," Lizzy said in quiet rebuke. "At almost nineteen, Miss Darcy is a woman grown." She viewed the stubborn tightening of his jaw and added, "I have four sisters. I know of what I speak."

"You do not know Georgiana, however," he bit out.

His love of his sister was all that it should have been and her heart softened somewhat toward him.

"That statement is unanswerably correct," she admitted. "Nevertheless, I must reiterate that I do not paint adults."

Mr. Darcy leapt to his feet. "Is it that your skill is unequal to the task?" he flashed back, his nostrils flaring.

Charles rose, too. He put a hand on their guest's arm. "Steady on," he said, his brows drawn together.

Darcy stiffened. His blazing expression shut down and he calmed his mind. He tugged on his waistcoat hem, nodded to

Bingley, and bowed to the ladies who both bore alarmed and shocked expressions.

"I beg your pardon. I must be more tired from my journey than I realized to offer such an insult." He took a deep breath and waited for his hostess's response. His one aim, to find a woman to paint Georgiana, could be lost entirely if Mrs. Bingley did not relent. She seemed to be equally against Miss Bennet painting his sister. *Why? What is the great mystery here?* "Pray, forgive me."

Mrs. Bingley was not proof against his plea. "Of course," she said, waving him back to his chair. "Please, sit and finish your tea before you take your leave and find some respite."

Darcy knew better than to sit without obtaining Miss Bennet's forgiveness as well. He looked at her. She had her head tilted to one side and her direct gaze stared into his. He stared back, willing her to relent. At last, she bowed her head and lowered her gaze.

He found his seat. Bingley returned to his own chair and passed him a plate of honeyed orange and almond sweetmeats. Darcy did not want one, but he took it for the peace offering it was meant to be. He placed it on his plate and picked up a fork.

"Miss Bennet," he said, squishing the round ball in half and spearing it on his utensil, "if I have not sunk below reproach, will you do me the honor of showing me your painting of Fountains Abbey? I would dearly love to see it."

Miss Bennet's face betrayed no alarm, but the color drained from her sister's. *Why?*

"Certainly, if you wish it. I have it in my room. Excuse me while I fetch it," Miss Bennet said, rising.

Darcy and Bingley both rose. Mrs. Bingley attempted to grab her sister's hand. Miss Bennet captured her hand, patted it, and let it go.

"You wish me to take Jeremy with me, I suppose," Miss Bennet said, a laugh in her voice. "I am not such a weak creature that I cannot carry a single painting back from my bedchamber. He will not be required."

Mrs. Bingley muffled a squeak behind her serviette.

“I shall send him in to set up the easel,” Miss Bennet said, heading toward the door.

Darcy hurried after her and reached the entry in time to open it for her.

“Thank you, sir. Ah, Jeremy,” she said to the young footman who had jumped to his feet from the chair kept beside the door for his comfort. “Kindly set up the viewing easel in the lounge. I am going to fetch my painting of Fountains Abbey.”

“Yes, miss,” he said, stepping aside to let her exit the chamber. “Do you need me to assist you, miss?”

“No, thank you,” she said, heading down the corridor.

He hurried after her regardless, took her key, opened a bedchamber door, and then returned the key to her. As soon as the door was closed, Darcy heard the key turn in the lock and Jeremy retraced his steps to the open door of the lounge where Darcy stood waiting.

“Sir,” the footman said, nodding to him. “May I pass?”

Darcy, instead of stepping back into the lounge, entered the corridor, intending to await Miss Bennet’s return. Bingley joined him.

“She says she needs no help, but the painting is fairly large,” Bingley said. “And, she always displays an unframed painting with a loose frame in front of it. To give a better effect, you understand.”

“Yes. The loose frame must be awkward to carry,” Darcy said, nodding. He glanced back into the lounge and watched Mrs. Bingley directing Jeremy’s positioning of the easel. She was still pale, but now she also appeared resigned. Once she was happy with the placement, the footman set a large, flat board upon it as a base for the painting. “Is the work done in watercolors? Or oil?”

“Watercolors,” Bingley said. “Ah, here she is. Lizzy is deucedly independent, you know. And, now, instead of asking for help, she is juggling the frame, her project portfolio, and the key, while she struggles to lock the door. It is as I thought, she needs help.”

"I shall help her," Darcy said and bounded down the corridor before Bingley could forestall him. "Permit me," he said, taking the loose frame from her grasp, preventing it from falling on the floor. "You look after the painting," he directed, taking her room key away, too.

"Uh, thank you," she said, backing away from him. Right into Bingley. "Oh, Charles. You, too?"

"I shall carry your portfolio," he said, tugging it out of her hands.

"Now I have nothing to carry," she protested.

"You may carry your key," Darcy said, holding it out to her.

"Thank you," she said, shaking her head at them, her lips pressed into a narrow smile, and taking the key. "Shall we, gentlemen?"

Darcy and Bingley followed in her wake as she swept toward the lounge. Mrs. Bingley met her at the door and Darcy could just make out her whispered words to her sister.

"The jackdaw!"

"I have not forgotten," Miss Bennet replied *sotto voce.*

Bingley must have heard, as well, because he said, in a rather too-loud voice, "Here we are, my dear, with the rest of Lizzy's trappings."

What are they trying to hide from me? What can they fear from a simple painting? Is it so poorly done that they are ashamed for me to see it? Jackdaw?

The footman came over to him and held out his hands for the plain wood frame. Darcy could think of no good reason not to let him have it, so he relinquished control of it. Mrs. Bingley approached Darcy and rested her hand on his arm.

"Let us turn our backs until Lizzy is ready for her work to be seen," she said, smiling at him. "Charles will assist her. He is quite the biggest admirer of her talent. Even more so than any member of her family. When she sells one of her paintings, he moans over the fact he will likely never see it again."

Refusing her wish was out of the question, particularly after his rudeness earlier. They turned their backs on the trio.

"That is truly something."

Perhaps it is through Bingley that I must go in order to convince Miss Bennet to paint Georgiana.

"If Charles had his way, the walls of Netherfield would be decorated with dozens of pets we did not know and children we had never seen."

Darcy chuckled.

"We are ready," Miss Bennet said from behind them.

"Are *you* ready, Mr. Darcy?" Mrs. Bingley asked him.

"I am," he said, feeling his heartbeat accelerate. Darcy could not remember a time when he felt so excited about a revelation. Very well, he could. Getting his first pony for his fifth birthday clearly beat this moment.

"Let us turnabout, then," his hostess said in a tight voice.

They turned and Darcy caught his breath.

He stared. And stared.

He had visited the ruined abbey before but he had never seen it quite like this. The stone seemed to glow with an eternal light, hinting at the holy work previously done there. Stone window arches remained as a testament to an inspired architect.

And the nave window…the huge nave window…

He remembered standing below it on the inside and his adult head had not even reached the sill. He had even stretched his arm up and could not touch the sill with the tips of his fingers. The window, then, had been empty—more of just a stone frame. No glazing remained. No stone munnions, either. The arch of the window had soared above the sill. He did not know its height, but he did not believe that it could be an inch less than fifty feet, and its width had been twenty-three feet.

In Miss Bennet's painting, the nave window no longer stood empty. Instead, a kaleidoscope of colors displayed a stained-glass window that may never have looked—could *never* have looked—exactly as painted. But he wanted to believe the window had once looked as beautiful as the painted version. The vision of that window struck his…his soul.

With immense effort, Darcy tore his gaze away from the

painting and looked at Miss Bennet. She was the only person in the room *not* looking at the easel. She was looking at him. Her eyebrows shot up. She was waiting for his response.

In a hushed voice, full of intensity, he said, "You *must* paint Pemberley House."

"Oh?" she said, folding her arms. "I thought you wanted me to paint your sister."

"I do," Darcy said. He pointed at the Abbey. "But I also want you to paint Pemberley. Surely, you can have no objection. Your talent is beyond anything I could have imagined. The green of the grass, the trees, the river, the stones. I cannot find the words to describe this work of art. Even the jackdaw…" his voice trailed away as Miss Bennet's gaze darted to the painting.

She blinked rapidly and tilted her head, then narrowed her gaze. "What jackdaw?"

Darcy frowned. He looked at the bottom corner of the painting while saying, "The one you painted in the…what? Where is it?"

Bingley looked at him. "What jackdaw?"

"Are you saying you did not see a jackdaw?"

Bingley shook his head. "No, no birds."

Darcy took a step back and scrutinized Bingley's expression and then that of his wife, and lastly Miss Bennet. *What is happening here?*

"Oh, I see it," Mrs. Bingley said, nodding at the painting. "In the bottom right-hand side. Husband, you must need spectacles."

Bingley pulled a face and examined the painting again. "Oh, right. There they are. Lizzy, surely you did not forget the jackdaw."

"Of course not," Miss Bennet said, chuckling. "I was jesting. Mr. Darcy, you should have seen your face. I do beg your pardon. It was not well done of me.

But Bingley also thought there was no bird, Darcy thought, studying the canvas again. The black and gray bird stood on the grass as before, appearing to be ready to hop away at any moment. *I must be tired.*

He shook his attention back to his desire and faced his quarry. "Miss Bennet, pray say you will paint my home. You could all leave from here and visit Pemberley. There is plenty of room."

Bingley moved so he blocked the painting as though he was banning Darcy from its beauty. "Is this a commission? Lizzy charges one hundred guineas for a landscape, whether you like the final result or not."

Darcy did not hesitate. "Done."

Miss Bennet had gasped at the price, but that was not what she commented upon. "Mr. Darcy, if we come to your home so that I might paint it, you must promise not to try and convince me to paint your sister."

"Of course," he said instantly. "And, I will not dictate the form the landscape must take. You will have complete artistic freedom."

Lizzy exchanged glances with her sister and brother-in-law. They were both frowning. To Mr. Darcy, she said, "Will you give us a few minutes of privacy to discuss our change of plans?"

"Certainly," he said, bowing his shoulders. "I shall wait in the corridor."

"And thus, forcing us to make a hasty decision?" Lizzy asked dryly. "We cannot permit you to be uncomfortable. We know your room number. Charles will bring you my answer."

Mr. Darcy bowed again and left without another word. As soon as the door closed, Jane rushed to her side and clasped her arm.

"Lizzy, you cannot. How can you risk it? I think Mr. Darcy is a powerful man, with powerful connections. What if he discovers your secret?" she asked, pale.

"Jane, dearest," Lizzy said, patting her hands. "I am not good for you. My talent is a drain on you. I know this commission is a great risk for me. I do not know what will happen when I paint Pemberley. I will not paint a single living thing in that landscape. Other than grass and trees, of course."

Charles cleared his throat. "Ahem. So sorry, but I saw the painting you did of Studley Royal Water Gardens. The statues of the wrestlers on the plinth had changed holds. I do not like to mention it, but feel that I must. Did some wrestling myself at Cambridge. Of course, it was just a minor little club off of Castle Street. That is why I recognized the change of position, you see."

"Oh, dear," Lizzy said, sighing. "I suppose I must keep statues out of the painting, too."

"Pemberley may be surrounded by statues," Jane pointed out. "There may be some on the roof."

"Or not. Mr. Darcy spoke of his home extensively and did not mention a single one," Lizzy pointed out. She clutched her hands together before her chest and said, "Think of how the one hundred guineas will greatly increase my nest egg. I will be able to buy my own little home even sooner and my troubles will no longer be yours."

"You are no trouble, my dearest Lizzy," Jane expostulated, releasing her arm so she could embrace her. "None at all."

"None at all?" Lizzy demanded, grinning. "What a plumper."

"No, sister," Charles said. "Jane is quite right. We love having you at Netherfield. You are not the least trouble."

"When you have shut off an entire double drawing room on your second floor just to house paintings no one but the family is permitted to see?" Lizzy scoffed. "Is that your idea of no trouble?"

"We cannot possibly need that drawing room," Jane said. "Netherfield has a separate ball room, as you know. We do not require those two rooms to form a makeshift space for dancing. Lizzy, dearest, you are worth any trouble. *Any*."

Tears pricked Lizzy's eyes and she blinked them away. How she loved her eldest sister, whose soft heart and loyal soul had engulfed her throughout her life.

"Thank you, Jane," Lizzy said, sniffing. She squeezed her

hand. "Nevertheless, I want to take this commission. I cannot say why this is so important to me—important enough to take such a risk—but I feel that this is the right thing to do."

"You *feel* it?" Charles said, frowning. "Like a premonition? Have you had those before?"

Lizzy nodded. "Most recently, I knew that our parents should not rush after Lydia. I urged them to wait for my uncle to arrive from London." She took a deep, steadying breath before continuing. "They would not listen. You know Mama. And…and they died."

Charles gravely examined both the lady's countenances. "Jane, my dear?"

Jane turned from them and found a chair. She sank into it, bowed her head, and covered her face with her hands. Charles rushed over and crouched down to embrace her.

"You see," Lizzy said, wringing her hands. "My poor sister is prostrate because of me. This cursed talent of mine! I must find a way to live freely and—before you say it, Charles—I will not accept an allowance from you. I must be independent. Mr. Darcy's one hundred guineas will be welcome. Most welcome, indeed. I want to take the risk."

Jane lowered her hands and nodded. Charles swiveled on his feet to look at Lizzy and said, "We agree to go with you to Pemberley," he said, attempting a smile. "I will fish in Darcy's lake—he has promised me great sport. And Jane will enjoy exploring the park and meeting a new friend in Miss Georgiana Darcy."

"And I will do my very best not to paint anything untoward," Lizzy promised. "Thank you, Jane. Charles."

"You must also promise to live near to us," Jane said, smiling weakly. "I could not bear it if you did not live close by. Promise me, Lizzy."

Lizzy solemnly placed her hand over her heart. "I promise. And Jane, even with this money, we shall have years and years together before I have accrued enough to move out on my own. And, if I attempt the adventure when I am too young, I shall have to hire a chaperone or a companion to lend me consequence and to keep me from falling beneath reproach. I do not want that."

Jane's expression lightened. "Yes, indeed. We shall have you under foot for at least another ten years."

"And we shall be heartily sick of you by then," Charles said, chuckling. He stood. "Shall I call Mr. Darcy in? I expect he did not withdraw to his rooms."

"Yes, please," Lizzy said. When the door opened and the man entered the lounge, she took a deep breath and said, "I will paint Pemberley."

Chapter Six

Darcy beamed. “Thank you. I am delighted.”

Miss Bennet held up her hand, palm forward. “Though I have agreed to paint your home, sir, we will not be returning with you directly to Derbyshire.”

Bingley glanced at her and raised his eyebrows.

“But…” Mrs. Bingley said, her voice trailing away.

Miss Bennet took her sister’s arm “Silly goose. Did you think I would force you and Charles away from all our planned pleasures? Are we not set on visiting the Minster church of St. Peter and St. Wilfred in Ripon on the morrow? I do not wish to miss its wonders either. It is supposed to be a magnificent edifice and the carvings of the misericords are said to be striking.”

“By Jove, it is,” Bingley ejaculated, grinning widely. “I have visited it before and long to see it again.” He fixed his attention on Darcy. “You should join us, if you have the time. We would enjoy your company.”

Darcy had little interest in the church, no matter how splendid it was, as he had viewed it on a previous visit to the North Riding. However, he nodded, and said, “I will be pleased to have an excuse to extend my visit. Will you bring your sketch pad, Miss Bennet?”

“I always do,” she replied, smiling a mysterious sort of smile that intrigued him.

“We mean to set out at nine, if that suits you?” Bingley asked, clearly pleased to add him to their party. “We want to arrive in good time, you see. The light is better in the morning and the landlord here has promised it will not rain. Our chaise should fit us all comfortably."

"Nine will be perfectly fine," Darcy said, inwardly doubting that the ladies would be ready so early.

But his silent prediction proved false. He presented himself at the Bingley's lounge door at the precise time and found the door open and all three waiting, the ladies already wearing their bonnets and pulling on their gloves. Jeremy, the footman, stood to one side, carrying a sketch pad and a box that looked like it might contain art supplies.

"There you are," Bingley said, hurrying forward to shake his hand. "Welcome."

"Thank you. Good morning, ladies," Darcy said, bowing his shoulders to the sisters.

"Good morning. How was your room, Mr. Darcy? Did you sleep well?" Mrs. Bingley asked, stepping toward him.

"Yes, indeed. Most comfortable."

"Excellent. Then, shall we?" she asked, gesturing toward the door.

Bingley offered his arm to his wife and Darcy held out his arm to Miss Bennet. She accepted it without demur. Once outside the inn, they paused for a moment and admired the cool, clear morning that boded to come on warm in the afternoon. Several other early-risers, out on their morning constitutionals, nodded a greeting to the party.

"Off on an excursion, Bingley, what?" a middle-aged man with great military whiskers asked, puffing out his chest and smiling at the ladies.

"Yes, Colonel," Bingley responded, straightening as though to attention. "Off to Ripon. To see the Minster church."

"Saw it yesterday. A fine building. Worth seeing." Then, without waiting for any further conversation, the colonel stalked off down the lane.

"It is nice to have his approval," Darcy said a trifle dryly.

Bingley chuckled. "He seems a bit of a tartar, but you should meet his wife and you will soon learn that he is a pussycat in comparison."

"Good Lord," Darcy said.

A groom held open the door to the chaise, a modern, well-sprung Berlin, upholstered in deep-wine leather. The ladies sat looking forward, leaving the gentlemen the rear-facing seat.

"We should only be on the road for about a half hour," Bingley said, settling in.

Jeremy passed the sketchpad and box to Miss Bennet and closed the door. The carriage swayed as the groom climbed onto the seat next to the coachman. They all lurched in their seats as the horses began their journey.

Darcy, sitting directly across from Miss Bennet, allowed himself a few minutes to admire her countenance, which appeared more and more pleasing to him each time they met. She glanced at him and noticed his regard, narrowing her eyes slightly.

"Shall we play Imaginary Hide-and-Go-Seek or some other game to pass the time?" she asked brightly.

Intrigued, Darcy tilted his head and repeated, "Imaginary Hide-and-Go-Seek? I do not believe I have ever heard of that one."

"It is very simple," Mrs. Bingley said, smiling softly. "You imagine where you are hiding and your fellow passengers must ask questions to discover where you are."

"When you are traveling with your family, you can limit the hiding places to within your own home," Bingley said with some enthusiasm. "However, if you have not grown up together, then the whole world is your hiding place. You can limit the places to countries or to cities."

"That sounds rather educational," Darcy said with a mock frown. "I expect a governess or a tutor came up with that variation."

Everyone chuckled and agreed that it seemed likely.

"If I may make a suggestion?" Darcy asked, his mouth quirking up at one side. "Let us converse, instead."

Miss Bennet raised an eyebrow. "Very well," she said and folded her hands in her lap. "May I ask how you know our new brother-in-law?"

Darcy stiffened and glanced at Bingley.

"Um, sorry. There are few secrets between husbands and wives and none at all between sisters."

Resigned, Darcy explained. "I have known Wickham since the earliest days of our childhood. My father stood as godfather to him. Indeed, he was named after my father. *His* father was *my* father's steward." He stirred in his seat at the memory of their past friendship. "After my father's death, I was charged in his will to provide for Wickham. The manner of that provision was left to my discretion. There was talk of a living we had in our purview going to him if he desired to enter the Church."

Miss Bennet interrupted him with a gentile snort. "A less fit person for the Church would be hard to find."

"Yes, so we agree. Instead, I settled two thousand pounds on him. Not a vast sum, I warrant, but certainly sufficient to support him until he obtained a position in whichever profession he found agreeable."

"I do not believe *any* profession would do," Bingley said, shaking his head. "Even the army seems to be merely a hobby to him."

"I am not surprised," Darcy said, pursing his lips. "Looking back as an adult, I can see the pettiness in many of his childhood behaviors."

"Is that why you fell out?" Mrs. Bingley asked, frowning. "His pettiness?"

Darcy shook his head. "No, he betrayed my trust most grievously." He held up a hand when Miss Bennet opened her mouth. "I beg your pardon, but I can say no more without betraying a confidence."

Her mouth snapped shut. Then, she commented, "It is amazing, is it not, that our paths have crossed. The chance of it is remarkable."

"I must agree," Darcy said, falling silent afterward. He stared moodily out the window at the passing countryside for a time before Miss Bennet spoke again.

"It is your turn to offer a conversational gambit, Mr. Darcy," she said. The carriage wheels rolled in and then out of a deep rut, making them all grab for the straps. "Whoops. Heavens. The roads are shocking." She shook her head and focused her attention on him again. "Come now. You wished to converse. What shall we talk about?"

"Very well," Darcy said, bestirring himself. "When did you begin drawing in earnest?"

"I have always drawn in earnest. From the moment I could hold a pencil."

"Oh, yes," her sister said, smiling widely. "Her drawings provided endless enjoyment for her sisters."

Darcy nodded at the sketch pad. "Do you have anything you would mind sharing with me?"

Mrs. Bingley seemed to hold her breath when Miss Bennet passed the sketch pad across to him.

Why is that?

He flipped open the cover and examined the studies in charcoal laid out upon its pages—an eye, an ear, a nose, a pair of hands. A church spire, a pair of headstones, a rose. He glanced up. "These are all very fine."

Miss Bennet raised her eyebrows in acknowledgment. He smiled slightly and turned a page without looking down. A flash of color caught his eye and he returned his attention to the drawings.

"Ah, a watercolor. The local church? I believe we drove past it yesterday." Light streamed down on the spire through billowing clouds as though God himself leant his blessing upon the structure. Darcy's mouth went dry when a nearly holy thrill swept through him.

"For the vicar," Bingley said, looking over his shoulders. He drew in a breath. "It is lovely, Lizzy. He will be thrilled with it."

"May I have it back, please?" Lizzy asked, holding out her hand. Mr. Darcy closed the pad with great reluctance and passed it across to her. She wanted it back before he could see anything unusual about it. Anything *more* unusual, that is. "Thank you."

"The vicar should be pleased with that painting, I should think," Mr. Darcy stated calmly.

If it does anything untoward after the vicar hangs it, he is likely to think it a miracle, Lizzy thought wryly.

She kept the thought to herself, however, and merely smiled and said, "Thank you. I shall have it framed in Ripon."

"Darcy and I shall look after that commission for you, if we may?" Charles offered. "We will set you down at St. Peters and St. Wilfred's with Jeremy to lend you consequence and to carry Lizzy's drawing box."

"But, dearest, then you shall miss viewing the church," Jane protested.

"Fear not. We shall soon catch you up," Charles promised, grinning widely. "If I know our Lizzy, here, she will park herself in front of a chapel and begin sketching. Let Charlie McMillan, the head verger, take you in hand. He has been a verger there for decades and knows all its history."

In retaliation for their abandonment, however long it may last, Lizzy stated as though out of the blue, "Charles recently informed us that he belonged to a wrestling club while at Cambridge."

Mr. Darcy skewed in his seat so he could look at Charles. "Which college?"

"Emmanuel," Charles said. "I suppose you attended Oxford?"

"Yes. Merton College. Wrestling?"

"Greco-Roman," Charles admitted, blushing a little.

Lizzy watched them while they discussed the sport. She had known that once she introduced the subject that the men would run away with it, leaving her and Jane to their own thoughts or discourse.

She did not open the sketch pad to examine the image. And she was not going to tell Jane anything about the painting. Most definitely, she would not be telling her that she had not painted the sketch. The color had just appeared out of nowhere, due to whatever influenced the caprices of her paintings. Had this happened before? She had never seen this variation of her talent. She had always thought her sketches safe from the results of her talent—except for the chipmunk. He would never sit still

Over the years, she had given away many sketches, believing no untoward revelation would occur. What if this proved to be an erroneous supposition?

Uncertainty swept through her. Surely, someone would have come to her if they had noticed anything strange about their sketch? Perhaps this was the first time? One thing was certain. Under no circumstance could she give this sketch-painting to the vicar. Or let Charles and Mr. Darcy take it to be framed. What if it changed again while they had it? What would Mr. Darcy think? What would happen to her commission to paint Pemberley? She imagined the one hundred guineas flying out the window, lost to her forever.

Lizzy slipped the sketch-painting out of the pad, held it toward her, and tore it in two. All eyes immediately fixed on her. She noticed that the paint disappeared, leaving her with only dark lines on the page. She tore the two sheets in half again, carefully keeping the sketch facing her.

"Lizzy!" Jane and Charles cried.

"Miss Bennet?"

Lizzy gathered the four quarter-sheets together and tore them again. And then again, and again, until she could not tear them anymore.

"Lizzy? What are you doing?" Jane asked weakly, collecting the few bits that had fallen to the floor. She turned them over, stared at them for a second, and then quickly covered them with her hands.

Lizzy tugged on the window, pulling it open with one hand. She thrust her papers out the opening, grabbed the ones from beneath Jane's hands, and threw them after the others where they would be ground under the wheels of the muddy road traffic. She swept her palms over her skirts as though clearing them of debris.

"There," she said in a mater-of-fact voice.

"Um," Charles said, his eyes wide. "Were you dissatisfied with your work?"

"After looking at it again, I realized I hated it," Lizzy stated, folding her hands in her lap and swaying with the motion of the carriage.

"It was lovely," Mr. Darcy said softly. "Really lovely. I was most struck by it."

To Lizzy's ear, he sounded as though rocked in shock. As well he might be. An astonished air filled the entire carriage. Neither of the men could believe that she had torn up the beautiful sketch-painting.

"I agree," Jane said, tucking her arm through Lizzy's. "It was not your best work."

"Perhaps not, I cannot say," Mr. Darcy said coldly. "But it was the most astounding display of wanton destruction I have ever witnessed."

Lizzy stared at him and lifted her chin, sniffing. "I am hiding. Where am I?"

Charles blinked at her so rapidly she thought something must have got into his eye. Lizzy exchanged a glance with Jane and knew that she understood why she had destroyed the sketch-painting. Jane rose magnificently to the moment.

"Are you hiding in Europe?" she asked.

"Yes," Lizzy replied. She looked at her brother-in-law. "Charles? What is your question?"

A long pause punctuated the silence and she wondered if he could make such a drastic shift in his thinking in order to avoid the topic of the torn painting.

"Um, Europe, eh?" he said, trying for time. "I have thought of a question. Are you east of France?"

Lizzy beamed at him. "Yes." She fixed her stare on Mr. Darcy. His expression remained stony. Would he be rude and refuse to play? "It is your turn, sir."

In a biting tone, he asked, "Are you south of Switzerland?"

Relieved, she answered, "Very good, Mr. Darcy. Yes."

"I wish I had a map," Charles confessed.

Everyone chuckled and the air inside the carriage lightened.

∞

Mrs. Little, the butcher's wife, stopped Georgiana in the street outside of their shop. Her generous body managed a small bob and she squeezed the edges of her apron with her hands.

"Good morning, Miss Darcy," Mrs. Little said, her smile stretching wide and accentuating the crow's feet angling out from her gray eyes.

"Mrs. Little," Georgiana said, smiling back. "It is a fine morning, is it not?"

"Yes, miss." She glanced up and down the high street before she said, "If y'll forgive me askin', miss, would thysen step into t'shop fer a bit?"

Georgiana nodded and then said to her footman, who walked with her, carrying her packages. "I shall be back directly. Kindly wait here."

When she came out of the shop a quarter of an hour later, she was frowning. *I will need to talk to Mr. Kearn. I shall invite him to eat with us tonight.*

She returned to Pemberley, her errands completed. In the entrance hall, she was greeted by Mellor.

"Did miss have a successful morning in Lambton?" he asked, directing the footman to take her parcels away to the morning room where Georgiana would go presently to distribute them. He accepted her bonnet and spencer.

"Yes, I did. Mellor? Will you send a request to Mr. Kearn to join my aunt and me for dinner tonight?"

The butler bowed his shoulders and left her.

Her aunt hurried down the grand staircase. "There you are, dearest. How was Lambton?"

"Lovely, thank you. I have invited Mr. Kearn to dinner," Georgiana revealed. At her aunt's twinkling frown, she added, "I have something to discuss with him and thought we might as well enjoy his company with our meal. Come with me into the morning room where Fred is waiting with my parcels."

"Of course," Aunt Sophia said. "Tell me all the gossip. Has the baker's daughter decided to marry that nice young farmer?"

Georgiana chuckled. "Indeed. The wedding is set for the autumn, after the harvest."

Once the parcels had been sent to their various destinations and tea served, the ladies were finally alone in the morning room.

Aunt Sophia set her teacup down and folded her hands in her lap, focusing her attention entirely on Georgiana, who lifted her eyebrows.

"Is something amiss, Aunt?"

"You will not mind me giving you a hint, I know," Aunt Sophia said animatedly, shifting forward a little on her seat. "You are young and inexperienced, while *I*," she paused and placed a flattened palm against her chest, "am not."

Georgiana frowned, confused. "A hint about what? I do not understand."

"My dear, a hint about Mr. Kearn."

Georgiana's heart skipped. She lowered her gaze and hoped her cheeks revealed nothing of her secret feelings. She picked up her teacup and took a sip. "Is aught wrong with our good estate manager? His family is well, I hope?"

"That is not the sort of hint I am talking about," her aunt said with mock asperity. "Come, look at me."

Georgiana schooled her expression and met her aunt's lively greenish-gray eyes. Beside the brightness found there, she could read a degree of soberness she had not expected.

"Tell me, are you developing feelings for Mr. Kearn?" she demanded, tilting her head. "Mind you, I cannot say I blame you. He is a handsome man, intelligent, hardworking, reliable, and...well...and so many other positive traits. His character is beyond reproach." She touched a curl lying against her neck. "Indeed, if I was a younger woman..."

"Aunt Sophia!" Georgiana exclaimed, blushing for certain now.

"Tell me the truth, now," her aunt said, shaking a finger at her. "You know he is ineligible."

"He is a gentleman," Georgiana said in a steady voice. "His father is an admiral."

Aunt Sophia shook her head and let out a long, loud huffing sort of breath. "I know you are only eighteen, my dear, but you know that the third son of an admiral is not a suitable match for you. You are an heiress. He is an estate manager. Your brother will never approve."

Georgiana set down her cup and rose to her feet. Slipping across to one of the long windows, she gazed, without really seeing it, at the ordered gardens beyond. She grasped the edge of one silk drape and held on as though keeping herself from falling.

In a gentle voice, her aunt continued, "It is not really fair, my dear, to give the man hope. I can see the way he looks at you. Soon, Fitz will notice too. You do not wish for him to lose his position, do you? Or, perhaps he would keep his position and Fitz would send us away until your come out, removing temptation."

"I believe you are mistaken about his feelings. He has never given me any reason to believe he has developed a *tendre* for me. Regardless, Mr. Kearn is a gentleman," Georgiana repeated softly. She swallowed before she said, without turning around, "He is not like Mr. Wickham. You need not fear a repeat of my younger self's folly."

She heard the rustle of her aunt's skirts and soon felt hands on her shoulders. It took all her fortitude not to shake her touch away.

"I have no fear of that," Aunt Sophia said solemnly. "However, you must maintain your distance. That is why he does not join us when your brother is away unless we are entertaining."

In a bitter voice, Georgiana said, "He must know his place and keep it."

"And you must help him do so. It is the kindest thing you can do for him."

Georgiana forced back the tears she felt stinging her eyes and moved away from her aunt, whose company she could not endure at the moment.

"I will send an invitation to the vicar and his family to join us for dinner tonight." Georgiana paused at the door, and half-turned toward her aunt, but she did not look at her. "The subject of my reason for inviting Mr. Kearn could easily be discussed before them."

"Thank you," her aunt said, but said it to the back of her niece and was uncertain as to whether Georgiana heard her. She sighed and murmured, "Oh, dear."

Chapter Seven

Yorkshire...

The Minster church of St. Peter and St. Wilfred proved to be as magnificent as reported. Built of a golden stone, it glowed in the morning sun. At the entrance to the town, they paused so everyone could step down and view the Minster from a distance. It had two superb square towers on the west end and a third, even more massive, square tower in the center of the building. The Minster dominated the skyline, drawing all eyes to it, and through it, to God. They climbed back into the carriage and drove on. Once inside the town, they passed through the market square, containing the newly built Palladian-fronted Town Hall on one side. It was slow going along Kirkgate Street, a narrow road that wound past shops until it opened up rather abruptly at the end, revealing the west face of the Minster.

Mr. Darcy offered his hand to assist Lizzy down from the carriage. She took it, paying little heed to him. Instead, once both her feet were firmly on the ground, she tipped her head back and stared up, and up, and up, to take in the glories of the two towers and the rows of stained-glass windows. They faced west, so their images could not be seen in the shade of the building.

"We should walk around to the east side," Lizzy said, holding out her sketch pad and box of supplies to no one in particular. Mr. Darcy took them from her and she murmured a distracted, "Thank you." Over her shoulder, she said, "Jeremy, I shall not need you."

"Yes, miss."

Slowly walking around the outside of the Minster, she gazed wonderingly up at it, taking in all its architectural wonders, including its buttresses and decorated Gothic window arches. Eventually, they reached the cemetery and the east window that displayed, to her eyes, brilliant colors as the sunlight struck it. She knew that Jane and Charles often did not see what she could and wondered what Mr. Darcy saw when he looked at the windows. Did he see brilliant colors, or would he only see those once they viewed the window from the inside where the light shone through each pane?

"Amazing," Jane said, coming to stand beside her. "There is such a sense of vastness. I can imagine a little more fully what Fountains Abbey must have looked like."

"Indeed," Lizzy breathed. She glanced away from the Minster and looked around at the wall surrounding and supporting the raised cemetery. The footpath sat at least three feet below the adjacent holy ground. "How do we get into the cemetery? Has anyone seen a gate or steps?"

"Not yet," Charles said. He grinned at her. "I am certain Darcy and I could lift you both up onto the wall."

"You will do no such thing," his wife told him with a smile. "There must be an entrance."

"It is further along the wall," Mr. Darcy informed them. "I recall it from a previous visit."

"We shall follow you," Charles said, sweeping his arm forward.

Mr. Darcy took the lead on the narrow, cobbled pathway. They found the entrance and proceeded to make their way through the ancient graves to a spot where they paused to admire the east nave window.

"It is very much like the window in your painting, Miss Bennet," Mr. Darcy said, looking at her, not the building. "Though your painting showed a level of brilliance we cannot see from the outside."

Ah, he does not see what I see. I am not surprised. No one ever sees what I see.

His attention continued to be on her instead of the window and that vexed Lizzy. What was she when such magnificence stood before them?

"Do you think there was some rivalry between the two orders as to who could build the more beautiful church?" Mr. Darcy asked.

"Human nature being what it is, sir, I expect so," Lizzy replied. "Is that your assessment?"

"Perhaps. If so, their weakness is our gain," he said.

"Indeed, it is. May I have my sketch pad?" she asked.

He handed it over. She also took the box.

"You may go ahead with Jane and Charles," she said, glancing around. "Where is Jeremy?"

"You told him you would not need him," Mr. Darcy said. "Did you forget?"

Lizzy frowned at him.

"Mr. Darcy is right. Jeremy stayed with the carriage, dearest," Jane said, moving over to her side. "I shall hold your box for you."

"Permit me," Mr. Darcy said, taking back the box. "I will stay with Miss Bennet while she sketches. Pray, Mrs. Bingley, do not be concerned for her. I will keep her company."

"It is not company she desires while she is sketching," Jane warned him. "Do not be surprised if she ignores you completely."

"I will be as quiet as a, ahem, church mouse," Mr. Darcy said.

Everyone chuckled except for Lizzy. She had found a bench facing the nave and now perched upon its edge. Lizzy opened the sketch pad to a new page.

"Mr. Darcy, if you are to be my assistant, kindly come closer and open my supply box."

"I am called," he said to the others, nodding to them before hurrying across the grass to her side.

Darcy sat on the other end of the stone bench, set the box on his lap, opened it, and held it out to her. She removed her gloves of York tan and set them to one side on the bench. From the box she took a pair of black cotton sleeve-guards, such as the type store clerks wore, and slipped them over her arms, protecting the delicate pink of her spencer sleeves from the pencil and charcoal dust. Next, she removed a folded apron, shook it out, and donned that.

She sat down again and lifted out a blue silk, narrow drawstring bag, opened it, and selected a silver *porte-crayon* from amongst the pencils inside. She also removed a pair of silver tweezers. She opened an inside compartment containing a jumble of artist's charcoal pieces, and used the tweezers to pick up a piece. After fitting the charcoal into the *porte-crayon* to her satisfaction, she turned back to her paper. Darcy put the box back on his lap, replaced the tweezers in the bag, shut the charcoal compartment, and closed the lid.

Then, he watched her sketch, remaining completely quiet and still. He marveled at how quickly the outline of the east nave window and structure appeared on the page. First, the strokes went on boldly and then, gradually, great delicacy of touch filled in the details.

He examined her profile, admiring the curve of her cheek and the sweep of her eyelashes. Lest he distract her from her purpose—he had noticed that she did not like it when he looked too closely at her—he stole his glances in between his appreciation of her work and the Minster. There was something compelling in her presence that he had never met in another female.

She still did not seem to like him very much. That did not surprise him at all, since he did not have the knack of easy association with others. If he made no effort, and if no other approached him, he had been known to sit still and silent and alone in a room amongst many knots of people conversing and laughing. He had no charm or ease of manner to recommend him to others. Only his wealth and position in society gained him any invitations at all. A wealthy, single man could always attain invitations to social events that held a bevy of eligible single women on the look-out for a suitable husband. The marriage mart—how he loathed the necessity of it.

He took a deep breath to clear away his gloomy thoughts, caught himself, and eased out his breath so he would not disturb Miss Bennet with the whoosh of air he wanted to release.

After about a half hour, Miss Bennet paused.

"Will you open the box, please?" she asked, and then blew on the sketch.

Darcy did as asked, holding the box out to her. She took out a soft brush and carefully swept her sketch free of particles.

"You will find a drawer in the bottom of the box. Kindly open it and give me a piece of tissue paper."

Darcy opened the drawer, pulled out a piece of white tissue paper and exchanged it for the brush. He tapped the brush against the side of the stone bench in order to dislodge any dust before replacing it in the box. Miss Bennet covered her sketch with the tissue before closing the pad.

"You make an excellent assistant, Mr. Darcy," she said, turning slightly toward him. "You must have found it tedious."

"Not at all," he said. "Rather, I found it fascinating."

"Will you hand me that white cloth?"

"Of course," he said, taking the cloth out of the box and presenting it to her. She used it to wipe her fingers before handing it back to him. "I expect there is no use in putting everything away, is there? You will wish to sketch again."

"You are right," she said, rising. "I will keep the apron and sleeve guards on as we view the rest of the building." Miss Bennet stood holding her sketchpad like a shield. She glanced down at herself. "I must look a ramshackle sort of person. Positively dowdy. Not elegant. Not nicely put together. Look at my dirty fingers—this charcoal will not come off completely without soap and water. Everyone we meet will think me a shopkeeper's sister or daughter." She laughed sardonically and pierced him with a look. "Will you be ashamed to be seen with me?"

Ah, a test.

Darcy was not such a cad as to answer in the affirmative. Besides, he did not feel ashamed to be with her, and that feeling surprised him somewhat. Instead, bowing slightly to her, he said, “It is my honor to accompany such a great artiste as yourself. Though, madam, I would appreciate it greatly if you would warn me the next time you mean to destroy one of your masterpieces. I do not believe my heart can take such a shock again.”

Miss Bennet chuckled and shook her head, but gave no promise.

“Are you ready to enter the Minster?” he asked.

“Yes.”

Lizzy walked beside Mr. Darcy, sneaking glances his way. She wondered, now, if she had been wrong in her initial assessment of his character. Perhaps he was not so very arrogant after all. He was certainly patient. She could not help smiling a little at the sight of him carrying her supply box as though he was her footman rather than her companion.

He raised an eyebrow. “You seem to object to my observations of you,” he said. “Should I object to your observations of me?”

Lizzy released a half-smile. “Perhaps. I will concede that a certain amount of observing must continue if we are to learn the measure of each other.”

“That is magnanimous of you.”

His dry reply sent an unexpected wash of delight through her. She enjoyed sparring with anyone worthy of her effort. Jane and Charles were both too kind to spar with, except in light-hearted banter.

“I have agreed to paint Pemberley House, a home that obviously means a great deal to you,” she said, testing the waters. “Do you love your home? Or, is it something other than love? Dreaded duty, perchance, wrapped up in clean linen so that even you may not recognize your secret antipathy toward it?”

Mr. Darcy stopped in his tracks. Lizzy paused and turned toward him, wondering if she had stuck her whole foot into the pond instead of just a toe. He stared stonily at her for a long moment before he replied.

"What have I said to make you think I might secretly hate my home?" he demanded, his brow furrowing.

"Nothing at all," Lizzy confessed, smiling slightly. "My understanding is that Pemberley is a great house and great houses require an enormous amount of work to maintain them. You must have scores of servants and workers of all kinds expecting their wages every quarter. How do you afford them? Is the estate succeeding so well that you have no fear of falling into arrears? Do not all these demands on your pocket, your energies, your time, weigh upon your mind? On your spirit? Are you never resentful? Or, could it be that *all* your work is a labor of love for you?"

"I will have you know, madam, that I am a man of considerable substance. When someone with sufficient funds looks after his family home, there is no need for resentment," Mr. Darcy stated firmly. "I am proud to be the means of providing a living for nearly fifty souls. Because of the wages my workers make, there are a further two hundred individuals who benefit from their employment. Wives. Children. Parents. Siblings. The nearest village."

"Ah, pride," Lizzy said, tilting her head to one side, trying to keep her inner exhilaration under control and beneath her expression. How would he feel about her challenging his thinking? "But pride is not love. It is *noblesse oblige*."

"There is no doubt that *noblesse oblige* enters into my actions," Mr. Darcy said sharply, biting out his next words as though he tore them out of granite. "However, I love my home. I *love* it. It is beautiful. It is productive. It has provided me with the happiest moments in my thirty years. It is my refuge."

Lizzy watched him fume until he gradually got his emotions under control. They stood in the shade of a magnificent oak. Birds chirped and flitted from branch to branch and the distant murmur of voices created a sort of barrier between them and the world. There was nothing intimate in the setting, yet their conversation was of a most intimate nature. She had struck a nerve, and his ability to respond to her queries rather than to snub her and stalk away gave Lizzy a better opinion of him.

In a low, intense voice, Mr. Darcy continued to respond to her accusation, "You reproach me for pride as though pride has no place in our lives. Proper pride keeps our homes in good repair, our persons presentable, our efforts driven toward the betterment of ourselves, our dependents, and if I may be so bold, even our country." He paused as though waiting for a reply. When she did nothing but raise an eyebrow, he continued in a more temperate tone. "Pride straightens our backs. It is the force behind our actions. Those with no proper pride are slovenly, careless of themselves and others, and are comfortable in their ignorance."

Lizzy blinked at him, very pleased with his argument. "I believe that is the longest speech you have made to date—in our company, at least," she amended without rancour. "I expect you rarely give them."

Mr. Darcy's breathing was a little rapid. He shook his head slightly, gazed up into the canopy at a scampering squirrel, and focused on her once he had restored the tone of his mind.

"You are correct," he replied tersely, and then resumed their path through the well-tended graveyard.

Lizzy fell into step beside him. She caught him casting her side-long glances.

"Have you no rebuttal?" he asked.

Lizzy shrugged and then opened her mouth to speak. Before she could do so, however, he made an observation.

"I suspect you are prejudiced."

Lizzy swivelled her head and stared at him. "Prejudiced? Against whom?" she demanded, smarting a little. "I am *not* prejudiced. I treat all men and women equally. In what way have I displayed prejudice?"

Mr. Darcy had the effrontery to harrumph. *A superior*

tactic, to be sure. He paused in front of an ancient monument and gazed down at it.

"I think that reads 1653," he said.

"Do not stray from the topic," Lizzy snapped. She rested her hands on her hips, her reticule slapping against her thigh, and glared at him. Then she laughed and shook a finger in his direction. "You make me take up arms, sir. Pray, kindly tell me why you believe me to be prejudiced."

"Hmm." He shifted the box and let it rest on top of the gravestone. "You objected to me from the moment we met. Without any knowledge of my character, you decided you did not like me. Is that not prejudiced thinking?"

"I did not dislike you," Lizzy said, huffing a little. "I was only being cautious in my evaluation."

"Cautious? Hmm. Tell me, do you resent my wealth? I have ten thousand a year."

Lizzy gasped. "As much as that? I had no idea, I promise you. Ten thousand," she repeated reverently. She smoothed the front of her apron. "The sum is difficult to contemplate."

"Do you find me a more desirable and attractive *parti* now that you know my worth?" Mr. Darcy asked, raising a single eyebrow and twisting his mouth into a grimace. "Is my company more acceptable?"

"A man's worth is not measured by the size of his pocket book," she stated tartly. "Permit me to quote Samuel Johnson. He said that, 'The true measure of a man is how he treats someone who can do him absolutely no good.'"

"A fine quote," he said, "but not an answer to my question."

"I am not prejudiced for or against you because you have more money than I could have imagined. Perhaps I should have compassion for you instead. You must be hounded relentlessly by every match-making mama in the *ton*."

Lizzy watched him shrug and no longer wondered at his stiff bearing.

"I spend a great deal of my time in Derbyshire," he replied dryly.

"It is a good thing you love your home," Lizzy observed calmly.

Mr. Darcy nodded once, glancing away.

She knew all about match-making mamas. Her own mother had been one such. Five daughters to find suitable husbands for had not made her the most pleasant woman to be around. When Charles Bingley and his five thousand a year had entered their social sphere, she had pushed Jane upon him without compunction. Fortunately, in this case, Jane and Charles had instantly discovered their mutual attraction. Their mother's attempts to marry Lizzy off to their cousin, Mr. Collins, had not born similar fruit. He had married Charlotte Lucas, Lizzy's best friend, instead. Then Lydia had run off with Lieutenant Wickham and they had been forced to marry—very quietly and while in mourning.

"Match-making mamas are a menace," Lizzy commented. "You have my sympathy."

Mr. Darcy appeared surprised and murmured a soft, "Thank you."

"My own mother was one such. Five daughters, you understand."

"A trial," he agreed.

"You are most fortunate that she is no longer with us," Lizzy said, then covered her mouth with her hand. "My blasted tongue. Oh, dear. Now I have cursed. Sometimes, there is no stopping it. Pray forgive me. I should not have said that about my mother. She meant well."

"A more damning observation would be hard to find," Mr. Darcy said. His mouth tipped into a half-smile. "My own mother was one such. When my cousin, Anne, and I were but babes in arms, Mother and Aunt Catherine made a ridiculous alliance between them that I should marry Anne."

"Your cousin? How extraordinary."

"Yes," Mr. Darcy said, sighing. "I shall not, however. Anne and I do not suit. She is sickly and I pity her. However, I do not believe one should pity one's wife."

"No, indeed," Lizzy murmured, shaking her head.

Mr. Darcy picked up the art box from the gravestone and said, "I do not know what has made me reveal my life to you in this way. Come, let us return to the others before you learn so much about me that you will never come to Pemberley and paint it. There are some fine misericords you will no doubt like to sketch."

He stalked off toward the church, leaving her behind to stare after him.

What does he mean by that statement? Does he think I will not like him if I know him better? How sad. Oh, dear. Now I *am pitying* him. *No, compassion is what I feel. Not pity.*

Chapter Eight

London…

Edmund Bissell stood in his bedchamber, staring at the sketch above the fireplace. His valet stood behind him, to one side. Today, the sketch should change to a watercolor painting. He folded his arms, stretching his black coat of Bath superfine across his broad shoulders. The curve of his wife's cheek enchanted him still. The coquettish look she cast from between her eyelashes continued to cause his heart to wring.

The madness of grief remained a part of him and this…this magical sketch-painting did not help. Yet, Edmund could not destroy it. The image was the only likeness he had of his poor wife.

He wanted to meet the woman who had sketched it. He needed to know how she had managed the trick of it.

After that? He could not say. This was his new goal. Afterwards, perhaps he would find another goal, and then another, until he rediscovered his ability to conduct himself in polite society. Perhaps then, mourning would have faded to a dull pain in the depths of his chest.

"Oh, sir," Clark said in a voice of awe.

In an instant, the sketch washed away from the top to the bottom, leaving the watercolor portrait in its place.

"Good Lord," Edmund whispered. "It never fails to amaze me."

"Yes, sir."

"We leave for Yorkshire in the morning," Edmund told his valet, continuing to stare at the portrait.

"Sir?"

"Lord Delta has had news from home and means to leave this afternoon. He is the last of my accursed guests to depart. I warn you, I mean to make an early start."

"Yes, sir. I've already begun packin'."

"Send Burrows ahead to Stilton immediately with the grays to make arrangements for our stop tomorrow night," Edmund ordered. "I shall use the grays for the second stage of our journey. They should be rested in time to continue by the time we need them. Arrange for two outriders."

"I'll talk to John Coachman, sir. He knows who t'hire that's reliable."

"Excellent."

∞

Derbyshire…

Georgiana entered the drawing room before dinner to discover Mr. Kearn and her Aunt Sophia already waiting with a glass of sherry in hand. Mr. Kearn stood when she approached and she shook his hand coolly.

He is so handsome. So kind. What am I to do?

"Good evening, sir," she said, smiling amiably, but without any particular degree of warmth. "Thank you for attending on us this evening. I have something to discuss with you and Mr. Franklin."

"Oh?" he responded, his eyebrows shooting up. "Some new project?"

In the pause before she could respond, they heard the front doorknocker.

"Ah, here they are," Aunt Sophia said, rising.

"Excellent." Georgiana turned toward the door, remaining at Mr. Kearn's side. "It is not a project, precisely. Rather it is a concern. Yes. A concern. We will discuss it when we are all together."

"I look forward to it," the estate manager replied.

He shifted his weight from one foot to the other, bringing

him slightly closer to her. Georgiana could not tell if he had done it deliberately—she secretly hoped he had—or if the move was merely accidental. She saw her aunt watching them together and took the opportunity to step away from him in the direction of the drawing room doors. Mellor opened them only a heartbeat or two later, so she prayed she had not offended Mr. Kearn.

I am a wretched creature. How am I to go on?

Their guests entered, the Reverend Mr. Franklin first, then his wife and daughter behind. Jennet seemed to have taken extra pains with her appearance. *Practicing for her come out next year, no doubt.*

"Welcome," Georgiana said with a wide grin and a graceful wave of her hand toward the center of the room. *No one must realize my heartache. I will not wear my heart on my sleeve the way I did with Wickham.* "Please come in, Reverend and Mrs. Franklin. And, Jennet, how pretty you look tonight."

Jennet flushed and looked conscious, nervously grasping her string reticule before her.

The Reverend Mr. Franklin was a man of middle years, having copious amounts of pure white hair, almost as though a fright had terrified the color right out of his locks. He had a pleasant, kindly look about him, neither carrying too much weight nor being distinguished by a lean habit.

His wife, smiling and relaxed, had smooth bands of dark-brown hair fastened at the nape of her neck and topped by a prodigious cap, edged with whitework of her own design. A tall woman, she almost reached the height of her even taller husband.

Somehow, however, their height had not been bestowed upon their eldest daughter. Shy, but capable, Jennet Franklin stood a head shorter than her hostess. She wore her smooth dark hair in graceful loops, drawn back from a high forehead and fastened at the crown of her head. An embroidered ribbon decorated this simple, but elegant hair arrangement. Her muslin evening gown of palest-blush suited her to perfection.

"We had not expected an invitation to dinner tonight, Miss

Darcy," Mrs. Franklin said, taking the hand Georgiana offered her. "However, we could not pass up an opportunity to enjoy you and your aunt's delightful company. And yourself, as well, Mr. Kearn," she said, holding out her hand to the estate manager.

"Apparently, Miss Darcy has much to discuss with us," Mr. Kearn said, shaking her hand and then greeting the vicar. "Mr. Franklin."

"Hallo," Mr. Franklin said, smiling, his white eyebrows climbing. "I am intrigued."

"As are we all." Aunt Sophia shook everyone's hands. She looked toward the door. "Ah, here is Mellor already. Shall we go down?"

They gathered in the small dining room where two footmen stood at the ready. Mellor joined them, ready to give the signal to start serving.

Tall windows overlooked the lake where swans glided in languid patterns beneath the evening sun. Shadows from specimen trees planted decades before by Georgiana's grandfather, a keen amateur botanist, lengthened and stretched across the rolling parkland.

"What a lovely aspect," Jennet said in her soft voice, pausing at the windows.

Aunt Sophia paused beside her. "Yes, indeed. It is one of my favorites. It almost makes up for the sound of cockerels in the morning."

Jennet chuckled. "Do you have a particularly annoying bird? We have one that positively relishes his duty to wake the entire world. Perchance he is related to yours?"

"You poor things," Aunt Sophia said.

"Pray, do not encourage my aunt," Georgiana said, taking her seat. "I live in dread of discovering she has dispatched our prize cockerel before my brother returns from Yorkshire."

"I will not run shy, I promise you," Aunt Sophia said, coming and taking her place at the table. "If I kill that bird, I will admit it readily and with relish, I assure you."

Everyone laughed.

"I hope you do not mind it, but we will dine *en famille,*" Georgiana explained. "I do not mean to stand on ceremony tonight, which is why I had Mellor remove most of the table leaves and the epergnes. I wish to be cozy."

"Delightful," Mr. Franklin said, holding his wife's chair while a footman held the back of his daughter's.

Once the ladies were seated, the gentlemen took their own seats, and the first course was served. It contained a wild mushroom soup, cod cheeks in cream sauce, Frenched green beans, potatoes Dauphinoise, a raised mutton pie, and a dish of braised new onions. Once the footmen removed their soup plates and served the remainder of the dishes, they stepped back and waited.

"This morning," Georgiana recounted after she had begun eating, "I met Mrs. Little on the high street. She asked me to step into her shop. I did so."

Everyone looked at her, their attention earnest.

"Please, continue eating," Georgiana urged. She took a bite of potatoes as an example. They followed her lead and the sound of cutlery on china punctuated the waiting silence.

When she could, she continued. "Mrs. Little informed me that Mr. Hornby—is everyone familiar with the cooper?" Satisfied with their nods, she went on with her story. "Mr. Hornby, Mrs. Little says, is in a bad way. He will not go to the doctor, yet he is afflicted with a most alarming cough. Sometimes, he is so wracked with coughing that he must sit down afterward and recover. His work is suffering. He has missed the deadline of two orders—one for small kegs, and one for a half-dozen buckets, and was financially penalized for his tardiness."

"He has no funds for a doctor?" Mr. Franklin asked. Then he shook his head. "Of course he does not."

"If he has consumption…" Mrs. Franklin said, her voice trailing away. She straightened her shoulders. "He must be made to see a doctor. He has a wife and five children. I have often observed that when consumption visits a household, another of the family may also succumb to its evils."

"It may not be consumption, my dear." Mr. Franklin sighed. "It may be something altogether different."

"Yes, we do not want to be alarmists," Aunt Sophia remarked. "Mr. Hornby's ailment may be nothing more than a putrid cold. He is not a Darcy dependent. Is it our business to interfere?"

"No, but, as he is the only cooper in Lambton, we must bestir ourselves," Mr. Kearn said emphatically. "We shall induce him to see the doctor and determine what must be done to get him well again. Dr. Barnes is a reasonable man. I will talk to him and convince him to take something in trade for his efforts. That will appease Mr. Hornby's pride. Everyone can use another bucket."

Georgiana nodded at him, cautiously appearing pleased, always aware of her aunt's scrutiny.

"That will answer, I believe," Mr. Franklin said, a bite of cod half-way to his mouth.

"Mrs. Little suggested, in a most self-deprecating way, that her cousin is a journeyman cooper and is looking to find a place where he might establish himself," Georgiana said. She tilted her head to one side. "Perhaps he could assist Mr. Hornby until he is better. However, our cooper is not an old man and if he fully recovers, as I am sure we all wish he will, what will Mrs. Little's cousin do then?"

"Perhaps Mr. Hornby might take him into partnership?" Jennet suggested shyly.

"I wonder. Is there a sufficient need for two coopers in the region?" Georgiana asked, frowning. "Mr. Kearn, how much work does Pemberley supply to Mr. Hornby?"

The estate manager swallowed, took a drink of wine, and answered her. "In the summer, before the harvest is upon us, we order extra barrels from him. And, throughout the year, there are occasional purchases. If the estate required more, we would engage our own cooper."

Mr. Franklin pointed his table knife at Mr. Kearn. "In the general way, it would be the responsibility of the journeyman cooper to prove himself worthy of becoming a partner. We should leave that part of the business to the two men."

"Agreed," Mr. Kearn said, nodding shortly.

Georgiana looked at both gentlemen, making sure her gaze did not linger too long on Mr. Kearn. "I am relieved that there is one aspect of this business for which we will not be taking responsibility."

She focused on the two ladies. "Mrs. Little mentioned that Mrs. Hornby is a fine lace-maker. Perhaps there is something she could make for the church? A new altar cloth, perchance? I would like to donate money for that personally, rather than from the Pemberley coffers." She cleared her throat and swallowed painfully before continuing.

"My mother…my mother once told me that it has been the pleasure of the ladies of Pemberley to be the benefactresses of St. Stephens. Our particular area of support has always been the soft furnishings of the building, including vestments, altar cloths, and so forth. You have yet to approach me with any request, so permit me to suggest this one. It will aid the Hornby family and the parish will obtain what I am convinced will be a beautiful new altar cloth."

Mrs. Franklin beamed. "I will visit her tomorrow and tell her of your bequest. I will also be able to see for myself what the situation is in their home."

Georgiana nodded, satisfied. She took a sip of her wine to fortify herself, and turned to Mr. Kearn. She discovered he was gazing at her with a degree of approbation that warmed her heart.

"Mr. Kearn, have you thought of a method of convincing Mr. Hornby to see the doctor?"

"I have. I will ride over to the doctor first thing in the morning and take him with me to the cooperage. As it happens, it is time for me to order our additional barrels. We will agree to a story that has the doctor with me quite by accident. If Hornby is coughing as badly and as often as Mrs. Little avers, then the doctor will simply step in and examine him. We will contrive nicely, I do not doubt."

"And we will pray that it is not consumption," Mr.

Franklin promised solemnly. His wife and daughter nodded.

"And Mrs. Little's cousin? What of him?" Georgiana asked. "Shall I suggest to her that he come and meet Mr. Hornby? Whatever happens after that shall be between the two tradesmen."

"I shall take on that duty," Mr. Kearn said.

∞

Yorkshire...

The next morning, Lizzy finished packing away her painting supplies and portfolios. Their footman stood in the doorway to her room, waiting. She stepped aside and waved Jeremy forward.

"These are the last of my things." Though Lizzy knew her words were unnecessary, she could not help but caution him. "Do stow them carefully within our carriage. I would rather lose my luggage than my paintings."

"Aye, miss," Jeremy said, carrying the items with exaggerated care.

Lizzy cast a final look around her room, picked up her reticule, and followed the footman out. Her sister was supervising the loading of their baggage and Charles was talking to the landlord. Mr. Darcy's carriage waited at the front of Charles' two carriages. The second carriage would transport his valet, his wife's maid, and Jeremy the footman. Arthur the groom acted as their second coachman. Two other grooms rode as outriders.

"Good morning, Miss Bennet," Mr. Darcy said, approaching her. He gestured at his carriage. "Bingley has agreed to keep me company on the first leg of our journey. You will, therefore, have more room for your sketch books and so forth. He tells me you prefer to keep them safely inside."

"I do, indeed," Lizzy said, smiling. "You are fortunate, sir, for you will find my brother-in-law an agreeable companion."

"I mean to," Mr. Darcy said, nodding once. "May I lend you my assistance?"

Lizzy approached the carriage and held out her hand. He clasped it firmly while she climbed up into the vehicle. She turned around and tried to retrieve her hand. Instead, Mr. Darcy kept a firm hold on it. Unaccountably, this caused her chest to tighten.

"Thank you for coming to Pemberley," he said, his voice solemn and earnest. "You will not regret it."

She felt he meant more than he said, but she did not know what to make of the depth of his gravity. Thankfully, she could fall back on civility.

"I am persuaded I shall enjoy painting your home immensely."

He seemed satisfied with her answer for he released her hand. Mr. Darcy turned to find Jane nearby.

"You have stolen a march on me, Mr. Darcy," she said, smiling gently. "I was going to suggest that my husband spend the day with you only to find that you have both arranged the thing between you."

"I hope you have no objection, madam?" Mr. Darcy asked gravely, only the slight sense of a smile in his voice.

"None at all," Jane said, holding out her hand as she moved to his side. "My sister and I shall have a comfortable *tête-à-tête* without the interference of male opinion."

Lizzy, seated now, leaned forward and looked through the carriage door. "They shall do the same, dearest, only they shall be thankful to have no female opinions."

"We shall not spoil your fun, Mr. Darcy," Jane said, taking his hand so he could help her into the swaying vehicle. "I predict that by the time we stop for lunch you will be firm friends."

"I have no doubt," Mr. Darcy said, releasing her hand and bowing his shoulders. "We shall stop in Wetherby for our first change of horses and for a meal. Ferrybridge is our goal for the evening."

He closed the door, leaving the women alone in the carriage.

The ladies settled themselves and soon the carriage rolled forward. Lizzy looked out the window and for a few miles they traveled without speaking. Wondering, at last, what her sister might be thinking, Lizzy turned her gaze away from the countryside and glanced at her, only to find Jane observing her in turn.

"What is it, dearest?" Lizzy asked, shifting somewhat toward her.

Her brow creased, Jane replied, "Why do you spar with Mr. Darcy so much?"

"Do I?"

"You know you do," Jane rebuked gently. "Can you not like him?"

Lizzy played with the fringe on her shawl, looking down. "I am not certain how I feel about him. Sometimes…" She shook her head. "I cannot tell. Now and again I am pleased with his company. And at others…" Lizzy paused, unable to articulate her feelings.

"At other times you want to rip and tear at him because of his air of self-importance," Jane supplied. She smiled a little. "Dearest, I am so thankful that you have held your tongue—mostly. I know you cannot abide conceit, but are you certain Mr. Darcy is so full of pride? Perhaps he is reserved, only."

Indignation rose in Lizzy's breast. "He told me he has no improper pride and then accused me of being prejudiced. Me!"

"That is very bad," Jane acknowledged. She tilted her head. "Prejudiced against what? Or whom?"

Lizzy folded her arms. "Against people with money, I suppose."

"Are you? I have never observed such opinions in you. Nor have you voiced them. What can he mean by it, I wonder?"

"I cannot perceive his meaning," Lizzy admitted, her lip curled. The carriage rolled through a rut and they both grabbed for the straps on the side walls. "I do not resent that Charles has money or that Mr. Darcy has money. And I pray that I have never displayed any vulgar jealousy of Sir William and Lady Lucas' financial solvency. Father had sufficient income for our needs, so why should I begrudge the wealth of others? It is a nonsensical notion."

"Yes, dearest," Jane said, linking her free arm with her. "I have no doubt Mr. Darcy is completely mistaken in his assessment of your character."

"Humph," Lizzy said with a sniff of disdain, looking away and out through the window.

"You may also wish to consider that you could be mistaken in *his* character."

Lizzy whipped her head around and stared at her sister. Jane looked steadily back at her. Lizzy released the strap and patted her arm.

"You are the kindest creature alive. I dare say you would have nice things to say about Lucifer's character."

Jane smiled and raised her delicate eyebrows. "Now you *are* being absurd. Do not let our cousin hear you speak so."

Lizzy chuckled. "I am immensely thankful not to be living with my cousin, even if he did marry my dear friend and then offered to have me stay at Longbourn after our parent's death. Charlotte is a saint to put up with his constant prosing."

"She is happy to have an establishment of her own."

"Agreed. Still," Lizzy said, shaking her head, "marriage to my cousin would not have suited me. I will marry for love, or not at all."

"Indeed, I hope you may," Jane said warmly. "But he must be blind."

Lizzy glared at her sister. "Am I so ill-favored?"

"No, you goose. If he is blind, he will not see what happens to your paintings."

They both chuckled, though Lizzy felt a stab of dejection. What if she fell in love with a man who feared her gift? Her curse? What if he insisted that she never paint again? She did not think she could bear to pack away her brushes and charcoals. She would have to leave her art with Jane and Charles and never have a single piece in her own home.

No, I cannot bear the thought of it. I suppose I shall never marry.

Having reached Wetherby in good time, they ate a

comfortable repast and then spent an hour walking about in order to relieve the tedium of their journey. They crossed onto the bridge over the River Wharfe and gazed down at the flowing water before turning their steps back toward the posting inn. Carts, carriages, horses and people often passed them by, for this bridge was part of the Great North Road that connected London with Scotland.

"Really," Miss Bennet said as they walked, "no matter how commodious and well-sprung one's carriage is, there is no escaping the fatigue that comes from being constantly jostled about."

"So true," Bingley said, taking his wife's hand on his arm once they left the confines of the busy bridge where they had needed to walk single file.

Miss Bennet's hand soon rested lightly on Darcy's arm. Throughout the time he had spent in Bingley's company, one part of his mind had been thinking of Miss Bennet in the carriage behind.

"May I suggest a change in our seating arrangements?" Darcy asked the others.

Bingley and his wife paused and all three looked at him enquiringly.

"I had a table fitted into my travelling carriage—the fitting of it is of my own design. I propose we travel in my carriage and while away the time playing whist or some other unexceptional card game."

"By Jove, the very thing," Bingley said, grinning widely. "What do you say, Jane? Lizzy?"

Mrs. Bingley glanced at her sister. Miss Bennet nodded.

"We would be delighted," Mrs. Bingley said, smiling kindly upon him. "We would like it above all things."

"I must warn you, Mr. Darcy, that I am a dab hand at whist," Miss Bennet said. "When Jane and I partner, we cannot be beat."

Her fine brown eyes twinkled in that disconcerting way that caused Darcy's heart to skip a beat. *Why does she have this effect on me?*

"Bingley and I shall not be cowed by your boast," Darcy claimed. "We shall strive to win every trick." He thought for a moment, smiled, and said, "In fact, I shall teach you a different way to play whist. It is called Norwegian whist."

"*Norwegian* whist?" Mrs. Bingley asked. "What is that, pray?"

"You shall see. I learned this variation from my father, who took the Grand Tour. He and his tutor spent several months in Oslo during the summer and played their version of whist into the small hours of the night."

Intrigued, the four hurried back to where their carriages were awaiting them. Ferrybridge was their destination for tonight, still some four hours away, giving the gentlemen plenty of time to thoroughly trounce the ladies.

∞

Bedfordshire...

"Will t'gentleman kindly step into t'coffee room?" the senior ostler asked, directing his underlings at the Red Lion Inn in Biggleswade to take charge of the fancy gentleman's four steaming horses.

"The gentleman is Mr. Edmund Bissell," the coachman said with a sniff. "And you take good care of 'is 'orses, you 'ear? Them there's prime'uns."

"I know it," the senior ostler said appreciatively. "We'll have a time of it matchin' these four."

"You won't do it," the coachman said proudly. "The grays brought 'ere yesterday will be the change."

"Oh, aye," was the phlegmatic reply.

Edmund heard them with only half an ear as he climbed down from his carriage. Exhausted by the eight-hour journey, he only wanted his supper and to rest. He turned and accepted the painting from his valet so he could climb down. Then, he handed it back to Clark to carry. He would not leave it in the carriage for someone to steal. Burrows, the second coachman, a big, burly man of fifty, with a bulbous red nose, heavy dark eyebrows, and an obsequious manner, rushed out of the inn and touched his knuckle to his cap.

"Everything's ready, sir," he said. "I've bespoke a private dining parlor fer yer honor's use. It's attached to yer bedchamber so all's convenient, like. There's a smaller bedchamber across the corridor fer Mr. Clark's use. You've made good time, sir, beggin' yer pardon."

"Yes. Thank you," Edmund said. "The chestnuts will have to be rested until the day after tomorrow. I do not know when I may return, so take them back to London in easy stages. I will use job horses on the return."

"You'll not like that, sir,"

"I dare say, but I will not leave you and my horses cooling your heels here waiting for me."

"Right you are, sir," Burrows said, knuckling his forehead again.

"Help John with our baggage."

"Sir."

I shall reach Colsterworth by tomorrow evening. Then Tickhill, through Ferrybridge, and finally, Ripon. It is a bloody long journey. Miss Bennet had best be there, or the trip may be for naught. I shall follow her trail until I find her. Or, until I must journey to Bristol to meet that blasted ship.

Chapter Nine

Derbyshire...

Georgiana smoothed her soft-pink cambric skirts and breathed deeply a few times before she lifted her hand to knock on Mr. Kearn's office door. She self-consciously touched the curl dangling free of her pinned-up hair, waiting for the door to open or for her to hear the call to enter.

It did not come.

Surely, he has returned from Lambton by now?

She knocked again. Louder.

"I am not in," a voice came from behind her.

Georgiana jumped and gasped. Her hand went to her throat. She swallowed and turned around.

The estate manager stood not two feet away. And he was smiling. His pale-blue eyes, ringed in dark-blue, twinkled engagingly. His full beard and mustache should have made him look much older, but, in fact, gave him a rakish air as though he was really a Viking in disguise. At any moment, he would reveal himself as a raider of old and they would both laugh.

How wondrous he is. Her heart tripped over at the thought.

"You startled me, sir," she said breathlessly.

"I beg your pardon, Miss Darcy," he murmured, bowing his shoulders. "Is there some service I can give perform for you?"

"I…I wondered if you might tell me the results of your visit to the cooper? With the doctor? Did Mr. Hornby agree to let our good Dr. Barnes examine him?"

Mr. Kearn begged her pardon and reached around her to open his office door. "We really should not be standing around talking in the corridor," he said quietly. "Will you come in?"

Georgiana nodded and entered before him. She liked his office. It felt used, and busy, and full of purpose. None of the dark furnishings were shabby, but they were not new, either. A large pair of windows illuminated the space, revealing bookshelves, filing cabinets, a faded Persian carpet, and four chairs other than the desk chair. Carefully drawn maps of the estate and the county hung from the wall opposite the windows. The room smelled nice, too.

Leather.

And that indefinable smell she associated with books.

Mr. Kearn's own scent accented everything—a mixture of pipe tobacco, soap, and a subtle touch of bergamot.

He waved her toward a chair, following her inside, but leaving the door wide open. Thankful for his discretion, she was betrayed into giving him a warmer smile than she had intended.

"Ah, there it is," Mr. Kearn said, grinning back at her. He sat behind his large, tidy desk. A pipe lay on top of a small silver salver. "I was beginning to think I had offended you in some unpardonable way."

Flustered, Georgiana felt a flush rise to her cheeks. "No…No, why should you say so?"

"Pray," he said softly, "do not be alarmed. We are old friends, are we not? I have known you for five years, ever since I rescued you from being stuck in a tree. What is there to alarm you?"

"Not a single thing," she said, ducking her head. "I promise you."

Georgiana reined in her emotions, tucked them away for later, and lifted her gaze to his. Mr. Kearn's eyes held such a look of understanding that dismay filled her belly.

He thinks I am infatuated with him...like a...like a silly school girl. He does not look on me as a woman grown. Instead, he thinks he is being kind to a girl who will soon grow out of her feelings for him. He thinks my love for him is a shallow thing. Like...like how I felt for Wickham. Something tepid and foolish. He is wrong, but there is no way for me to tell him so. How shall I bear it?

Determined not to let him see anything of what she thought and felt, she asked, arching her eyebrows, "Now, did Mr. Hornby permit Doctor Barnes to examine him?"

Mr. Kearn clasped his hands on the arms of his oak chair. "He did. During our drive to the cooper, I mentioned our fears of consumption to the doctor. This caused him grave concern. He told me that Lambton has had no cases of consumption for ten years—after old Mrs. Peters died. He would like to keep Lambton free of the disease."

Leaning forward, Georgiana asked, "Did he promise to let us know what is wrong with poor Mr. Hornby?"

Mr. Kearn shook his head. "Only if it is consumption. He desires to retain patient confidentiality."

Georgiana nodded. "Indeed, I must acknowledge that Mr. Hornby deserves his privacy. When will we know?"

"He promised to send me a note this afternoon."

Georgiana watched, almost mesmerised, as the estate manager began to stroke his beard. She wanted to be the one to smooth the beard, to see what it felt like on her fingertips. On her palms. Against her cheek.

Aghast at the direction of her thoughts, Georgiana jumped up from the chair, her fingers intertwined.

"Thank you for seeing to this," she said, hating the breathlessness of her words. "Kindly let me know what the doctor says as soon as the note arrives."

Mr. Kearn stood, frowning a little. "Of course, Miss Darcy."

Georgiana gave a jerk of her head and left the office as sedately as she could manage it. The moment her feet carried her around the first corner in the corridor, she hastened her steps until she was almost running.

I am fleeing him. Fleeing! Me! What has come over me?

On the road to Pemberley...

"Everyone must sit before the table is put in place," Mr. Darcy explained, indicating that Jane should sit facing forward. Then, to Lizzy, he said, "No, Miss Bennet, you will be paired with your sister so you must sit next to Bingley."

Charles climbed in first and held out a hand to Lizzy. She accepted it and sat beside him on the navy-blue, leather-upholstered seats. Before he entered, Mr. Darcy reached into a compartment beneath the forward-facing seat and retrieved a walnut box measuring approximately twelve-by-eight-by-six inches, handsomely painted, with swirling motifs and flowers of ink in the Persian style. Fat felt circles adorned the bottom of the box. He gave this to Charles, closed the compartment, and sat down next to Jane.

"Give me the table now," Mr. Darcy said to his groom.

The young man passed him a rectangular table top. Mr. Darcy fitted the smoothly finished piece of wood into a cleat beneath the door window between Jane and Charles. A wide and flat folded leg was let down and two pegs at the foot of the leg fit into small round holes in the floor.

"How ingenious," Charles praised.

"Yes, indeed," Lizzy said, smoothing her gloved hand over the lip along the edge of the table. "How comfortable this will be."

"Thank you," Mr. Darcy said. He nodded to his groom. "We shall do. Ferrybridge is our final stop today, Jermyn."

"Aye, sir," the middle-aged groom said, and he closed the door.

Within a few moments, the carriage set off, jostling the passengers. Charles set the box on the table and Mr. Darcy drew it toward himself, sliding it across on its felt feet. He opened the lid and took out a folded piece of green baize fabric. He handed this to Charles, who unfolded it and laid it upon the table, smoothing it in place. The baize fit exactly within the confines of the table lip.

The inside of the box had been lined in blue silk, divided into multiple compartments, four of which contained packs of playing cards tied together with black ribands. An ivory cribbage board occupied one long compartment. Two compartments held markers, fish-counters, paper, and several pencils. The final one held dice. Mr. Darcy took out a deck and set it on the table.

"What a lovely box, Mr. Darcy," Jane said.

"Thank you. My sister Georgiana painted it," he said, releasing the cards from their bindings and revealing their lovely, stenciled backs. Each card had been identically decorated with a bunch of blue morning glories and green leaves. "And she stenciled the backs, as well."

"Quite an accomplished young lady," Jane expressed with a gentle smile. "The common practice of playing with unpainted cards can lead to unintentional dishonesty when the white backs become smudged and dirty. We had one such pack when I was a girl and Kitty knew all the interesting marks that indicated a preferred card."

"That is why, in the clubs, a dealer may call for a new deck at any time," Mr. Darcy informed her. "A steady hand is needed to decorate the backs identically—or, as identically as is possible, even when a stencil is used."

"By Jove, Lizzy," Charles said, examining the backs of the cards. "Imagine how fascinating a pack of cards painted by yourselves would be. And, confusing, I warrant. Frogs leaping about on Lily pads. Birds flitting from back to—"

Charles yelped and Mr. Darcy frowned at him.

"My dear," Jane said, smiling at her husband with her eyes wide open and her expression minatory, "Lizzy has quite enough to occupy herself with in her portraits. She does not need another project."

"I just thought she might like…" Charles swallowed his next word as understanding washed over his features. Shrugging a little, he glanced at Lizzy. "I forgot. Sorry." He looked at their host. "Carry on, Darcy. Teach us this new way of playing whist."

Mr. Darcy nodded, a slight frown of curiosity pulling his brows together. He did not ask them what Charles had meant, however. Instead, he set aside the box, tucking it next to him on the seat.

"No whist counters?" Lizzy asked brightly, choosing to act as though her brother-in-law—the kindest creature imaginable, but sadly shatter-brained at times—had said nothing untoward.

"Oh, right," Mr. Darcy said, reopening the box and collecting a piece of paper and a pencil. "For this type of whist, we need only keep score." He wrote 'Us' and 'Them' at the top of the paper and drew a line between them, creating columns.

"And there is no trump?" Charles asked, sounding suspicious.

"No trump," Mr. Darcy replied. He began to shuffle. After a moment, he set the pack down. "We shall cut for deal. Highest card wins."

Everyone lifted a section of cards off the pack and turned them over, revealing their cut. Lizzy had an ace and she collected the cards and reshuffled.

"Deal out all the cards, just as in regular whist," Mr. Darcy directed. "Once we have our cards, we should divide them into suits."

"Now, Jane, dear," Charles said, quizzing her, "you and Lizzy must play fair. No giving of hints, groaning over your cards, or giving each other nudges under the table."

"Oh!" Lizzy protested in lively dismay. "How can you accuse us of such tactics, sir?"

"He is only teasing," Jane said, smiling a little. She looked at her cards and said, "Goodness."

Charles pointed his finger at her. "Ja—ane," he said in a warning voice. "None of that."

"What?" she asked, her eyebrows climbing. "What can my sister infer from that single word?"

Lizzy laughed and looked at Mr. Darcy, her hand spread open and clasped carefully close to her chest. "Our cards, such as they are, have been sorted and we are ready for our next bit of instruction."

Charles muttered, "'Such as they are.' Humph. Beware, Darcy. We are amongst the most dastardly set of players you will ever hope *not* to meet."

"I will take your warning," Darcy responded. He glanced around the table and found them all waiting for his instruction. "Highest card takes the trick, as long as it is in the same suit as the first card laid down. You must follow suit." He paused while Bingley gave each of the ladies a minatory glare.

"We shall remember," Mrs. Bingley promised. "We are not ninnyhammers, you know."

Bingley gave a slight snort and Miss Bennet nudged him in the arm.

Deepening his voice, Darcy said, "Behave, children."

Miss Bennet sat up straighter and managed an angelic expression.

"The first order of business is for us to decide whether we want to take tricks or we do not want to take tricks. This is called 'passing', if you think you cannot take at least seven tricks, or 'grand' if you think you can." Darcy watched for their nods of understanding. When he had collected all three, he continued to explain the advantages or disadvantages, scoring wise, of each type of play. "If we are agreeable, we shall play to fifty, since the day is long."

"I assume we cannot consult our partner before we make the decision to 'pass' or 'grand'?" Bingley asked, frowning once more at his wife and sister-in-law.

"You are correct," Darcy said. Miss Bennet appeared courteously attentive and Mrs. Bingley blinked at him, waiting. "Are we prepared to begin?"

"Who states their preference first?" Miss Bennet asked.

"The player after the dealer. Once someone says 'grand', then there is no need to ask any further. The player behind the 'grand' player begins the play. If we all 'pass' then the player after the dealer begins."

"Let us start," Bingley said, grinning. "We shall learn fastest by playing. Darcy, what say you? 'Pass' or 'grand'?"

Darcy checked over his hand. He thought he could take only two tricks. "'Pass'," he said, keeping any inflection out of his voice. He looked at Mrs. Bingley, waiting for her declaration.

She took a deep breath, sighed mightily, and tsked her tongue before she finally said, "'Pass'."

Bingley glared at her, saying between his teeth, "'Pass'."

Miss Bennet shook her finger at her brother-in-law. "Charles, you told us not to make noises and give clues and here you are, talking through your teeth as though you would rather not 'pass' but instead declare 'grand'. If you think you can take enough tricks, then *say* 'grand' instead of hissing. That was a warning to your partner if ever I heard one."

Bingley rolled his eyes. "It was not a warning."

"Hmm," she replied skeptically.

"Miss Bennet?" Darcy said. "What do you declare?"

She smiled, showing her teeth. "'Grand', of course."

"Very well. Bingley, you may begin."

His new friend piously pressed his lips together and laid down a two of clubs. Miss Bennet immediately laid down a two of hearts. Sluffing. Bingley stirred in his seat, but said nothing about following suit. So, Miss Bennet was short-suited. *No wonder I have so many clubs. Third man plays high,* he reminded himself and played his king, even though an ace could take it, depending on his partner to have the ace to play on another hand so Mrs. Bingley could not take it. Mrs. Bingley, however, had the ace, and took the trick. She gathered the played cards, turned them over and arranged them in a neat pile. Then, she immediately played a heart, returning to Miss Bennet's sluffed suit.

Darcy had rarely seen a pair of players who seemed to intuit so well what their partner held. The ladies claimed nine tricks of the possible thirteen. At the end of the second 'pass' hand, they had eight tricks. The cards seemed to go their way through most of the game, until, by the end, the ladies won with fifty-eight points to the gentlemen's thirty-two points.

"I enjoyed that," Lizzy said, smiling widely. "It is simpler than long whist. Shall we go again?"

"You have a natural talent, Miss Bennet," Mr. Darcy praised.

"And you are an excellent loser," she replied, passing him the rest of the cards on the table.

"Thank you," he murmured. After shuffling, he began to deal.

"My sisters and I used to play often, using fish-counters only, instead of money," Jane said.

Lizzy struggled to keep her attention on the play, discovering she could look at him as often as she wished without feeling the least self-conscious because everyone was preoccupied. Occasionally, he laughed out loud and his expression softened, causing her to catch her breath. Then, she had to be reminded to watch her cards. How had she not noticed how handsome he was before now?

When the carriage jostled them, his knee rubbed against hers, sending a shock of awareness through her system. *What is this sudden attraction? Is it because we are sitting in such close proximity? No other man has ever made me feel quite this way. Breathless. And lightheaded.*

When their opponents won the second game, Mr. Darcy seemed to display no pride, merely smiling slightly when Charles crowed. He was not humble, but he did not flaunt his win like he might have.

Charles grinned at his wife and Lizzy. "Perhaps you would like to change games?" he asked. "Now that you have lost, I mean."

"Oh, ho!" Lizzy cried, grinning back. "We are tied, are we not? We shall win the rubber."

I must, however, pay better attention instead of focusing so often on the inimitable Mr. Darcy.

"After letting you win the way we did," Jane said dolefully, "We are obligated to play our best to win this round."

"*Letting* us win?" Charles cried, laughing. "We shall see. Whose turn is it to deal?"

"In our family, losers of the game always begin the next round," Lizzy said, holding out her hand for the pack. Charles passed it to her.

Lizzy kept her mind on the game, not without some difficulty, and the ladies won the rubber.

∞

Pemberley...

Georgiana heard the sound of footsteps on gravel and glanced up from where she sat in the garden, within the shade of an elm. It was Mr. Kearn. She set her embroidery project—a sampler containing a bible verse for Mrs. Franklin to hang in the Sunday school room wall—on top of her sewing basket, folded her hands in her lap, and waited for him to approach.

He is a fine walker, she thought, admiring his steady gait and the set of his shoulders. *He walks with resolution, but without arrogance. He is a considerate companion on any walk, as well. He matches his steps with his company. Mr. Wickham had been a nervous walker, pressing ahead and then falling back and apologizing and even scampering around you as he talked animatedly. She had giggled when he had done so, but she had found it tiring too. Oh, why am I thinking of that foolish man?*

Georgiana sighed, supposing that a comparison between her only two loves was bound to occupy her mind on occasion. Though, there were never any true parallels, not in the essentials. Mr. Kearn was honest. Wickham was not. Mr. Kearn was honorable. Wickham was not. Mr. Kearn was selfless. Wickham was not. He only thought of himself and whatever he could turn to his advantage.

The closer the estate manager became, the more Georgiana's heart raced. All thoughts of the hated Mr. Wickham drained away. Recalling her aunt's words to her, she tightly reined in her galloping emotions and smiled in a composed way at him.

"Mr. Kearn? Has our good doctor sent us reassuring news?" she asked, waving at the empty end of her bench.

Mr. Kearn nodded and sat down. "How is your sampler coming along?"

Georgiana, blushing a little, unfolded her work. "I am about half way through the verse."

"Which did you choose?"

"Isaiah 40, verse 8. It reads, 'The grass withereth, the flower fadeth: but the word of our God shall stand for ever.'"

"An excellent choice," Mr. Kearn praised. "You have a delicate hand."

His praise caused Georgiana's chest to tighten. She could hardly breathe and managed only a simple, "Thank you."

He took a piece of folded paper from his pocket.

"The message only just arrived. I shall put you out of your agony of apprehension," he said, unfolding the paper and passing it to her.

Georgiana tore her gaze away from his beloved countenance and looked down at the missive now in her hand. She read,

Dear Mr. Kearn,

After your concern for the possibility that Mr. Hornby's poor health might be the result of having contracted consumption, I agreed to examine the cooper, gratis. He was resistant to our efforts, as you recall. However, between us and his kind wife, we managed to convince him to be examined. After you left, I spent a good half-hour with him, discussing his symptoms and listening to his chest when he breathed and when he coughed. He swore that he had not been anywhere near anyone that may have had that dread disease. We cannot depend on this assurance, unfortunately, since we know little about how an individual contracts consumption.

You and Miss Darcy were quite right to be concerned, for it is an insidious disease that we have thankfully not seen in our community for more than a decade. I am able to reassure you that Mr. Hornby does not have consumption. I have given

him a regimen of care that will encourage him to make a full recovery within a couple of weeks. He needs to rest, however, and he does not seem to be the type of man capable of doing so. He frets about his obligations. It is unfortunate that his eldest son is not old enough and skilled enough yet to take over the business until his father recovers. I will visit him again in a few days.

Your Servant, sir,
Doctor Oren Barnes.

Georgiana rested the letter on her lap. "This is a relief, is it not? Though, I do not know why he could not have simply said that Mr. Hornby's complaint was not consumption at the beginning of his note. I was in agonies of apprehension through-out until he relieved me of it."

Mr. Kearn smiled, making his mustache shift. "Yes, he does have a loquacious style of writing, does he not? I wonder how long his letters to his family are."

"They must be pages and pages long," she said, covering her mouth when she chuckled. "But," she added in mock severity, "we should not laugh at him so. His letters must be a great comfort to his friends and family."

"No doubt," Mr. Kearn agreed, grinning now.

And then someone called out, startling them out of their comfortable cose.

"Georgiana! Yoo-hoo!"

Chapter Ten

Pemberley...cont...

Georgiana's eyebrows shot up, as did Mr. Kearn's. They both turned as one from facing each other to look out over the flower gardens, resplendent in riotous color, to the white gravel path where her Aunt Sophia waved. Heat flushed Georgiana's cheeks.

What does my aunt believe we are doing here in plain sight of the house, of the gardeners, and of any other passing servant? Does she think Mr. Kearn is making love to me here where any might see? Does she think I am so lacking in conduct that I would permit him to do so?

Mr. Kearn rose to his feet. "She must wish to know the result of Dr. Barnes' examination as well."

"Yes. That must be it," Georgiana said, also rising. "What will she think of his style of writing, I wonder?" Before he could answer her rhetorical question, she asked, "Have you spoken to Mrs. Little about her cousin?"

"I have. He is coming for a visit and should arrive in Lambton tomorrow. I said that I thought Mr. Hornby could use some interim help but that her cousin must endeavor to convince the cooper to hire him on his own, since we do not know her cousin's character and so would be unable to vouch for him." He added with a half-smile, "She was effusive in her appreciation."

Aunt Sophia approached them and he bowed his

shoulders.

"Good afternoon, Mr. Kearn. Have you heard from Doctor Barnes?" she asked, smiling sunnily. "Is that why you are sitting out here so cosily? Reporting to Georgiana on this lovely afternoon? Tell me, I am eager to know."

"You have caught me out, ma'am," Mr. Kearn said, smiling back. "You are correct. We have heard from the doctor and our minds may be easy. Mr. Hornby does not have consumption."

Georgiana held out the letter to her as evidence. "Indeed, the doctor believes he will be well within a couple of weeks as long as Mr. Hornby follows his regimen."

Her aunt rolled her eyes and took the missive. "He will not. They never do. Men, I mean. They fall into two categories, my dear. There are men who will fall sick and forever think they are dying. It takes forever to convince them they are well enough to get out and about again. Or back to work, whatever their case may be. Then there are the men who refuse to take sensible care of themselves when they are ill so that it takes forever for them to get well again. Our cooper seems to be of the latter fraternity."

She glanced down at the letter and quickly read it through. "Well," she said when she finished it. "He writes a comfortable letter. And, there, do you see?" She pointed at one part. "He agrees with me that the cooper will not be an easy patient."

"Mr. Kearn has already been to see Mrs. Little about her cousin," Georgiana informed her aunt, anxious she believe that they had been enjoying unexceptional conversation when she had virtually forced herself upon them. Then, Georgiana chided herself for being so ungracious in her thinking.

I am being foolish beyond permission to think that my most beloved aunt cares for anything except my happiness. She does not know that Mr. Kearn is the author of all my happiness. She cannot know it...or else she will take me away from Pemberley until she thinks I am over my feelings for him. That will never happen. I will always love my Mr. Kearn.

"Excellent. I came out in the garden, dear Georgiana, to

tell you that Mrs. Franklin has just now left. She came to tell us that Mrs. Hornby has agreed to make the altar cloth we commissioned. That was an excellent idea, my dear," Aunt Sophia praised, smiling widely. She glanced down at the work basket on the bench. "Are you finished embroidering for the afternoon? I was thinking of sending a nice tidy box of early plums to the Hornbys. What do you think? Will their children like them?"

"Undoubtedly. I shall take them myself," Georgiana said, collecting her embroidery work. "In my gig. I will be careful and not go in the house. Mrs. Hornby will come out to me, I am sure."

Mr. Kearn bowed. "I will order the gig to be readied." He took the letter back from her aunt. "And I will file this. I do not scruple to tell you that I am relieved by the doctor's news. My own grandmother died of consumption."

In a shy voice, very conscious of her aunt's presence, Georgiana said, "I am sorry about your grandmother." Then, after a heartbeat, she added, "I am grateful to be in a position to help others in need. It is a blessing."

Mr. Kearn smiled kindly at her. "Yes, it is."

∞

On the road to Pemberly…

The Darcy, Bennet, and Bingley party spent a comfortable night's repose in a Ferrybridge coaching inn. After breaking their fast and taking a short walk to admire the stone bridge with its three arches, they climbed into Mr. Darcy's carriage once more.

"I saw you had a cribbage board in your games box," Lizzy said. "Shall we teach you how to play crib-to-lose?"

"Crib-to-lose? What is that, pray?" Mr. Darcy asked, clearly perplexed. Then, "Surely you do not mean that the goal is to lose the game?"

"Exactly," Bingley said, grinning. He looked at his wife. "You, however, will not pair with Lizzy. Switch with me and Darcy shall be your partner and Lizzy shall be mine,"

"As you wish," Jane replied. "I am all amiability."

"Indeed you are, sister dear," Lizzy praised with a lively grin. "Charles, you will both have to step out of the carriage to manage the switch."

Fortunately, Mr. Darcy's groom still stood at the open door, waiting for instructions. Jane climbed out of the carriage, her husband following, and then she climbed back inside first. Charles settled himself beside her.

"Tickhill next, Jermyn," Mr. Darcy ordered. "We shall stop for refreshment there."

"Aye, sir," the middle-aged groom replied, and he shut the door.

"Now, how do we play crib-to-lose?" their host enquired as he took out the cribbage board, in the form of a box with a drawer. He placed the box on the table and opened the drawer beneath, retrieving another set of painted cards and the four requisite pegs.

With an almost trembling hand, Lizzy traced the painted image of a thatched cottage residing in the center of the diamond board. The cribbage board she had painted when she was twelve now stayed on a shelf in the 'special' collection at Netherfield. The three pigs in a muddy pen that she had painted rolled about and blew dirty bubbles at each other—a totally distracting display.

If only I could control this…this gift. Even my portraits of children and pets expose the very best of the darlings—though they do not move, thank the good Lord. Or melt. Or turn to dust and reincarnate themselves.

Jane touched her hand and they exchanged an understanding look. Jane knew the cause of her distress.

Lizzy contained her sigh and held out her hand for the cards. "The painting is lovely. More of Georgiana's talent?"

"Yes," Mr. Darcy said. "Have you ever painted a cribbage board, Miss Bennet?"

"By Jove, has she ever!" Charles exclaimed, his expressive eyes alive with delight. "You should see it. Three of the liveliest spotted little piggies you have ever seen. Oxford Sandy and Blacks, I think. They wallow in the mud and—"

Charles jumped in his seat and stared at his wife accusingly. Whether or not he would have revealed their secret in his admiration for the painting, they could not know. Her brother-in-law's amiable, cheerful, open nature, occasionally made keeping a secret difficult. What did Mr. Darcy think of Charles' reaction to what Lizzy considered must have been a sound pinch? She glanced up at him and saw frowning intrigue reflected in his expression.

Oh, dear. Charles is sweet, but he...well, I love him like the brother I never had. I will not love him less if he continues to be a gabble-monger.

"The cards, Mr. Darcy?" Lizzy asked, continuing to look at him.

It took him a moment to reply because he was still observing the admonitory looks Jane and Charles were exchanging. Finally, he caught her gaze in his and Lizzy felt as if she was falling down a long tunnel. Sound did not intrude. Her stomach swooped and her knees trembled. She prayed he did not notice the latter, since they sat so close together. He blinked, and broke the spell.

"Of course," he replied

His fingers brushed her palm when he handed them to her and a shiver of awareness caused her to catch her breath. This reaction alarmed her. She did not understand it. No other man had ever made her feel this way. Did he have any reaction to her? Lizzy dared herself to glance at him. He was looking at her, waiting for her explanation, seemingly calm and not at all affected by their accidental touch.

Why should he be? Who am I to him? I am just a painter who refuses to paint his sister. I am a woman who has accepted a commission from him—he is paying me. In a way, I am in trade. What a lowering thought. Art tradesman. Tradeswoman. Would Father have approved? I cannot say. Heavens. Think instead of your lovely potential cottage by the sea.

Lizzy took a calming breath. "Well, the idea is very simple, though the execution, as you will find, is much more difficult."

Jumping in, Charles continued, "The goal is to have as few points in your hand as possible. The first team who reaches the end, loses the game."

"Quite simple," Mr. Darcy agreed. "Five cards?"

"Yes, we start with five cards as usual," Jane said.

They cut for deal and the game began. Darcy, very conscious of the woman sharing the bench with him, looked over his five cards and discovered he had two fives, two fours, and a six. Normally, he would discard one of the fours, leaving him with a double run worth eight points plus an extra four points. Twelve possible points, even if the turn-up card was of no use to him. Too many points. Of course, one card had to go into the 'crib', which went to the dealer. In this case, the dealer was Bingley, his opponent. Strategy, Darcy realized, was even more important in this version of the game. He passed over the six, placing it face down in front of Bingley, breaking the runs, and leaving his own hand worth a possible four points, instead.

When Mrs. Bingley cut the deck and her husband turned over the card, almost everyone groaned. It was a three. Darcy could not believe that there was a single time when a sixteen-point hand had caused him anything but jubilation.

"Very nice," Miss Bennet murmured beside him.

Bingley had a pleased grin on his face as well. Mrs. Bingley displayed a slight frown. Miss Bennet smiled like a cat with a live mouse beneath her paw.

Why does she affect me so? She is pretty, granted, but I have been plagued by more beautiful women than she. Is it her lively mind? Her air of mystery? The fact that she does not seem to like me? Am I so shallow that I must have the only woman who appears not to want me?

"You play first," Bingley reminded him.

Darcy, called to order, laid down a five, hoping to trick Miss Bennet into laying a card worth ten points so the two would add up to fifteen, whereby his opponents would have to peg two points.

"Six," she said, laying down an ace.

"Nine," Mrs, Bingley said.

"Twelve," Bingley said.

"For two," his wife reminded him.

"Charles," Lizzy said in mild exasperation. "Mind your doubles."

"Oops, sorry," Bingley said, looking sheepish and pegging two points on the board.

"Sixteen," Darcy said, laying down a four. Perhaps Miss Bennet would lay down a two or a five, making a run and giving them three points to peg.

"Twenty-five," she said, laying down a nine of diamonds and thwarting his hopes.

"Go," Mrs. Bingley said, indicating that she had no cards beneath a seven.

Bingley sucked in his breath and laid down a six. "Thirty-one for two."

He pegged his points and Darcy began the round again. After all the cards had been displayed and the pegging points totted up, Miss Bennet and Bingley were ahead by seven points. Or behind, Darcy supposed.

While they added up the points in their hands and in the 'crib', Darcy asked, "Where did you learn this variation? Or, did you make it up yourself?"

"No," Jane said, smiling sadly. "An excellent friend of ours, who has died recently, introduced us to it. We often played it. In turn, we taught Chinese crib to Susan."

"I am sorry for your loss," Darcy said gently. The ladies nodded. Sensitive to their melancholy mood, Darcy began shuffling the cards in silence. Finally, he said as he dealt, "I have not heard of that variation either."

"We shall teach it to you and your sister one night at Pemberley," Miss Bennet promised. She sighed, picked up her cards, and opened them. "Heavens," she whispered.

When the Darcy and Mrs. Bingley team won handily, never even crossing the skunk line, Mrs. Bingley pronounced herself well-pleased with her new partner. Her husband playfully scowled at her and they all laughed.

Darcy realized in that moment that he had rarely enjoyed playing cards more. *I have never laughed as much in one sitting than with these three individuals, either.*

A Tickhill posting inn enjoyed their company for an hour and a half, where they ate a delightful repast of cold meat pies, pickled cucumbers, and dill-sprinkled carrots, followed by a steamed peach pudding covered with lashings of custard. The party split apart for the afternoon with the two sisters in the Bingley carriage and the two men in the Darcy one. Just as they were pulling away from the posting inn, another carriage whipped around the bend and careened into the yard. The Darcy and Bingley coachmen pulled on their reins, cursing. They shook their fists at the reckless driver before proceeding on the last leg of their journey.

∞

Mr. Edmund Bissel jumped down from his carriage as soon as the door was opened. "We have made good time, John," he said to his coachman. "I meant to sleep here tonight."

"Aye, sir," the man said, touching his forehead. "Will we eat 'ere, sir, and press on t' Ferrybridge before nightfall?"

"Yes. Be ready in an hour," Edmund ordered.

"As y'say, sir," his driver replied.

"Mind my things," Edmund said.

"O'course, sir."

"Very good," Edmund replied and turned to stalk into the dark-beamed inn, calling for the landlord. When the heavy man came through to the hall, Edmund enquired after something to eat.

The man pulled on his forelock. "Beggin' yer pardon, sir, if you'll sit 'ere for half a mo', we'll be tidyin' our private parlor fer ye. We jist 'ad a party depart. They're off t' Derbyshire, they are."

Edmund glared at him. "Are you going to tell any strange traveler *my* business after I have left?"

"No, sir. I won't, sir," the landlord promised, his porcine expression crestfallen. "I do like a bit o' a chinwag now and now, but I can keep me tongue between me teeth if I 'ave to."

"Take care that you do," Edmund said testily. He sighed, heartily sick of traveling. "While I am waiting, kindly have someone bring me a glass of stout."

"At once, yer honor," the landlord said, scurrying away.

Edmund sat down on a straight-backed chair next to a narrow table against the wall. The place smelled of age and beer. The occasional waft of air through the open door brought the pungent smell of the stables inside to mix with the rest. He devoutly hoped that the private parlor would face away from the yard.

His glass of stout was brought to him by a buxom young woman who strongly resembled the landlord. *She must be his daughter.*

"'ere ye are, sir," she said, setting the glass of dark beer before him.

Edmund nodded and passed her a coin. She curtsied and hurried away into the recesses of the building.

Soon. Soon.

∞

Derbyshire...

A substantial stone gatehouse marked the entrance to the Pemberley House estate. The keeper hurried to the gates, pulling them wide before standing to the side and doffing his cap as the Darcy carriage drove through. His plump wife joined him and bobbed a curtsy at each of the three carriages.

Lizzy and Jane leaned closer to their open window and watched excitedly for their first sight of the great house that Lizzy would soon paint. They rolled on a remarkably smooth drive through a beautiful, natural woodland of silver birch, English elm, pine, and ash. Gravel crunched under the carriage wheels. Birdsong could just barely be heard above the. The trees gradually thinned and their first glimpse of the pale, Palladian-style stone mansion brought small gasps to their lips.

Once they left the veiling influence of the trees, the

ground opened up into grassland and the full magnificence of Pemberley House could be appreciated.

"Is it not superb?" Lizzy breathed. "Perhaps I should paint it from here."

"I expect you will need to see it from many angles before you find the one that you prefer the most. Mr. Darcy is bound to have a gig you could borrow," Jane replied. "It is a happy aspect, to be sure. I thought Netherfield magnificent and infinitely grander than our home at Longbourn. But this?"

Six columns adorned the center front, soaring two floors from the porch floor to the peaked pediment above. Though the house sat on a significant rise across a shallow valley, there was only one sweeping step up to wide, double doors, flanked by windows. Two square-topped wings stretched to each side, two storeys tall. Great windows punctuated the walls, some with Palladian arches decorating their tops. Huge chimneys, carved and decorated, thrust out of the roof-top. Wooded hills—the home wood—framed the house from behind.

The carriages rolled over a slightly arching stone bridge, crossing a wide, natural stream of some significance. It widened before the house into one end of a lake, and then narrowed again as it disappeared into the woods beyond. Lizzy saw several wide foot bridges, created for easy passage from one part of the gardens to the next. Nothing seemed forced or unnatural and she found herself well-pleased with the estate so far, seeing great potential for her paints and brushes.

They arrived at the front door at last. The carriages drew to a halt and liveried footmen hurried forward to open the doors and assist the passengers. Soon, they were all standing on the marbled porch floor. A tall young lady with a pronounced resemblance to Mr. Darcy, hurried forward and embraced him. Another older lady, stylish and full of vivacity, hurried forward to greet Lizzy and Jane.

"Hello, and welcome to Pemberley. I am Mrs. Sophia McDougall, Fitzwilliam and Georgiana's aunt. Widowed, unfortunately. You must be horrendously exhausted by your journey and I will take you up to your rooms directly. We received a letter this morning telling us of the treat my nephew was bringing home and here you are. Georgiana and I love visitors."

Jane took her hand first. "I am Mrs. Jane Bingley and this is my sister Miss Elizabeth Bennet."

"Miss Bennet, welcome. I understand you are to paint our beloved Pemberley."

"Yes, I am," Lizzy replied, shaking her hand.

The gentlemen approached.

Mr. Darcy had his sister on his arm. "Before you take them away, Aunt Sophia, I must make the ladies known to Georgiana. Mrs. Bingley, Miss Bennet, this is my sister, Georgiana Darcy."

Lizzy and Jane both shook her hand. Georgiana smiled widely and seemed genuinely pleased to meet them. She was taller than both sisters and had smooth, lovely skin and kind, rich hazel-brown eyes. Tendrils of dark hair—the same color as her brother's—framed her lovely features. She was a young woman bursting into womanhood and much too old for Lizzy to safely paint.

"Have you come to paint my portrait?" Miss Darcy asked. "Shall I have to sit for hours and hours?"

Lizzy shook her head. "I am not here to do your portrait. I am sorry, but I am here to paint Pemberley House."

Miss Darcy looked from her to Mr. Darcy and then clapped her hands together, clasping them afterward. "What a splendid idea. We only have the architect's sketch and much has changed since that was done. And, I must say, that I am somewhat relieved that I will not be sitting for hours at a time."

"You will have to sit when I find a portraitist that satisfies me," Mr. Darcy reminded her. "Perhaps I will lure François Mulard from Paris. I have seen his work."

"I have a reprieve, then," Miss Darcy said, laughing up at her brother. She looked at Lizzy, still smiling. "Come, Miss Bennet. I will take your arm and lead you to your room. Aunt Sophia will accompany your sister."

She did just that, linking arms with Lizzy and leading her

into the house. When they were fully into the grand entrance hall, Lizzy stopped moving and listening to Miss Darcy's chatter. Instead, she halted in place on the grey and white marble-tiled floor and pulled her arm free so she could turn and stare.

Chapter Eleven

Pemberley...

A domed roof light flooded the interior with light. Everywhere she looked, examples of great art washed her senses in wonder, even from the ceiling. Portraits formed the majority of the paintings, stacked three high, one row above the other. Men and women from previous centuries stared out at their descendants and their guests. One enormous portrait hung on the landing wall, directly opposite the front door. In it, a handsome gentleman of the previous century stood, his spaniel at his feet, looking autocratic with his magnificent white wig of curls.

Three niches on each wall, except the outside wall, held marble busts. Several plinths sat to the side, each holding a full-sized example of Ancient Greek or Roman statues—one was a woman holding an urn and the other was a common soldier, at ease, both hands resting on his standing spear as though he was supporting himself with it.

Lizzy struggled to take it all in. She thought she could stand here for hours examining each masterpiece and even envied the doorman with his straight-backed chair, because sitting in this glorious space was his *job*.

She peripherally noted that the staircase must be twenty-feet wide, adorned in blue, gold, and cream carpet with brass stair-rods holding the adornment in place. Several doors led off from the grand entrance hall. Some were open, but she did not care what lay beyond their entrances when such a display of splendor lay before her.

I believe that is a Gainsborough, she thought, taking a step toward the right-hand wall so she could examine the painting more closely.

Georgiana soon realized she had lost her guest and returned to her side. Looking up at the painting of her great-great aunt which Miss Bennet appeared to be admiring, and then around the hall, she said, "Awe inspiring, is it not? So much work and effort and skill. Did my ancestors deserve such exertions, I wonder?"

"Oh, my," Miss Bennet said on a sigh. "I cannot say if they deserved the distinction of having their portraits painted, but they chose their artists well. They are all exquisitely done. Quite exquisite."

"Thank you, Miss Bennet," Fitz said, joining them, Mr. Bingley at his side. "Our dining room is decorated with landscapes only. Our father removed the portraits there, claiming he would not have his insides curdled by the stares of a bunch of rum touches."

Georgiana laughed, though her brother should not have used such a phrase in front of ladies.

Miss Bennet chuckled. "I look forward to seeing the landscapes," she claimed, still smiling. "*And* the rum touches," she added daringly.

"It will be my pleasure to accompany you," Fitz said, bowing his shoulders.

Georgiana's gaze popped to her brother, examining his countenance. She had never heard him talk in such a warm manner to any woman other than the ladies in his family. And Nanny. And Cook. And Mrs. Reynolds, their housekeeper since before Georgiana's birth.

Well, well, she thought, returning her attention to Miss Bennet.

"Shall we continue?" Georgiana asked, indicating the stairs. "There is just enough time left for us to change for dinner. Did you bring your maid?"

Miss Bennet shook her head. "We left her at home. My sister's woman usually does for me when we travel."

"I shall have Mrs. Reynolds assign a girl to help you," Georgiana promised, linking her arm through Miss Bennet's again. She glanced to the right where the housekeeper waited. Mrs. Reynolds nodded and hurried away.

"You are too good," Miss Bennet murmured.

"Nonsense," Georgiana replied, smiling widely. They started up the stairs "I predict that you and I shall be great friends. Now, we have put you across the corridor from your sister and her husband. We thought you would be more comfortable knowing they are near. Pemberley is larger than any house has a right to be."

Miss Bennet chuckled. "Perhaps, but you have so many walls on which to hang art. Surely that cannot be deemed a superfluous excess?"

"You would not think so, of course," Georgiana said with a soft, lady-like snort. "If only Fitz and I had been closer in age. Then, we could have played hide-and-go-seek together. Mother died when I was young, but I remember her ordering Fitz not to play the game with me because she feared I would be lost amongst all the rooms."

"My sisters and I often played. We squealed and giggled so much that my father would come out of his book room and send us into the home wood to play."

"Are your parents still alive?" Georgiana asked.

Miss Bennet sighed. "No, they died in a carriage crash two years ago."

They had come to the next floor and Georgiana slowed her steps. She hugged her guest's arm. "My dear, I am sincerely sorry. So recently, too."

Miss Bennet nodded. "Thank you."

Georgiana cast about for another topic and found one instantly. "Did you play games on your journey here? In our carriage?"

"Yes, indeed," Miss Bennet said, smiling up at her. "The

game box was beautiful. Your talent in decorating it was much admired, I assure you. The painting of the cards was exquisite."

Heat suffused Georgiana's cheeks. "I have little talent in comparison to yours, I am sure," she said shyly. Directing their path toward the third door down from the landing, she quickly added, "Ah, here we are. I do hope you like the room."

"I am certain I shall," Miss Bennet said politely. "Did your mother do the decorating?"

"Some," Georgiana said. "I have refurbished a few rooms—with my aunt's assistance. And my brother's, as well. You would not think it, but he has a keen eye for color. Besides, he has seen the London salons and I have not. My aunt has not been used to moving in those elite circles, either. Between the three of us, I believe we have managed very well."

"No doubt. Everything I have seen so far is beautiful," Miss Bennet praised.

They entered the bedchamber and Georgiana nodded at the young maid who must have raced up the backstairs to get there ahead of them.

"Oh, my. Look at this room," Miss Bennet said, smiling widely. "White and gold. So pretty. And the light from the windows is magnificent."

"Thank you," Georgiana said, tucking a stray curl behind her ear. "Ah, and this is Fiona."

The wide-faced, freckled girl, a few years younger than Georgiana, bobbed a curtsy. Her frizzy red hair peaked out from her cap and her bright-green eyes sparkled with excitement. Georgiana's own dresser had been training a few interested maids in the art of being a personal servant. This would be Fiona's first chance to prove herself worthy of the honor of waiting particularly upon a Darcy guest.

"I will leave you now in Fiona's care. She has been training to be a lady's maid so pray, be patient with her. I am confident she will do her best. We dine at six, Fiona."

The maid bobbed another curtsy and Miss Bennet smiled

reassuringly at her. Georgiana squeezed her guest's arm and hurried away, anxious to begin her own preparations for the evening meal.

∞

North Riding, Yorkshire…

Bissell's carriage drew to a halt in front of the Yorkshire inn that had enjoyed the patronage of his quarry. Damn tired of traveling, he quickly descended to the drive. Several male patrons crossed his path, nodding and touching the brims of their hats. He returned their salutes automatically and hurried into the building the moment the way was clear. A substantial desk, behind which stood a woman built upon a magnificent scale and of indeterminate age, occupied one wall of the large foyer. She wore her graying hair tucked beneath a starched white cap. She smiled in greeting.

"Good afternoon, sir," she said. "My name is Mrs. Lidd. How may I assist you?"

"Good afternoon," Bissell said, though he would have said they were closer to evening. "I have come to inquire after a friend whom I understand is a guest here."

"And who might that be, sir?" she asked, her tidy eyebrows rising in an arc.

"Charles Bingley," Bissell informed her. "He is staying here with his wife and sister-in-law."

"Miss Bennet?" She beamed. "The artist?" Without waiting for his reply, she pointed to a framed sketch on the wall behind her. The image depicted a terrier sitting in the yard of the inn. "She drew that, she did. Barty never looked so good, for he's a terrible scamp, he is."

"It is charming," Bissell said automatically, struggling to contain the swoop of excitement that flowed through his chest. *She is here!* He assumed a sangfroid that he did not feel. "Pray tell me that the Bingley's and their guest are still here."

Her lips turned down and she shook her head. "I cannot, sir. They left this morning."

Bissel's heart plummeted. "Have they returned to

Hertfordshire?" he asked, a disappointed frown marring his brow. "I have just come from there, you see. I was sure they meant to stay away all summer."

She considered him for a moment, no doubt taking in his fine person, his cultured manners, and likely wondering if he was truly a friend of their former, and favored guests. He waited patiently, offering a smile.

Finally, she said, "Mr. Bingley did not confide the location of their next destination with me. However, I was chatting with the head ostler, who is my brother, you understand, and he said they were bound for Derbyshire."

Bissell's brows drew together. *Derbyshire?*

"They like to visit local manor houses," the woman mentioned. "Perhaps they mean to visit Chatsworth. It's said to be magnificent. And then, there is Pemberley House." She paused and blinked a few times. "Say, the owner of Pemberley was here and they met with him. I remember him especially because his man came in and insisted on our best suite. Perhaps Mr. Darcy invited them for a visit?"

Bissell's shoulders relaxed. Tomorrow, he would push on to Derbyshire. At least he was headed in the right direction to meet the ship in Bristol. To the clerk, he said, "I am sure you are right. Now, do you have a room for me and some place for my people?"

She pursed her lips. "Ooh, let me see," she said, opening up her ledger. "It's a busy time of year, it is."

"I shall be happy to take the suite that the gentleman of Pemberley used."

Her expression cleared. "Of course, that set of rooms is available. How long will you be staying with us, sir?"

"Only one night."

"Can I tempt you into staying an extra night, sir?" Mrs. Lidd enquired while reaching for a pen. "You have traveled a fair distance and your coachman will be exhausted, he will."

Bissell thought for a moment, glanced around the comfortable-looking inn, and considered how tired he felt. *I have the time. I could spare an extra day.*

“It should be a fair day tomorrow,” Mrs. Lidd added when he hesitated. “You could take a walk around Fountains Abby. ‘Tis a peaceful place, it is. A good place to let the dust blow off you, if you take my meaning, sir.”

He had never seen the ruin and he had heard it was magnificent. Bissell sighed, and said, “I believe I would enjoy that. Yes, I will stay for two nights. Thank you for the suggestion.”

“You will not regret it,” she promised and dipped the pen in the ink before handing it to him so he could sign the ledger. “No one who goes to the Abby regrets their visit.”

∞

Pemberley...

Before their meal that night, Lizzy thanked the footman who had shown her the way, and entered a small drawing room. Her hostess, her sister and her husband, Mrs. McDougall, and another man stood in two groups talking quietly. Lizzy quickly glanced away from Mr. Darcy, struggling to keep her pulse calm.

He is not even looking at you! How can you react like such a school girl just at the sight him?

Lizzy took one step inside the threshold and then paused, delighted by the décor and wishing to take a moment to admire it. Rich, yellow damask walls had been adorned with wide white cornices and white wainscoting below a luscious chair rail, trimmed with gold leaf. Paintings of women from across several centuries hung on every wall except for the silk-draped window wall. Lizzy gravitated toward the nearest portrait, but Miss Darcy distracted her as she hastened toward her.

“Here you are,” she said, smiling widely. “This is the saffron drawing room. We usually meet here before going into the family dining room. Unless there is a large party, of course.”

Lizzy smiled and gestured. “It is a beautiful room, Miss Darcy.”

“Thank you,” she replied. “Come, you must call me Georgiana, for, as I said, I believe we shall be great friends.”

Lizzy flushed with pleasure. "I am Lizzy, then."

"You have met my aunt, but you have not met our estate manager, who is joining us for dinner," Georgiana said, touching her elbow and drawing her further into the room toward the group also containing her aunt.

A man in his mid-thirties, Lizzy thought, a little taller than Georgiana, sporting a fine dark beard and mustache, below eyes of icy-blue, stepped toward them. He bowed and smiled.

"Miss Elizabeth Bennet, may I introduce Mr. Kearn? He is the son of Admiral Kearn," Georgiana said, folding her hands in front of her.

Lizzy detected a hint of pride in her hostess's voice and wondered at it. Was she proud of who his father is, or of the man himself? *Perhaps he is an exceptional estate manager?*

Instead of a curtsy, she held out her hand. "I am pleased to meet you, sir. Did you not wish to follow in your father's footsteps and join the Royal Navy?"

He took her hand and shook it warmly. Chuckling, he explained, "I must confess that I get seasick every time I step aboard a ship. Or a boat. Or a dingy. My father tried repeatedly to rid me of this affliction, and so my childhood was replete with opportunities to hang my head over the gunwales. When I reached my thirteenth birthday and could still not bear to sail without being ill, he admitted defeat and sent me to Shrewsbury School."

"He must be proud of you, nevertheless," Lizzy offered. "Being the manager of an estate like Pemberley must be considered a significant achievement."

"Compared with captaining a ship in the Battle of Trafalgar?" Mr. Kearn replied with a grimace. "There is no parallel."

Lizzy tilted her head. "An elder brother?"

"Indeed."

"*We* are happy to have you here with us," Georgiana said. She looked over Mr. Kearn's shoulder at her brother. "Are we not, Fitz?"

"We are. Very pleased," Mr. Darcy said, joining their

group. "I stole him out from under the Vice-Chancellor who was trying to make him a fellow. Just at the eleventh-hour, too. Old Mr. Wickham was due to retire and he needed to train his replacement."

"Mr. Wickham?" Lizzy asked, her brows drawing tightly together. "Surely Wickham is not such a common name. Is he related to Lieutenant George Wickham, my brother-in-law? Whom you said you know?"

Georgiana stiffened beside her, color draining from her cheeks. Mr. Kearn stilled, and Mr. Darcy's eyebrow lifted. Lizzy did not know how her simple question could have elicited such a response.

"I beg your pardon," she hastily said, blinking rapidly. "I did not mean to—"

"You have no need to apologize." Mr. Darcy rubbed the side of his nose with his finger. "Old Mr. Wickham's son is Lieutenant George Wickham. We do not speak of him in this house. He disgraced his father's good name."

"I am not surprised to hear this account of his character," Lizzy mused. "I confess that I am ashamed that he is now a member of our family."

Mr. Kearn stirred and addressed Georgiana. "Perhaps, Miss Darcy, Mrs. Bingley and Miss Bennet would enjoy seeing the rose garden tomorrow?"

"I…yes. I will be delighted to show them," Georgiana said, her color returning. The door opened and she glanced over her shoulder. "Ah, here is Mellor calling us to the table. Fitz, you will take Miss Bennet in, please, and put her to your right, opposite Aunt Sophia. Mr. and Mrs. Bingley will follow you, and I will come in on Mr. Kearn's arm. Aunty, you will take Mr. Kearn's other arm, if you please. Is that acceptable to everyone?"

No one demurred and they were soon seated in a comfortably-sized dining room, at a table shrunk down so that it held only eight individuals. Georgiana sat at one end, her brother at the other. Jane and Charles were directed to the places at her left and right. Mr. Kearn sat beside Jane, next to

Lizzy.

"We are one short, unfortunately," Georgiana said, frowning a little, and then she smiled widely. "But we are dining *en famille* tonight, so we may all be comfortable. I mean to talk across the table and give you all permission to do the same."

Lizzy, pleased with her hostess's directions, watched her nod to the butler and the meal began.

As their first course of roasted peaches with some nicely melted stilton cheese on top was consumed, the tension of the last few minutes in the drawing room dissipated. Lizzy praised their cook and partook of fried sardines with parsley-caper sauce, dishes of braised celery, boiled potatoes, and candied parsnips. Everyone talked and laughed together, getting to know each other while delicious courses were offered, the next being roasted chicken and escallops of pork, breaded with crumbs, pine nuts, and lemons. Charles told everyone the story of how he and Jane had met and of how his sister, Caroline, had tried to keep them apart.

"We did not listen to her naysaying attitude," Charles declared, helping himself to several pieces of finely roasted chicken, adding mashed turnips—sweetened with maple syrup—wilted cabbage, apple and walnut salad—dressed with mustard, olive oil and vinegar—creamy lemon-ginger spinach, and braised radishes with bacon and shallots. "I knew she was the wife for me the first time I laid eyes upon her. That was at a village ball. She was the most beautiful woman in the room."

"I am not surprised," Georgiana said, smiling at Jane. Looking around the table, including everyone in her glance, she said, mischievously, "You know, Fitz is a wonderful dancer." He grimaced at her and she laughed. "He does not like to do so very often. But he taught me."

"And why is that, Mr. Darcy?" Lizzy asked, leaning to one side to accept a slice of chicken breast from the footman. "Surely, you have been to balls where there are not enough men to squire the ladies on the dance floor."

Mr. Darcy only lifted an eyebrow and took a bite of his

food, offering no excuse.

"Once," Mrs. McDougall said, casting a sly look at her nephew, "he told me he did not want to lend consequence to gauche young ladies whom other men had overlooked."

Everyone at the table gasped comically.

"You did not!" Lizzy exclaimed. "What am I saying? Of course, you did. Mr. Darcy, you would not have been popular at the Meryton Assemblies." She shook her finger at him. "For shame."

Darcy's nose twitched, but he could not be drawn out. Instead, he directed Mellor to refill their glasses.

Charles, his face lightly flushed with his pleasure in the evening, laughed. "I enjoyed the assemblies immensely. So many pretty ladies and many with great vivacity, too. I think Meryton, and its environs, must be the happiest place to live."

"Thank you, Charles," Jane said in her quiet way. "I am certain Derbyshire is an equally happy place to live. What do you think, Mrs. McDougall? Have you lived in Derbyshire long?"

Georgiana's aunt swallowed her food and then answered, "No, only a few years." Mrs. McDougall cut her meat and then added, "I am well-pleased with the county—except for the cockerels. They have the loudest cockerels it has been my misfortune to hear. Georgiana and I have taken great pains to place you in the wing furthest from the home farm." She glanced down at the piece of chicken on her fork. "I could not convince Alfonse to cook ours. We would have had a lovely wine and mushroom sauce on him. Slow-cooked, you know, to make the meat tender." Her frown intensified and she scowled. "I could have wrung his neck myself."

Lizzy laughed and asked, "Alfonse? Or the cockerel?"

"Both!"

Even Mr. Darcy laughed at her war cry.

Chapter Twelve

Pemberley…

Darcy, wearing riding dress in anticipation of the work his estate manager would put him to, walked across the broad expanse of lawn to where Miss Bennet sat on a stone bench. She was staring up at his home, a thoughtful expression on her face and a sketch pad in her lap. Her footman stood near-by, her artist supplies on a portable table beside him. She was prettily attired in a pink day-dress dotted with tiny flowers. A villager straw bonnet protected her complexion. Her familiar apron lay draped across the bench beside her.

"Good morning," he said when he drew close enough. She smiled at him and he caught his breath. "Uh…have you begun already? I thought you would take a day or two to recover from our journey."

"I am doing some studies," she said, tilting her pad for him to see.

The large sheet held six sketches. One was of a first storey window. The second showed the intricacies of the flashing and cornice above the second storey windows. The third, fourth, and fifth sketches displayed three different chimney shapes. He pointed at a sixth, very small drawing in the lower, right-hand corner.

"What is that?" Darcy asked, his lips twitching. "Is it a mouse?"

"No, it is a chipmunk," Miss Bennet confessed, a

delightful pink tinge coloring her cheeks. "They are native to North America, though there is a cousin that lives in Asia, I believe. I saw a painting of one at a lecture on the fauna of that continent, and the little creature charmed me."

"He is like a striped field mouse," Darcy observed. "But with a wider tail." Then he frowned. "But…" he pointed at the tiny drawing. The chipmunk now sat on his haunches in the *middle* of the page, next to one of the chimneys. He blinked rapidly. *I am seeing things poorly. I must be.*

"Oh, I know his tail is not as magnificent as a squirrel's," Miss Bennet said, sweeping her hand across her drawing. "But I think him adorable."

Seemingly, she chased the drawing back to where it belonged, in the bottom right-hand corner of the page, because that is where the chipmunk now sat, staring out at them. *It did not just blink.* Darcy forced himself to look away from the page before he saw anything else out of the ordinary.

Clearing his throat, he swerved the conversation back to her efforts to record his home. "Will you be moving about the grounds as you make these studies?"

"I will," she said, sounding a little breathless. "I need to choose the best angle and situation before I begin to paint. I expect to have many pages filled with studies."

"Of course." Darcy risked a glance down at the page. Miss Bennet's hand now hovered over the chipmunk. He looked away and up toward the sun before looking down at her once more. "We have a small marquee that can be erected on the spot where you decide is the best place for you to set up. It will keep some of the weather off you. I believe we also have an enormous Chinese parasol that can be moved about with you while you are sketching. The end is pointed, you see, and can be pushed into the soil. I shall send one of the gardeners over with it." Darcy waved around at his parkland. "Keep him with you. He can stay busy with the shrubbery or flowers whenever you stop to draw."

Miss Bennet smiled at him and he forgot about the odd behavior of the chipmunk sketch.

"Thank you, you are most kind." She hesitantly held out her free hand.

Darcy took her warm, soft hand. It felt instantly at home within his grasp and he did not want to let it go.

"I admit that finding shade is not always possible," she said, slowly withdrawing her hand.

"Once the parasol arrives, you will no longer need to go to any extraordinary lengths," he replied, nodding brusquely before striding away across the lawn.

Darcy discovered that once he was away from Miss Bennet, the thought of the *active* chipmunk sketch intruded. He shook the idea out of his head. Drawings did *not* move. *Could* not move.

I must not have slept as well as I believed. Ah, here is Carmichael.

His head gardener straightened his tall and powerful frame to face him and said, "Master." He touched his cap with a gloved hand.

"Carmichael, I have promised my guest that she might have the use of that large parasol my sister sometimes uses when she sits in the garden."

"Aye, sir. I'll send one of t'lads wi' it," he said.

"Just my thought. Have him assigned to Miss Bennet for the duration of her stay, or until she no longer has need of him. He can move the parasol about the place for her and generally make himself useful. When Miss Bennet is busy with her sketching, he can attend to nearby garden needs. He is to report to Mr. Kearn each morning for orders."

"Aye, sir," Carmichael said, frowning a little in thought. His brow cleared. "I'll send me own son, Alphy. He's strong at work and won't be a bother t'the lady while she's workin'."

"Thank you. She is sitting on one of the benches on the south lawn at the moment."

"I'll tell 'im, sir."

Darcy nodded and headed toward the side door that led to the estate offices. Once inside, he found Bingley, wearing country riding dress, sitting and chatting with Kearn in his office. They both stood up to greet him on his arrival. Darcy nodded to both men.

"Good morning. I am glad to see you here," Darcy said, smiling. "I have come for the list of duties I am to perform this morning—Kearn is a great one for lists. If he had joined the army, I am convinced he would have been a regimental colonel by now."

They all laughed and Kearn picked up a piece of paper from off his tidy desk and handed it to Darcy.

"There are just a few items, sir," Kearn pointed out. "The most important is a visit to review the repairs on the Applegate farm cottages. Since the day is fine, and the workers will be about their business, I am hoping your presence will spur them on to greater speed. They are needed elsewhere soon."

"I shall do my best," Darcy promised. "Shall I look stern, or pleased?"

Kearn stroked his beard. "Uh, both?"

"Very well," Darcy said, nodding. To Bingley, he asked, "Would you care to accompany me? We shall ride, if you like. I can mount you on a fine bay gelding."

"Capital." Bingley grinned widely and waved at his clothes. "As you see, I was hoping for a chance to ride about the estate."

"You shall have it," Darcy promised. He glanced at Kearn, who had begun to sit back down. "Will you have some lemonade taken out to where Miss Bennet is working?"

"Miss Darcy is already attending to that, sir," Kearn replied, straightening up. "She told me so when she collected her list."

Darcy frowned. "I thought you sent her list to the room where she breakfasts?"

"Yes, but she came before I had a chance to do so. It appears that Miss Bennet is an early riser and Miss Darcy wished to be beforehand in her attentions."

"Of course." Darcy turned to his guest. "Come, Bingley, if we get through our chores, we shall be able to join the ladies for their afternoon tea."

Bingley followed him, seemingly pleased to agree to any regimen his host suggested. They exited the house and walked toward the stables.

"By Jove, that Kearn is a treasure, is he not?" Bingley commented. "His explanations on all manner of estate related questions were so clear and perfectly understandable. I wonder how hard it will be for me to find a similar fellow when I buy a place. Deuced hard, I should think."

"When you find an estate that you want to buy, it may already have a manager." Darcy signalled to Jermyn, who was walking across the stable yard carrying some tack. "Saddle Javador for me, please, and Brustin for Mr. Bingley."

The groom touched his cap and hurried off.

"You may like him well enough to keep him on," Darcy said, continuing their conversation. "If you must hire a new manager, I recommend you find a man who is a gentleman—the younger son of a member of the landed gentry, perhaps. He needs to know his business, be able to command the respect of your tenants, if you have any, and offer intelligent intercourse. You, my friend, have the sort of easy disposition that allows you to like anyone. Therefore, you must be extra cautious about whom you hire or else he will take advantage of your kindness and rob you."

Bingley blinked rapidly. "Surely not?"

Darcy shrugged. "I have a more cynical nature. If you wish, I will assist you when the time comes."

Bingley flushed, clearly pleased. "Thank you. Your…expertise in the matter will be most welcome."

Darcy nodded. He shifted his feet so he could look out at the paddocks where some of his horses were grazing. In a nonchalant way, he said, "I saw your sister-in-law in the gardens. She was sketching studies of Pemberley House. Her skill is remarkable and so accurate." He turned back to face Bingley and pinched his thumb and forefinger together until they were about an inch apart. "She had added a delightful little sketch of a chipmunk to the group."

"Ah, yes," Bingley said, grinning. "He is a little devil, that one."

He is a little devil?

"I beg your pardon?" Darcy asked.

Bingley coughed behind his fist before he replied. "L…Lizzy draws him often. In the m…most devilish poses, too. Jane and I are often in whoops at his antics."

His antics? Who controls the drawing? Miss Bennet? Certainly. Then, why does Bingley talk of the critter as if he is alive and in control? Darcy raised an eyebrow. The little chipmunk had been so cleverly drawn that it had almost capered across the page. His own fancy had got the better of him so he imagined it doing so. Sketches of chipmunks could *not* move on their own.

"I am disappointed that Miss Bennet will not be painting my sister," Darcy said, instead, skewing their conversation away from the rodent.

"Miss Darcy is much too old," Bingley assured him. "You may see her as a child still, and nearly nineteen is young, I grant you. But anyone can see that she is a grown woman. My Jane was much struck by her poise and kindness. As was I. You must be very proud of her. Has she been presented?"

Darcy shook his head. "No. Not until this December. Will you come to town for the winter season? We will send you all an invitation to Georgiana's ball, if you are."

"We have not made any plans and so are free to come," Bingley said. "No doubt, Jane will want a new gown."

"And Miss Bennet? Will she not want a new gown? I assure you that she will also receive an invitation," Darcy promised.

Bingley's brows knitted together. "There is an issue, there. Lizzy does not like to spend her money on expensive gowns. She has a nonsensical plan to buy a seaside cottage and live there. If she does not marry, of course." His expression had turned pensive, but suddenly he appeared conscious stricken. "My tongue does run on so. I should not have spoken of her plans to you. Pray, disregard my revelations."

"I will pay them no nevermind," Darcy promised. "As to

her ball gown, you have only to gift her with it for Christmas. Surely, she will not refuse a gift?"

Bingley's brow cleared. "Yes, indeed. That is a capital idea. Ah, and here are our horses. That *is* a magnificent bay."

∞

Georgiana had just finished directing the footmen in the positioning of the chairs in their elegant music room, while her guests and her aunt stood to one side and watched, when the doors opened and the men joined the ladies. She had told her brother not to let the men linger too long over their port because she had a surprise in store for them.

"Ah, there you are," she said, smiling widely. "Come in and take a seat. Mr. Kearn, will you sit at the desk?"

"Of course," he replied, hurrying over to the one chair pulled up to the graceful walnut lady's desk, facing the rest of the group and angled so the evening light from the tall windows would fall onto it.

A single slender volume lay unopened before him. Two others rested in a pile on the desk in one corner.

"Mr. Bingley, will you sit with your wife? Fitz, kindly seat Miss Bennet, sorry, Lizzy. Aunt Sophia, please sit here, with me," Georgiana directed, pointing at the two chairs on the left of the semi-circle before the desk. Once everyone was seated, except for herself, she said, her voice vibrating with excitement, "We are in the music room because I had meant to play for you. However, Mr. Kearn has graciously assented to read for us tonight instead. He has an exceptional reading voice and we have enjoyed many evenings together listening to him."

"What is the book?" Fitz asked, raising an eyebrow. "Not a romance, pray."

Georgiana laughed. "No, brother, it is not a romance. Fear not. I ordered the book months ago but the story proved to be so popular that I only received my copies of the three volumes today." She glanced at their guests and hesitated. "I beg your pardon, but I did not think to ask if you had already read it."

"Perhaps we have," Mrs. Bingley replied, smiling gently.

"But no story so excellent as to be popular can fail to please, whether we have read it or not. What is the tale called?"

"It is 'Guy Mannering'," Georgiana said, her eyes wide and questioning.

"'Guy Mannering'!" Mr. Bingley exclaimed. "Our copies have not yet arrived from the publishers, so, of course, we are behind times. This is a chance, is it not?"

"We have heard how wonderfully the story is written," Lizzy said, smiling widely, obviously excited.

"You naughty puss," Aunt Sophia said, grinning. "The package arrived this morning and you told no one?"

Georgiana waved one hand at Mr. Kearn. "I told one person, but I managed to keep the secret to myself, otherwise."

"Shall we begin, Miss Darcy?" the estate manager asked, picking up the volume before him. "I am ready."

"Mellor will bring tea shortly," she promised him and he smiled back at her. Georgiana sighed inwardly with pleasure. "So your mouth will not get too dry," she explained and then wished she had not since the reason was so obvious.

I am going to sit and immerse myself in the story. I am not going to act like a silly school girl any more. I will not display my feelings so that Fitz notices. I will not...

And Mr. Kearn began. His mellifluous voice calmed her and she folded her hands in her lap and watched him read.

"'*Guy Mannering; or the Astrologer*,'" he read, and then explained. "It is written anonymously. It begins with an excerpt from *Lay of the Last Minstrel.*

'Tis said that words and signs have power
O'er sprites in planetary hour;
But scarce I praise their venturous part,
Who tamper with such dangerous art."

Mr. Kearn continued for three hours, pausing occasionally for a sip of hot tea. He stopped once an hour for his listeners to discuss what they had heard so far. Everyone stood and took a turn about the room before they settled for the next hour of reading. During the second break, Lizzy approached Georgiana.

"Mr. Kearn is a remarkable reader," Lizzy said, shaking her head in wonder. "The characters come alive as he speaks. I do not believe I have ever heard anyone better."

A flush of pleasure swept through Georgiana's person, almost as though the compliment had been meant for herself. Her pride in Mr. Kearn could not be matched.

"Indeed. When we have performed amateur theatrics, he is a great favorite to play the most dramatic parts."

"I am not surprised," Lizzy said, looking at her searchingly.

Have I betrayed myself? Does she suspect?

Lizzy sat down in her seat as soon as Mr. Kearn returned to his. Mr. Darcy sat next to her and his arm brushed the side of hers. She drew in a slow, steadying breath. This morning when he had walked across the lawn toward her and she pretended to barely notice him, she experienced a frisson of anticipation. Mr. Darcy had a fine figure and a confident walk that appealed to her more than she had been willing to admit. His rich-brown riding dress and gold waistcoat had fitted him to perfection. He seemed more relaxed here in Pemberley and his expression had been warm and friendly.

Her frustration with what she had assumed to be his prideful nature had blinded her to his superior traits. Two days in his company while they had traveled to this beautiful estate had shown him to have many positive qualities.

He had played their games with apparent enjoyment, exhibiting no ennui, false or otherwise, like she thought he would have. She could tell that Charles liked him, as did Jane, but then that was no surprise since they could find the best in most anyone. What did surprise her was Mr. Darcy's enjoyment in Charles' company, who was at least five years his junior. Also, Mr. Darcy's care of his sister was all that it should have been. And, his people liked him.

Then, he touched her hand.

With just the tips of two fingers.

And she stopped breathing altogether.

He instantly withdrew his touch and she felt its loss.

Her gaze flew to his. Serious brown eyes looked down at her.

"You were wool-gathering," he whispered. "Kearn is about to begin again."

"Oh," she said stupidly. "Yes, of course. Thank you." *That* is why he touched her hand.

I should have known.

"I did not wish you to miss any of the story."

"Thank you," she whispered, and forced herself to break her gaze away from his.

Lizzy focused her attention on Mr. Kearn, who had already picked up the volume and opened it to the page where he had left off. He began and she heroically managed to maintain her focus and get lost on the story once more.

Chapter Thirteen

Lizzy dismissed her maid, pulled a shawl around her shoulders, and took her sketch pad and charcoal box to bed with her. She piled up the pillows, lit several extra candles on the bedside table, and climbed between the sheets. Sitting with her back against the headboard, she opened her pad to a fresh page and began to sketch.

Georgiana.

Though she would continue to refuse to paint the young woman, Lizzy felt compelled to sketch the winsome and youthful beauty.

First, she captured Georgiana as she had stood in the entrance hall, staring up at the paintings lining the walls—a three-quarter profile. An engaging smile displayed her natural charm. After completing that drawing, Lizzy flipped the page and began another. Georgiana took shape beneath her deft talent, sitting in the music room listening to Mr. Kearn, another smile hovering on her curved lips—a full profile. The next drawing showed Georgiana clasping her brother's arm, resting her head on his shoulder, obviously pleased at his return home—a straight-on, full image of her face.

Lizzy's hand slowed as she tackled Mr. Darcy's hard-angled handsomeness. The relation of the two subjects could be readily seen, but, while Georgiana's cheekbones were softly rounded, her brother's displayed defined shadows and highlights. His was a masculine face, tempered by the love he bore for his much younger sister.

"Hmm," Lizzy hummed slowly, gazing longingly at Mr. Darcy. She suddenly snapped the pad shut. "That is enough daydreaming out of you," she told herself. "You should be ashamed."

I shall burn those pages when I get up in the morning.

Lizzy set the pad on the bedside table, put her box of charcoals on top of it, blew out the candles, removed a few of the pillows from behind her back, and settled down to sleep.

And I shall not lie here thinking of him until morning, she swore to herself. Instead, she counted backward in the peculiar pattern she found useful in tricking herself into slumber. *100, 98, 99, 97, 98, 96, 97, 95, 96, 94, 95, 93, 94, 9…*

The next thing Lizzy knew, Fiona was pulling back the drapes. Morning sun spilled in, filtered through fine voile panels.

"Good mornin', miss," she said, turning toward the bed and picking up Lizzy's rose-colored cotton robe from the chair near to the bed. "I hope you slept well, miss."

Fiona held it out for Lizzy to put on when she stood. Lizzy sighed and climbed out of bed.

"Yes, thank you," she said, permitting the maid to help her don the robe.

"That's good, ain't it?" Fiona said in the jolly sort of voice that came from a person who had already spent several hours out of her own bed. "Are you goin' to draw some more today?"

"I will. After eating." Lizzy moved over to the dressing table and sat down. She removed her light cotton summer cap and placed it to one side. In the reflection of the mirror, she noticed Fiona pick up her sketch pad and charcoal box. Forgetting the sketches of Georgiana and her decision to destroy them, she gave the maid direction. "Please, put those with the other supplies. Jeremy will come and fetch them while I eat, just like yesterday."

"Of course, miss."

Once done that chore, Fiona poured a can of hot water into the porcelain basin, wet a cloth, and brought it to Lizzy. She took it and began her morning ablutions.

Afterwards, she dressed in a day gown of rose Pompadour and white striped cotton, lined with white cotton sarcenet. A turquoise ribbon bound the skirts beneath her breasts. A white fichu filled in her décolletage. Long, straight sleeves would protect her arms from the sun.

"It'll be a warm day today, miss. Do y'want the turquoise spencer? Or a shawl?" she asked, holding up both offerings. "You may not need either to my way of thinkin'."

"The pink shawl," Lizzy said, taking it from her and draping it over one arm just as a knock sounded at the door.

Fiona opened it, bobbed a curtsy, and admitted Jane, who was gowned in lovely Pomona green and primrose yellow.

"Good morning, dearest," Lizzy said, smiling widely. "I am finished, as you see."

"Yes, and you look charming. Lizzy, do you want my company today while you sketch?" Jane asked. "Only, Georgiana asked me to join her on a visit to the vicarage, and to a number of tenants. Duty calls, you know."

"I do know, and no, I do not need company."

Lizzy nodded to Fiona, who bobbed a curtsy, and then Lizzy left the room with her sister.

"Dearest, you would be very much in the way."

Jane chuckled. "I thought that is what you might say, but I wanted to be certain."

"I am always lost in my own world when I draw, as you know. I expect you would be bored rigid if you followed me around the gardens."

Jane tugged on her arm when Lizzy paused to gaze admiringly up at a still life oil painting of a bowl of fruit. "Come along, my dear. I woke up famished. The toast and chocolate Gibb brought me was insufficient." Lizzy allowed her to pull her onward. Jane continued their conversation by adding, "I know you well. If you had wanted company, I would have brought my stitchery."

"So you would. And what are the men up to today?" Lizzy asked.

"They left early to do some fishing," Jane said.

"Afterward, Charles is to accompany Mr. Darcy about the estate again."

They started down the main staircase and Lizzy stared in awe at the masterpieces surrounding them, paying little heed to her feet so that she almost slipped. Jane grabbed her arm.

"Hold onto the banister if you are going to look at the paintings instead of at your footing," Jane admonished. "Otherwise, you are going to fall. You gave me a fright."

"I am sorry. I will not fall," Lizzy murmured, grasping the mahogany banister. "I am reminded of our visit to Whitby and the walk down those stairs from the abbey, past the Church of St. Mary. The view of the town and the harbor was magnificent, but the uneven steps forced us to watch our feet more than the view."

"I recall. There were one hundred ninety-nine stone steps and Charles actually stumbled twice. These treads are not uneven, though, so you have no excuse for stumbling except your inattention."

Lizzy chuckled at her dryly spoken admonishment. "I promise to spend the next rainy day inside, examining each work of art so that I might become inured to their charms."

Jane smiled. "I suppose I can ask for nothing more. But, do you truly believe you could ever become accustomed to them? Even if you lived here for the remainder of your life?"

Lizzy shook her head. "I expect not."

Georgiana glanced up from her plate when she heard her two guests arrive in the breakfast parlor. She stood immediately and went to their side, smiling widely.

"Did you both sleep well?" she asked.

"I did," Lizzy replied, nodding.

"As did I," Mrs. Bingley said, smiling gently.

"Come, eat." Georgiana said, drawing them further into the room. "We like big breakfasts here at Pemberley to sustain us while we are out and about. My aunt has been down already and she is at the home farm, remonstrating with the farmer."

"Oh, dear. The cockerel?" Mrs. Bingley asked, heading

toward the sideboard.

A substantial meal had been laid out. It included dishes of braised kidneys, poached eggs in hot milk, stewed fruit, and crumpets sitting alongside a joint of ham. Beside the ham, two cakes, one plum, the other almond, rounded out the offerings. Mrs. Bingley loaded up her plate. As did Lizzy.

"Yes, indeed. She is enjoying an ongoing war with the poor farmer. He has won, on behalf of Pemberley, of course, many ribbons for his prized bird and he will not be bullied into killing it. She once constructed a tiny muzzle for it out of leather, but Farmer Bender refused to put it on him. Aunt Sophia claimed the cockerel need only wear it during the night and could have it removed later in the morning. He did not like that concession either."

The sisters laughed at the image, which pleased Georgiana immensely. She was not often the hostess of ladies older than herself. The Darcys did not entertain largely except for the neighbors whom she had known her entire life. She returned to her own meal with them. Mellor filled their cups with tea or coffee according to their desire.

"I expect your aunt enjoys the battle," Lizzy said, buttering a piece of toast.

Georgiana chuckled. "I think you are right. If she moved to a room across the corridor, then her window would face the front of the house. But she says she will not be routed by a cockerel."

"When I am in the gardens today, perhaps I will meet this famous bird and paint him as a gift for your aunt," Lizzy offered before she addressed her plate of eggs and kidneys.

Frowning, Georgiana slowly said, "I am not certain she would appreciate the gift as much as she should."

Mrs. Bingley exchanged a look with Lizzy that Georgiana could not interpret.

"Maybe your aunt would learn to love the bird after she receives the painting," Mrs. Bingley said. "Lizzy's animal paintings are quite spectacular."

Georgiana opened her eyes wide. "I think I should like to

see one."

Lizzy smiled mysteriously and took a sip of tea.

Leaning forward eagerly, Georgiana asked, "Shall I commission a painting? Then, she will not be angry with you, she will be angry with me. I am not afraid of her tongue."

Lizzy frowned and appeared to hesitate. "It is a pet, really, is it not?"

Georgiana nodded.

"Then…"

Georgiana put her hands together as if in prayer. "Come, what is a fair price? If my aunt repudiates the painting, I shall give it to Farmer Bender. He will love it for certain."

"For a watercolor?" Mrs. Bingley asked, resting her hand on her sister's arm. They exchanged a look and finally Lizzy nodded. Mrs. Bingley focused once more on her hostess. "Shall we say ten guineas?"

"Done," Georgiana exclaimed. "Ten guineas it is. I am so looking forward to seeing how your skilled hand recreates the animal. Thank you, kindly."

"You are most welcome," Lizzy said solemnly. "I hope your expectation matches reality."

Georgiana squirmed in her seat with happiness. "I am certain it shall."

ꕤ

Darcy, having paused for a little while from his turn about the estate with Bingley, went in search of Miss Bennet. Interestingly enough, he found her on a knoll above the home farm. Or, at least, he found the parasol and her table, her easel, and her footman, Jeremy. But Miss Bennet was nowhere to be seen.

"Where is your mistress?" he asked the footman.

Jeremy touched his hand to his forelock. "Sir. Miss Bennet 'as gone to see the farmer who looks after the 'ome farm. Shall I fetch 'er, sir?"

Darcy looked at the able young man and imagined that standing nearby while an artist draws, or paints, must get extremely tedious. Therefore, instead of going himself, he nodded.

"If you go, I will not have to listen to Farmer Bender complaining about my aunt," Darcy confessed in an unusual moment of revelation.

Jeremy ducked his head to hide his smile—a singularly futile attempt. "Sir," he said, and headed off toward the barns.

Darcy sat upon Miss Bennet's chair, prepared to wait. He saw that she had prepared some paper for painting and that her easel had been rotated to the horizontal. He assumed a watercolor was in the offing. Her position did not lend itself to painting Pemberley House, however. He saw her sketch pad nearby and reached to pick it up. His hand hovered over the closed pad, wondering if he should not look for fear of committing a gross impertinence. Surely, one's drawings could not be considered in the same light as a diary, he reasoned. He would never violate Miss Bennet's privacy by reading her diary. That went without saying.

However, in spite of his argument, he glanced around to see if Miss Bennet was nearby, saw no sign of her, and only then picked up her pad. He wondered how she was progressing with her studies of his house, so he flipped to the back pages. His efforts brought him to the first sketch of his sister.

But Miss Bennet claims she will not paint Georgiana, he thought, mildly confused. *And why has she drawn her so pensive? So...sad?* He flipped the page and examined another sketch of his sister. *So haunted.*

Darcy touched his sister's cheek with a gentle finger as though to tenderly comfort her. *What is this? How does Miss Bennet draw such emotions out of her subjects? And, what does she see in my sister that would make her depict Georgiana with such misery on her countenance?*

The third sketch of his sister made him catch his breath, for it contained a portrait of himself, as well. His expression showed fond emotion and acceptance. He had never thought of himself as so…well…so appealing.

Miss Bennet has made me more than I am. That is, indeed, her great talent. No wonder her skill demands such a high price.

Truly uninterested in his own appearance, he turned his attention to Georgiana. His sister leaned her head against his shoulder and clutched his arm as though pleased to see him. Yet, instead, her expression held such painful yearning that Darcy snapped the pad shut so he might close away the poignant reminder of all his Georgiana had lost.

She must have loved Wickham more than I thought. That bastard.

Darcy set the pad down on the worktable and clasped his hands in his lap, tightening their hold until his knuckles showed white. He breathed deeply in an attempt to rid his heart of rancor. Once he felt himself more in control, he relaxed his grip and closed his eyes.

But, stay, is it possible Miss Bennet has drawn only what she imagines must be my sister's emotions? Perhaps Miss Bennet has guessed, knowing Wickham's character so well herself, that Georgiana had been the most wronged by his actions two years previously? Yes, that must be it. My sister cannot go about so lively and with such grace of manner and bearing if she still holds a tendre for the blaggard.

Impossible.

Recklessly, but with care, Darcy reopened the sketchpad and removed the sketch of himself and Georgiana. He might never have a portrait by Miss Bennet, but he claimed this sketch and would not relinquish it to anyone. Gently, he rolled the drawing tightly shut and tucked the tube away inside his waistcoat.

Movement caught his eye and he stood up to watch Miss Bennet leave the farmyard. Her footman carried a large wicker cage containing their prize cockerel. Darcy's left eyebrow lifted. He stepped away from her easel to meet her.

"Miss Bennet," he said, bowing his shoulders. "Have you captured Mr. Pitt? Aunt Sophia will be ecstatic."

"Is that his name?" Miss Bennet asked in a laughing voice, looking lovely and pink after her mild exertions. "After the Right Honorable William Pitt? Our former First Lord of the

Treasury?"

"Indeed. Farmer Bender is a staunch Tory," Darcy revealed. "He always names his cockerels after famous party members. He will not thank you for absconding with his favorite."

"Absconding? Do not think it, sir," Miss Bennet rebuked. "I have stolen nothing. Farmer Bender caught him and put Mr. Pitt in the cage himself—with the help of Jeremy, here. All while explaining Mr. Pitt's excellent points. His rose comb is over three inches long and two and three-quarter inches across, for instance. And look at his vibrant plumage. Rust, turquoise, and black. Even white."

"I know all of Mr. Pitt's good points," Darcy replied. "His coloring is considered as magnificent as his crow. Do you plan to paint him?"

"Yes. Georgiana has commissioned a watercolor of him to give to your aunt as a gift."

Darcy stared at her, unblinking. He automatically moved to one side while she came around to her chair. Finally, he found his voice. "She cannot mean it."

"I assure you, she does," Miss Bennet said, twinkling up at him. "Georgiana swore she will give the painting to Farmer Bender if Mrs. McDougall does not want it."

"I…I do not know quite what to say," Darcy admitted, and then covered his mouth to hid his delicious and irreverent grin. With great difficulty, he managed to gravely say, "I shall be certain to be at home, and present, when my sister gifts our aunt with your painting."

Miss Bennet laughed delightfully, appearing to take his meaning with perfect understanding. "I have never had a painting of a pet repudiated," she promised him.

"I have no doubt. However, I am entirely certain that Aunt Sophia does not see Mr. Pitt as a pet, even though I am equally certain that Farmer Bender does," Darcy retorted lightly.

"Oh, dear," Miss Bennet drawled softly.

She looked at him so solemnly that neither could keep their countenances straight and both burst out in merry laughter. This so exacerbated the cockerel's sensibilities that he ruffled his feathers and crowed.

Darcy, entirely enchanted by this interlude, captured Miss Bennet's hand, leaned over it, and pressed a lingering kiss onto her smooth skin. Her fingers tightened around his before he reluctantly released them and took a step back.

"I must leave you to your commission," he said, sounding breathless to his own critical ears. "Bingley and I are joining Kearn for a drive about the estate."

"So, I understand," Miss Bennet murmured. "Good day, sir."

"Madam," Darcy said, nodding his head to her before turning and striding away, unaccountably pleased with the world.

∞

On the road to Pemberley…

Edmund Bissell and his valet, Clark, had spent a good deal of time on the road saying absolutely nothing to each other. This morning, however, Edmund broke the silence.

"Tomorrow, we shall reach Pemberley House."

"Sir."

Edmund glanced at the portrait beside him, still wrapped up in brown paper and tied closed with a string. It bounced when they drove through a rut. Steadying it, he stirred in his seat, tightened his lips, and then looked at his valet.

"We should not have dawdled in Aldfield. The painting will revert to a sketch tomorrow and we must be at Pemberley when that happens. It is our proof." He clenched his right fist on the carriage strap. "I must be in Liverpool in a week to meet the ship. I simply cannot linger at Pemberley for ten more days, waiting for the sketch to turn back into a painting."

"It changes after the noon hour, sir," Clark reminded him. "We shall be there in good time."

"As long as the traces do not break or a horse does not throw a shoe," Edmund snapped. He dry-washed his face with his hand before saying, "Pay no heed to my poor humors, Clark. This has been a damnably long journey."

"Indeed, sir," his valet replied stoically. "If I may, sir? What d'you hope to gain by confrontin' Miss Bennett? What if she claims that the magic is none of her doin'?"

"There can be no other explanation," Edmund bit out. "There is nothing magical in my house. The frame is not responsible, for we changed frames, did we not? And the image continued to alter. No, she will be made to see that it is her doing."

Edmund stared out the window, silently urging the job horses to greater speed. Without turning his head, he said, "Surely she must realize. Is it possible that this is the only one of her sketches that has changed? I cannot believe it. It is a nonsensical notion."

"Yes, sir."

"Yet, I have heard of no other drawing or painting of hers that has caused the sort of furor that could not go without notice."

Clark frowned. "You've told no one, sir. Perhaps it's the same for others."

Edmund scowled and thought about it for a moment before giving a curt nod. "There may be something in what you say."

Chapter Fourteen

Georgiana, thinking of her guests and staring down at a note for the cook in her hand, hurried around the corner of a hallway on the way to the kitchens.

And ran directly into someone, dropping the note.

"Oh," she cried softly, reaching out to catch herself. A strong male hand clasped it and she looked up to see who had bumped into her.

Mr. Kearn.

Oh, my.

He took her elbow, too, and smiled warmly down at her. "In a hurry, Miss Darcy?"

"I…I…" She could scarcely breathe. Coming to herself, she stepped away and he released both her elbow and her hand. "Um…Mr. Kearn, I did not expect to find you here. Are you not accompanying my brother and Mr. Bingley about the estate?"

"We have come back to collect a map," he explained in a soft voice without increasing the distance between them.

Georgiana swore she could feel the air between them charge like the air before a thunderstorm.

She wanted him to kiss her.

She wanted to kiss him.

She wanted to feel his arms around her.

But it could not be.

If her aunt discovered them?

If a servant saw them?

What then?

Oh, my Lord, what then?

But she knew what then and her greatest fear brangled about inside Georgiana until she could not contain it.

"I might be sent away," she blurted out and then covered her mouth with her hand and hastily glanced around the empty corridor. *What have I revealed with those five words?*

Mr. Kearn straightened. "*Sent* away? What is this? Why?"

"Because…I mean…Fitz has not noticed how I…but…if he did? I could not b…bear it," she cried softly.

He seemed to gather his defences about him. "There is nothing for him to notice. There *can* be nothing for him to notice. Pray, forgive me for distressing you."

Georgiana, her heart wringing, nodded. "My aunt…she has…oh, dear. She said it was impossible…and she said…Oh, I cannot say…I *cannot*. Mr. Kearn…I…I am wretched…most, most wretched…"

The man she loved clasped her elbow again and leaned closer—close enough that she could smell his scent. No other man's scent had affected her in this wild and joyous way. How could she feel like this in the midst of her misery?

"I beg of you not to be wretched on my account," he said in an undertone that could not be heard beyond their intimate circle. "I do not pretend to misunderstand you, my dearest girl. I am fourteen years your elder. In a few months you will go to London and be presented. There, you will find a suitable husband who will spend his whole life endeavoring to be worthy of your kindness, your accomplishments, your soft heart. Oh, of so many other qualities that makes you an estimable woman. A 'pearl of great price'."

He breathed deeply and she struggled to keep from crying out against his words. His entirely sensible words.

In a harsher voice than any she had previously heard from him, he added, "And you will forget me."

"I…I…Never!"

His voice dropped to a gruff whisper. "You must."

Desperation made Georgiana bold. Heedless of their

exposed position, she reached up and pressed the palm of her hand against the side of his face, feeling the texture of his magnificent beard against her hand for the first, and possibly last, time. He stilled.

Footsteps and voices sounded from around the corridor corner. Georgiana and Mr. Kearn hurriedly broke apart.

"Come," he whispered, grabbing her hand.

Mr. Kearn opened a door a little behind her, and pulled Georgiana into a large linen closet. A window high on one wall lit the space. Racks lined three of the walls, filled with sheets, pillow cases, towels, and coverlets. It was the closet reserved for the linens for the servants' quarters. They should not be disturbed there, for these linens were changed once a week, three days hence. Mr. Kearn closed the door and leaned back against it, still holding Georgiana's hand. They listened in pregnant silence while the servants passed by.

Georgiana permitted Mr. Kearn to take her other hand and raise both of her palms to his lips in order to kiss each one. She curled her fingers into his beard and sighed with pleasure.

"I h…have long wanted to touch your face," she admitted in a trembling voice. "The f…feel of it pleases me."

"I am a cad to permit it," Mr. Kearn whispered. He heaved a shuddering sigh. "My dearest girl, we must not…My income is not sufficient to keep you. Would you be happy in the estate manager's small manor house that does not even belong to me? That contains only four bedchambers and one drawing room? Pemberley has so much—"

Georgiana interrupted him. "Yes, I would," she stated unequivocally.

He shook his head. "We would have no great parties or balls. Everyone would say you had married beneath you. They would stare at you."

"I would stare back," Georgiana said, lifting her chin. "My true friends would not abandon me. Here, in the neighborhood where I am well-known? The thought makes reason stare."

"Your brother will not permit it," Mr. Kearn said in the

manner of a clincher.

Georgiana frowned and fell silent, staring not into his beloved face, but at the top button of his waistcoat. He folded her hands together and held them against his rapidly beating heart.

Slowly, she said, "I am not certain you are correct, sir. Fitz loves me very much. He will want me to be presented at court—I cannot deny that. I think…I think, also, that he will wish me to meet other potential husbands."

"There will be a plethora of gentlemen vying for your hand," Mr. Kearn stated in a pained under-voice. "My love for you is a paltry thing in comparison to all another might offer you."

Georgiana's heart fluttered like hawkmoth wings. *He loves me. He loves me. He loves me,* she told herself. She could not think of anything else for a dozen heartbeats. Then, she contained her flights of ecstatic wonder and concentrated on the subject at hand.

"Your love is not paltry to me. It is the most wondrous, most joyous thing I have heard. And, my love for you matches it." Georgiana paused while she enjoyed a warm hug from Mr. Kearn. He released her, but kept his hands on her shoulders. "However, I agree that we must be sensible. Do you think Fitz will demand that I marry a man of his choosing?"

Mr. Kearn shrugged and then slowly shook his head. "No, but he will not permit you to marry an unsuitable man, either. He will think me highly ineligible. My income is less than six hundred pounds per year, and half of that comes from my employment here. My home belongs to Darcy. If he should dismiss me, I would have no home to bring you to. I have no property other than the two small farms I have acquired during the last five years. I have been frugal and I mean to purchase a mill in the spring, if I can get it at the price I wish. Darcy may put me out for my impudence. I cannot take you from all this to a two up and two down farm cottage." He heaved another sigh. "Besides, both of the farms are tenanted and I will not evict them."

"You know this is nonsensical fustian," Georgiana lovingly offered. "My brother is not an ogre. He values you highly as an estate manager and as a friend, I have no doubt. Besides, I have a great deal of money of my own, the income of which will provide us with fifteen hundred pounds more a year."

"I would not use your money," Mr. Kearn said tightly.

"As I expected."

Georgiana's short reply caused him to stare at her keenly. In a hesitant voice, she added to it, "We…we will save it f…for our children. Though, if you have no objection, I think we should buy a house for ourselves first, and then put the remainder aside for our…our children."

He brushed her hair away from her face with a gentle hand. "You speak such sense for a young woman of almost nineteen. But, there are too many hurdles. Too many obstacles."

"Is it not part of your…occupation to overcome hurdles and obstacles?" she asked. "I have faith that you will find a way. An honorable way." They stared into one another's eyes, hope glimmering deep within each pair. "Make a list, my darling Mr. Kearn. I know how you love to make lists."

He nodded once. "A list. Yes. An excellent suggestion." He glanced around, as if coming to himself out of a dazed trance and realizing where he stood. "I must get back. Your brother and Mr. Bingley await my return with the map. We will speak of this on the morrow."

Georgiana lifted her lips for a kiss, but he merely pressed one on each of her palms again. Without speaking another word, he left the closet.

For a long time, Georgiana stood in the cool space, pressing her palms to her cheeks and breathing deeply, struggling to bring calm and order to her mind. She opened the door to leave the linen closet and discovered the housekeeper right outside, blinking at her in surprise and holding a piece of paper in her hand.

"Ah, Mrs. Reynolds. You have found my note for Cook.

Thank you. Would you give it to her, please?"

"O' course, miss."

"Uh, I…I was just wondering about the state of the pillowcases for the servants' rooms," Georgiana said, inventing an excuse for her presence in the linen closet.

"I went through them last week w' the laundress, miss," Mrs. Reynolds said, entering, requiring Georgiana, perforce, to back into the closet again. The housekeeper pointed to a nearby shelf. "This here stack needs new cuffs for t'edges are frayed."

Georgiana clasped her hands together in a relaxed pose and said, "This would be an excellent opportunity to add some cheer into the servants' bedchambers by using colored cuffs, instead of white."

Mrs. Reynolds raised her eyebrows. "Colored cuffs, miss?"

"Yes, indeed. A soft blue or yellow would be lovely. We can gradually change over the others as their cuffs need replacing."

"I understand, miss," Mrs. Reynolds said. "I'll order the bolts so we'll 'ave the colors on 'and."

"Excellent," Georgiana said, smiling widely. "I shall leave the choice of the color up to you. But, no brown or gray, mind. Nothing dreary."

He loves me. He loves me. He loves me. Oh, how will I contain this happiness?

"O' course, miss," the housekeeper said, nodding. "Miss? Yer aunt 'as been lookin' for you. She wanted to know if you'd like to join 'er and Mrs. Bingley on a drive."

"An excellent scheme. It is a lovely day for a drive in an open carriage. Kindly let her know that I will be with them directly."

∞

Lizzy's portrait of Mr. Pitt progressed nicely. In her painting, the cockerel stood at attention on a pristine white background, his deep nut-brown head lifted and self-satisfied, as though proud of his rose crown. His dark-turquoise-black tail plumage arched high and proud and he looked about to crow. Lizzy touched her paintbrush to the paper, applying a dab of black to his eye, making him look suddenly mischievous.

When she felt the first pangs of hunger, she turned to look around for Jeremy, her footman. She saw him standing near the portable table. He gestured down and she discovered a plate of small, cold meat pies, cheese, and plums ready for her.

"Thank you, Jeremy," she said, smiling. "I am famished. Have you had something to eat?"

"Yes, miss," he said, stepping away from the table.

"Good."

Lizzy picked up a pie with her left hand and began to eat while she continued to paint. "Mmm. Tasty."

"That it is, miss," Jeremy replied.

Mr. Darcy found them later in the afternoon, just as Lizzy put the final touches on her watercolor.

"There," she said, dropping her brush into a jar of water. "Jeremy, please take Mr. Pitt back to the home farm. I think he is tired of being confined."

"Yes, miss," he said, stepping forward to pick up the cage. The cockerel fluttered his wings in annoyance. "And here is Mr. Darcy, miss."

Lizzy swiveled around, looking for her host. He was crossing the lawn, walking confidently, a smile hovering on his lips.

Goodness, he is handsome. Why am I so pleased to see him? Not many days ago I did not like him at all. How is it possible that my regard for him has altered so much?

A slight breeze riffled her curls, bringing with it the spicy scent of the pinks growing in a sweeping bed near the stream. Lizzy took a deep breath of the fragrant air to calm her senses.

"Mr. Darcy," she said, raising her voice so he could hear her and then smiling back at him.

He raised a hand in salute. Lizzy stood to greet him, gifting him with a slight curtsy.

"Well met, Miss Bennet. Have you finished?" he asked, reaching her side and glancing down at her work.

Lizzy indicated the drying portrait with one hand. "As you see. I decided to keep the background clean so as not to distract the eye from your famous bird."

Her host leaned over to examine the horizontal image. After a moment, he shook his head.

Lizzy raised an eyebrow. "You are not pleased? Is something amiss?"

"You have painted the ideal, Miss Bennet," he said, a frown in his voice. "Do you always paint the ideal?"

"Painting the ideal is not difficult when such a specimen is available," Lizzy replied tartly. "Mr. Pitt is worthy of every ribbon tacked to the wall of the barn."

"Granted," Mr. Darcy said, turning his head with apparent reluctance from the magnificent image revealed through her art. He focused his attention on her. "But, surely, every pet or child you paint is not so perfect as our cockerel. I have heard from several sources that you have a deft touch at providing superlative images—something beyond what is really there."

Lizzy considered him for a moment and then slowly said, "When I paint a child, Mr. Darcy, what we see is the divine potential in that individual. I hope you do not believe me blasphemous, sir, but I hope I am painting them as our good Lord sees them—through the eyes of his love for his children. You know the scripture, I am sure. 'Suffer little children, and forbid them not, to come unto me…'"

Mr. Darcy completed the quote. "'…for of such is the kingdom of heaven.'"

"Yes."

"Hmm," he said, tilting his head. Boldly, he took one of her hands and turned it over as though examining the paint smudges.

Lizzy held her breath.

"And the pets? What of them?" he asked, drawing her hand through his arm and leading her away toward the path that approached the stream.

"Uh…" Lizzy could hardly think, could hardly breathe. *I am being so foolish.* "In pets," she began, concentrating furiously so as not to sound like an idiotish school girl, "what I aim to show is their innocence. Even naughty puppies and irascible elderly cats have innocent hearts."

"I see," he said in a deep, calm voice. "I am not certain everyone would agree with your assessment. I have known a few barn cats that will swipe at anyone that crosses their paths. Evil is what I would call them. When will you start on the house? Have you found the aspect that pleases you most?"

"I have. I need to do some more studies. I expect to be able to begin within the week," Lizzy said. Stealing a glance up at him, and then swiftly looking away when she encountered a warm look in his eyes, she said, "I have decided to do the work in oils. I must mix my paints. Is there a place where I can prepare what I need? There are some smells that may annoy others, so a place a little separate would be best."

"You may use the ballroom."

Startled at the offer, she cried out at his suggestion. "Oh, no. The ballroom? Surely not. I do not require nearly that much space."

Mr. Darcy patted her hand and then held it over hers as they strolled. "Nevertheless, I shall turn the room over to you as a studio while you are here. There is plenty of light and a half a dozen doors that can be opened for ventilation. My grandfather had the good sense to place the room on the north side of the building so it should not be too hot in there during the day. I shall ask Mr. Kearn to find some drop cloths to protect the floor."

"Wise," Lizzy said, pleased. "The drop clothes, I mean. I shall need at least one large old table—nothing fancy."

"I am certain there must be one or more about the place."

Darcy stopped their walk at the center of one of the bridges that crossed the stream. With their backs to the sun, they watched the play of light across the quick flowing water. He kept his hand over top of her small, talented one.

"Pray, pardon the impertinence, but are you happy living with your sister and Bingley?" he asked.

She glanced up at him, frowning. “Whatever made you ask such a question? Of course, I am happy living with my dearest sister. And Charles is a darling, you must admit. I do not think I have a bigger admirer of my art than Charles—his regard is at least on par with Jane’s.”

“And when you marry?” he asked daringly.

Miss Bennet tugged her hand free and took a half-step away from him. “I would not live with them anymore, would I?” she retorted.

“I suspect you would miss Jane enormously.”

“I would.”

Darcy had no doubt that her terse reply was meant to put him in his place. He decided to switch their conversation to something less contentious. “Bingley has an open and confiding personality, does he not? I find I like him very much. He is considering buying his own estate.”

“Yes, I know. He cannot decide whether to buy Netherfield or to buy another estate in a different county.”

“I would be most pleased if he considered Derbyshire,” he said, following her off the bridge and back toward where her easel waited, with her footman standing at the ready.

“I must admit it is pleasant country. It is a shame that Derbyshire is landlocked.” Miss Bennet paused to gaze around her. “You have a beautiful home, Mr. Darcy.”

“Thank you. Perhaps I should purchase a second, smaller place, at the seaside?” Darcy reached out and took her hand again, drawing it back through his arm. “Do you, perchance, favor a particular seaside location?”

“Somewhere with cliffs and a promenade,” she said, smiling now, and looking into the distance. “Near a small resort, perhaps. Not Brighton, though, because that watering hole is too big and busy. I would rather travel to the sea in the spring, than to London.”

“Do you dislike London? Will you not come for Georgiana’s come-out ball in December?”

“I do not dislike London, but I prefer short visits. And, I shall be delighted to come to Georgiana’s ball,” Miss Bennet said, turning her far away gaze up to his and grinning. "And you shall dance with me, shall you not?"

Darcy, dazzled by the brightness of her eyes, bowed his shoulders. "It would be my pleasure. A waltz. Two waltzes. And, I shall be honored to take you into supper as well."

"Perhaps you presume too much," she said softly.

"Do I?" Darcy held his breath and waited.

Miss Bennet blushed and shrugged. Instead, she indicated the easel with one graceful wave of her hand. "Here we are. Ah, the picture is dry. I shall take it inside and show Georgiana. I hope she will be pleased with it."

"Undoubtedly. She, your sister, and my aunt returned from a drive just before I came outside. She will probably be in her bedchamber by now, changing for dinner."

"Good, then your aunt will be as well. I shall hurry up to Georgiana before I also change for dinner. I had no idea the time had grown so late." She detached her painting from the easel and held it carefully with the image toward her. To her footman, she said, "Jeremy, will you tidy up for me, please?"

"Yes, miss."

"Permit me to escort you, Miss Bennet?" Darcy asked. "I know a shortcut."

She nodded.

"This way," he said, taking her arm. "I know all the best ways into Pemberley. During my childhood, I often bypassed my tutors and Nanny so I could run about the orchard or look for polliwogs in the pond in the middle of the home wood."

"Were you a naughty child?" Miss Bennet asked, grinning. "I can imagine it."

"Can you?" he asked, hurrying her along toward a small door in Pemberley's south wall. "Most people cannot."

"Perhaps they have not had the advantage of seeing you here at Pemberley. You are comfortable here. Relaxed. Comfortable enough to be naughty as a boy. Are you usually stiff in company?" Lizzy asked, entering his home before him and finding herself on a miniscule landing at the foot of a long stretch of stairs. He shut the door, turning the small area into a gloomy place and forcing Lizzy to climb a step to give him room. "You were stiff the first time I met you."

She turned a little, waiting for his answer and found herself able to look directly into his face. She held her breath, searching the shadowed planes of his countenance. He lifted his hand and brushed the back of two fingers across one of her cheeks. A caress.

In a whisper, he said, "Your skin is so soft."

Lizzy shifted the painting in her hands, hearing it crinkle in her nervous fingers. "Uh, thank you," she whispered in turn.

Will he kiss me?

He should not…but…

"Now, up you go," he said in a normal voice. "Straight up the stairs. Shall I carry your painting so you can hold your skirts?"

"I…yes, thank you," Lizzy said, hiding her disappointment—hoping she hid her disappointment.

No kiss.

She passed the paper over and grabbed a handful of her skirts before starting to climb. "You did not answer my question, you know."

"What question?" he asked, following. "Oh, I remember. Yes, I am usually reserved in company. I should not say I am stiff, precisely."

"The line between the two behaviors may be too fine to be easily discerned."

"Perhaps."

Lizzy paused and glanced over her shoulder. There was still only the light that came from a single small window near the top of the stairs. However, she could see his grim expression. "Why are you so reserved? Are you secretly bashful?"

His brows drew together and he came to a stop. "Bashful? I do not believe so."

Lizzy began to climb again. "Then, you do not make the effort."

Mr. Darcy took several steps before he replied. “Do you think I should?”

“Most certainly. You are a gentleman and being pleasant to be around is a gentlemanly skill. No one likes a grump.”

“A grump? Indeed? I am reserved, remember?” With a harrumph, he repeated, “A grump.”

“Are you insulted?”

“I believe I may be,” he answered.

Lizzy laughed. “Famous.”

To her surprise, Mr. Darcy also laughed.

And her heart melted at the sound.

Chapter Fifteen

Booth gave Darcy a patently impatient, patient look when he entered his bedchamber to dress for the evening. His tall, spare frame stood at attention beside the bed where Darcy's evening rig had been laid out.

"No evil eye from you, if you please," Darcy said to his valet. "I am not so late that I deserve that."

"As you say, sir," Booth said, at his most urbane. His sudden arrested attention honed in on Darcy's chest. "What do you have in your pocket, sir? Nothing I put there."

Darcy frowned and patted his jacket. He felt the rolled-up sketch and drew it out. "Ah, this." He unrolled it while asking, "What do you say to this, Booth? Miss Bennet sketched it and I must say that I am well pl—"

Darcy stared at the image of himself with Georgiana. She was smiling. Not just an ordinary everyday sort of smile, either. A radiant smile. *But…I would have sworn Georgiana's expression had shown painful yearning. Not this glowing happiness.*

"It is an excellent likeness, sir," Booth said, glancing down at the paper. "Miss Georgiana looks particularly fine."

Darcy blinked rapidly, trying to make the sketch appear as it had earlier. However, it stubbornly refused to alter.

"Indeed," he mused, his brows drawn together.

His valet reached out to take the paper. "I shall put it on your writing table, sir. With some books on top of it to flatten out the curl? I expect you will want to frame it."

Still flummoxed, Darcy slowly said, "I will."

I must be imagining things. Like the chipmunk. Perhaps my own worry about Georgiana's emotional state overlaid the true image. That must be it.

Yet…

Lizzy knocked on Georgiana's bedchamber door. Her maid opened it a little and gave a small curtsy when she saw who stood there.

"Miss," she murmured. "Miss Georgiana has begun dressin'."

"Who is it?" Georgiana asked from within the room.

"'Tis Miss Bennet, miss."

"Let her in."

"Yes, miss," the maid said, pulling the door to and stepping back. "I'm Fern, miss."

"I am pleased to meet you, Fern," Lizzy said, smiling at her. "Have you been with your mistress long?"

"Two years, miss," she said.

Lizzy nodded and slipped into the large, beautifully finished bedchamber. A cream and pink Aubusson carpet, woven with dark and light-pink roses, graced the floor. Georgiana, dressed in a wrap of royal blue, appearing to be radiantly happy, stood next to the Adams four-poster bed. It was hung with rich silk-velvet curtains—rose and gold. Chinese silk wallpaper—cherry blossoms on slender branches, painted on a background of robin's egg blue—adorned the walls. In spite of the beauty of the room, Lizzy's gaze was immediately drawn to the multitude of frames on the wall.

"Heavens, Georgiana, did you paint all of these?" Lizzy asked, sweeping her hand before her. "Landscapes and portraits and stills. My dear, I am impressed. Perhaps you should paint your own portrait."

Georgiana laughed softly. "No, I do not think so. But, thank you," her hostess said shyly. "I am certain they are nothing to yours. I see you have brought a painting. Is it of our famous cockerel?"

Lizzy turned the painting around and presented it to her. "Mr. Pitt proved to be an exceptional sitter. He preened and looked haughty as though he were a peacock instead of a chicken."

Staring at the picture, she gasped. "Lizzy," Georgiana said, drawing out the name. She took the painting in trembling fingers. "How…how did you manage to…I cannot find the words…Lizzy, he is magnificent!" she exclaimed softly. "Aunt Sophia *must* love him."

Delighted, Lizzy laughed. "I am hesitant to believe that the image of her tormentor will influence your aunt's opinion, regardless of how beautiful she thinks him."

Georgiana chuckled. "You may be right." She glanced around her walls. "I think I have a frame that will fit this." She pointed at the wall beside her bed. "Yes, there. That watercolor of the pond in the home wood. I will switch out the paintings." Impulsively, she turned back to Lizzy. "I say, do you need a carpenter to help you with framing your canvas for the landscape of Pemberley House? We have one on staff. He is excellent and knows just how to go about the business. He keeps a number of frames on hand for me. You could look over his supply and see if any would suit."

Lizzy's eyebrows shot up. "What a marvelous suggestion. You are so generous. Thank you."

Georgiana waved away her thanks. She held up the watercolor. "Thank *you.* So much. I am more pleased with the painting of Mr. Pitt than I can say." She hurried over to her dressing table, set down the paper, and retrieved a lock box from a drawer. Georgiana opened it with a key and took out ten paper notes and counted out ten shilling coins. Hurrying back to Lizzy, she said, "I hope you do not mind small denominations? I have always thought carrying large banknotes makes no sense, since who can give one change?"

Lizzy struggled not to blush while taking the money and nodded quickly in agreement. "You are so right. How can we expect a shopkeeper to change a ten-pound note? He may not make ten pounds in an entire month."

"Precisely. I am delighted we are of like mind." Georgiana then clapped her hands together, clasping them at the end of the gesture and holding them against her chest. "I think we had better finish dressing for dinner. We have only a half hour remaining."

"Yes, indeed." Lizzy turned and hastened to leave the bedchamber, not precisely embarrassed—because she had successfully finished the commission and felt proud of her work—but a little flustered anyway. She focused on her growing bank account and straightened her shoulders. At the door, she gave Georgiana a slight curtsy. Georgiana, grinning widely, returned it.

Darcy, Bingley, and Kearn joined the ladies in the music room after having let the port go around only once. Georgiana had warned him that they were to hear more of Guy Mannering tonight and he was not to let the men linger at the table.

"Fitz, please sit beside Miss Bennet again tonight," Georgiana said, waving them toward the chairs pulled forward for everyone. "Mr. Bingley, pray sit with your wife, if you will. Aunt, will you sit with me?"

"Of course, my dear," Aunt Sophia said, taking her seat. "I am all excitement to hear more of the story. Ah, here is my tatting," she said, finding her work box set beside her chair. "I find listening so much easier when my hands are busy. You are so thoughtful, dear."

"Thank you," Georgiana said. "Do you have sufficient light from the windows?"

"I can see well enough, thank you."

Darcy watched his estate manager take his place at the desk, thinking he looked unusually grave. And yet, the gravity was offset with…with something else. A certain softening around the mouth, perhaps? *And, what is causing that? Is he looking forward to the story? No, that cannot be it. Surely, he would look more excited if that were the case.*

"Are you ready?" Georgiana asked Kearn, drawing Darcy's attention to her.

He considered her expression and it reminded him forcibly of the one she held in the sketch. *Oh, Lord. Not again.*

"I am," Kearn said.

Darcy quickly switched his regard to him and tightened his lips reflexively. *At least he is nothing like Wickham.*

"What is amiss?" Miss Bennet whispered from beside him.

He glanced down at her and smiled slightly. He shook his head and forced himself to relax. "I was trying to remember what has gone before in the story," he dodged.

"Is your memory already afflicted by your advanced age?" she teased softly. "I shall be searching your hair for silver strands before long."

Chagrined, he quickly whispered, leaning so close that his breath swayed the fine hairs next to her ear, "My valet already found one. He yanked it out forthwith, I promise you. I believe he found its presence an insult to himself."

Miss Bennet released a breathy chortle, making his heart trip, but also drawing Georgiana's attention.

"Brother, are you ready to listen?" she asked from where she still stood before the desk, her eyebrows arched, her countenance glowing.

Called to order, he and Miss Bennet straightened in their chairs. "We are," he promised. Darcy would have preferred to continue the pleasant interlude with Miss Bennet, even though he had enjoyed the reading the previous night.

"Very well," she said with mock severity. "Mr. Kearn, if you are ready, so are we."

Kearn opened the volume, waited for her to sit, and began.

∞

Mr. Edmund Bissell's coach drew up before the Inn-at-Lambton, in the center of the village nearest to Pemberley House. He climbed down after Clark, heartily sick of traveling. The mid-evening sun slanted across the village green, throwing houses and gardens in relief. The homes and shops that encircled the green were of a brick and light-colored stone construction, most with slate or tile roofs. Window frames were almost universally painted white. The church, with its square Norman bell tower, occupied one end of the green, surrounded by carefully tended gravestones. The vicarage could just be seen down a short drive, only steps from the church.

"I'll procure us some rooms, sir," Clark said and hurried into the inn.

Edmund strolled along the street a way to work out the kinks in his frame caused by the constant bumps and thumps of the road. He admired the look of the village, recognizing the careful husbandry of the near-by big houses, whose owners supported their local businesses, hired staff from the village, and generally kept a close eye on the welfare of those they considered their own. They had driven past at least a half-dozen manor houses dotting the countryside. Beside the cottages, he noted several substantial village houses where the local doctor might live alongside the village solicitor, the retired sea captain, and the wealthy widow.

"Sir?"

Edmund turned around. "Clark. Are there rooms to let?"

"Yes, sir. A meal's bein' prepared for you in the private dinin' parlor."

"Very well. Let us go in."

They proceeded into the tidy country inn. The landlord showed them upstairs to a large, comfortable bedchamber beneath the eves. His baggage had already been deposited onto a chair under an open window. The brown-paper wrapped sketch-painting lay on the bed. A large elm overhung the inn, providing shade and keeping the room relatively cool.

"Thank you. This will do," Edmund said to the portly landlord who wore a white apron buttoned to his shirt and wrapped around his ample frame.

"Right you are, sir," the landlord said. "I'll have dinner laid out fer yer 'onor in a trice."

"I am looking forward to it. Tell me, if you will, if Mr. Darcy is in residence at Pemberley?"

"That he is, sir."

"Very well, thank you."

Once the landlord bowed and left, closing the door behind him, Edmund turned to Clark. "Have the groom take one of my cards around to Pemberley House. Hold, I will write on the back."

Edmund took a pencil from his card case, wrote a short note on the card back, and handed it over to his valet. Clark put it in his own pocket and helped his master change before he sought out their groom.

∞

Mellor brought in their tea at ten-of-the-clock. The evening light had faded and two footmen entered to light the candles. Once the substantial tea had been set out on a side table, the butler approached Darcy. He held out a small silver salver. A visiting card lay upon it.

"This came earlier, sir," he said. "After Mr. Kearn had begun to read. The groom did not wait for an answer, but I believe his master is staying at the Inn-at-Lambton."

Darcy nodded, took the card, and read it to himself. The front read, "Mr. Edmund Bissell". The back read, "May I have the honor of calling upon yourself tomorrow at one-of-the-clock?"

He held the card in his hand for a moment, thinking. He thought he might know of this gentleman, but he was reasonably certain they had never met.

To Mellor, he said, "Send one of the older stable lads into the village with a reply. I will see Mr. Bissell tomorrow at one."

"Yes, sir," the butler said, bowing slightly and leaving the music room.

After a hearty tea had been consumed, the ladies retired. Lizzy changed into a light, white cotton nightrail with short, capped sleeves. She dismissed Fiona, picked up her sketch pad and pencil and climbed into bed, shoving a few pillows behind her back. She wanted to draw Mr. Kearn sitting at the desk, reading for them. There had been something arresting about his expression tonight—something that had caught Mr. Darcy's attention, too.

She flipped through the pages and paused at the first drawing of Georgiana. Narrowing her eyes, she closely examined the image. Lizzy had to admit that her hostess's countenance had changed. The pleasant expression, touched with a stroke of melancholy, which she had previously drawn, now displayed a joyous happiness full of hope—without a trace of sadness.

"Well, well," Lizzy softly murmured.

Then the image wiggled her nose as though it itched.

"Goodness. I will not be able to show you to anyone."

Lizzy looked up, staring, but unseeing, into the dim corners of the room, reviewing the evening. *Georgiana looked like this tonight. Something has happened.*

Turning the page, Lizzy considered the second drawing. The same change of expression had occurred. This image, however, scratched her nose. *What nonsense is this? An itchy nose? What does that mean, pray?*

Then, Lizzy turned the page to examine the last image of Georgiana and her brother.

It was gone.

Lizzy took deep, quick breaths.

Gone.

How could it be gone?

Who could have taken it?

Lizzy traced the torn paper at the spine with one trembling finger. *No one cares about these sketches except for...except for Georgiana and...and Mr. Darcy. Oh, Lord. Mr. Darcy. Today. When I was away from my easel.*

Lizzy struggled to calm her breathing, feeling light-headed and nauseous.

What if he sees it change? No, wait. He may not have seen the original. If he took it today, then maybe the drawing had already altered.

And if it changes again? What then? What shall he think? Who will he tell? Will he laud it about, saying "Look! Look!"

or will he tear it up and tell no one? And, will he worry that the landscape he has bespoke will change and he will be unable to display the finished piece? Shall I lose my commission? She gulped. *And, shall I lose his...his regard?*

Casting aside her sketch pad as if it had offended her somehow, Lizzy hugged herself.

Why do I care so much if I lose his regard? Lizzy recalled the cold implacability she had observed in Mr. Darcy's features when he thought of George Wickham, her brother-in-law. She suspected that once lost, his regard—his respect—would be difficult to regain.

Lizzy dashed an impatient hand across her cheeks to dislodge a willful tear. She was not going to lay here weeping because of a possible revelation of her talent. Tomorrow, before the sketch had a chance to change again, she would confront Mr. Darcy and ask for her property back. What right had he to take the drawing? None.

A frontal assault required a good night's sleep so she removed several pillows and flung them aside. After blowing out the candles, she snuggled into her remaining pillow and determinably closed her eyes. A restless hour passed, however, before she finally succumbed to exhaustion.

Darcy entered his bedchamber at midnight. He and Bingley had sat up after the ladies went to bed, and Kearn had begged to be excused since he always rose early. Subsequent to his first brandy, Bingley had easily been led into a discussion of Miss Bennet's art.

"You can have no idea, dear sir," Bingley said, stretching his legs out before him, "of the lengths we have gone to accommodate Lizzy's talent. We have set aside an entire double-drawing room just for my dear sister's artwork. We packed everything in the room into boxes and stored the stuff in the attic. Then, we painted the walls white. Once that was done, we brought in crates and crates of Lizzy's art from Longbourn House and began hanging her work."

"Is everything hung now?" Darcy asked, rubbing a finger

along his jaw.

Bingley snorted and shook his head. “We installed filing drawers—you know the type? The ones for maps?”

Darcy rested his head on his hand and nodded.

“I think there are twenty drawers,” Bingley mused, grinning. “At least half are full of sketches and watercolors.”

“Do you like everything Miss Bennet produces?”

“Indeed, I do. Everything,” Bingley reiterated with evident satisfaction. “There is one that I am particularly fond of. She painted it as a young woman. Even then, her remarkable talent was evident.”

“What is the subject?”

“A floral still life.” Bingley shook his head, apparently seeing it in his mind’s eye. “Remarkable. So real. So believable. More than real, if you understand me. More beautiful than any flowers that might have inhabited this earth, except perhaps those of Eden.”

“I would dearly love to see it,” Darcy said, lifting his eyebrows. “A vase of flowers capable of captivating your admiration so well must be worth seeing.”

Bingley hardly seemed to be listening to him. His half-closed eyes gazed into the distance. “And when it…”

Darcy waited for him to continue. Finally, he asked, “When it what?” He waited. “Bingley?”

His guest started and blinked rapidly. “What? I beg your pardon. What was I saying?”

“You were about to tell me about something that happens to the painting.”

“What painting?” Bingley asked a touch suspiciously.

Holding onto his patience, Darcy managed to speak calmly. “Miss Bennet’s still life.”

Bingley frowned. “Which one? There are dozens.” He set down his brandy glass and abruptly stood up, stretching a little. “You know, Darcy, you will have to excuse me. I am dead tired. I cannot keep a thought in my head.”

And then he had walked out of the room without saying another word—almost as though he was fleeing.

What had he been about to say, Darcy wondered, handing Booth his coat and waistcoat. The valet set them to one side and accepted the remainder of Darcy's clothes. These joined the first and the valet held up a navy-blue, light cotton banyan. Darcy shrugged into it.

"You may go," he told Booth, tying the robe around himself.

"Sir," the valet said, bowing slightly. He collected the clothes and disappeared into the dressing room.

Darcy padded over to the wide-open windows, seeking a breath of cool air, for the night was warm. He leaned his hands on the sill and drank in the night scents—roses and lake water. A hint of the stables. The heavy-feeling air presaged a storm, he was sure of it. He thought he saw a flash of light in the distance and had the satisfaction of knowing he was right. Darcy turned from the view and hurried over to pick up his writing table chair and take it to the window, where he sat down to watch the storm.

Does Miss Bennet like thunder and lightning? I hope so.

He thought the storm would pass before morning, so he expected it to be no hindrance to her plans of continuing to sketch studies of Pemberley House. Darcy could hardly contain his excitement to see the finished product. The painting of Fountains Abbey had been extraordinary.

The soft sound of distant thunder mumbled across the vista. The breeze, so slight before, picked up speed and ruffled the curtain edges and found its way into the front of his robe. Darcy closed his eyes and focused on the feel of the cool breeze against his hot skin.

Light flashed through his lids and he opened his eyes in time to see the last stroke of an impressively long and forked lightning display. Within a few seconds thunder rolled—no longer a mumble, but a mighty rumble. Darcy grinned.

"Excellent," he whispered.

Another great fork of golden power slashed downward, illuminating the angry clouds. The responding clap resounded through the room like a cannon roar. Darcy's excited laugh

broke off.
He heard a cry.
A fear laden cry.

Chapter Sixteen

Lizzy tossed in her bed and suddenly cried out. She sat up, breathing heavily, her eyes wide and staring.

"Miss Bennet?" A slap sounded on her door. "Miss Bennet?"

The call of her name seemed unanswerable. She clutched the bedsheet to her chest and continued to take in great gulps of air.

The door opened and someone raced across the bedchamber to her side. She shrunk instinctively away. Lightning flashed, illuminating the man looming over her. It was Mr. Darcy. Thunder clapped and she jumped, crying out involuntarily.

"It is only a storm," Mr. Darcy said, sitting down on the side of her bed. "You are not afraid of storms, are you?"

Lizzy shook her head. He reached out to her and she tumbled easily into his arms. His closed about her and she snuggled against his chest, still clasping her hands between her breasts. He felt so strong and solid. The steady beat of his heart beneath her ear reassured her. She never wanted him to let her go.

"A nightmare," Lizzy confessed and heard the chattering of her own teeth. She drew in a ragged breath.

"Tell me," he ordered, rocking her a little.

He had done this before, she could tell. With Georgiana?

"It is fading now. I remember being on a battlefield, searching for someone amongst the dead. It was foolish, really.

Like most dreams. I have no…no family who died in the war with France." She paused to take in a shuddering breath. "And then a canon went off and I must have…must have cried out."

"I expect the thunder invaded your dreams," he said in a practical tone of voice. "I assure you that the last big crack was as loud as a canon."

"Was it? I love storms. Truly," she swore. "I wish I had been awake for it."

"So do I," Mr. Darcy murmured softly.

"Lizzy? Was that you?" Jane called softly. "Why is your door open?"

Lizzy turned and looked toward the open doorway and saw the soft glow of candlelight. Jane entered the bedchamber, carrying a candle whose flame danced in the breeze coming from the open windows. She wore a light-blue woolen shawl around her shoulders, which she held closed over her white cotton nightrail. A lace-trimmed cap sat atop her blonde hair.

Suddenly, Lizzy felt the impropriety of her position and pulled back. Mr. Darcy instantly released her.

Jane came closer, an expression of shock on her face. "M…Mr. Darcy?"

"I came in only just now," he assured her, standing. "In response to her cry. I thought she might be afraid of the storm."

Jane frowned seriously and observed him. "Lizzy loves storms."

"He just arrived," Lizzy said quickly. *Oh, dear. Thank goodness it is only Jane who has found a man in my bedchamber.* "I had a nightmare, dearest. It was positively horrid."

Addressing Mr. Darcy in as disapproving a tone as Jane could ever manage, she said, "Even so, you should have collected me first. I was sleeping, dearest," she explained as an aside to her sister, "or else I would have come sooner."

He bowed his shoulders. "You are correct, of course. Pray accept my apologies. I shall withdraw. Now that you are here, I am certain Miss Bennet will soon be soothed and ready for sleep again. Good night, Mrs. Bingley. Miss Bennet, your servant."

Lizzy nodded, struggling to maintain some dignity though she felt heartily embarrassed. "Thank you, Mr. Darcy. I am sorry to have disturbed you."

"Not at all, madam," he said and turned on one bare foot to stalk out of the room.

Jane followed him and closed the door. She returned to the bed and sat down.

"Are you well?" she asked, reaching out and brushing back a lock of Lizzy's hair from her forehead.

"Yes. Quite well, now. Thank you." Lizzy sighed. She smoothed her bedclothes about her. Another roll of thunder sounded, bringing the nightmare back. "Jane, what a dream I had."

"You are trying to turn my attention," Jane accused. "Lizzy, dearest, if I had been Father, he would have demanded that Mr. Darcy marry you."

Lizzy's eyebrows shot up. "Father?"

Jane chuckled. "Very well. If not Father, then Mama."

Lizzy laughed. "Mama, certainly." She shook her head. "Mr. Darcy behaved most gentlemanly. He treated me as though I were his sister. Really, Jane, I might have been Georgiana for all the effort he made to make love to me."

"*Lizzy*," Jane said on a sharp exhalation. She pressed the flats of her hands against her cheeks.

"We must not make more of this than it was," Lizzy admonished. "Do not tell Charles. He might think he needs to do something noble."

Jane opened her eyes as this thought sunk in. "No, he would not." She paused. "Would he? Not a *duel,*" she whispered. "Not Charles."

"Men have such odd notions of honor," Lizzy commented. The room brightened for a moment. "Oh, we missed a good one." She flicked open her sheets. "Draw the curtains wide and come and watch the lightning with me. Ah, there is the thunder. The storm must be right above us now."

Jane set her candle down on the nightstand, hastened over to the windows and drew back the drapes. Returning to the bed, she climbed beneath the sheets. They lay together, their heads close, and one arm linked with the other's.

"I will tell Charles you had a nightmare," Jane said, and gasped lightly with her sister when another fork shoved its way across the sky. "We cannot have a duel. And I do not wish to spoil his friendship with Mr. Darcy over a trifle."

"Thank you, dearest," Lizzy said, squeezing her arm.

She decided in that moment to ignore the missing sketch of Georgiana and her brother. Lizzy would not worry Jane with the possibility that Mr. Darcy had discovered the secret of her talent. Time would tell.

"I have learned—oh, very nice—and listen to that thunder—why I have been so tired lately," her sister said, her voice suddenly shy.

"Why is it?"

Jane whispered her answer. "I think I am…increasing."

Lizzy squealed and hugged her.

Darcy returned to his chair by the window. *What was I thinking? Sitting on her bed? I must be mad.*

His concentration on the storm was broken. All he could think of was the feeling of holding Miss Bennet in his arms. Such trust she had to fall into his arms so readily, trembling in the memory of her nightmare. Darcy rubbed his hand across his chest. He had wanted to hold her there forever, revelling in the warmth of her spirit. He smiled involuntarily.

So much spirit.

So much talent.

He had never considered that a person's personality and character could be bound so much in their talents. But then, artists were often measured and defined by their skill at their craft. Miss Bennet, though, seemed to give so much to her work. She revealed something to the world with each stroke of her pencil, pen, and paintbrush. Somehow, her lively wit appeared on the paper and canvas, too. Her pleasure in the absurd abounded as well.

That thought brought the sketch of the chipmunk to his mind. As much as he tried to dismiss the odd behavior of the tiny rodent, he could not. It should not even *have* a behavior.

Darcy leaped up from his chair and moved to his writing table where Booth had placed the sketch. He removed the heavy books from on top of it and picked up the flattened piece of paper. He took it over to his bedside where several candles burned. Darcy tilted the drawing so he could examine it closely. Georgiana looked exactly as she had done earlier—radiantly happy. He glanced at his image.

Have I changed? Yes! I look...worried.

Darcy sat down on his bed, so surprised at the change that he could not even consider why he looked worried. Then the rain came and he set aside the sketch so he could speedily close the windows.

∞

Lizzy and her sister entered the breakfast parlor together the next morning, surprised to see that the men had joined them. Their usual habit was to eat earlier and to go riding about the estate.

Georgiana and Mrs. McDougall, already seated, smiled broadly at them. Both Charles and Mr. Darcy rose from their places and crossed the room to greet them. Charles led Jane to the sideboard. Mr. Darcy took Lizzy's hand and pressed it warmly.

In a low voice, he asked, "You have recovered from your nightmare?"

Warmth tingled in her cheeks. "Yes. Thank you, Mr. Darcy."

"I am pleased."

The apparent truth of his statement could be told from the sincerity in his voice. He certainly knew how to make himself agreeable when he wished to. He led her toward the sideboard.

"You must try a slice of plum cake." Mr. Darcy bent his head closer and said quietly, "I am not partial to it, but Georgiana is."

"I shall be delighted. And some ham, if you please, and toast."

"A baked egg?"

"Not today, thank you," Lizzy said, shaking her head.

He continued in a less intimate voice. "I have spoken to Kearn. The ballroom is being arranged according to your direction. The room should be ready for your inspection later this afternoon. The drizzling rain appears to be here to stay, so you may wish to confine your activities to the house until it lets up."

"I now have an excellent excuse to spend my time examining the art you and your family have collected," Lizzy said, picking up a plate. "Mmm, peach tarts. Yes, please," she said, pointing to the plate laden with golden deliciousness. "Cream, too. Thank you."

"An excellent choice. Cook has a way with peach tarts. They are my favorite. I have already eaten two," he confessed, grinning down at her and holding her gaze for a moment before he continued to fill her plate according to her desires, including a slice of plum cake. "The main gallery is on the first floor, immediately above us. I shall escort you there after we eat as my study is off the gallery."

"You are too kind, sir," Lizzy said, smiling.

She moved toward a place at the dining table. Mr. Darcy held her chair as she sat. Then, he returned to his own chair and resumed his seat. A footman offered her coffee and she accepted.

Having apparently overheard Lizzy's plans, Georgiana spoke up from beside her. "I find I must go into Lambton this morning on an errand. Perhaps, Mrs. Bingley, you and your husband will have no objection to keeping Lizzy company as she examines our paintings? Unless art bores you, Mr. Bingley? I believe many men find art tedious."

"Not at all, Miss Darcy," Charles said, grinning at her. "I find art fascinating." He addressed his wife. "What say you, Jane? Shall we while away a few hours examining the riches of Pemberley?"

“Yes, indeed,” Jane said, nodding.

“I shall accompany Georgiana,” Mrs. McDougall announced. “The milliner promised to show me a particularly fine length of lace that she ordered. If I like it, she will add it to the cap she is making for me.”

“Did you sleep well, Aunt?” Georgiana asked, a mischievous smile playing across her lips.

Mrs. McDougall smiled widely. “That dratted cockerel seems to have been intimidated by the storm, for I heard nothing from him this morning. I slept two extra hours and I feel wondrously refreshed.”

“Excellent,” her niece said. Georgiana leaned closer to Lizzy and said in an undertone, “I mean to give her the painting this evening when we gather before dinner. I framed it this morning.”

Lizzy grinned and picked up her fork. “I look forward to her response.”

Georgiana covered her mouth and giggled.

“Mmm, this plum cake is nice,” Lizzy said, sparing a quick glance toward the head of the table. Mr. Darcy responded with twitch of his lips.

“And what secrets do you two whisper over?” Mrs. McDougall asked, reaching for the silver dish of sugar to add to her coffee.

Lizzy returned her attention to Georgiana. They both chuckled softly and shrugged.

Seemingly pleased to keep their secret, Mr. Darcy said, “Ah, I believe ‘nothing’ is the answer.”

“Is it not always the answer?” his aunt asked, rolling her eyes.

“I believe it is short for ‘nothing of any import’,” Jane suggested.

“Or, ‘nothing that we wish you to know’,” Charles added, smiling and shaking a finger at Georgiana and Lizzy.

“Or, ‘nothing worth repeating’,” Mr. Darcy contributed.

“That is quite enough out of you, brother,” Georgiana retorted. “I have a good mind to tell stories of your childhood to our guests."

"You would not!" Mr. Darcy said in mock horror. "Pistols at dawn."

Georgiana giggled into her napkin.

"And, here I leave you," Darcy said, stopping in front of a pedestal lectern near the beginning of the long gallery. A thick, brown, leather-bound book sat upon it. "Index" had been stamped into the cover and painted with gold leaf. He pointed at the book. "This is a record of all the art in Pemberley. The first third is a description of the paintings. The last third represents curios, statues, and carvings."

"That is excellent," Bingley said, shifting closer. "How is it catalogued?"

"There is a table at the front of each section and the table references the pages where more information can be found." He pointed at the frame of the nearest painting and the brass plaque found there. "The works are listed by the title found on their frames."

"How informative," Mrs. Bingley said, smiling.

Miss Bennet did not comment for she had already strayed and was staring enraptured by a large oil. She leaned closer and read aloud in an awed voice, "Francisco de Goya…" She looked at Darcy. "How did you manage to get one of Goya's works?"

"My father acquired it on a trip to Spain. He met the artist," Darcy explained.

She returned her attention to the painting, a slight frown accentuating her features—features that became increasingly lovely to him with each passing hour.

"I shall leave you now for a few hours. I have some work to do," he said, gesturing to the door further along the gallery. "My study is just there, if you need me. And, if you would like some assistance with something from a footman, the bell pull is here," he said, pointing to the blue and gold brocade strip, tipped with a gold tassel, hanging from the ceiling, near the wall behind the lectern. "Take the book with you and have a footman return it when you are finished."

Mrs. Bingley and her husband nodded. Miss Bennet, enthralled by the art, barely lifted a hand as he passed.

That shows how important I am to her, he thought sardonically. *I cannot compete with a masterpiece.*

However, he glanced back down the gallery when he reached the open door to his study and caught her watching him. He nodded and she dropped the slightest of curtsies. His mood improved.

Perhaps I can.

He entered his study with a smile playing across his lips. Movement by the window caught his attention and he saw that Kearn had already arrived for their meeting.

"Ah, Kearn," he said, closing the door behind him. "How are you this morning? Has there been any damage from the storm last night?"

"Very little," Kearn said, moving away from the window.

Darcy strode across the olive-green Persian carpet, woven with designs of animals and huntsmen in a jungle, to his large oak desk. He was pleased that he had taken a moment earlier to lock the sketch of himself and Georgiana away in the top drawer. Otherwise, Kearn would have seen it while he waited. Darcy waved at the guest chair and sat on his own chair behind the desk.

"A beech tree at the edge of the home wood was struck, but fortunately, the rain came and put out the fire before it could spread," Kearn said, coming to sit.

"Will the tree be in Miss Bennet's painting?"

Kearn shook his head. "I expect not. It is behind the house. It can be seen from the ballroom, however, so the forester will be cutting it down as soon as the rain stops."

"You do not think a blackened tree will add to the atmosphere of the place?" Darcy asked, his mouth twisted into a half-smile.

Kearn, who should have laughed, merely shook his head. "I do not."

Darcy straightened, clasped his hands before him on the

blotter, and leaned forward. "What is it? You seem out of sorts this morning."

"Sir," he replied. His estate manager, and friend, smoothed his hands across the tops of his thighs. He glanced up at Darcy once, revealing a sort of burning brightness in his remarkable light-blue eyes. Then, he attempted to soothe himself by stroking one hand over his full beard, as was his wont, while he stared at the rows of books on the shelves lining the walls.

Darcy patiently waited for Kearn to get his thoughts in order. Regrettably, an iron-heavy foreboding clunked into the pit of Darcy's stomach. Certainty replaced confusion.

Georgiana.

And Kearn.

"She is too young for you," Darcy said before Kearn could speak.

The older man's gaze fixed on him. "I am only thirty and three. The difference is not so outrageous that society would be alarmed. My own father married a woman fourteen years his junior and none were scandalized."

"Your station—"

Kearn clenched his fists on his knees and stated the obvious. "I am your estate manager and not a man of means."

"Your connections—"

"My grandmother was Countess von Krier of Luxembourg," Kearn informed him stiffly. "My father is—"

Darcy interrupted him. "I know who your father is."

Kearn leapt to his feet. "If you think I want Georgiana because she is an heiress, then…"

Darcy slowly rose. His voice was stern when he asked, "Then?"

"Then you would be wrong," Kearn said, sweeping his flat hand between them. "She is the sweetest, the most caring, the most talented, and the kindest woman I know. She is a darling and I will work tirelessly to deserve her. I care nothing for her money. Indeed, I wish she had none. It is an impediment, rather than a benefit. Good Lord, do you think me the type of man who wishes to live off his wife's money?"

Darcy shook his head. "I do not. Nevertheless, the money exists. Kearn, you must know that she has not been about in the world much. That damnable Wickham, her cousins, and yourself, are the only unattached men she has been intimately acquainted with. Wickham was no proper example. Her cousins are her family. And you are—"

"A servant," Kearn said bitterly.

Darcy pressed his lips together and shook his head. "Not precisely a servant. Shall we say an employee? A highly valued employee."

Kearn made an inarticulate sound and turned away, presenting his back to Darcy.

"Surely, you realized when you took this post, that you were limiting your marital prospects?"

"Of course," Kearn said in a wooden, stiff voice. "I am suitable as a husband for the daughters of vicars or lawyers or doctors. But not for the daughter of the big house."

"No," Darcy replied. He stirred and pressed his fingertips to the desk surface. "Look, Kearn, I—"

"You have no need to say it," Kearn said with stiff formality. He turned and faced his employer. "I shall begin looking for a suitable replacement for my services immediately. I believe John Hardcastle is looking for a new place. He wrote that he is tired of the Highlands and wishes to live closer to his family. Perhaps we can exchange positions. I will write immediately. No doubt you will send Georgiana away until I am gone." He bowed perfunctorily. "Good day, sir."

"You mistake me," Darcy said forcefully, speaking again to Kearn's back. "I do not wish you to go. I value you too highly. But you are right about one thing. I shall take Georgiana and my aunt to London and establish them there. They would have left in six weeks or so to prepare for the winter season and her come-out ball in any case. There, she will meet other eligible men and begin to know her own mind."

Kearn said nothing and strode from the room, leaving the door partially open. Through it, Darcy overheard Mrs. Bingley greet him.

“You look pale, Mr. Kearn. Are you well?”

“Perfectly well, thank you, ma’am,” Kearn replied. “If you will excuse me?”

“Of course.”

In the study, Darcy sat with a thump and thought, *this is a damnable business.* After taking a few deep breaths, he rose and crossed the carpet to the door so he could close it. Then, he paused, lifted his hand from the doorknob and stepped further behind the door, shamelessly listening. His guests were hiding something and he was determined to find out what.

Chapter Seventeen

Lizzy looked away from a Rembrandt—*a Rembrandt*—to watch Mr. Kearn exit the gallery, then, she returned to her examination of the painting.

"I will never be able to paint like this," she said with a sort of moan in her voice. "Look at those strokes. The color. The expression. The light."

Charles approached, passing the study doorway. "You, my dear sister, have a different talent. A better one, if I may say so, than any of these great artists."

"Better?" Lizzy asked, shocked. "You are permitting your partiality for me to overcome your good sense. My talent is so…so…capricious. I cannot trust it, yet I cannot stop."

"Stop? Never." Charles continued in a voice of great excitement. "You bring your subjects to life! I look at these pictures and they seem dull and ordinary to me in comparison. What am I saying? There is no comparison. They have no life, no spirit. Their beauty is flat. Your paintings and sketches are vibrant and animated."

He grabbed her arm and pulled her over to the Constable on the opposite side of the study door. Jane trailed behind. Lizzy looked at her and saw the growing wonder in her countenance. She was looking at her husband as though she was seeing him in a whole new light.

"Consider those cows. They are skillfully done, I grant you, but all they do is stand there. If you had painted them, they would turn and look at us, maybe even walk closer in that way cows do when you are standing by a fence."

Lizzy had to acknowledge that her farm animals never stayed still. She grinned. "Remember that painting where sometimes it is raining and the sheep all huddle together in the corner of the croft?"

"Remember it?" Charles laughed. "It is one of my favorites. Do you know that when I am feeling a little low, all I need to do is visit the gallery? I look to see which ones are in the process of changing. And I know I will look at the painting of Fountains Abby any time I need to feel calm and at peace." He paused and when he continued, it was with a little difficulty and his voice throbbed with emotion. "Lizzy, I am filled with wonder and awe every time I view your work. I have spent *hours* looking at your renderings in our gallery at home. Am I to be fascinated by a de Vinci? A Rembrandt? A…a…" Charles paused and leaned over and read the plaque of a near-by painting, "Turner? They are ordinary. They are mundane."

"Oh, Charles," Lizzy said, laughing a little. "You cannot mean that. Look at this," she said, waving at the Turner painting. "There is splendid light in his work. Can you honestly say that I have the same skill as he?"

Charles shook his head. "No, but then none of these great painters have the same skill as each other. Why should yours be the same as theirs? Your paintings touch peoples' souls." He stared at her eagerly, clearly hoping that she understood how he felt.

"These do as well," Lizzy argued.

"It is not the same," he said, making a face. "Not at all." Charles continued in a grave voice. "I think, sister, that you are ashamed of your talent. Not everyone in the family despises your art. Your father found great joy in it. Whatever magic would appear with your newest work delighted Lydia. And Kitty? She cannot wait to see what is new in the gallery every time she comes to Netherfield."

Jane crossed the few feet between them and embraced her. "If anyone deserves to feel ashamed, it is I. No, listen. I have always loved your art, but I have not been as supportive of you as I should have been." She pulled back and lovingly stroked a strand of Lizzy's hair back from her face. "I am so sorry, dearest. I allowed fear of revelation to cloud my enjoyment of your work. Indeed, I secretly visit the gallery as well. I have been foolish beyond permission."

"I—"

Charles interrupted her. "Lizzy, dear sister, if it would not cause hilarious havoc, I would throw open the gallery at Netherfield to all and sundry so that everyone could appreciate your great talent."

Both ladies gasped and said, "Oh, no!"

"No, you are right," Charles admitted reluctantly. "You know, I would lay money that your painting of Mr. Pitt will make Mrs. MacDougall love him."

"I have not your faith in human nature," Lizzy retorted. "I will keep my money, thank you."

Charles laughed. "Lizzy, you have a great talent. A gift from God."

"What sort of gift is it when I have to hide away most of my work?" Lizzy demanded in a harsh whisper. "Mr. Darcy saw my chipmunk move. I am sure he has convinced himself that he did not see it, but even so."

"Your painting of Pemberley House will be magnificent, I am sure." Jane warmly clasped Lizzy's arm with both hands. In a soothing tone, she said, "There are no statues and you will paint no people and no animals. You have no reason to fear. Think on your painting of Fountains Abbey. Except for the jackdaw, it was perfect. Mr. Darcy loved it."

Lizzy wrung her hands. "And the window? I have not looked at the image since. What if the window is gone?" She dropped her voice to a mere whisper. "And, what if Mr. Darcy notices the chipmunk again? What if I lose his regard? I could not bear it, Jane."

Jane shared a look with her husband. She responded to her sister's worry with her own whisper. "Dearest? You care about him, do you not?"

Lizzy nodded, wretchedly worried. "I am a fool. A fool.

Oh, Jane. Charles. What shall I do?"

Charles was the one who responded first. Quietly, he said, "There can be no distrust in a true marriage of minds and hearts."

"Marriage?" Jane whispered in awe.

"We are ahead of ourselves," Lizzy cautioned. She took several deep, calming breaths. She continued to whisper. "There has been no talk of that between us. Why should he ask me? Who am I above other more eligible females? I am no one."

"The longing of the heart is not reasonable," Charles said in ready sympathy.

"But *I* must be," Lizzy said in a more normal voice. She sighed and pulled away from them to glance around the gallery. "My work is so different—in the result. Perhaps there can be no comparison. If only I could control the outcome."

"I think the outcome is the work of Providence," Charles said, folding his arms. "Why else would the results be so different, so often? The phoenix flowers—so brilliant as if they had been plucked from Eden itself. And, remember the painting of the regatta on the Thames? You caught a moment in time, but the viewer can watch the painting until the race is won. The mischievous chipmunk. The wrestling statues that change position. There are so many and I love them all." With his eyebrows high and his expression earnest, he presented a suggestion. "Perhaps, dear Lizzy, you will gain more control if you accept your gift. Even so, never, ever, be ashamed of being astonishingly wondrous."

"Oh, Charles. Jane," Lizzy said, feeling as though a knot in between her shoulder blades had come unravelled, "I do not deserve you."

Charles pointed a finger at her and shook it, saying loudly, "Do not say that!"

Jane jumped and glanced around, a worried frown suddenly drawing her brows together. She gasped softly and pointed to the side at the open door of the study. In a whisper, she said, "Hush, Charles."

Her husband looked at her and then at the gap. He grimaced and took both ladies' arms. In a carrying voice, he said, "Shall we leave the gallery and examine the paintings in the entrance hall? There are statues there, as well."

"Yes, let us go there," Lizzy said, thinking her response sounded stilted. She looked around Charles at her sister, wondering what she thought of her performance. Jane, however, seemed to be thinking more of her husband's.

"I am all compliance," Jane said in a normal voice, shooting exasperated looks at Charles. "Bring the book, husband."

Darcy stood behind the open study door, transfixed, listening to their retreating footsteps. He slowly closed the door. Turning on his heel, he hurried across the room, fumbling in his pocket for the desk drawer key, eager to see if the sketch had changed. He finally managed to find the key and unlocked his desk drawer. He tugged it open and drew out the sketch. It shook in his trembling fingers.

A quick examination of his own features showed new wonder. However, Georgiana's joy had faded a little. Her jawline appeared stiffer and her narrowed eyes displayed determination. And stubbornness. He remembered that stubbornness from her childhood. Her obstinacy had mostly disappeared once she had grown old enough to listen to reason, but it had not gone entirely.

Darcy dropped the picture back into the drawer and closed it again, locking it. *No one should have the power to look into another person's secret emotions like this. It is so…underhanded. Ungentlemanly.*

He sat, leaned back in his chair, stroked his knuckle along his chin, and considered what he had overheard. He wished he had been able to hear everything. However, the whispered part of his guest's conversation eluded him. There was so much in what he could hear that he easily pushed aside what he had not heard.

How is it even possible for Miss Bennet to have this

talent? I have never heard of such a thing. It is fantastical!

If any of her portraits of children and pets had changed, all of London would have known of it. Darcy thought again of Miss Bennet's refusal to paint Georgiana because she was too old. And she had referred to Mr. Pitt as a pet, not as livestock. Somehow, he reasoned, those two subjects did not alter after she painted them.

Why?

It seemed that even Miss Bennet did not know the reason. Clearly, she had no control over the outcome of her accomplishments. Though wonderment swelled inside Darcy, he was not as certain he could ever be as sanguine about Miss Bennet's unusual talent as Bingley appeared to be.

What of his feelings for Miss Bennet?

Darcy scraped a hand across his face. Every time she walked into a room or he heard her voice, his heart seemed ready to burst out of his chest. He had never felt this way about any other woman. What was he to do with these feelings if he concluded that Miss Bennet's talent put them at risk for scandal and notoriety? Mrs. Fitzwilliam Darcy—the woman who painted mad images. He had no trouble envisioning the ridicule and scorn his family might have to endure if anyone outside of it discovered the strangely behaving paintings.

Looking back, he recalled Miss Bennet's odd behavior in the carriage when she had torn up the sketch of the local parish church. What had happened to that sketch? What had she been worried someone might see?

Darcy ran both hands through his hair and then stilled.

What will happen to the painting of Pemberley House? Will it become a painting I have to hide away from prying eyes? But, no, Miss Bennet must feel she can paint the landscape with at least a moderate degree of equanimity. Otherwise, why has she taken the commission? Why put her talent at risk of discovery?

He considered for a moment.

Ah, yes. For the money.

Darcy folded his arms and bowed his head, his brows

crimping. *It is a gamble. A potentially disastrous gamble—for herself. And for the Bingleys.*

"Bloody hell," he whispered.

His gaze strayed toward his desk and the locked drawer. Darcy swore again beneath his breath and added in a tight whisper, "I will *not* check the sketch for any new changes."

Then, the study door banged open, causing Darcy to jump. He uncrossed his arms and glowered at the doorway where Georgiana stood. She scowled at him in turn and hurried inside, slamming the door behind her.

"Is this raucous behavior absolutely necessary?" her brother coldly demanded, rising to his feet. "If you cannot maintain some decorum, you may retire to your chamber until you have restored the tenor of your mind."

"I will be nineteen in seven weeks and no longer a child, Fitz," Georgiana snapped, storming across the room. "I am angry—a perfectly normal reaction to your interference in my future life and happiness. I am *not* having a tantrum."

"Hmm, the two behaviors seem remarkably similar. Pray tell, how am I to tell the difference?" he drawled.

"Do not take that tone with me," Georgiana said through gritted teeth, shaking a finger at him. "How could you?"

"How could I what?"

With an enormous effort of will, Georgiana resisted the urge to stamp her foot. "You know perfectly well. How could you refuse Mr. Kearn without even consulting my wishes? I thought you were more reasonable than that. I thought you would have at least talked to me first before telling him of your precipitous plan to remove me from Pemberley."

"You must have realized that possibility existed," Fitz said, one of his eyebrows arching upward in that infuriating manner of his. "It is clear to me that you and Kearn have discussed this issue already—before he came to me, in fact."

"Of course, we realized it," Georgiana retorted. "And *of course*, we discussed it first. This is 1815, not the Dark Ages. I was uncertain how he felt about me and he was equally unsure if I loved him. How could he come to you before he knew if I welcomed his suit?" She wrung her hands, stared over her brother's shoulder with unfocused eyes, and muttered, "He was *supposed* to make a list itemizing how we should proceed, but his eagerness overcame his usual good sense." Georgiana blinked rapidly, and then fixed her brother with a pleading glare. "Surely, his enthusiasm only indicates the fervor and honesty of his intent."

Fitz took a deep breath and held it before releasing it slowly. Calming himself down, she hoped.

"I do not mean to impugn Kearn's integrity. I have great respect for him."

Georgiana opened her mouth, but shut it again when her brother held up his hand.

"He is significantly older than yourself, but not bizarrely older. If you were twenty-one, I would have no argument with the age difference. By twenty-one, you will have more worldly experience and so be able to make a proper decision."

Georgiana gasped and planted her fists on her waist, arms akimbo. "You wish us to wait *more than two years*? That is wholly unreasonable."

"If you will permit me to finish?"

Chastened by his biting tone, she nodded. *There is no point making him crosser.*

"Your age difference is not the only reservation I have against you marrying."

Georgiana wrung her hands again. She bit on her bottom lip to keep from speaking.

"I am also concerned about the differences in your fortunes."

"It is not as though Mr. Kearn has *no* money," Georgiana countered in a rush.

Fitz's frown deepened and she clapped both of her palms over her mouth.

He folded his arms. "I am aware that he has begun to build a property portfolio. I applaud him for his excellent intentions in that regard. And, he said his intent is not to live on the income from your 30,000 pounds, so—"

"I know you do not wish me to speak, but I must take leave to inform you that *our* intentions are to buy a modest manor house with my money, and then set aside the remainder for our children." Georgiana heard the pride in her own voice and hoped Fitz heard it, too.

"An admirable scheme."

Her brother's praise momentarily stymied her. How was she to answer that?

"My third objection," he said, filling the momentary lull in her protestations, "is the difference between your social standing. Kearn is a working man. His situation is an honorable one, but when he became an estate manager, he removed himself from our level, making his connections moot."

"I do not care a single jot for that," Georgiana scoffed. She glowered at him, trembling inside. "The truth is, you believe me to be fickle. You do not trust my ability to make good choices. More than three years have passed since that disastrous near-elopement. Have you not forgiven my stupidity, yet?"

In a quiet voice, her brother said, "I did not think you stupid."

A tear leaked out and ran down Georgiana's cheek. She dashed it away with the back of her hand. "Surely, Fitz, you must agree that Mr. Kearn is a much superior choice for a husband than Wickham?"

"I cannot deny Kearn's superiority," Fitz acknowledged. "There can be no true comparison between their characters. Kearn is by far the better man."

He hurried around the desk and approached her. Georgiana faced him and permitted him to clasp her shoulders.

"But Georgie," he said intently, using his childhood nickname for her, "I simply cannot permit you to marry Kearn before you have even been presented." He quickly spoke again when she opened her mouth. "Or to become engaged to him."

Georgiana clenched her jaw together, willing her

swimming tears not to fall. She took a ragged breath. "Will you promise me you will not force me into a marriage with someone *you* deem more suitable?"

Fitz stiffened, but did not release her. "I would *never* force you to marry where you had no regard."

Georgiana wrenched herself away and poked him in the chest with her index finger. "I do not want *regard*, Fitz. I want *love.* Mr. Kearn loves me and I love him. I will not go looking for something I already have." She watched his expression darken and hastily held out her hands, palm forward. "However, I am willing to go to London for the winter season as planned. To please you, I will dance with the gentlemen hanging out for a wife. I expect the experience will do me good." Stepping forward, she placed a palm on her brother's chest. "I will prove to you that my feelings are constant and true."

Fitz held her gaze with his for several excessively long heartbeats. Finally, he spoke.

"We will leave for London when the painting of Pemberley House is complete."

Georgiana's heart lurched. "So soon?"

Her brother nodded. "I expect we shall be on the road by the end of August."

"We were to leave at the end of September," Georgiana said in a small voice. "A whole extra month in London…I shall miss Mr. Kearn terribly."

"We shall be home between Christmas and Easter." Fitz lifted her chin and kissed her on her forehead. "*That* is when we shall revisit the possibility of you and Kearn marrying."

Georgiana impulsively hugged him. His arms encircled her and he hugged her back.

Darcy watched his sister hurry out of his study. No doubt she intended to rush to Kearn's side and tell him her news. She had used her most potent weapon on him. Her tears. Or, more exactly, it had been her valiant effort not to cry that had wrung his heart.

He sighed and went to look out the raindrop spattered window at the watery image of the park beyond. Georgiana's happiness meant more to him than even his own. In the end, he knew he would succumb to her desire for Kearn, but Darcy was determined she would have her London season first. Then, not only would *he* know that her interest was fixed, but she would know it too.

I must make certain Kearn gets that mill at the price he wants. There is a tidy manor for sale at the edge of Lambton that might be perfect for a small family. Perhaps as a wedding gift? No, Kearn would never countenance such interference.

Darcy shook his head at his own machinations. *I am as bad as Aunt Catherine. Oh, Lord. Aunt Catherine...what will she say if I permit Georgiana to marry my estate manager?* His lips stretched into an unholy grin. *That would be something to hear.*

He allowed himself a few moments of reverie before he stamped down his enthusiasm for such a scene. Georgiana would not like it at all. She rarely visited their aunt simply because she quailed under that gorgon's flaying tongue. Whenever Lady Catherine swept down upon Pemberley for a visit, dragging poor Anne behind her, Georgina was notably quiet and withdrawn.

Is it any wonder she has a reputation of being shy?

If...if I permit Miles Kearn to marry Georgiana, the banns will be read locally and the wedding will be quiet. No announcement will be made to the London papers until after the event. Perhaps Aunt Catherine will not hear of it until it is a fait accompli.

"I need one of Kearn's lists," Darcy muttered to himself as he considered all the ramifications of such an unequal alliance—should it occur. A knock sounded at his door and he turned around, saying, "Come."

Mellor opened the door, carrying a silver salver with a card resting upon it. He crossed the room and held the salver out. Darcy retrieved the card. It read, 'Edmund Bissell' on the front with nothing on the back.

"Shall I show Mr. Bissell up, sir?"

"Is it one already?" Darcy glanced at the clock next to the door. "Yes, I see it is. Very well, have him come up."

"Sir." The butler hesitated. "Uh, sir," he said, pointing at his master's head.

"What is it?"

"Your hair, sir," Mellor said. "It is in disarray."

Darcy frowned and crossed to the mirror over the fireplace. He pressed his lips together and used his hands to pat his hair back into place.

"There," he said, and turned back to look at the butler, but Mellor had left.

Chapter Eighteen

Darcy waited to meet his guest in front of the cold fireplace. His butler opened the door, entered the study, and stood to one side of the doorway.

"Mr. Edmund Bissell," Mellor announced in a calm monotone.

A gentleman crossed the threshold, approximately ten years older than Darcy, appropriately dressed in elegant country attire—brown and green tweed jacket, hunter-green waistcoat, buff-colored doe-skin britches, and umber-topped black boots—carrying a rectangular brown paper-wrapped package. Darcy's eyebrow rose as his curiosity increased three-fold—the package appeared to be a framed painting. Mellor withdrew.

"Mr. Bissell," Darcy said, holding out his hand. "Welcome to Pemberley."

"Sir," he said, giving a firm, business-like handshake. "You have a magnificent home."

"Thank you," Darcy said, making his way around to his side of the desk. He waved him toward one of the two chairs in front of his desk. "How may I be of assistance?"

"I have travelled from Islington," he said, setting the package carefully onto the other chair. He sat, crossing his legs. "Pemberley contains many superb pieces of art. I, too, have a gallery. Though it is, of necessity, significantly smaller than your own."

Darcy reached his chair and faced Bissell, confused by

this conversational gambit. He wondered if his guest wished to sell the painting hidden by the brown-paper wrapping.

"My family has been collecting for generations. My grandfather particularly enjoyed acquiring," Darcy said, adjusting his chair to his liking. "Have you come to show me a painting?"

"As to that? No. I have come to speak with Miss Elizabeth Bennet. I understand she is your guest?"

Darcy paused, half-way down into his desk chair. He looked keenly at Bissell and straightened again. Deep, sorrow-filled lines ravaged his visitor's determined countenance. Gray eyes shone with a fervor that Darcy wanted to categorize as anxious but feared might be more closely allied with zeal.

Keeping his words clipped, Darcy said, "She is."

Bissell leaned forward. "May I see her?"

"What is the nature of your relationship with Miss Bennet?"

The man waved a hand between them as though to wipe away any improper implications regarding the reason for his visit.

"There is none. Not really. She was a guest at one of my departed wife's garden parties. Their friendship was of the slightest kind. A mere acquaintance, actually."

"Then I fail to see any reason for you to undertake such a long journey. Could you not have waited until she returned to her home before seeking an interview?"

"I could not wait." Bissell looked away and focused his attention on the package. After a moment, he said, "Do you have an objection to Miss Bennet sparing a few minutes of her time for me?"

Darcy considered him for long enough that Bissell rose. He took a turn about the open area between the door and the desk, never straying very far from the chair holding the package.

"You understand that while Miss Bennet is a guest in my home that I am responsible for her welfare?"

Bissell chin bobbed. "Yes, of course. I have not travelled

all the way to Derbyshire—nay, Yorkshire and then Derbyshire—for a matter of trifling import. I assure you, sir, that I mean no harm to Miss Bennet."

Darcy nodded as though he believed him, but said, "Frankly, sir, I do not know you. May I know your particulars? Who are your family? What is your circle of interest?"

"Very well." Bissell pulled out his watch and snapped it open. "We have some time to spare. Let us get to know one another a little."

Darcy sat, gesturing that his guest should sit again. Bissell did and then explained his history, who his connections were, and that he was a man of affairs, with significant shipping interests. His gaze strayed often to the package as though he feared someone might sneak into the study and carry his prize away from beneath their noses.

Bissell ended his discourse by saying, "My reason for seeking an audience with Miss Bennet is of a private nature."

"Miss Bennet has a great talent, has she not?" Darcy asked, setting aside his guest's statement.

Bissell started. He crossed and re-crossed his legs, finally nodding reluctantly.

"Indeed," was all he said, however.

"I saw a portrait she did of some spaniels," Darcy continued conversationally. "I have never seen anything to match it. So…life-like. So…so delightful in every way. After viewing their portrait, I wanted to hurry home to Pemberley so I could play with my own dogs."

Bissell fixed his attention entirely on Darcy, his expression intense and probing. "Indeed? Was there anything…unusual about the likeness?"

"Unusual?" Darcy held his breath, waiting for a reply. When none came, he finally probed, "In what way?"

"I meant nothing by my question," Bissell said, managing a creditable, but nevertheless unbelievable, shrug of insouciance. "I was merely interested."

Darcy captured and held his gaze. "Tell me, sir, is there something *unusual* about the painting you have brought?"

Bissell forced a laugh. “It is a sketch, not a painting.” Then, beneath his breath, he added, “For now.”

Enjoying excellent hearing, Darcy had no trouble discerning what his guest doubtless wished he had left unsaid. “For now?” His eyebrows shot up. “Are you wishing Miss Bennet to paint over the sketch so you have a proper portrait of your wife?”

“That will not be necessary,” Bissell said with a mild snort. He indicated the package with a flick of his wrist. “This sketch is a masterpiece. I would count it a crime if Miss Bennett painted over it.”

“To use it as a template, then?”

“No, no.”

The impatient and hastily said answer intrigued Darcy. He folded his arms and rested them on the desk. “You have piqued my curiosity. Will you show me the sketch of your wife?”

Bissell stared intently at him, and Darcy thought a refusal trembled on the rim of his lips. Then, the man rose slowly and approached the chair holding the package. He picked it up and pulled on the string bow binding the paper to its secret. The paper fell back onto the chair seat, the string tumbled to the floor, and Bissell rotated, the framed sketch held before him like a shield.

Darcy stood and adjusted his position so he could see the sketch without the reflection on the glass from the afternoon light coming through the windows. Instantly, he was struck by the beauty of every pencil line. The genius of Miss Bennet’s talent clearly shone from each mark. It seemed impossible to him that anyone could display another person’s vitality, strength, and…and soul with nothing but black and white.

Miss Bennet had drawn only Mrs. Bissell’s shoulders and head. The lady sat half-turned away, but looking back at the viewer, a laughing smile on her lovely features. Darcy experienced a hitch in his chest and he wondered at the feeling. How could he feel such…such charity toward a woman he had never met in person?

“She is exquisite,” Darcy said in a hushed voice.

Bissell heaved a sigh. "She was. In person and in character." He turned the frame around so he could look at it. His expression softened into poignant longing. In a quiet voice, he said, "I am not surprised God wanted her back."

Darcy let that sentiment seep into the atmosphere before saying, "I can see why you would not want anyone to paint over her."

"It would be an unnecessary exercise."

That is an interesting comment, Darcy thought, watching as Bissell re-wrapped the sketch. *Does something happen to the sketch? She does not move, like the chipmunk. What magic is there in* this *sketch?*

"Will you permit me to see Miss Bennet?" Bissell asked, finishing his task. He removed his watch and checked the time.

"Are you in a hurry, sir?" Darcy asked, frowning a little. "Or do you simply have a compulsion that requires you to look at your watch every quarter hour?"

Bissell shook his head. "There is still time. Pray, will you give me your answer?"

"Can you tell me nothing more about the reason for your visit?"

"I cannot. Pray believe me that I mean Miss Bennet no harm."

Feeling a powerful desire to know the reason for this unorthodox visit, Darcy decided to trust that he could protect Miss Bennet from anything this man might reveal, or request, or divulge.

"We shall go down to the drawing room and invite my guests to join us for tea," Darcy said, rising. "Afterward, Miss Bennet must judge for herself if she is willing to give you a private word."

∞

When the butler cleared his throat, Lizzy reluctantly tore her concentration away from the painting she, Jane, and Charles were examining in the dining hall. Charles had procured, through a footman, a free-standing spiral library ladder for her use so she could get closer to the masterpieces and examine their brush strokes in detail. She rested a hand on the brass finial of the turned pilaster support and twisted in place so she could look down at Mellor.

"Yes?" Charles asked.

"Begging your pardon, sir, but Mr. Darcy requests your presence and that of Mrs. Bingley and Miss Bennet, in the blue drawing room for tea. A guest has arrived."

"Tea?" Jane said. "How delightful." She looked up. "Lizzy?"

"Yes, please," Lizzy said, climbing down. "A hot cup of tea would go down a treat on this damp day. Who is this guest, pray?"

"Mr. Edmund Bissell, miss," the butler explained.

Lizzy frowned, wondering where she had heard the name before.

"His name sounds familiar. Do you know him, Charles?" Jane asked.

"I have never heard the name before," her husband admitted. He grinned. "I am always pleased to meet new people."

"As am I," Jane said, taking his arm.

Mellor led them to the blue drawing room, a room they had yet to see. Linen wallpaper, dyed indigo and painted in repeated pale-blue ogee patterns, with sprays of flowers in their centers adorned the upper two thirds of the walls. Lightly stained wainscoting finished the look. The chairs, sofas, and divans had been upholstered in creams, blues, and golds. Lizzy, as ever, regarded the artwork on the walls and was fascinated to discover that the images were of architectural features, such as examples of carved Greco-Roman columns, charts of capitals, and illustrations of various types of architraves.

Movement in the room drew her attention toward the occupants and she discovered that Mr. Darcy and his guest had been joined by Georgiana, who looked strained, and Mrs. McDougall, who appeared determinedly cheerful. Lizzy's gaze instinctively sought out Mr. Darcy's.

He seems oddly grave, she thought. *Why?*

"Mrs. Bingley, Mr. Bingley. Lizzy," Georgiana said, hurrying across the room to them, ahead of her aunt, who also stepped forward to greet them. "Please, come in and meet our guest."

They followed her, their footsteps hushed by the pale-blue Axminster carpet, to where a strikingly handsome gentleman stood next to Mr. Darcy. She kept the frown off her face, but inwardly she wondered again where she had met him before.

"This is Mr. Edmund Bissell, from London. I understand, Mrs. Bingley, that you and Miss Bennet knew his wife," Mr. Darcy said, nodding to her and then looking searchingly at Lizzy.

Turning her attention from Mr. Darcy to the tall, dark-haired gentleman, Lizzy suddenly remembered him. She had only met him fleetingly on the day of his wife's garden party.

It seemed Jane also remembered him, for she said, holding out her hand, "Mr. Bissell, kindly let me express our deepest regret over the passing of your beloved wife. And…and your baby, too. Mrs. Bissell was a charming woman with a lovely temperament. You must miss her dearly."

Jane's gentle and heartfelt commiserations seemed to touch Mr. Bissell's heart. He smiled in a melancholy way and his stiff shoulders relaxed.

"Thank you, Mrs. Bingley," he said, taking her hand. He shook Charles' hand next and Lizzy's last. "Miss Bennet, I have come to the north specifically to speak with you."

"With me?" Lizzy asked. From the corner of her eye, she spied a brown paper-wrapped package on the gold and blue long divan pushed up to the wall at her right. She struggled not to turn her head and stare at it. Her stomach muscles roiled with tangled anxiety. Sunnily, she said, "I am all astonishment. Why ever for?"

Mr. Bissell retrieved a gold watch from the pocket of his fawn waistcoat, flipped it open, and then put it away. "We have time to partake of tea, and then perhaps you will permit a private word?"

A private word. Yes. Private.

Lizzy opened her mouth to agree, when Jane stepped in.

"My sister does not meet with gentlemen in private, Mr. Bissell. You understand?" Jane smoothed the front panel of her aquamarine day-dress, looking down at the floor before meeting his gaze. "My husband and I will stay for the interview."

"As will I," Mr. Darcy said, steel in his voice.

Georgiana regarded the four of them and immediately piped up. "I should also like to stay."

Mr. Darcy frowned at her and she glowered back before gifting their guest with her brightest smile. "Lizzy is my friend. Come, Mr. Bissell, what can you possibly have to say to Lizzy that the rest of us cannot hear?" She ignored her aunt's faint outraged gasp and continued in a lively manner. "Is it a commission? Do you wish her to do a painting for you? You shall have to wait if you do, for she is here to paint Pemberley House. I am certain it shall be a masterpiece."

"I have no doubt," Mr. Bissell said politely, bowing his shoulders at Lizzy. "You have quite the reputation amongst the *haute ton*. And amongst other levels of London society. Everyone I spoke to had nothing but praise for your talent, Miss Bennet."

Heat tingled across Lizzy's cheeks. "You are kind to say so, Mr. Bissell."

"Not at all," he murmured.

"We are excessively proud of her," Charles said, beaming. "You will not regret it if she accepts a commission from you."

"Thank you, Charles," Lizzy said, somewhat flustered by all the attention. She turned to Mr. Darcy and Georgiana. "Thank you for your concern, but I am certain Jane and Charles will be sufficient chaperones for my private interview with Mr. Bissell. We could talk in the yellow drawing room—if you have no objection?"

Mr. Darcy, still looking grave, bowed his shoulders. "No objection at all. However, perhaps the library would be more appropriate?" He pointed at a nearly hidden door in the corner.

"It can be accessed through there. You will find the light excellent at this time of day, in spite of our overcast sky."

"That should do nicely," Lizzy said, struggling to present a serene smile, something copied from her sister's repertoire. In spite of her efforts she was reasonably sure she had not managed to display anything but a strained grimace.

Does he sound disappointed? No, why should he? Lizzy could determine no good reason other than nosiness and she did not think him nosy.

Georgiana, however rampantly curious she might be, was too well-bred to press for any explanation. "I will have a fire lit to take the damp chill off of the room," she said, smiling. "Ah, I think I hear the tea coming."

The door to the drawing room opened and Mellor entered. He supervised the two footmen who followed in the laying out of a substantial tea upon a long mahogany sideboard. Georgiana approached him and gave him a soft order. He nodded and spoke in turn to one of the footmen, who left immediately.

Mr. Bissell shifted his position so that he stood closer to Lizzy. In an undervoice, he said, "Truly, Miss Bennet, I believe what we have to discuss would be best done in private."

"Perhaps," Lizzy said quietly. "But, I have no secrets from my family."

"Of course."

Lizzy nodded to him and slipped away to assist Georgiana and Mrs. McDougall in preparing the tea, doing her part by swirling hot water around the teapot to warm it before pouring the water into the waste vessel. She handed the teapot back to Mrs. McDougal, who unlocked a rosewood tea caddy and measured out the precious black tea leaves from within and into the pot. Georgiana poured the steaming hot water over the leaves.

Has Mr. Bissell discovered my secret? How? That package must be a painting. But…I did not do a painting of Mrs. Bissell. Nor one for Mr. Bissell. Perhaps it is a painting that belongs to someone else?

But, who?

I have been so careful.

So very, very careful.

No one outside of the family has a painting that is not of a child or a pet. Except for Charlotte. And she never shows anyone the miniature of her parents inside the locket she wears around her neck.

Lizzy bit her lip, recalling that the painting faded away and reappeared at regular intervals, returning with the image reflecting Charlotte's parents' new age. But Lizzy firmly believed her friend would never say anything, or show it, to anyone. Undoubtedly, Mr. Collins did not even know.

They handed around the cups of tea and then the platters of prepared delicacies. Warm Buxton pudding was greeted with sighs of pleasure, alongside fidgety pie, slices of blue cheese, and leek fritters.

Lizzy, however, could only nibble at an oatcake, unable to swallow anything without forcing it down with a sip of tea.

Thank the Lord that Mr. Bissell has sought a private interview. What if he is about to reveal something about the painting in that accursed package? I am being foolish beyond permission. Perhaps he has merely brought a bequest from his wife. Could that be it? Now I am being even more fanciful. Why should Mrs. Bissell leave anything to me?

Lizzy glanced over the top of her teacup at Mr. Darcy. He still looked grave and had also eaten little.

Could he know? Did he overhear our conversation in the gallery? Oh, Lord, how will I bear this agony of uncertainty?

Fortunately, even a substantial tea could only prolong the inevitable so long. By the time the footmen came and cleared away the repast, Lizzy was well beyond wishing to wait.

Mr. Bissell pulled out his watch, read the time, nodded, and retrieved the package. Lizzy, Jane and Charles rose to their feet. Mr. Darcy also, though he did not move from his place. Lizzy clenched her fists and then relaxed them.

Everything will be all right, she told herself.

"Follow us, Mr. Bissell," Charles said. To the rest, he said, bowing his head, "Kindly excuse us."

"I will wait here in case you have need of me," Mr. Darcy said, his tone implacable.

"Thank you," Charles murmured.

He led them across the room and opened the door to the library. They passed by him and into a library as grand as any Lizzy had ever seen in a private home.

Tall, northeast-facing windows brightened the room, revealing row after row of leather-bound books, chocolate-brown leather club chairs, mahogany desks, and a long mahogany table in the center, surrounded by chairs as though waiting for a meeting.

Mr. Bissell headed for the table. He waited until Charles closed the door before he laid the package on the surface. Lizzy hesitated to cross the room. She wanted to turn and run away and then called herself a craven fool. What could he do to her?

Nothing.

Lizzy stiffened her spine and took up a strategic position with her back to the windows so she could clearly see Mr. Bissell's face while her own would be in shadow.

"Kindly explain to us what has brought you into Derbyshire," Charles requested, coming to stand at the head of the table. Jane joined him and put her hand through his arm. He patted her hand.

"I am prepared to do so," Mr. Bissell promised.

He pulled on the string bow. He opened the wrapping on the package, revealing that it did indeed contain a picture. He turned the frame around so they could see the image. It was a sketch.

"It is your wife?" Charles asked. "She was beautiful. Lizzy, this is one of yours, is it not?"

Lizzy nodded dumbly at her brother-in-law, so relieved. He was grinning as she expected. Her hand clutched the wood back of the Adams chair beside her. She remembered the sketch now. She had drawn it after attending Mrs. Bissell's garden party. Upon completing the drawing, she had kept it for a week before sending it to the subject, wanting to be certain that nothing extraordinary would happen to it first.

"Yes, it is," Mr. Bissell said, cutting through Lizzy's remembrances. "Firstly, Miss Bennet, I want to thank you for this sketch. I have no other image of my wife."

Lizzy swallowed and then smiled. "You are most welcome. Did you come all the way to Derbyshire to thank me? You could have sent a letter to Netherfield."

"A letter could not have described my feelings adequately," Mr. Bissell said with earnest gravity.

His praise affected her deeply. Lizzy pressed the back of her hand against her suddenly hot cheek. She had liked Mrs. Bissell exceedingly and it pleased her to no end that her simple sketch gave her husband so much pleasure.

And then Charles and Jane gasped. Lizzy's gaze darted to them and then to what they were staring at.

The sketch was changing.

Starting from the top of the image, a shimmer washed down over it. The pencil marks disappeared, replaced by the same image, but now gloriously and stunningly glowing with water color paint.

Good Lord.

Impossible.

Jane moaned.

"Look at that!" Bingley cried with great excitement. "Sensational."

Lizzy said nothing. *But I waited a week—a whole week. How could this have happened? And, why has Mr. Bissell waited so long to confront me about it?*

"I promise you, this is no trick. I have done nothing to accomplish this…this miracle," Mr. Bissell said. He held one hand out in entreaty. "Permit me to explain."

He was looking at her. Lizzy nodded and he sighed with apparent relief.

"Soon after my wife's death, I longed to see her face again, so I went to my gallery to look at the only image I had of her. To my surprise, the pencil sketch that we had sent out to be framed was no longer a sketch. I thought, in my ignorance, that my wife's friend," he gestured at Lizzy, "had sent her a completed watercolor. I was delighted, as you can imagine. I decided to hang the painting in my bedchamber. Two weeks later, it had changed back into a sketch. And two weeks after that, into a painting again. Then a sketch. And so forth. Every two weeks. Exactly, to the minute."

In a whisper, Lizzy said, "I have never seen..."

"Miss Bennet, are you saying this is none of your doing?" Bissell asked, his eyebrows high and his attitude one of incredulity.

"Surely," Jane said in her gentle way, "someone would have seen this change before? If not yourself, then perhaps a servant, or your wife? We attended your wife's garden party several years ago—before our parent's passing. Has no one seen it change?"

"If anyone saw it, they did not inform me, or my valet."

"Could it have been triggered by your wife's death?" Charles asked, gazing raptly still at the portrait.

"I…I…" Lizzy blinked rapidly, her gaze swiftly scanning the room in the same attitude a cornered animal has when looking for an avenue of escape. *What should I say? Should I admit that my art is…blessed somehow? Should I reveal that I have an entire gallery of paintings that change in numerous ways?*

"I know nothing of metaphysical matters," Bissell said, his frown deepening. "It never occurred to me that the change only started recently. Miss Bennet, have you ever sketched another portrait that behaved in this fashion?"

"No, I have not," Lizzy said, confident, choosing to forget the sketch of the church that she tore up and threw out the carriage window without fully examining. "It is fantastical. I had the sketch for a week before I sent it to your wife. Nothing transformed during that time."

"Only a week," Bissell mused. He fixed her with a searching gaze that caused Lizzy to lean away slightly. "Did you make other sketches of my wife? Have you seen any changes in them?"

Lizzy thought for a moment and then shook her head. "No. I only did the one sketch."

Mr. Bissell's expression of intense hopefulness transformed into tragic disappointment. He rallied to ask, "How can this be? What did you do to make this miracle? You must explain it to me. I have travelled all this way for an explanation." He turned the painting around so he could gaze at his wife's image. "I am haunted by my ignorance. I need to know, to understand. You must tell me."

I cannot find the words. I do not know what to say to him. This is my worst nightmare. I cannot tell him. I cannot!

Lizzy's eyes met Jane's in mute appeal. "Jane…"

Jane instantly hastened to her sister's side. She took one of Lizzy's hands in both of hers and faced their accuser. "Mr. Bissell, kindly refrain from harassing my sister."

Bissell took a slight step backward. "Madam, you misunderstand my intent. I do not wish to accuse Miss Bennet of anything. I merely long to know how this is possible. How? I cannot sleep for lack of understanding. None of your admirers have warned me that your paintings reflect any metaphysical properties. No one in London spoke of anything untoward happening to their paintings. I am the one that needs to comprehend this phenomenon."

Lizzy licked her lips and shook her head. "There is no understanding it."

"There *must* be an explanation," Bissell insisted.

Lizzy shook her head.

Bissell opened his mouth, but Bingley interrupted his attempt to expostulate further.

"It is *force majeure,* Bissell," he said. "An act of God, if you will."

"*An act of God*?" the man said, his mouth hanging open, his eyes wide. He recovered himself and asked, "Has this happened before? To other sketches?"

Lizzy swallowed, wishing he would stop staring at her and

just go away. She finally could do nothing but shrug. "I have already explained that I have noted no other changes like this to my other sketches."

She thought he did not believe her for he looked at each of them with narrowed eyes.

"It must be an aberration," Charles stated in his cheerful way. "Clearly."

Bissell stared at him. "*Clearly?*"

"Of course," Jane said, waving a negligent hand. "How could there be more than one?"

Bissell's lip curled into scornful incredulity. "You want me to believe there is only *one* act of God? Even though Miss Bennet was tempted to admit to more?"

Lizzy lifted her chin and looked kindly at Bissell, her gaze straightforward and unwavering. She hated having to disabuse him of his belief in her metaphysical talents, but she could not—she really could *not*—allow him to leave Pemberley thinking anything else.

"I was about to admit nothing. The behavior of my simple sketch held me in thrall for a moment. That is all. Now that I have collected myself, I can say with certainty that my sketch of your wife is the first and only one that has switched to a painting in this wondrous fashion." She released Jane's hand and moved forward to stand next to Charles, keeping the table between her and Mr. Bissell. "Now, if we are to ascribe to Providence the creation of this phenomenon, then I kindly suggest you take up the meaning of the changes with God. Perhaps, though, you might consider thanking Him instead of questioning His gift."

Bissell set the portrait down in a measured, careful manner. He picked up the brown paper, wrapped the painting in it, tied it with a string, and then held it against his chest.

Lizzy watched his actions in silence.

"You must tell me," Mr. Bissell said quietly, his head bowed. "You must explain. I swear to you that I will never tell another living soul. I *must* understand."

"Why?" Charles demanded. "Why do we have to

understand it?"

"How is anyone to understand a phenomenon like this?" Lizzy asked, keeping her voice steady and soothing. "It is beyond my comprehension."

"I do not have much time for God," Mr. Bissell admitted, shifting from one foot to the other. He looked at Bingley and then focused on Lizzy. "God has always seemed too capricious for my liking."

"Are you asking yourself why He would give you this gift?" Lizzy asked gently, clasping her hands before her in as relaxed a manner as she could manage.

The poor man jerked his head into the semblance of a nod.

"I do not know. I cannot tell you," Lizzy said softly. "There is no explanation possible. I wish I knew how I did it. I wish I understood as well. How I would like to make this happen again and again. I am not a wealthy woman, Mr. Bissell. I could make my fortune if my sketches turned into paintings to the delight of my clients. Though, I expect, once enough people had one, the novelty would wear off."

"I have the only one?" Mr. Bissell asked, though his question was more a comment of wonder.

"You lucky dog." Charles moved around the table and grasped one of Bissell's arms. He shook it lightly. "Or blessed dog, I should say."

"Blessed." Mr. Bissell frowned, adding, "Yes, perhaps." He sighed and focused his attention on Lizzy. "Miss Bennett, I shall keep your secret. Thank you for my sweet wife's portrait. I shall treasure it always."

"You are most welcome, sir," Lizzy said, sighing inwardly with relief. "Might I suggest you take steps to insure no one discovers its miracle?"

"You could put it in a locked cabinet," Charles suggested, grinning. "You will become a man of mystery to your servants. I have always wanted to be one, but I am too open and guileless."

"Those are good traits, my dear," Jane said, smiling at him.

"Are they?" He waggled his eyebrows. "I am not so certain. Your father thought all our servants would cheat us. Do you remember?" To Mr. Bissell, he asked, "Are you returning home now?"

He shook his head. "Bristol. I must meet an investment ship." He rubbed his cheek with one palm. "And I must order a lockable cabinet—something I can keep above my fireplace in my bedchamber. I shall write a letter directly after I return to the inn."

"Is your valet to be trusted?" Charles asked, concern drawing his brows together.

"Clark was my scout at Oxford. I trust him utterly." He bowed to the ladies. "I shall take my leave, now. Pray forgive me for speaking too heatedly. My emotions have been close to the surface since my wife's death."

"Of course they are. No forgiveness is necessary," Lizzy said, dropping a curtsy. "Have a safe journey."

"Thank you." He hugged the painting to his chest. "And for this, too."

"You are most welcome," she said.

"Come, I shall walk you to your carriage," Charles said, indicating the library door that exited onto the corridor.

Mr. Bissell changed the portrait's position to one hand. He lowered it to his side, pushed his other hand through his hair, tugged on his waistcoat, and only then reluctantly followed Charles, taking one last look at Lizzy before he left.

As soon as the door closed on the men, both ladies found chairs and sank into them.

"What am I going to do?" Lizzy asked in a whisper.

"Do?"

"How shall I go on now?"

"Why, the same as always," Jane replied in a similar fashion.

Lizzy moaned. "But someone knows my secret. Do we dare trust Mr. Bissell?"

"We must. We have no other choice."

They sat for several long minutes, both looking pensive.

Then, sitting forward, Lizzy grinned.

"I have a thought."

"Oh?"

"We could kill him."

"Lizzy!"

Shrugging, Lizzy settled back in the chair and closed her eyes, unutterably tired. "It was just a thought."

"Not a very good one," Jane retorted.

Lizzy snorted.

Chapter Nineteen

Edmund Bissell climbed into his carriage and set the painting down on the leather seat opposite him. The door shut, the vehicle swayed, jerked, and he began his journey back to the Inn-at-Lambton.

He scraped a hand over his face and shook his head in mild disgust. *What a bumblebroth. Tomorrow I must hie off to Bristol with naught to show for my time.*

The anti-climactic result of his adventure weighed heavily upon him. After traveling many days, and after many hours of speculation, he was coming away with…nothing. He had not learned the reason for the astounding behavior of his wife's portrait. He did not know, for certain, if anything like this had happened to Miss Bennet's other sketches. She claimed not. Regrettably, he doubted her word. She had been too tense, too watchful.

What could be done about her deception? He rubbed a spot above his eyebrow and sighed. Nothing. She could not be forced to reveal more to him than she had. Clearly, her family knew and they were not about to divulge her secret.

Perhaps one of their servants knew something? Edmund grimaced. He would not stoop to turning Clark into an interrogator. He could imagine his valet's stare if he suggested such a thing.

I have given my word to keep Miss Bennet's secret. I cannot go back on it. Delving into her private affairs goes beyond the pale. I shall have to accept the situation as it is. Do

I care about any of her other works? No, not at all. I only care about this one sketch-painting. Then, her prevarications also mean nothing to me.

Harrying after her has been an act of near-madness. What was I thinking?

A new thought occurred and he opened his eyes wide with it. *I should have asked her to paint a proper portrait of my beloved wife.* Edmund cursed beneath his breath and considered having his driver turn the carriage around. He leaned forward to rap against the carriage ceiling and then hesitated. Frowning, he fell back into his seat, deciding that the polite thing to do would be to send Miss Bennet a letter, requesting her to paint the portrait. He longed to have a painting that he could hang openly in his library.

Edmund glanced at the cherished package resting on the opposite seat and supposed he would probably have to leave it behind with Miss Bennet so she could refer to it while she painted. It seemed unlikely that she remembered his wife well enough to paint her from memory. His gut twisted into knots.

No. No. I cannot leave it behind.

If I cannot leave it with Miss Bennet, then I will have to forgo another portrait.

Edmund looked up at the black carriage ceiling and blinked back sudden tears of disappointment. Yet, at the same time, his shoulders relaxed and his guts unwound themselves simply because the likeness of his most adored wife would remain in his possession. When he got back to the inn, he resolved to unwrap the sketch-painting and gaze upon his wife's image while he drank a glass of brandy to sooth his nerves. The interview with Darcy, and then with Miss Bennet, had been most trying.

∞

Darcy heard the carriage pull away and realized that Mr. Bissell had left Pemberley without seeking further intercourse with himself. Both Georgiana and his aunt had already withdrawn, going about whatever business they had planned for the afternoon. He waited for the Bennet sisters or Bingley to come back from the library. When ten minutes had passed and they had not, he went to the library door, knocked, opened it, and discovered an empty library. He moved through to the corridor entrance and almost ran into Mellor.

"Sir," his butler said, moving back a step.

"Mellor, where are the Bingleys and Miss Bennet?"

"The Bingleys are walking in the garden, sir and Miss Bennet is in the ballroom."

"I am going riding. Send someone to the stables and then direct Booth to me."

"Yes, sir," Mellor said, stepping to one side.

Darcy hurried past him, climbed the stairs two at a time, and continued to his bedchamber. By the time his valet arrived, Darcy had almost completely disrobed. He wore only his white shirt.

"Your corbeau riding jacket, sir?" Booth asked as soon as he entered.

"That will do," Darcy said. "And buckskin trousers."

"Sir."

Booth bustled into the dressing room and returned with the clothing. Once dressed, Darcy sat on a chair while his valet, wearing white gloves to keep finger marks from the dark-brown leather, helped him on with his riding boots.

"If I may say so, sir, everyone below stairs is right pleased with our new friends," Booth said as he stood and retired a few steps in order to give Darcy room to stand.

Darcy blinked at him, surprised that the tall, spare man had ventured to speak on this subject. His servants—fiercely loyal—had always closely associated themselves with anyone the Darcy family had brought within its sphere, seeming to 'claim' any of his friends as their own, as well. They also felt deeply about anyone who betrayed the family—such as George Wickham—as though the servants had been betrayed as well.

Darcy hesitated, and then said, "I am also pleased with them. They are easy to like. Bingley in particular."

"Very gentlemanly, if I may say so," Booth expressed in a careful voice. "Their people, too, sir, have pleased us in the rooms."

Darcy merely nodded, wondering how his servants would feel if they knew Lydia Bennet was married to Wickham. Booth further surprised him—though perhaps he should not have been surprised—by his next words.

"We understand, sir, that Miss Bennet's youngest sister has an unfortunate history."

Darcy scowled at him and decided to be firmer than he might normally be. He could not have his servants gossiping about Miss Bennet's family. Inwardly, he sighed, supposing that there really was nothing he could do to prevent it. "I permit you a great deal of latitude, Booth, but this familiarity is unseemly."

Booth bobbed his head, but did nothing more than clasp his hands behind his back, neither retreating, nor putting himself forward.

"Well?" Darcy tilted his head to one side. "Have you been designated the spokesperson for the rest of the staff? Is that not Mellor's role?"

"In a matter of speaking, I have," Booth said, bowing slightly. "Mr. Mellor refused to take on the role in this case, believing me to be in a better position to inquire."

"Perhaps you should make his behavior your example."

Booth frowned. "I've considered doing so, sir. But the staff is anxious."

Darcy shifted his weight, folding his arms. "Anxious about what, pray?"

The valet took a deep breath and straightened his shoulders as though girding his loins for a grim duty. Booth gave an infinitesimal shudder before he explained in a rush of softly spoken words.

"Sir, the staff are worried that we'll be required to wait upon Mr. Wickham again."

Darcy stiffened. In a harsh voice that reflected more on his antipathy for the subject than his annoyance with his staff, he said, "That man will never be permitted to cross Pemberley's threshold. Not in my lifetime, or in the lifetime of my sister, or my future children, or grandchildren. My feelings on this matter have not undergone an iota of change, in spite of my friendship with his in-laws. Is that understood?"

"Even if…?"

"Even if I ally myself more closely with the family," Darcy said in a tight voice. "This is beyond what I would usually allow, Booth. Mind yourself."

Booth nodded and his shoulders relaxed. "Yes, sir. I do beg your pardon. Please, forgive my presumptuousness."

Darcy waved a hand.

"Thank you, sir, for your tolerance. Do I have leave to ease the staff's mind, sir?"

"You may. However, speak nothing of a possible alliance with anyone."

"Of course, sir," Booth said, bowing more deeply. He turned away and picked up his master's favorite crop and black riding hat. After handing them to Darcy, he opened the bed chamber door.

Darcy stalked out, his lips pressed into a thin line. He never understood how servants learned the way the wind blew without anyone telling them aught. At least they did not seem to know anything about Miss Bennet's curious talent.

He hastened out of the house before his guests waylaid him. His horse awaited him at the bottom of the steps, Jermyn at his head.

"Thank you," Darcy said, accepting the groom's assistance in mounting.

"Sir," Jermyn said, touching his hat brim.

"I shall be back in an hour or so," Darcy said. "Kindly inform my aunt or my sister."

"Aye, sir."

∞

Georgiana raced through Pemberley's corridors toward the estate offices in as seemly a fashion as she could manage. She nodded and smiled at the servants as they paused and gave her little bows or curtsies. This would be her first chance to meet with Mr. Kearn since her talk with Fitz and she could not stroll.

Georgiana reached the estate office after what seemed an interminable time. The door stood ajar and she could see him sitting behind his desk, looking grave, and still. Even though he held a pen over a ledger, he did not move to write in it. Her stomach lurched and her heart ached for him.

He must have felt her presence for he glanced up. The shadows in his countenance evaporated. He smiled and stood with a jerk as though he could not help himself.

Georgiana entered the room and closed the door behind her. She wanted no one to overhear their conversation.

"I have talked with Fitz," she said before he could warn her to open the door again—for propriety's sake.

Mr. Kearn frowned. "Yes?"

Georgiana scurried across the office to his side. She rested her hand on his arm. "Do not be vexed with me, please," she begged, lifting her face to his.

He touched her cheek with his fingertips. "No, how could I be? What did your brother say? Did you give him a good scolding?"

Georgiana felt her cheeks flush. "I did. Now, my dear one, I have agreed to go to London for the winter season."

Her beloved nodded gravely. "I thought as much. I am afraid there is no way to avoid it." He took a breath. "I shall miss you terribly."

Her heart melted and she leaned into him. He put his arm around her and kissed her temple.

"I shall extract a promise from Fitz that we may write to each other," she said, sighing deeply.

"You must tell me all about the wonderful parties you shall attend."

Georgiana nodded. "I mean to visit some museums, too, and I am to study for a few hours with Signore Muzio Clementi—Fitz arranged it."

"You will enjoy that."

She grimaced. "Perhaps. I expect he shall scoff at my poor attempts but I shall endeavor to learn something from him in spite of that. I would not be surprised to learn that he thinks female pianists are only fit for drawing rooms where their listeners will clap politely and exclaim at how well *our dear Miss Darcy plays*."

Mr. Kearn chuckled. "I shall be busy as well, so before we know it, you will be home for Christmas."

"Yes," Georgiana said, hoping she did not sound as soulful as she felt. She lifted her gaze to his. "You will not fall in love with our good vicar's daughter while I am away?"

He took her in his arms and kissed her, leaving her in no doubt about the sincerity of his affections. When he drew away, they were both breathing heavily.

Mr. Kearn rested his forehead against hers. In a whisper, he promised, "There is no chance of that."

A sharp rap sounded on the door and it opened before they could pull apart. Fern, Georgian's maid, poked her head around the door edge and Georgiana heaved a sigh of relief. She stepped out of Mr. Kearn's embrace.

"What is it?" she asked.

"Miss," Fern said, her gray eyes wide with understanding. She pushed the door all the way open so it would look from the corridor as though the door had not been shut. In a soft voice, she explained why she was there. "Mrs. McDougall has been lookin' for you. She's been all about the house, she has. There's nowhere else to look than here."

"Has something happened?" Georgiana asked, her eyebrows shooting up.

"Mr. Darcy's favorite hound has got into the kitchen, miss, and carried off the joint you was to have fer yer dinner," Fern said. She began to wring her hands. "Mrs. Reynolds is visitin' Nurse at Firelight Cottage and can't calm Chef Alphonse down like she usually does, miss—her speakin' French and all."

"My aunt speaks French," Georgiana said, frowning and moving toward the door.

"Aye, miss, but she's been talkin' about how t'would be a good time to cook that cockerel, miss. And, I must say, Chef

Alphonse is in agreement with her. He's beggin' Mr. Mellor to give him a bottle of Burgundy. He wants some brandy, too, miss," she added in a hushed voice. "Mrs. McDougal done say that when she finds you, she's goin' to make you support her and force Mr. Bender to kill Mr. Pitt."

"Oh, heavens," Georgiana said. She shooed her maid before her and exited the office, saying, over her shoulder, a radiant smile on her lips, "Pray excuse me, Mr. Kearn."

∞

Darcy climbed the worn, wooden stairs of the Inn-at-Lambton to the first floor. They creaked with each careful footfall, making him smile a little. As a young child on vacations from Eton, he used to visit the inn often, running through it and playing with the son of the landlord. The landlady used to give them cake and hot milk.

He walked along a short corridor and knocked on the white-painted door of Bissell's parlor. He listened to muffled footsteps approacheing. The door swung open, revealing a tidy, small man of about forty-five, bearing the indefinable stamp of a gentleman's gentleman.

"Yes, sir?" the valet inquired.

"Mr. Bissell, please. I am Darcy."

At the sound of his name, Bissell, who had been hidden from view by the high-back of his upholstered chair, leaned forward and looked around the wing. He rose the moment he saw his guest.

"Darcy! I did not expect you to call. Come in."

The valet bowed, held the door open further, and closed it after Darcy entered the familiar private parlor, stepping to one side to stand inconspicuously next to the table in front of the bay window.

Darcy bowed his shoulders to Bissell, and then crossed the faded brown and gold carpet to shake his hand. However, half-way across the space, he spied the painting Bissell had placed upon the carved wooden mantel. The image was identical to the sketch Darcy had viewed earlier. Even the frame matched.

The hand meant for Bissell rose instead to point at the

portrait. “What is this?” Darcy asked in a shocked voice. He dropped his arm to his side and stared at Bissell’s beautiful wife, dumbstruck and unable to clarify his question. There was something about the image that pulled at his soul, creating a yearning—not for something inappropriate, but with a desire to be near her, to sit beside her, to lean his being into hers so that they touched and shared wonder. Darcy did not understand his own feelings. How could he feel this way?

Bissell spoke. “It is difficult to look away from her, is it not?”

In a hushed voice, Darcy replied, “Miss Bennet told me she did not paint adults. I can understand why, now, if all her portraits cause this sensation.”

“You see it too, then?” Bissell asked, turning around to fully face the portrait.

“That she is like…like an angel on earth,” Darcy whispered. “Like I have known her before I was born and that she is like a long-lost friend, who loves me more than I can ever understand. My, Lord.”

“Yes, that is it. She was, of course.” Bissell took a step toward the painting and lifted his hand as though to stroke her cheek. “However, this shows more.”

“Perhaps it is blasphemous to say so,” Darcy said, frowning a little now, “But she looks as if God had painted a beloved daughter.”

Bissell nodded.

“Where is the sketch?” Darcy asked, tearing his gaze away from the painting.

Bissell cleared his throat and looked down at the floor, seemingly unable to answer. Darcy stared at him for a long, drawn-out moment and still Bissell said nothing.

Looking back at the portrait, Darcy considered it with his eyes narrowed, struggling to be objective about it. The subject sat in the same chair, in the same pose, with the same expression on her face. He pursed his lips, turned his back on the distracting image and sighed.

“This *is* the sketch, is it not? Somehow, the sketch has

transformed into the painting," Darcy stated and then waited for Bissell's response. When he said nothing, Darcy pressed him gently. "Am I correct?"

"Like a miracle," a voice full of awe said from behind Darcy.

"Clark!" Bissell shushed.

Chapter Twenty

Darcy turned around to face the valet. The man looked at the floor, his expression turned wooden.

"Clark spoke out of turn," Bissell said in a stern voice. "He is going to retire now and attend to the business of our departure tomorrow."

"As you wish, sir." Clark bowed low, turned on his heel, and left the parlor without another word.

Darcy cocked his head to one side and considered Bissell.

"Is this why you have come to see me? To ask about my interview with Miss Bennet? You have wasted your time, for I will say nothing about it. And nothing more about my wife's portrait," the man said, his expression relaxed, but steady. "My silence is a matter of honor and I will not break it. Not for you, not for anyone."

Bissell moved toward the window and looked out over the village beyond. Darcy followed him and they stood companionably for a moment, watching the business of the village pass beneath them. He wanted to grab the man and shake him until he told him everything he had discovered in the library when he had spoken to Miss Bennet. But he could tell Bissell meant every word when he said his honor prevented him from speaking about her secrets. Darcy would learn nothing from him.

"You understand that I leave for Bristol tomorrow? I must meet that ship I mentioned," Bissell said.

"Important business," Darcy acknowledged. He sucked in

a breath and then slowly released it. He abandoned his view of the village and looked at Bissell. "May I call on you the next time I am in London? I would be honored if you agree to count me as one of your friends."

Bissell looked at him and immediately nodded. "It would be *my* honor." He held out his hand and Darcy shook it. Bissel frowned and finally said, "I will say this to you, however. Miss Bennet has a talent like no other. It is essential that she is treasured and safeguarded from the…the…" Bissell paused, pressing his lips tightly together, seemingly unable to find the right word.

"The 'world'?" Darcy suggested.

Bissell slowly nodded. "Yes. From the 'world'. There are too many who would not understand her talent, and then there are those who would revere her as something, well, something angelic, perhaps? Witness the behavior of my own valet. She could easily be hounded from all sides. Imagine such a creature being inconvenienced by the scaff-and-raff of the world, as well as from those who should be her peers, or her betters. She must be protected."

"She will be," Darcy stated in a firm, emphatic voice.

"Good." Bissell held out his hand again. "Until we meet again, then?"

Darcy took his hand in a firm grip and shook it. "Indeed."

Edmund watched Mr. Darcy ride away before he turned to the writing table. He sat and drew out some paper. After unstopping the ink, he dipped a pen into the black liquid and set pen to paper.

∞

Georgiana, having sorted out the troubles in the kitchens, went in search of her guests. She decided Lizzy was the person she would like to speak to most. Therefore, she slipped along Pemberley's corridors until she came to the double doors of the ballroom. Jeremy, Lizzy's footman, sprung away from the wall and opened one of the doors for her.

Georgiana paused at the threshold and spied Lizzy

standing alone at a worktable covered in tins and bowls, wooden spoons, and several mortars and pestles. She wore an apron over her gown, sleeve protectors over her arms, and gloves upon her hands. Drop clothes protected the floor beneath her and the large easel that awaited the canvas their carpenter would provide. No one else occupied the makeshift studio.

Speaking loud enough to be heard across the large space, Georgiana asked, "Mixing paints?" Jeremy closed the door behind her, remaining in the corridor.

"Hello," Lizzy said, turning her head and smiling widely. "Yes, that is exactly what I am doing."

"I hope you raided my art cupboard," Georgiana observed, crossing the ballroom. "You will need a great deal of linseed oil for the amount of paint needed to cover the size of canvas being prepared." The closer she came to the table, the more she could smell the intoxicating aroma of art-in-the-making. The pungent scent of spirits of turpentine tickled her nose. "Or, do you prefer walnut oil?"

"I use both," Lizzy said, setting down the pestle she had been using to turn a vermillion pigment cake into powder. "Thank you for the offer, but I have enough with me."

Georgiana nodded. Lizzy was watching her, a quizzical expression on her face.

"Is something amiss?"

Georgiana sighed and chuckled a little. "One of Fitz's dogs got into the kitchens and stole the joint we were to have for our evening meal. The chef was in a tizzy and my aunt thought this would be a perfect day to cook up Mr. Pitt."

Lizzy laughed. "Did you save him?"

Georgiana gave a lady-like chortle behind her hand. "Fortunately, Farmer Bender has taken to keeping Mr. Pitt in his own back garden so I had to do little to save him. It is walled and Aunt Sophia cannot get to him without forcing her way through Farmer Bender's house, and even she does not have enough effrontery for that enterprise."

"Are you certain?" Lizzy asked, her lips twitching and her

eyebrows high.

"Pretty certain."

Georgiana recalled the reason for her visit and her humor faded. She folded an arm across her stomach and grasped the other arm. Instead of looking at Lizzy, she wrinkled her brow and stared at the worktable top, then through the row of windows to the back garden, until finally she peeped at Lizzy. Though they had met so recently, Georgiana already felt a kinship with this lively, talented woman.

Tentatively, she began, "I wonder if you have noticed the attraction—yes, I will call it that, though there is so much more than that paltry emotion—if one can call 'attraction' an emotion…um…" Georgiana stopped talking and took a deep breath, silently scolding herself for her rambling start. Her cheeks flushed hot with embarrassment.

"Perhaps you should begin again," Lizzy said gently. "Without any roundaboutation."

Georgiana nodded and then blurted out her explanation. "Mr. Kearn and I are in love and Fitz is making us wait for at least a year, maybe more, before he will permit me to marry him."

Lizzy blinked. "Heavens." She tugged off her gloves, laid them beside her mortar, and took Georgiana's arm. Leading her over to a sofa set to one side of the vast room, Lizzy drew her down and they sat turned toward each other. All she could think of to say was, "Oh, dear."

Twisting her fingers together in her lap, Georgiana continued to elucidate. "Fitz thinks I cannot know my own mind. But I do, I promise you. This love is not like the other time I fancied myself in love. My feelings for Wickham were nothing, *nothing* compared to my feelings for Mr. Kearn. And…and *before*, Wickham was not half the person Mr. Kearn is. My Mr. Kearn is a *true* gentleman. He has great presence of mind and a flawless character. He is honorable and kind."

Lizzy, not unnaturally, was wholly shocked at discovering the name of Georgiana's former love. "*George* Wickham?"

Georgiana blinked. "Why, yes. His name is not usually spoken of in this house. He is a vile, despicable creature and I cannot believe I ever thought myself in love with him. But, I was only fifteen." She shrugged, and then stared at Lizzy. "Do you know him?"

She swallowed hard and opened her mouth to speak, and then shut it again. After licking her lips, she finally managed to say, "He is my brother-in-law. Georgiana, I am terribly sorry to have to tell you this. Two years ago, he came with the militia into our county. There, he charmed our neighborhood and ended his triumph by sweeping my youngest sister, Lydia, away. He had no intention of marrying her. I expect he lured her away from family and friends because he could. In the end, he had to be forced to marry her."

Georgiana's color faded. She took several quick, rapid breaths, and then unexpectedly slumped backwards as though in a faint. But she was not swooning. Instead, she was laughing.

Laughing!

"I do not know what there is in my story for you to find amusing," Lizzy said, folding her arms and tapping her foot. "My sister's husband is no fit person for anyone to marry."

With the heel of her palm, Georgiana wiped the tears off her face. She straightened up. "I do beg your pardon. You are right. It is not amusing. I am merely relieved. So relieved that he can no longer approach me and try to make me go off with him again. I have been fearful every time I went to town that he would find a way to importune me. Can you understand my feelings?" She visibly shuddered.

Lizzy relented and nodded. "The experience must have been horrid for you. Let us discuss Mr. Wickham and Lydia no longer. Let us return, instead, to your immediate predicament. You and Mr. Kearn wish to marry and Mr. Darcy forbids it."

Georgiana, recalled to her situation, picked up where she had left off. She scowled. "Fitz is being horrid about everything!" She swept the back of her hand across her cheek as though wiping away angry tears, though none had fallen.

"No, no. That is not fair of me. He is being, well, typical. Highhanded. A little."

"Only a little?" Lizzy prodded. "Has he forbidden you to speak with Mr. Kearn?"

Georgiana shook her head. "No, he has not. But we are going to London sooner than planned because Fitz wants to separate me from Mr. Kearn. Even though Fitz said he would permit me to write to Mr. Kearn while I am in London, I am afraid my brother will frown at me and growl and make me feel sick to my stomach with his dark looks." Georgiana scowled. "Fitz thinks that I will find another gentleman whom I will like better just because they will dance with me at balls and routs. I imagine they will take me to the theatre, too."

"I expect they will," Lizzy said, holding back a smile. "All those activities will be full of gaiety and fun, of course."

"Oh, I know. I am sure I will enjoy them excessively. Even so, there is no substance to those activities," Georgiana pointed out. She tipped her head to one side. "How will I know I love a man if I do not witness his good character? Any gentleman knows how to be polite. That is no measure." She scowled. "Scoundrels can be polite."

Thinking of George Wickham, Lizzy dryly replied, "They can indeed."

"And how will I know that the prospective gentleman will love me for me and not for my money? It is a great curse to be an heiress. I would much rather have a smaller portion."

Lizzy could see her point. However, she would have been grateful, indeed, if her measly fifty pounds a year portion had been five hundred pounds instead—a very comfortable independence.

"Do you think Fitz will make me wait until I am of age to marry Mr. Kearn?" Georgiana asked, gazing at her with hope in her eyes.

Startled to be asked such a question, Lizzy shrunk from giving an opinion.

"Please, what are your thoughts?" Georgiana pleaded.

Lizzy took a breath before answering. "I am afraid I

cannot help you. I have no idea if Mr. Darcy will make you wait. We are not on those sorts of terms. He does not share his views with me."

Georgiana's shoulders slumped.

"Pray, do not be disheartened," Lizzy said, resting a hand on her arm. "I believe your brother will keep his word and if you follow his rules, he will honor his promises."

"I do not wish to wait so long." Georgiana unfolded her arms and took Lizzy's hands. "Pray, will you speak with him? Will you plead my case to him? He likes you. I know he does. He will listen to you."

Alarmed, Lizzy's eyebrows shot up and her eyes widened. "I could not be so presumptuous."

Georgiana nodded vigorously. "You could. I know you could."

Lizzy released a half chuckle, half groan. "Your praise touches me to the quick."

"Oh!" Georgiana bit her lip and looked down at her lap. "Pray forgive me."

"You are forgiven. My dear, try to set aside your emotions and consider what must be your brother's point of view," Lizzy urged gently. Georgiana released her hands and would have stood, but Lizzy grabbed her hands and held them snuggly within her own. "I believe your brother may merely wish you to gain a little town bronze, as they say—a little more experience before you marry Mr. Kearn, who is a mature gentleman. You must admit that your suitor has been about in the world much more than you have. Would you not prefer to come to your marriage with a greater understanding so that your match will be more equal?"

Georgiana leaned away, her eyes open and staring. "I had not thought of that side of the issue."

"You say that your love is fixed on Mr. Kearn—oh, no, do not poker up at me," Lizzy said as a laughing admonishment "A fixed love cannot be dislodged by a few months parting. Remember that Shakespeare sonnet? *'Love is not love which alters when it alteration finds, or bends with the remover to remove.'"*

"*'O no! It is an ever-fixed mark that looks on tempests and is never shaken'*," Georgiana replied, quoting the next two stanzas. She took in a great breath and grinned as she released it. "Lizzy, you are a wonder. Thank you. You have calmed my trepidation."

"I am so glad," Lizzy said, her own anxiety lessened. She had not wanted to discuss this extremely private subject with Mr. Darcy.

Georgiana tipped her head to one side. "Lizzy, I am consumed by curiosity. Please, tell me, what did Mr. Bissell want? What was in the package?"

Having anticipated this question, Lizzy had prepared an easy and ready fabrication that she hoped would satisfy Georgiana's inquisitiveness.

"It was a framed watercolor painting of his wife," she said, smiling sadly. The portrait would be a watercolor for two more weeks and he meant to leave for Bristol on the morrow. Lizzy dared not say it was a sketch because Georgiana could possibly see the painting before Mr. Bissell left the neighborhood and then her secret would be revealed. "He wished to commission me to use it as a template for a portrait in oil. Unfortunately, I had to disappoint him. As I have previously explained to your brother and yourself, I no longer paint portraits of adults."

"Was he very disappointed?" Georgiana asked, her mouth turning down.

"Yes," Lizzy admitted, sighing over the lie as much as over Mr. Bissell's distress at discovering that he would learn nothing from her about the mysteries of his sketch-painting. "However, he is resigned."

Georgiana rose and Lizzy followed suit. "He could have sent you a letter and then met with you at your home instead of searching you out here. Did he provide a motive for this chase?"

Lizzy shrugged. "He is in mourning. That must needs be reason enough."

"Indeed. You are right. Poor man." Georgiana touched her on the arm. "I shall leave you to your preparations. Thank you, once more, for helping me reason out my course going forward."

Lizzy flushed a little at the younger woman's earnest gratitude. She smiled and gave a short nod. Georgiana left her and Lizzy returned to her preparations. The drizzle had finally stopped, but the ground was too damp to be traipsed over today. Tomorrow she would return to sketching the studies of Pemberley House. But, this afternoon, she would prepare her dry pigments.

The ballroom door opened and Jeremy entered, bringing her a letter.

"It just arrived, miss," he said, holding out the silver salver. "One of the ostlers from the Inn-at-Lambton brought it.

Lizzy frowned a little and took it. "Thank you," she murmured, taking the folded letter. Jeremy bowed and left her. Lizzy unfolded the letter.

"Miss Bennet,

I wished to write you a note of assurance. My fervor in seeking you out must have alarmed you. I had no intention of causing apprehension. I do beg your pardon. I must ask to be excused on the grounds that I continue to mourn my wife and child's passing most grievously. Finding you and discovering the answer to our mystery became almost the sole focus of my life. After our discussion, I realized that I had nothing more to learn from you. I have no interest in any of your art other than the great gift you gave to us. And, in that, I am more than satisfied. The image of my wife gives me great solace. Be assured that I shall never break my word to you and that you may count me as one of your friends. Be careful, and be safe.

I will ever be, a most ardent admirer,

Edmund Bissell."

"Goodness," Lizzy whispered, blinking away moisture in her eyes. His letter had, indeed, reassured her and she honored him for it.

∞

As per their habit, they gathered in the saffron drawing room before their evening meal. Darcy waited for their guests to come down. Aunt Sophia stood near the fireplace talking with Kearn. Georgiana sat nearby, facing the fire. He was pleased to see both his sister and his estate manager behaving with great circumspection. If he did not know differently, Darcy would have thought their relationship unchanged from before he had discovered their regard. He could not even tell if Georgiana had confided their news to Aunt Sophia. He suspected not.

When the door opened to admit their guests, Darcy walked across the room and welcomed them inside.

"Bingley. Mrs. Bingley. Good evening. Miss Bennet, come closer to the fire," he said, taking her hand and putting it into the crook of his arm. "There is a chill in the air from all of the rain, is there not?"

"Not in here, sir," Miss Bennet said, smiling up at him. "It is wonderfully cozy."

Darcy's breath caught in his throat. How could he have ever thought that just her eyes were fine? Every line of her face pleased him. Recently—since his thirtieth birthday, in fact—he had begun to think that the time had come to find a wife. Darcy could not imagine anyone else other than Miss Bennet filling that role. He narrowed his eyes in a smile. And, she needed his protection. There could be no doubt of that.

She leaned in to him and whispered, "Has Georgiana brought the painting I did of…of you know who?"

"I have not seen it. My sister arrived from her room before I entered. Our aunt came in after me." He glanced around. "I warrant she has it hidden behind a chair. Does she mean to give it to her before we eat?"

"That is what she told me earlier," Miss Bennet replied.

"Whispering is altogether too unsocial," Aunt Sophia said in a lively voice that carried throughout the room. "Darcy, pray tell me all."

"Demanding to know the private conversations of our guests is far worse, Aunt," Darcy teased.

"Oh, pooh!" Aunt Sophia cried. "Surely, I am old enough to speak my mind?"

"If you are not careful," Darcy cautioned, "You will turn into Aunt Catherine."

"Fitz," Georgiana said, laughing behind her hand, "that is a horrid thing to suggest. Our dear Aunt Sophia will never be like Aunt Catherine." To their guests, she explained, "We are speaking of our mother's sister. She is very strict and always claims more than her fair share of the conversation. She terrifies me."

"Mr. Darcy has mentioned her to me," Miss Bennet said. "I believe she is the same Lady Catherine who was formerly the patron of my cousin, Mr. Collins. I should have met her, I expect, if I had gone to visit my dear friend, Charlotte Collins. However, that was not to be. Lady Catherine sounds like a veritable gorgon. Your aunt deserves a reward for being nothing like her."

Georgiana's eyebrows rose. However, she smiled at her aunt and said, "As it happens, as a reward for how nice of an aunt you are, I have commissioned a painting for you. It is quite spectacular and I hope you will like it exceedingly."

"For me?" Aunt Sophia asked, frowning and touching her chest with the flat of her hand. "Something by Miss Bennet? What is the subject? It cannot be you or Darcy. A landscape?"

"Lizzy painted it yesterday," Georgiana said, grinning. She moved over to an upholstered chair, reached behind it, and drew out the framed painting, draped in a magenta and green paisley shawl. "It is not a landscape, and, no, it is not of either Fitz or me. However, I am convinced that you will love the most extraordinary subject."

Their aunt's gaze narrowed, suspicion flashing across her features. "Georgiana? Am I going to want to box your ears when I see it?"

His sister shrugged and held out the package to her. With obvious reluctance, Aunt Sophia took the painting.

"I cannot wait to see it," Bingley said, his eyes wide with glowing expectation. "Have you seen it yet, Jane?"

"No, my dear."

Darcy felt the hand on his arm tighten. He glanced down.

In a whisper, Miss Bennet said, "She will not like it."

"If she does not, the fault will be with the subject, not the artist," he promised gently.

"What a gallant thing to say," she replied.

Darcy admired the flush in her cheeks and could have continued to watch her expressions, however, his sister and Aunt drew his attention.

"Aunt, why are you just standing there? You cannot be afraid of a painting," Georgiana teased. "Do you need help to uncover it?"

"I have had an awful premonition," their aunt revealed, staring down at her gift with her eyes wide.

Then, she shook herself, chuckled, and juggled the painting until the shawl slipped away, tumbling to the carpet. She gaped at the painting and no one spoke as they waited for her reaction.

Finally, she said, "Oh. My. Lord."

"At last," Georgiana said, grinning still.

"This is Mr. Pitt, is it not? He is splendid. Truly splendid," Aunt Sophia said, her voice thick. She swallowed hard and then wailed, "How unfair of you to make me love that accursed bird! I have immensely enjoyed ranting about him. How shall I vent my spleen now? You dratted girl!"

"Do you mean me?" Georgiana asked. "Or Lizzy? Which of us is a 'dratted girl'?"

Aunt Sophia sniffed and turned the painting around to show everyone. "Both," she said tartly.

"By Jove," Bingley said, leaning over at the waist to bring his face closer to the watercolor. He straightened and looked at his sister-in-law. "You have done it again, Lizzy."

"Who would have thought that a cockerel could look so amazing?" Mrs. Bingley asked.

"And I wanted to eat him tonight," his aunt said, blinking rapidly as though to stop tears from falling.

"If you look at too many of some of Lizzy's animal

portraits, you might not be able to eat meat again," Bingley warned. He shook his head in memory. "Our home farm has a pet calf. Eventually, he will be eaten because we do not need another bull, and so I begged Lizzy to promise not to paint him. I like a nicely roasted joint, and have no desire to swear off beef. Or pork. Or venison. Or chicken. Dear me," he moaned and swung on his heel to move away from the fireside gathering, stopping at a window. Without turning around, he added, "Tell me when the painting is covered."

Darcy laughed, startled by his new friend's behavior.

"Oh, you may find this amusing," Bingley said, leaning his hands on the window ledge, "but, I know of what I speak. If you keep staring at that painting you will never be able to eat chicken again. And do not hang it in any of your dining rooms."

"I shall hang it in my bedchamber," Aunt Sophia said, shaking her head at the younger man's antics. "Every morning when Mr. Pitt wakes me, I shall gaze upon his image and smile."

"Do you think that will help you return to sleep?" Darcy asked.

"Perhaps. Perhaps not." She lifted one shoulder. To Georgiana, she said, "Thank you, dear one. I shall always treasure it."

"You are welcome, Aunt," his sister said, beaming. She held out her hands. "Give it to me. Your maid can take it to your rooms. The footmen are all busy in the dining room." She turned and walked out of the drawing room with it.

Mellor entered. Darcy looked at him.

"Dinner is ready, sir."

"Excellent. What are we having? I understand the joint disappeared under suspicious circumstances?"

"It did, sir. Chef recovered and has made a delectable *Tourte au Poulet*, containing mushrooms and black olives."

Bingley groaned and turned around to face the room. "Chicken pie." He gulped dramatically before he commented, "Well, at least we shall not have to look it in the eye."

Aunt Sophia took a hasty step toward the butler. “It is not Mr. Pitt, is it?”

Chapter Twenty-One

"I do beg your pardon, madam, but no."

Her eyes closed. "Thank you, Lord."

Darcy could not hold in another chuckle. He covered Miss Bennet's hand with his own and looked down at her. "Shall we?"

Lizzy surreptitiously watched Mr. Darcy all through their evening meal. Something had changed. She could not tell what it was exactly, but whenever he glanced her way, she detected a softening of his facial features. The expression was rather disconcerting. What could he mean by it?

Surely...he cannot be...surely not. He is merely getting used to us, that is all, Lizzy told herself, experiencing an errant swooping delight that rocked her core. She ruthlessly thrust her own escalating feelings deep inside herself, covering them up with pragmatic and sensible reasoning.

He is wealthy—far too wealthy for a country gentleman's daughter to aspire after.

He is proud. Yes, far too proud for my liking.

Lizzy inwardly squirmed. She had admitted to herself that his pride was not improper, as she had at first thought, so she could not use that character trait to reject his charms.

What charm? He has no charm of manner. At least very little of it. Or, well, he uses it for his family and close friends only.

Who am I to attract his notice? She huffed silently. *Even* *if he is developing a regard for me, I cannot permit myself to return it. I will be exposed. I cannot hide my talent from so astute a man. And I will not...*cannot*...stop painting.*

Not for anyone.

"Are you well, Lizzy?" Jane quietly asked her.

"Quite well, thank you," Lizzy replied, frowning a little and looking at her sister, who sat to her left.

"I only ask because you are stabbing your slices of liver," Jane said, smiling. "They are already dead, dearest."

Lizzy examined her plate and set down her knife. The braised lamb livers, served with baby onions and parsnip rounds, had been further butchered by her unthinking hand until they lay across the plate in grayish, unappetizing lumps, surrounded by an eddy of equally gray sauce. Though she did not like to waste food, she could not force herself to eat another bite. The dogs were welcome to it.

A footman, on a signal from Mellor, removed her plate. A different footman gave her a clean one in preparation for the sweets course.

"I believe I have another three or four days of sketching to do before I will begin the painting of Pemberley House," Lizzy said very quietly. "I am beginning to have the feel of the building and the place inside me now. Indeed, I hope to be gone from here within two weeks. You must stay out of the ballroom, dearest. The aromas may not be beneficial to the baby. I will finish up quickly and then we shall have you home before traveling becomes onerous for you."

Jane's eyebrows lifted. "You sound very confident. I understand the canvas will be of an extraordinary size. Ten days of painting does not seem sufficient."

Lizzy nodded. "I am confident."

Her short answer caused her sister's frown to deepen, but Charles spoke to Jane and she turned to reply, giving Lizzy relief from interrogation.

"Miss Bennet?" Mr. Darcy sat at the head of the table, to her right. "I thought we might set aside 'Guy Mannering' for one evening and you can teach us how to play Chinese crib as you promised."

Lizzy beamed. "Gladly. How many cribbage boards do you have? With Mr. Kearn playing, we can make up three pairs, but there will be one left out."

"Earlier, I set Mrs. Reynolds to find our supply and she has found eleven boards and an equal number of playing card packs. She reminded me that when my father was alive, we had a small tournament of sorts. Amongst the local gentry, you understand."

"I do." Lizzy thought for a moment and then suggested, "I am glad you have so many because each of us will need our own crib board. The counting is different than regular cribbage. Please, excuse my presumption, but might we send a groom down to the parsonage and see if Reverend and Mrs. Franklins, and Jennet, too, would care to join us? Three more players will make the numbers even. Jane and I taught Charles ages ago. Each of us will take a pupil and the other pairs can sit close-by and learn that way."

Georgiana turned from conversing with her aunt and said, "Are you talking about our card evening? I already sent a groom to the parsonage and the Franklins have kindly agreed to join us. They will arrive in an hour."

"Excellent," Mr. Darcy said.

Georgiana glanced at their butler, gave him a nod, and said to the table at large, "Ah, here is the sweet course. Chef promised to make us *gimblettes de fleurs d'oranger.* They are a specialty of his."

Several plates of golden, knotted biscuits, redolent of orange and anise, were set down on the table, along with dishes of nuts, sweetmeats, fruit, Chantilly cream, and fancy marzipan fruit. The footmen left the room, indicating that they were to serve themselves. The butler remained, however, ready to assist.

"They look delicious," Lizzy said, reaching for one and placing it on her plate. "I do not believe I have eaten them before."

She added a handful of pistachio nuts that rattled nicely

when they hit the porcelain. Mr. Darcy then offered her a plate of delectable treats.

"Here, Jane," Lizzy said, taking the silver salver of tiny saffron sweetmeats and presenting them to her sister. "You love saffron. And these little cakes are bathed in honey, too."

No sooner had the aroma of saffron and honey reached Jane's senses than she drew back sharply and covered her mouth with her hand. Lizzy instantly handed the plate back to Mr. Darcy without looking away from her sister. He took it from her and passed it to his sister.

"Breathe through your nose, dearest," she advised quietly. "You know that does you good when you are unwell."

Jane nodded and followed directions. After a moment, she said in a quiet, unsteady voice, "Mother once said she could not abide certain favorite foods during her time. I suppose I am the same. I do not know how I could stomach the liver, but not the honey."

"Perfectly natural, I dare say," Lizzy said sensibly. "Would you care for peaches and cream, instead? Or, here are marzipan grapes."

Jane swallowed, inhaled shakily, and finally managed to say, "Nothing, thank you."

Lizzy patted her arm and left her alone to compose herself, knowing perfectly well that Jane disliked being fussed over—particularly in company. Glancing at Mr. Darcy, she saw him raise an eyebrow. His eyes flicked to her sister and then back to her. She smiled reassuringly but gave no explanation. It was not her place to inform him that Jane was increasing.

∞

They repaired to the safari saloon after their meal. Georgiana led the way while Darcy followed behind everyone. In spite of being at the rear, he managed to hear Mrs. Bingley's appreciation of the décor.

"What a lovely room," she praised when they entered. "And look at the carpets."

Darcy discovered her and Bingley turning away from their

admiration of the monkey and jungle toile wallpaper gracing the walls to the floor coverings.

"My father collected these carpets while on his Grand Tour with my uncle," Darcy said. "Each of the six hunting-themed carpets is of the Early Ottoman period—from Persia, I believe—except for that one over there." He pointed to the one nearest the fireplace. "That one is from Turkey and does not have scenes of animals being hunted from horseback. Its geometric pattern does not quite fit with the theme, but since it is a collection from my father's Tour, we have always had it in here."

His guests spent a few minutes examining each of the six carpets. Mrs. Bingley did her perusing from the comfort of one of the green upholstered chairs that stood against the perimeter. She still looked a little pale. Georgiana, being an excellent hostess, sat beside her, pointing out her favorite images.

"Spectacular," Miss Bennet said, looking up from the floor at the art on the walls. She gestured at a painting next to the fireplace. "That tiger looks ferocious. How does one play cards when there are teeth like that hovering above one?"

"He is a trial to concentration for some," Darcy acknowledged, approaching her and standing close enough to smell the violet scent she wore. "Georgiana could not bear the sight of him while growing up."

She turned her back on the Chinese watercolor and moved away from him toward the baize-topped mahogany folding card tables arranged in the center of the large room. A collection of crib boards and packs of cards rested on one of the tables.

Is she as aware of me as I am of her? Is it possible that she might care for me?

"Let us rearrange these tables so that four are beside each other where one teacher can explain to three students," Miss Bennet said, pointing to two tables, and then to two others, drawing the other players' attention from the carpets to the game. "Charles, Mr. Darcy? Will you oblige us? Spread the tables out so that the teaching at one will not disturb the others."

"Right you are," Bingley said. He moved with alacrity to the nearest table. "Come, Darcy, these two first."

Darcy smiled to himself and assisted his guest in rearranging the tables. He enjoyed seeing Miss Bennet feel comfortable enough in his home to give directions.

She will fit in well here. If she accepts me. He inwardly snorted. *Of course, she will accept me. Why would she not? I am rich, powerful enough to protect her, and she loves...my home. She does not appear to hold me in disgust, so why would she refuse? She will not.*

By the time they had completed the task set to them, the door opened to admit the butler and the Franklins. Georgiana and their aunt hastened across the room, skirting the tables, to welcome the parson and his family.

"We are so grateful to you all for coming to make up our numbers," his sister said, drawing them into the room. "We are excited to learn this new variation to our familiar cribbage game. You remember our other guests? Miss Bennet and Mr. and Mrs. Bingley?"

"Indeed, we do," the Reverend Mr. Franklin said, bowing his shoulders to the room at large. His wife and daughter executed slight curtsies. "We were yawning over our meal, wondering what we could do to liven up our evening, when your invitation arrived, so we thank you for rescuing us."

"You are most welcome," Georgiana said graciously. "Shall we find our seats? Miss Bennet will take one table, Mrs. Bingley will teach at a different table and Mr. Bingley at another. Lizzy? Where would you like us?"

"Charles will teach Mr. Kearn," Miss Bennet said, pointing to the table with only two chairs. "I will teach Mr. Franklin, Jennet, and Mr. Darcy at these tables, facing that tiger, I think. That leaves Georgiana, Mrs. Franklin, and Mrs. McDougall to be taught by Jane, there. Everyone take a crib board each and one pack of cards between two players."

Darcy chose his crib board, pleased that Miss Bennet had chosen him to be at her table. However, he was too well bred to show any outward sign that he was extraordinarily delighted with his teacher. He watched Miss Bennet whisper something to her sister. Mrs. Bingley smiled and nodded, then shook her head slightly. Miss Bennet held her sister's chair while she sat, indicating that her pupils were to take their seats.

Lizzy and her students sat down at their joined tables. She took the pack before her and began shuffling. Mr. Darcy sat opposite her while Jennet paired with her father, who was at Lizzy's right. Mr. Darcy's complete attention threatened to tangle up her mind. She refused to allow his intensity to fluster her, however. Instead, she concentrated on her lesson.

The first thing Lizzy showed them was where to place their pegs on their own boards.

"You will be counting for your opponent on the board before you. Your opponent will count for you on the board in front them," Lizzy explained.

"I see," Mr. Franklin said. He leaned forward and smiled at his daughter, saying in a kindly voice, "You will enjoy this, my dear."

"I am not at all a good cribbage player," Jennet admitted nervously, glancing shyly at Lizzy. "Having my own board is rather odd. I fear you have a poor student in me, Miss Bennet."

"Chinese crib allows the new player, or the hesitant player, to learn how to put together hands and how to count," Lizzy explained, smiling reassuringly. "It is also an excellent game to visit over, because we do not have to lay down our cards and count as we go. Instead, all counting out is done at the end of the hand and chatting is possible. This, of course, occurs once one is proficient at the game."

"I am ready to begin," Mr. Franklin said. "How many cards do I deal?"

"There is no dealing," Lizzy said. "Lay down four cards on the table in front of you, face up and in a row, like this." She watched while her pupil followed her example. "These are the beginning cards of your four hands."

"Four hands?" Jennet asked.

Lizzy nodded. "Yes. Next, we will throw one card to the side as our cribs."

Both the reverend and Lizzy did so.

"Now, we will begin the second row of our four hands, laying down a card below each of your other cards, one per row, overlapping the cards slightly. Decide for yourself where you want the card. Here, I have an eight, see—you have no need to hide your turned over card. I will put it on the seven because that will give me fifteen-two and the possibility of a 'run'. I will put this jack on my queen, and this five on the king. My last card is a three and it goes on the eight, the final one of the first row whether I like it there or not." Lizzy watched Mr. Franklin as he placed his cards. Then, she admonished her students, "You may not switch a card's place once you have turned over the next card. Or rearrange any card in a previous row to your liking." Everyone nodded their understanding. "Now, another discard to the crib pile."

Lizzy watched Mr. Franklin place his cards and throw away the crib card. "Well done," she told him. Glancing at Mr. Darcy and Jennet, she asked, "Are you following so far?" They nodded. "The next two rows are laid down just like the first two."

Lizzy struggled to stay focused. She could feel Mr. Darcy's gaze upon her. To distract herself, she looked between him and Jennet at her sister to check if Jane was managing. With satisfaction, she saw that Jane's color was returning. Lizzy returned her full attention to her own table. Mr. Darcy's gaze met her own and his held an intensity of expression that caught her focus until she was called to book by Mr. Franklin.

"Now what, Miss Bennet?"

Lizzy cleared her throat. *I will not admit to having lost concentration. To do so would be rude.* In a composed voice, she said, "We have laid out all four rows and have four cards in the crib, so we count each hand, and the crib, while our opponent pegs for us. Our goal is to get at least thirty points. If we have less then we peg backward. When we get more than thirty points, we move forward."

She began counting out her cards and Mr. Darcy pegged for her. Lizzy had thirty-five points so he pegged forward five holes on her behalf. Jennet conscientiously pegged for her father, who only had twenty-eight points and therefore went back two points.

"Our pegs will go forward and backward throughout the game until one player finally pegs out, winning the game," Lizzy explained. "Now, we pass the pack over and our opponent repeats everything we did." She passed the cards to Mr. Darcy. His strong fingers brushed against her hand and she swallowed. *Heavens.*

Jennet accepted the cards from her father, clumsily shuffled them, and then began to lay out her first row of cards, requesting hints from her father on how to play after every few cards. Mr. Darcy quickly and efficiently laid out his cards, needing no help from her. Lizzy recalled how well he played from when they traveled in his carriage.

They continued to play for an hour. Jennet, after some extremely fortunate hands, won their game. This pleased her enormously. She and her father chose to watch Mr. Darcy and Lizzy's game instead of starting a new one of their own. They laughed and groaned at the turning over of good cards and of useless cards.

"Will this game ever end?" Jennet asked when Mr. Darcy's hands forced him to go backward by twelve points. He had been ahead but now he was trailing. "Mr. Darcy, you had only five pegs to go."

Lizzy, scooping up the cards and shuffling them for her turn, said, "This is my chance. I am going to have a brilliant hand, I can tell."

Jennet gasped. "Do not ever say that! Oh, you have doomed yourself now. You will go back for certain."

The other players in the room glanced their way. Mr. Kearn and Charles, who had just concluded their own game, stood and gathered around them to watch. The others at Jane's table also came over. Mr. Kearn stood beside Georgiana. Charles stood beside Jane. Mrs. Franklin stood behind her daughter. Lizzy glanced up from shuffling at Mr. Darcy. His eyebrow rose in challenge, causing a shiver to dance down her spine.

Lizzy smirked at him and laid out her first row of cards without even looking at them. After she fed the crib, she turned over the first card for her second row so everyone could see it. Everyone sucked in their breath. She looked at the card. *An ace.* There was no good spot for the ace. She held the card over the six.

"Ooo," Mrs. Franklin said, shaking her head. "Not the six. Put it on the king. You might get a four."

"She might get an eight," Mr. Kearn pointed out.

"Put it on the four," Charles said. "Then you would have a five in case you get a ten."

Lizzy tilted her head to once side. "I might even manage a run if I get a two and a three. Very well, Charles, you have convinced me. I shall put it on the four."

Mr. Darcy shook his head and scowled at his guests.

"I am certain they shall help you, too, Mr. Darcy, when it is your turn again," Lizzy said, smiling saucily at him.

"I do not require assistance."

"I am not so sure of that," Georgiana said with a mocking laugh. "You are the one behind at the moment."

Lizzy nodded sagely when a five turned up. She placed it on the king, crying, "Hah!" in triumph. Her turn continued at speed. An accomplished card player, Lizzy placed her cards quickly and efficiently in spite of some "But..." and "You should have…" comments. When her points were totted up, she discovered she had won at last.

"Congratulations," Mr. Darcy said. "That was a hard-won victory."

"Thank you," Lizzy said, rising from her seat, feeling a little flushed by her success.

"Yes, and thank you for teaching us this new way of playing cribbage," Mrs. McDougall said. "The men in my husband's regiment had a slew of variations, but I have never heard of this one before."

"You must teach me some of them one day," Lizzy said. "Have you all enjoyed the game?" After everyone gave their assent, she asked, "Does everyone want to switch around their opponents?"

They shuffled their seats about so that they still had one of the teachers nearby and the next round of play began. Lizzy did not know if she was pleased when Mr. Darcy chose to continue at her table, though his new opponent was Mr. Kearn.

At ten of the clock, Mellor and two footmen brought in their tea. A few of the players had to agree that the person ahead had won their game since not all the games had been completed when the tea arrived.

Just as the party was breaking up and the Franklins were leaving, Lizzy discovered Mr. Darcy at her elbow.

"Miss Bennet?"

"Yes?" She hated that her voice sounded breathless. *I am merely tired.*

"Tomorrow morning, before you begin sketching, will you do me the honor of joining me for a walk about the lake?" he asked her, his tone formal and rather daunting. "I believe the morning will be fine."

"Um, well, of course, sir."

"Thank you," he said, bowing his shoulders stiffly and walking away.

Lizzy watched him bid farewell to the Franklins, alarm settling in the pit of her stomach.

Chapter Twenty-Two

Four evenings later, instead of retiring immediately after his guests had, Darcy set off for his study further down the gallery. Shadows from his candle danced along the walls, folded over the sides of picture frames, and merged with the dark spaces between. The beam of the single flame reflected off the paint whenever he came close to the masterpieces lining Pemberley's walls.

Once he reached his private domain, Darcy used the candle to light a lamp on his desk. He took the key from his waistcoat pocket and unlocked the drawer where he had placed the stolen sketch. Though he had promised himself not to look at the drawing again, he longed to once more view the proof of Miss Bennet's curious talent. They had spent a portion of each morning in gentle exercise, walking around the lake, through the home wood, and amongst the trees of his orchard.

They had conversed, of course, mostly about Pemberley and his life. Miss Bennet had not talked overly much about her own upbringing. She had spoken warmly of her father and with some constraint about her mother. He suspected this might be due to Miss Bennet's curious talent. Mrs. Bennet must have lived in constant fear that her daughter would be found out.

The drawing rustled when he drew it forth, loud in the quiet of a house mostly settling into sleep. He placed the sketch on the desk surface, sat, and examined the changes in the expressions of the two occupants on the paper.

Georgiana's mien had undergone another change. Subtle,

but there. Her image still displayed determination, but it had been softened by…hope? His own expression had altered more dramatically. His sister's resolve had transferred to his image. Even the hands were clenched.

How is this possible? What if unscrupulous individuals forced Miss Bennet to sketch their business adversaries, or their spouses, or their enemies? What knowledge could they glean? She must *be protected. Bingley does not have the power or the influence to keep his sister-in-law's secret forever. How many times has he almost told me the whole?*

Darcy pressed his lips into a grim line full of determination, unconsciously mimicking the image on the page. Or did it mimic him?

A knock sounded at the door and he frowned. He thought everyone had gone to their bedchambers. Darcy replaced the sketch inside the drawer before he spoke.

"Come."

The door opened, revealing Bingley, dressed in a burgundy silk banyan, wrapped and tied over his shirt and pantaloons. He had replaced his shoes with curly-toed embroidered slippers.

"Hey-ho," he said, grinning. Then his smile drained away. "I say, you look rather bleak. Is aught amiss?"

"Nothing at all," Darcy said, rising and leaning over his desk to look down at Bingley's footwear. "What do you have on your feet?"

Bingley held up a leg, displaying the blue and gold slippers. The toe end curled monstrously long, being at least six inches in diameter, tapering to a lean point tacked with a gold rosette to the instep so it could not flop down and be trod upon.

"Do you care for them? They are Turkish, you know."

Darcy smothered a smirk. "My dear fellow, they are magnificent."

Bingley laughed, entering the room and closing the door. "You are teasing me, I suppose. But they are whimsical and I like them. Life is too short to bow to the conservative views of the *beau monde*." He paused, and then added with a crooked grin, "At least, I need not bow to them while in the privacy of my own bedchamber."

"Pray, sit," Darcy begged, waving him to one of the chairs in front of his desk before he sat. "I thought you meant to retire."

Bingley sat and crossed his legs, folding his hands across his middle. "I had a letter this morning. I do not know why my accursed butler sent it on because I do not want it." He scowled. "I should have instructed him to consign any letters from my brother-in-law to the fire."

"Do you not have a secretary?"

"I do, I do," Bingley assured him. "He must have taken advantage of my absence to hook it. I shall give him a good scolding when I get back, I assure you."

Darcy doubted he would do anything of the sort. The man did not have it in him to scold a flea.

"I did not think Mrs. Bingley had any brothers," Darcy commented.

Bingley shook his head. "Not Jane's brother. Lydia's husband. I have mentioned her before. Wild to a fault, that one. Even so, I would not have wished Wickham upon her."

Darcy stiffened. "As I said previously, we prefer not to speak of that man in this house."

Bingley frowned and sat forward. "I would not injure you for the world, sir, but I cannot talk about this with my wife or with Lizzy. The man is constantly asking me for money. I expect when I give it to him, he only gambles it away."

"I have no doubt that your fears are well grounded," Darcy said, his words issuing out of his mouth through clenched teeth. "You would do well to have nothing more to do with him."

Bingley nodded miserably. "It is Lydia who suffers. She is but eighteen, you see, and very silly."

"When you wed one member of a family you wed them all." Darcy stirred in his seat. "If only he had joined the regulars. Then, he might have been sent overseas."

"Oh, did you not know? He left the militia and joined a northern regiment. In the regulars. He is not even a lieutenant anymore." Bingley frowned. "We are so used to referring to him as lieutenant that it never occurs to us to call him by his new rank. It is ensign."

Darcy snorted. "He must love being the lowest ranking officer."

Bingley smiled. "Not a bit of it." Then he scowled. "He cites his lower pay as the reason for plaguing me for money." He scraped a hand over his late-night stubble. "I have wondered if the best course would be for me to make them an allowance. Say, fifty pounds a quarter? To augment his pay, you understand."

Grimacing, Darcy sighed. "Will sending the money to Lydia do the trick? I know you said she is a silly girl, but can she keep household?"

"I cannot imagine it." Bingley rose and took a turn about the room. As though as an aside, he said, "Jane is increasing."

"Congratulations," Darcy responded, grinning. "This is good news, indeed."

Bingley nodded. "Yes, but you can understand now why I do not want her worrying about Lydia."

"I do." Darcy pulled at his bottom lip. "I fear that your money will disappear without any material gain to your sister-in-law. Could you not, instead, pay for their lodging? Then you need never fear that they will be thrown into the street due to non-payment. Your man of business could arrange it. Or, if you permit me, I will have my man in York look into it. He can discover where they live, the price of their lodging, and if they need to find rooms, or a small house, better fitting their situation. The rent on a small house may only put you out of pocket for ten to fifteen pounds per annum."

Bingley pointed a finger at him. "That, sir, is an exceedingly excellent idea. I welcome the assistance of your man in York. I shall leave you with Wi—Lydia's direction. And, if it is possible, perhaps there is a purveyor of goods that can provide them with food hampers and…and…candles and such every week?"

"My man will look into it." Darcy watched the weight of worry lift off of his new friend's shoulders and was pleased. "If I may make another suggestion?"

Bingley waved grandly at him. "Sir, I am willing to hear any of your excellent notions."

Darcy chuckled. *I must encourage him to find a home nearby. Hertfordshire is much too far away. I need a friend like Bingley.* "Shall I direct my man to find a woman—a retired housekeeper perhaps—who will choose the necessities? She will cost you only ten pounds a year. She need never come in contact with Lydia and her household and so would not be influenced by their desires."

Bingley frowned. "Do you think she might?"

"Wickham might bribe her to sell the goods and give him the money, paying her a percentage."

Bingley's eyes opened wide and he blinked rapidly. "Surely, not? He cannot be such a scoundrel."

A surge of alarm swelled in Darcy. He rose to his feet and came around the desk to face Bingley. "Sir, you have no notion. Your good nature precludes you from considering any man to have so black a heart as to allow his wife to starve while he sits gambling. But I assure you in the strongest possible language, that Wickham is capable of anything. *Anything*. I cannot allow you to continue to suffer under any misapprehension that George Wickham is capable of changing his foul nature."

"But…but cannot any man—"

Darcy interrupted him with a snarling reply, "Not *him*." He drew in a deep breath, noting Bingley's startled expression, and continued in a calmer voice. "That man has attempted atrocities which would have ruined the life of an innocent if his plot had not been discovered in time."

Darcy observed Bingley's mouth open and he hurried to add, "I am honor-bound to say no more about the incident." Bingley's mouth shut. Darcy shook his head at him. "Must I remind you of how your wife's own young sister was led astray by him? He continues to run up debts, does he not? And gamble?"

"He does," Bingley said solemnly. "What a despicable man." He pressed his lips together and thought. "Too charming by half, as well." He sighed. "Since there is no trusting him, and Lydia is so young, your man of business must find a respectable, honest woman to choose the goods for the hampers. He must make certain she knows she is not to have anything to do with them."

Darcy nodded, feeling much relieved. "He shall look into it. *And* keep an eye on the situation." He backed away a few steps and leaned his hips against his desk, drained.

Bingley beamed, walked toward him, took his hand, shook it, and clapped him on the back at the same time. "Thank you for trusting me enough to tell me what you could about my brother-in-law's past misdeeds. I am honored." He managed a sort of sickly chuckle. "I knew I should find help if I talked this through with you. I thank the Lord that you came looking for Lizzy."

"You are most welcome."

Darcy watched him leave his study and knew that whatever the result of the interview he meant to have with Lizzy the next morning, he must keep in close contact with Bingley. The man did not have the strength of will to resist Wickham's machinations. *If I had revealed to the world what type of man he is, Lydia Bennet would never have fallen into his power. Even though such a revelation was impossible, I am sorry for her. Life will never be easy for her with a husband like Wickham.*

∞

Rising from her bed the next morning, Lizzy marveled that she had slept so well. Her last thoughts the night before had been of the interview Mr. Darcy had requested of her that morning at the end of their walk. Today was the first day of painting, so they could not have talked on their walk. He was joining her in the ballroom.

Her heart, usually such a reliable organ, had skipped

alarmingly with his application. So formally put forth, her first thought had been that he wished to ask for her hand. This she had immediately dismissed with secret reluctance. The alliance, so unequal, would open him to censure by his friends and family. Surely, they expected him to marry an heiress.

Once her first thought had been shoved aside, the second thought came to her that Mr. Darcy wished to alter the terms of the commission.

Mayhap he wants to make another attempt to convince me to paint Georgiana. If I refuse, will he cancel the painting of Pemberley House?

"Good mornin' to ye, miss," Fiona said, turning from pouring the can of hot water into the wash basin. "Did ye sleep well?"

Lizzy brought her thoughts back to the moment and smiled at the cheerful maid. "Yes, thank you."

"'Tis a fine day, miss," Fiona promised. She approached her charge and assisted her with the removal of her white cotton nightrail. "They say in t'rooms that yer about ready t'start paintin'. We're all that excited, miss. T'see what it will look like," she explained.

"I am ready," Lizzy said, picking up the washing flannel. She dipped it in the water and progressed with her morning ablutions. "To that end, please lay out my plain gray dress."

"The one with t'paint on sleeves?" Fiona asked, displaying just a hint of disapproval.

"Yes. I would not like to get paint on one of my good dresses, would I?"

"Nay, miss," Fiona replied, moving toward the wardrobe. She opened a drawer and retrieved the dress. She shook it out, looked it over, and clicked her tongue. "M'worse dress is better than this one, miss. It don't seem right, it don't. An' you goin' down t'breakfast in it."

Lizzy shrugged. "I shall go down to the ballroom directly and take a plate of food in there this morning. Pray attend to it. A pot of tea, too."

"Aye, miss."

∞

Hand hovering over the container of walnut oil, Lizzy paused to consider whether Mr. Darcy would arrive soon. He had not given her a specific time for their interview. If he had not surprised her so much with his request, she would have asked him. Once she started painting, she preferred to have hours and hours of uninterrupted work. She glanced toward the closed ballroom doors.

Should I wait before mixing the paints?

Lizzy glanced at the canvas the carpenter had delivered that morning. It was at least eight feet wide and five feet high. He had brought along a selection of easels to set it upon. This would be the largest canvas she had ever painted. She stepped away from her work desk and positioned herself so she could see the entire canvas. In her mind's eye, she sectioned it off, delegating a certain amount to the sky, some to the foreground, and then to the spot where she would place Pemberley House.

Not right in the middle, she thought. *No, lower down and to the right a little so the windows appear to be looking out into the distance, into the future. Yes, like that.*

Almost in a daze, as though a third eye had opened in her forehead, making reality and the invented spar for supremacy, Lizzy moved back to the workbench and reached for the oil. She could see the image she wanted to produce. It was time to start painting.

And then someone touched her arm.

Lizzy jumped, sloshing some oil onto the table. She dropped the can back in place, gasping in shocked surprise.

Turning to the person who touched her, she cried, "What are you about, to almost scare me out of my wits?" Recognizing her assailant as her client, she tamped down her ire and spoke again in a more temperate manner. "Oh, Mr. Darcy. I beg your pardon. I was lost in contemplation."

"So, I see," he replied, smiling slightly. "Forgive me."

"Of course," Lizzy said, pressing a hand to her chest, feeling the rapid beating of her heart beneath her palm. She concentrated on calming her breathing.

"Are you quite recovered?" he asked solicitously.

"Yes, thank you." She grabbed a rag and blotted up the spilled oil. "I was just about to mix my paints. You came at the right time. Once I start, I like to work for hours uninterrupted."

Mr. Darcy said nothing. He waited patiently until she had finished with the rag. She dropped it on the table, swiped her hands over the front of her apron and faced him again.

He waved at the couch where she and Georgiana had sat. "Shall we sit?"

"Yes, of course."

Mr. Darcy nodded, taking her elbow as though she might faint. Once they were both settled, turned slightly toward each other, Mr. Darcy unexpectedly rose and paced a path in front of her.

Silently.

Without looking at her.

With his hands clenched at his sides and a rather fierce expression on his countenance.

What does he mean by this odd behavior?

"Is aught amiss?" Lizzy asked finally. "Have you decided you do not wish me to paint a…"

Mr. Darcy swung to face her, making her blink and lean back a few inches.

"You must give me leave to tell you how much I most ardently desire to protect you and care for you."

Lizzy gasped. *What is this? Surely he cannot mean what I think he means.*

He started pacing again. "I have struggled to overcome my feelings on this matter, but it simply cannot be done. Keeping your amazing talent from prying eyes is essential. I have the power and the influence to be certain no one ever knows about it."

"Knows about what? I do not take your meaning," Lizzy claimed, frowning fiercely.

"About what happens when you paint, of course."

He speaks in such a backhanded manner as though this issue is not of paramount importance to me. Can he not even look at me when he speaks of my talent? Is he that ashamed of it? Is he so mortified by me that he cannot offer marriage?

He faced her again. "You must understand, I—"

Lizzy jumped to her feet. "Must I? *Must I*? Why must I?"

Seemingly taken aback by the ferocity of her response, Mr. Darcy's mouth opened but no sound came out.

"You wish to be my protector? My *protector!* I am not a…a…lightskirt who will fall at your feet in gratitude for your protection," Lizzy ground out, tears smarting. "How dare you, sir?"

Pale, now, Mr. Darcy replied, "You choose to misunderstand my meaning. I—"

"Your meaning is perfectly clear." Her chest heaved with indignation.

He took a step toward her. "If you will kindly permit me to finish my sentence?"

Lizzy pressed her lips into a thin line and jerked her head in a nod.

"Thank you," he said with grave calm. "I know I am making a mull of this, so pray forgive me. I did not mean to offer you anything less than my name. You need protecting and I am offering to marry you."

In a cold voice, with a heart shrivelled and dying, Lizzy asked, "To *protect* me?"

Mr. Darcy nodded. "Surely you realize that you cannot keep the secret of your remarkable talent forever? If you continue to do commissions for clients, your secret will soon be out. Bingley told me of your desire for independence, and that you are funding it with your commissions. I cannot allow you to put yourself in that sort of danger."

So he wants to keep my remarkable talent from prying eyes, does he? All *my painting?*

"*You* cannot allow me?" Lizzy was shaking so hard with terrified fury that she did not know if she could remain standing. "Tell me, if you please, what right you have to claim the privilege of allowing, or forbidding me to do anything? You are not my husband, or my father, or my guardian." She took several long, deep breaths. Clasping her hands before her waist to disguise their trembling, she said in a moderate, polite voice, “I am conscious of the great condescension of your offer—”

“Do not speak of my condescension,” he ordered, slashing one hand to the side as though it would strike the word from her memory.

“Very well. Of the great *honor* of your offer,” Lizzy said, heavily stressing the changed word. She squeezed her hands even tighter. Glancing down, she saw that her knuckles were white. Swallowing, she finished, “However, I cannot accept. I will not marry you. I have no intention of *ever* marrying.”

“And *that* is your answer?” Mr. Darcy replied, his body stiff, his chin lifted and working.

“It is.”

“You are throwing my offer into my face without an explanation?” he asked through gritted teeth.

Dear Lord, he has not said he loves me. I will not *endure the indignity of asking him.*

“I am not required to provide one,” Lizzy replied stiffly, her heart breaking.

Mr. Darcy bowed reflexively, turned on a heel, and stalked from the ballroom. Lizzy watched him go, wishing there were not so many steps between herself and the door. She wanted to call him back, to beg him for the loving words every woman wished for during a declaration of intent. But, she would not. Those words had to be freely given, not entreated for.

I will not marry without love. Not even if it means financial security. I will not live in a gilded cage. I would rather live simply in a cottage by the sea where I will be free.

And I cannot stay here.

I must go.

I must go home!

Now!

The door slammed, galvanizing Lizzy into motion. She lifted her skirts and flew across the room. Cracking the door open, she checked for Mr. Darcy's presence. He had already reached the great front hall. She heard him call for his horse while he stormed out of the house.

"Miss?" Jeremy, her footman, said, stepping away from the wall toward her. "Do y'need me?"

Lizzy pulled the door open. "I do. Kindly, collect my painting things—only my own, mind—and pack them up. Collect your own things, too. Make haste for we are leaving Pemberley almost this instant."

Chapter Twenty-Three

Lizzy burst through the door into her sister and brother-in-law's suite with hardly a knock. Fortunately, she did not find them *en déshabillé*. They were both fully dressed and sitting on chairs in front of the window, a small table between them. Their Persian backgammon board rested on the table. Charles, surprised by her sudden entrance, dropped the dice onto the floor.

"Lizzy!" Jane exclaimed, starting from her chair. "Whatever is the matter?"

Charles stood and leaned over to pick up the dice and then leaned away to avoid being knocked down when Lizzy sped across the room and into Jane's arms.

"We must leave Pemberley immediately," Lizzy cried. "Make haste, make haste. Call for our carriage. We have to pack. Jeremy is collecting my art supplies."

"What has happened?" Charles demanded.

Lizzy gasped out her answer between deep, heaving breaths. "Mr. Darcy proposed." She swallowed hard. "I said no." *Oh, dear, what have I done?* "I—"

"Lizzy, you are teasing us," Jane said, grabbing her by the shoulders and shaking her a little. "You must have misunderstood. Mr. Darcy has not proposed! Not after so short a time. He could not have."

"He did, he did. And…and…" Lizzy managed to squeak out.

"You must calm yourself," Charles admonished kindly.

"You will make yourself ill."

Lizzy swallowed again and forcibly brought her breathing under control before she spoke again. "I am quite well, thank you. But we must leave here. I cannot stay at Pemberley now that I have refused Mr. Darcy. Surely, you see that? He is angry. Most angry. He has gone riding. Let us go before he returns."

"I can appreciate that seeing him again will be exceedingly uncomfortable," Jane acknowledged. She glanced at her husband and then back at her sister. "Would you have us depart without seeing Mr. Darcy and thanking him for his hospitality? He has been generous and kind. As has his sister and aunt. It distresses me to think of offering him this insult."

Lizzy wrenched herself away from Jane and paced, wringing her hands. "He knows. *He knows.*"

The color drained from Jane's cheeks. "How?" she asked. "Did Mr. Bissell break his word?"

"I cannot believe that he would," Charles objected. "Surely not."

"I do not know how he has discovered my secret, but he has." Lizzy folded her arms tightly around herself as though her stomach ached. "One of my sketches has gone missing from my sketch book. I think he took it."

"That is very bad," Charles said gravely. "What was the sketch of?"

"Him and Georgiana," Lizzy confessed.

"Lizzy!" Jane gasped in an awful voice. "How could you have sketched them?"

"I did not expect anyone to meddle with my sketches, did I?" Lizzy asked in wretched tones. "I wanted something to remember them by. Why should that be wrong? And…I am not sure…but he may have seen my chipmunk friend."

Jane moaned. "I have told you and told you not to keep drawing him."

"I know, I know."

"I expect Darcy took the sketch because he wanted an image of Georgiana," Charles said, turning to straighten up the backgammon pieces and dice. He scooped them into a velvet sack, flattened the sack so it fit inside the board, and then folded it shut, flipping the tiny hook that held it closed. "He loves her very much, you know."

Lizzy nodded distractedly. *Oh, good. He is packing.* "We will make our farewells to her and Mrs. McDougall. I pray that Mr. Darcy has gone riding for an exceedingly long time. I will not see him again."

"I do not like the furtive feeling of this type of a departure," Jane said, heaving a breath afterwards. "But I agree with you, we must leave before he discovers even more about your talent."

She looked at her husband, and Lizzy saw the entreaty in her gaze. Lizzy moved back to her sister's side, clasped her hand in both of hers and stared up at her amiable brother.

"Charles?" Lizzy said. "I know you have become friends with Mr. Darcy, and this must go much against the grain with you, but please, may we return to Netherfield?"

Charles pressed his lips together and thought before answering. Finally, he said, "I will write to him, expressing everything that is proper. Let us ring for our servants and help them with the packing. Graham will probably make me sit to one side while he does all the work and that is when I shall write our excuses."

"Thank you, Charles," Lizzy said, impulsively hugging him. "You are the best brother ever."

"And husband," Jane added before hastening over to the bell pull. She yanked on it. "Lizzy, off you go and summon Fiona."

Lizzy ran from the room and then into her own bedchamber. *We must be gone before he gets back. I cannot bear to see him again.*

∞

Darcy stalked into Pemberley House through a side door. He climbed a set of back stairs two at a time, clutching his riding gloves in one hand. He had only a half hour to dress before dinner. He would not go down smelling of horse sweat.

What a fool I have been to allow my pride to take over my reason, he thought. *I cannot expect Miss Bennet to love me all at once. My feelings are mine alone. I shall convince her to love me. And she is not going to do so if I smell and I act like a cantankerous bear.*

Darcy fully expected to find Booth awaiting his arrival, his evening dress laid out. His valet, though, was in the corridor outside his room, not inside it.

"I know I am late," Darcy said, holding up a hand to forestall a measured rebuke. He passed over his gloves and his hat. "We shall make it."

"Miss Georgiana has pushed back dinner, sir," Booth said, stepping toward the bedchamber door. He opened it, adding, "She wishes to speak to you first."

"There is no time for a *tête-à-tête*," Darcy said, entering the room at a sharp pace. The door closed behind him. He glanced back and saw that Booth had not entered with him. A voice caused him to swivel around to face the speaker.

"'Time is the wisest counselor of all,'" his sister, said, quoting Pericles. She rose from the armchair set before his fireplace. She had already changed her dress. "There is no rush."

Darcy frowned. His sister rarely came into his bedchamber. "What is amiss, Georgie? Are you still angry with me? I must wash and change. Can we talk after dinner?"

"As I said, there is no urgency." She pursed her lips and shook her head at him. "You have made a complete mull of it, Fitz. The Bingleys and Lizzy left three hours since. So, you see, we have no guests for dinner and you may wash and dress at your leisure."

Darcy, who had been walking across the room to where clean, steaming water awaited him in his washbasin, stopped. "What?" He turned to face her square on, his mind reeling. "What did you say?"

"The Bingleys and Lizzy left three hours since," Georgiana repeated. She put her fists on her hips and glowered at him. "What did you say to Lizzy? You must have insulted her for them to leave so suddenly. The Bingleys are far too forgiving to be injured by your poor behavior."

"I shall go after them," Darcy stated, turning toward the door.

"You cannot go riding *ventre à terre* after them. Consider how that would look to the servants. And, surely, Lizzy needs time to calm down. At least, do not leave until you have answered my question. Please, Fitz, what did you say?" Georgiana repeated forcibly. "I care for Lizzy. Why would she tear out of here as though she feared we would stop her from leaving? You must have said or done something. Did you have an argument?"

Darcy paused, half-way to the door. He clenched his stomach and stared up at the painted and embossed ceiling, seeing none of its beauty. He felt a hand on his arm and looked down into his sister's pleading countenance. Concern shone in her hazel-brown eyes.

"Please, tell me."

Darcy's frown deepened and he wondered if he looked as bleak as he felt. He sighed.

"I asked Miss Bennet to marry me," he confessed.

Georgiana ginned.

He shook his head. "She refused."

Blinking rapidly in surprise, his sister said, "You told her of your love and she refused you?"

"I…"

She narrowed her gaze. "*Do* you love her?"

Her fists were back on her hips.

"This is a highly inappropriate conversation."

Georgiana glared at him. "You thought it appropriate to talk to me about my feelings for Mr. Kearn. How is it inappropriate for you to talk to me about your feelings for Lizzy? Do not treat me like a child and do not close yourself off behind that wall of silence in which you wrap yourself. You may trust me with the truth." She took several deep breaths and finally restated her question. "Do you love Lizzy Bennet?"

Darcy replied to her impertinent question with a simple nod.

"And did you tell her you loved her?"

Darcy scraped his palm over his face, feeling the rough evening growth of hair on his cheeks.

"I am not…sure."

"How can you not be sure?" Georgiana asked, puzzled. She put her hand back on his arm and squeezed it. In a quiet voice, she probed further. "What *did* you tell her?"

Darcy swallowed. "I said I wanted to protect her."

"Protect her? Why should she need protecting? She has her sister and Mr. Bingley. And several uncles and a cousin, too. She is not unprotected."

He realized that his innocent young sister did not recognize the implication of his poor word choice in the same manner as Miss Bennet had. Georgiana took his words in the manner he had intended. He would have to explain to Georgiana if he wanted her to understand why Miss Bennet needed protection. However, there was no way to explain about her curious talent without giving a demonstration. He took his sister's hand.

"Come with me and I will show you."

Georgiana allowed him to lead her out of his bedchamber, past his unflappable valet, through the long empty corridors to his study. Thankfully, she remained silent for the entire distance. Once they entered his sanctum, he released her hand and moved around behind the desk. While he unlocked the drawer, he began his explanation with a warning.

"You must never, ever, tell anyone about this. Not even Kearn. This is Miss Bennet's secret to tell. Swear it."

Georgiana nodded solemnly. "I swear it. You may trust me."

"I do," he said, meeting her eyes.

She flushed with gratification.

Darcy withdrew the sketch, took one look at the paper, and passed it to his sister. Her fingers trembled slightly upon receipt of the image.

"It is a sketch of us," she said unnecessarily. "Lizzy did it, did she not? But, Fitz, why does your image appear so…so…desperate? Why would she draw you like this?" She looked up from the sketch and stared at him.

"She did not draw me like that," Darcy said, sitting with a thump. "When she drew me, I looked like I usually look."

"I do not understand. How can that be? Has she altered the original?"

"Georgie, the images change according to our moods. Study your own image."

Georgiana frowned and obediently examined her expression. "I look worried…and a little perplexed. I remember this day. It was the day you arrived with our guests. I did not look like this…I am sure of it. I was happy to see you. And pleased to meet new people."

"Do you feel worried and perplexed?" he asked.

She moved to one of the chairs facing the desk and sat. "I do."

"After you and I argued about Kearn, your image looked determined," he revealed. "Frankly, I thought you would be weeping. I was relieved when I saw your expression of resolve."

Georgiana glowered. "I am not certain I like that you can see my moods every time you look at this sketch."

Darcy shrugged. "I am determined not to use it as an emotional barometer, I assure you." He leveled a keen gaze upon her. "Is that all you have to say, though? Are you not amazed? Astonished? Can you not see how this talent of Miss Bennet's, if it becomes common knowledge, would ruin her?"

Georgiana nodded. "I am, of course. Astonished and amazed, I mean." She thought for a moment and then asked, "Does something happen to every sketch or painting she does? Surely it cannot, or else everyone would already know about Lizzy's talent."

"Though I do not know the reason of it, I suspect that the danger must be more significant when she paints or draws portraits of adults," Darcy mused. "Which is likely the reason why she would not paint you."

"What about Mr. Pitt? Has anything untoward occurred to it?"

Darcy shook his head. "Miss Bennet stressed that the cockerel must be regarded as a pet. She paints pet portraits for the *haute ton.* They must be safe." He then told her about imagining that he saw the tiny sketch of the chipmunk move around on the page. This caused her eyes to widen.

"How…extraordinary. And when she paints landscapes?" Georgiana asked.

Darcy cocked his head to one side and made a splayed hand gesture that silently admitted that he did not know. "I have only seen one significant piece—Fountains Abbey. It was magnificent." His frown deepened. "You know, Georgie, at one glance there had been a bird in the lower corner and in the next, the bird was gone and I thought I had imagined it."

What would have happened to the painting of Pemberley House? Will I ever know? I must get her back!

"Troubling," Georgiana acknowledged. She examined the sketch again. "It has changed once more." Placing it gently on his desk, she stared him in the eyes. "Having this talent must be terribly difficult for Lizzy. Being required to constantly hide the curious aspect of her talent, I mean. Surely, her parents must have known. How did they react, I wonder? Did they want her to stop doing her art? Was she punished when a painting or a sketch changed?"

Darcy's scowl deepened. "I hope not."

"As do I," Georgiana replied. "The poor woman. Always frightened. Continually on tenterhooks. Yet, I must admire her determination not to be a drain on her sister. Foolishness, really, because clearly Mrs. Bingley adores her, and Mr. Bingley loves her, too. Not romantically, of course, but as a beloved sister. And, living on her own will put Lizzy in *more* danger, not less. She will be regarded as an oddity, I think. And oddities in a village garner attention. I have seen it here, in Lambton."

Darcy picked up a glass paperweight, and then placed it

back on the desk, an inch further to the right. He grimaced. "It is what I fear."

"So, this is why you forgot to tell Lizzy that you loved her?"

Darcy heaved a sigh. "Yes." He clasped his hands on the desk and hung his head. "I do not know if I can simply permit her to drive away."

"Permit?" Georgiana repeated sharply.

Darcy met her gaze. She had one eyebrow raised. Her expression at that moment resembled Miss Bennet's so much that he inwardly cringed.

In a whisper, as though he were confessing something both wondrous and wrenching, he revealed his inner self to his sister. "I cannot bear it."

Georgiana straightened in her chair and dropped her chin so her gaze penetrated through the haze of his loss.

"This is what I think you should do," she said briskly. "I think you should wait a week before y—"

"A week!" Darcy cried, retreating back in his chair to glare at her. "A whole week?"

She glowered at him. "You want me to wait *years*."

Darcy leapt to his feet. "This is hardly the same case."

Georgiana stood, her cheeks tinged pink, and wagged a finger at him. "I think you need to wait so that Lizzy has a chance to think about you, about what she is missing by refusing you. Then, you can follow her. Do not expect to stay at the Bingley's, though. Find a nice inn."

"I am not such a ninnyhammer as to expect Bingley to put me up," Darcy said harshly. "And I do not need a slip of a girl giving me advice on how to court a lady."

Georgiana put her nose in the air and sniffed. "You are not doing so well at courting for a man of your advanced age, are you? I would think you would welcome some female advice, particularly from someone with your best interests at heart."

She turned on her heel and left him, saying at the last moment, her back to him, "Dinner will be served soon, so I suggest you change."

Darcy locked the damning sketch in his desk drawer and headed to his bedchamber to change.

Under normal circumstances, the counsel of a sister more than ten years his junior would hardly impact him. But this time, he wondered if she might not be right. She *was* a female. He admitted to himself that he had bungled the entire proposal so badly that perhaps Miss Bennet did require time to calm herself.

Could she not trust me? Is she so afraid of anyone knowing about her talent—of me *knowing about her talent—that she would rather live alone or with her sister rather than be wed to me?*

Darcy attempted to shrug off that uncomfortable thought. He entered his bedchamber to find Booth just as he had expected to find him before. His valet approached and handed him a letter.

"I found this on the mantel, sir," Booth said. "After you and Miss Georgiana left."

Darcy took the letter and broke the seal, unfolded it and began to read while Booth began undressing him.

"*Darcy,*

Thank you for all your kind attentions, which began when we first met in Yorkshire, to the present. I am delighted that we have become friends. The thought of concealing important information from a friend naturally causes one's feelings to revolt. I gather that you have discovered our great secret. Its significance cannot be overstated—which I am certain you appreciate—and therefore you will forgive me for holding it so close to my breast. I know there have been a few moments when my own loose tongue has caused your curiosity to rise, and so I beg your forgiveness for my easy ways."

Darcy switched the letter to another hand so Booth could tug off his jacket and waistcoat from that side of his body. *His loose tongue? Yes, indeed. There were a few times when he almost revealed all. My dear Miss Bennet does not have the best protector in her brother-in-law in spite of his clear affection.* Darcy switched the letter to the other hand again to continue reading.

"Knowledge of this secret has put you in a difficult position. Your honor has led you to make an offer for my dear sister, Elizabeth. Allow me to know her character better than you, sir, and believe me when I say the manner of your offer greatly offended her and caused a level of fear in her that I have rarely been a witness to. Lizzy has a lively disposition and has a strong sense of the ridiculous, but your offer of 'protection', though misunderstood, could only make her furious. Her fury, as I hope you have realized, was fueled by her fear."

Grimacing, Darcy had to confess to himself that he had not given enough credence to her fear. Only his own. For her. Until his talk with Georgiana, he had thought Miss Bennet did not care enough for him, yet, to agree to an alliance.

"Kindly step out of your pantaloons, sir," Booth ordered.

Darcy obeyed. Then, he had to set the letter down on the bed while his valet tugged off his shirt. He immediately picked the missive up again, determined to finish before he set it aside to wash.

"However, do not despair. I can tell that Lizzy holds you in high regard. She has not expressed her true feelings to me, but will no doubt tell my dearest Jane. I have watched her with you, hoping that she might have found the gentleman to whom she might give her heart. I have seen much between you that is encouraging. I have not given up. Nor should you. The long drive to our home will provide Lizzy with many hours of reflection.

"When you come after her, as I expect you are planning to do, pray seek me out first. I have something marvellous to show you. I know I can rely on your discretion. You need not reply to this letter unless you have decided to give Lizzy up, which I hope you do not mean to do. I will expect you in ten days' time. There is an excellent inn in Meryton—The Golden Fleece. I shall tell them to expect you.

Your Hopeful Friend,
Charles Bingley.

Darcy folded the letter and set it on the nightstand. Both Georgiana and Bingley counselled patience. Well, he would be patient.

Somehow.

Chapter Twenty-Four

Netherfield Park, Hertfordshire...

Lizzy sunk onto her own bed, her shoulders slumping, and heaved a mighty sigh. *Thank the good Lord that I am home at last.*

Somehow, the drive home seemed to have taken an age. Every moment she had expected Mr. Darcy to catch up with them and demand further explanation about her feelings for him—about her refusal of his suit. She had begged Charles to use only the quietest posting inns, hoping to avoid any chance of encountering Mr. Darcy. He had complied without any fuss and so Mr. Darcy had not caught up with them.

Saying good-bye to Georgiana had been heart-rending. The poor girl had no idea why they had to leave so abruptly. Their explanation that they were homesick had sounded like a lamentable invention even to their own ears. Mrs. McDougall had looked searchingly at her and then said everything that was gracious and generous, setting an example for her niece. They had not even asked about the abandoned commission to paint Pemberley House. Lizzy was grateful for this unanticipated kindness.

A knock sounded at the door, and Anna, the young Irish maid who did for her, entered the chamber and gave a small curtsy.

"Welcome home, miss," Anna said. "Sure, an you must've had a grand time of it, so brown as ye are."

Lizzy nodded.

"Ye look done in, though," Anna said, frowning. She shoved a stray red curl up under her mob cap. "I'm thinkin' ye'd like to lie down fer a while, ye would. Let's get ye out o'those travellin' clothes of yers and get ye tucked into bed fer an hour or so. Sure, an I can unpack while yer at dinner, I can."

Lizzy almost objected, but could not muster the energy to do so. Soon she was lying beneath the cool sheets and closing her eyes.

She slept and dreamed.

Of Mr. Darcy.

She dreamed that his strong arms were wrapped around her and that he was stroking her hair, which lay loose about her shoulders.

"You will become accustomed to not painting, my dear," he said. "As lady of the manor, you will be busy with good works. Georgiana will show you the way of it. And when our children arrive, you will have much to occupy yourself. You will not even miss your talent."

Not miss my talent? What is his meaning? I cannot reason it out. He cannot be saying that I must stop painting? Impossible.

"My love, my talent is part of me," Lizzy argued, fighting to keep her voice measured and reasonable. "I could never stop sketching and painting."

"It is too dangerous," Mr. Darcy said in a gentle voice that was, nevertheless, wrapped around a steel core.

"But, if I am careful, there is no danger," she pointed out, trying to draw away from him so she could see his expression. His arms tightened, keeping her from moving. Panic surged through Lizzy. She felt trapped.

"There will always be danger."

Lizzy struggled in his arms. "No!"

"It is precisely because you think there is no danger that I have destroyed all your art supplies. There is not a pencil in the house, either. And you will only use ink under my supervision."

She gasped. "I shall order more."

"No one will take your order," he stated in a hard voice. "I am the master of Pemberley. This is for your own good, my dearest Elizabeth. I shall keep you safe. I shall protect you."

No more painting?

No more drawing?

No more painting!

No more drawing!

No more...no more...no more...

Lizzy reared up in her bed, panting and wild-eyed.

I cannot love a man who keeps me from painting, was her immediate thought.

Tears leaked out and drifted down her cheeks. Lizzy sniffed and used the sheet to wipe the salty tracks away. Her love of Mr. Darcy had hardly managed to coalesce in the far reaches of her heart before he had asked her to marry him. Not because he loved her. Only to protect her.

Lizzy scowled. "I do not need his protection," she whispered to the empty room. "I will be more careful."

Determined to prove herself, she climbed out of bed and padded across to her art supply cabinet. She took a key from around her neck and unlocked it. From one of the shelves, she retrieved a fresh sketch pad and chose a *porte-crayon* from another. It already held a piece of sharpened charcoal. She locked the cabinet once more.

"I shall draw him," Lizzy murmured. She moved to the window seat, sat, drew her knees up to rest the pad against, and opened the pad.

Using quick, sharp lines that spoke of the force of his presence and the strength of his personality, she quickly sketched Mr. Darcy, concentrating with all her might.

It is just an image. Lord, I need this to be just an image. Nothing more. I do not want it to change. I do not want...I do not want...I do not...

She paused to consider the drawing. With a strangled, lady-like curse, she tore the page from the pad and crushed it into a ball. Then, she threw it across the room.

Immediately, she began another sketch. She put Mr. Darcy on a horse this time, willing the horse to remain merely a horse and for the rider to remain merely a man. When her first flush of deft movements ended, she paused again.

This one will be better.

It was not.

The paper ball joined the other one.

What is wrong with my art? Why do my sketches look lifeless and dull?

I shall draw my chipmunk. He is always lively.

Lizzy sketched the little animal, giving him an acorn to hold and putting him on a branch. She finished and held the drawing away from her, examining it critically. She grimaced, baring her teeth in frustration. *A child could have drawn this better!*

The chipmunk sketch, uncrumpled, floated unsatisfyingly until it landed on the floor with the other two disappointing drawings.

A church this time. St. Stephen's church in Lambton. Or something like.

The square tower, with finials atop each corner, came into shape with practiced ease. Then, the belfry, the nave, and the transepts came after. A graveyard surrounded the church, old gravestones listing to the side. A path wound through the graves to the narthex.

*Better. But...*Lizzy gritted her teeth. *There is nothing here! The image evokes nothing—no emotion, no sentiment!*

She ripped out the page and threw it down on the floor with the rest. A dozen more joined the other failures.

What is wrong with me?

Lizzy tried once more—Mr. Darcy as the subject again. This time, she did not rush. She worked cautiously, believing desperately that she could draw safely without losing that certain something that made her work astonishing.

Inwardly, in that spot where she kept her resolve, an ember struggled to live. She fought with it, feeling as though spiders crawled over her skin and that she could not breathe without the spark.

Though she longed to be a 'normal' artist, and exhausted by her efforts, Lizzy could not help but rebel against the dying of the spark—that spark that enlivened her art. The excited contentment she usually felt when she created could not be dampened down without causing harm to her soul.

Relenting at last, Lizzy closed her eyes and kept drawing, permitting the ember to glow. The dreadful sensation of spiders on her skin left her. Peace returned.

"My talent is a gift," Lizzy whispered. "My talent is a gift."

When she lifted the charcoal from the page after the last stroke, she opened her eyes and gazed down at the newest sketch of Mr. Darcy.

He was smiling.

And her heart lurched.

He is so handsome.

His arms were folded and he was leaning on a drystone wall, grinning out at the viewer. He was dressed for riding, but in this sketch, he wore a cap. She found this rather interesting, having never seen him wear one before. His usual head attire was a curly-brimmed beaver.

Lizzy stood and returned the sketch pad to the art cabinet. She did not close the pad, however, for tonight, before she went to bed, she would look upon his image again, torturing herself with what her talent had cost her. She picked up the failed drawings and set only the two images of Mr. Darcy on the bed to take down and show Jane and Charles. She tore up the other drawings and threw them in the waste bin just as Anna returned to her room to assist her with dressing for dinner.

Gowned that night in midnight-blue, split over an underdress of blue and white striped muslin, Lizzy entered the Periwinkle drawing room. The Netherfield Park inhabitants gathered before their evening meal in this intimate space. The walls had been plastered and colored periwinkle-blue. Classical paintings of Grecian temples and frolicking Greek ladies adorned them.

Jane and Charles stood before the long windows overlooking the bow lake where a family of swans had taken up residence this year. Charles glanced over his shoulder at her arrival and waved her over.

"Come and look, Lizzy," he said, waving down at the lake. "There are still seven signets. My, they have grown while we were away."

Lizzy, clasping the smoothed-out failed sketches of Mr. Darcy in her hand at her side, obediently observed the mother swan gliding along the smooth surface, her babies behind her. "They are almost half the size of their parents. Where is the father?"

"Over there, in the reeds," Jane said, pointing.

"I shall paint them before they fly off. Have we been feeding them?" Lizzy asked.

"Only vegetable scraps from the kitchen," Jane promised. "Cook looks after it herself. They like lettuce and potatoes, she said. They come right to her when she goes out. The signets like the carrot scrapings."

"Then they are pets," Charles said with some satisfaction. He smiled at Lizzy and noticed the crumple-damaged pages in her hand. "What is this?"

"Pray, take a look at my efforts to draw *without* my talent," Lizzy said, handing one of the sketches to Charles and another to Jane.

Her sister and brother-in-law stared at the failed sketches.

"Who is this supposed to be?" Jane asked, frowning. She held the one with the horse. "It is not Mr. Darcy, surely?"

"I think mine is Darcy," Charles said, puzzlement in his voice. He peered at the sketch in his wife's hand and showed her his. "Yes, they are both supposed to be him."

"They are awful. Most awful," Lizzy stated. "Why should I take the trouble to paint or sketch if this is the result? It would be better if I stopped all together."

Charles immediately protested. "On no account!"

Jane took both the sketches and tore them up, saying,

"Dearest, I second my husband's objections. Remember the parable of the three talents? Two servants took their talents and magnified them. The third did nothing with his."

"The talent in that parable is money, though," Charles pointed out.

Jane smiled gently at him. "You are right, my dear, but I believe the parable is meant for all of us, for all types of 'talents'."

Her husband immediately nodded.

Looking back at Lizzy, Jane continued, "I know I have always been fearful on your behalf, and I am still, but you cannot bury your 'talent'. There is so much joy in every one of your paintings—even the paintings that age, like the miniatures in Charlotte's locket. Will you deny us the joy we feel when we view them?"

Lizzy shook her head. "I cannot. I cannot deny you, or myself." She rubbed her hands up and down her arms, remembering the sensation of spiders crawling over her skin. "You cannot imagine the feeling that came upon me when I tried to draw without my talent." She shivered.

Jane hugged her, the torn sketches in one hand. "Everything will be fine, dearest. You shall see."

Nodding, Lizzy hugged her back. "I am going to paint Pemberley House. I shall start tomorrow."

"Are you certain?" Charles asked, his eyes wide with surprise. "Shall I arrange for a large canvas to be stretched?"

"I have one," Lizzy said, withdrawing from her sister's arms. "It is not as large as the one I was to paint…before…but it will be easier for the cartage company to take. And to frame."

"We will send it in a box and let Darcy frame it to his liking," Charles said, smiling a little.

"A good plan," Jane said gently. "Shall we go in? I heard the gong."

Later that night, Lizzy unlocked the cabinet and took out the sketch. She tilted it to one side so she could see it better in the light of the branch of candles on the mantle. A *chapeau de bras* now adorned Mr. Darcy's head. Everything else in the sketch appeared identical. The absurdity of a sketch where head gear changed made her smile.

Tomorrow, I will begin the commission. Not because I want the money, but as a gift.

∞

Pemberley House, Derbyshire…

Six days into his ten days of waiting, and the day before he was to leave for Meryton, Darcy rose from his seat at the dining table, startling the ladies.

"Shall we take a walk around the lake instead of spending this beautiful evening indoors?" he asked, looking around the table. "You too, Kearn."

The estate manager nodded.

His aunt took one look at his face and smiled. "What a wonderful suggestion. Georgiana and I must change our slippers, however, for walking shoes."

They assembled on the terrace. Instead of offering his arm to his sister, Darcy held it out to his aunt, leaving Kearn to offer his to Georgiana. Darcy noticed the glowing look exchanged between the pair and was satisfied. He and his aunt led the way, strolling down to the lake path from the terrace.

"You were right, Fitzwilliam," his aunt said. "It is much too beautiful an evening to spend it all indoors."

Frogs sang and a song thrush sounded from the edge of the home wood. A light breeze rustled the reeds that lined lake. Only a slight murmur of voices could be heard from behind them where Georgiana and Kearn had fallen back some.

"I have put this off for some time, but I believe the time has come for me to, perhaps, warn you," Aunt Sophia said in a low voice. "Your sister and Mr.—"

"I am aware, madam," Darcy said stiffly. Then, repentant of his tone, he patted her hand where it rested on his arm. "Georgiana has not discussed our arrangement with you?"

"What arrangement?" she demanded, frowning. She glanced behind her as though making certain the other strollers had not heard. In a quieter voice, she repeated her question. “What arrangement have you made with Georgiana? Does it have to do with the reason we are leaving for London so soon?”

“It does. I am departing for Hertfordshire tomorrow. Mr. Kearn will make every arrangement for your journey. You will leave in ten days. He has agreed to escort you in my stead. I will join you in London as soon as I may.”

“I am sure he will be an efficient and enjoyable escort, but are you certain you wish for him and Georgiana to be so much in each other’s company? There is danger there,” his aunt cautioned. “He is a fine man, no doubt, but Georgiana can expect to receive offers from gentlemen of fortune and influence. What does Mr. Kearn have to his credit?”

“He has connections.”

“Connections?” she scoffed softy. “What could they be, pray?”

“His grandmother was Countess von Krier of Luxembourg.”

Aunt Sophia snorted. “A dead countess. A dead, *foreign*, countess. What aid or introduction can she give him? None.”

“Admiral Kearn, his father, however, is not dead.”

His aunt shook her head. “An admiral is a fine thing, but if you permit your sister to marry Mr. Kearn, she is taking a step down from her current position in society. You cannot deny it.”

Darcy stiffened. “She will always be *my* sister and her children will be *my* nieces and nephews.”

“As you say,” his aunt said in a placating voice. “What *is* the exact arrangement you have made with Georgiana?”

“I have given my word that if she participates in the upcoming London seasons, and remains constant, I will permit Mr. Kearn to pay his addresses.” He added as a caveat, “If he, also, remains constant.”

“Who is he to meet, here? The vicar’s daughter is too young—even younger than Georgiana.”

“He might fall in love with you, Aunt Sophia,” Darcy

quipped.

"*I* am too old for *him*," she retorted. "Seven years older, I believe. Besides, I will be in London most of the next nine months."

"You will be home for Christmas and three months afterward before the season begins again in the spring."

"I thought the plan was for us to be home for only a month at Christmas?" Aunt Sophia asked, frowning.

"We must observe Georgiana and Kearn," Darcy explained, maintaining a reasonable tone. "We cannot do so if they are never together. I must be absolutely certain of their hearts."

"And your own heart? You said you are leaving for Hertfordshire tomorrow. You will see Miss Bennet?"

"I will."

"You are going to press your suit?"

Darcy nodded. He spied a weasel against a fallen log dangling out over the lake. He pointed at it. "Look."

"I see it. Pray, do not change the subject," his aunt ordered. "You are as foolish as Georgiana. Miss Bennet is a charming woman, but she is no more your equal than Mr. Kearn is your sister's."

"When did you become so high in the instep?" Darcy harrumphed and continued before she could respond. "Miss Bennet is the lady I love. There can be no other. I shall count myself blessed, indeed, if she agrees to be my wife."

His aunt remained silent for a half-dozen steps, but finally said, "If you marry into that family, you will be related to George Wickham."

"I am aware," Darcy said tightly.

"Is Georgiana?"

"She is."

"Well," Aunt Sophia said, clearly dumbfounded.

"You sound more and more like Aunt Catherine," Darcy charged.

His aunt took a deep, affronted breath. "You take that back."

Darcy shook his head and found relief in a bark of laughter.

"I am *nothing* like your mother's sister," Aunt Sophia stated emphatically. "I pity her husband."

"You never met him."

Aunt Sophia sniffed. "Still, dying must have been a relief to him."

Darcy laughed again. "You are outrageous. Perhaps you will find someone to marry when you are in London."

His aunt clicked her tongue, but he could tell his words had pleased her.

"I will be too busy fighting off the fortune hunters."

"That will be my duty," Darcy said in a hard voice. "I have been cultivating a stare."

Aunt Sophia snorted in a perfectly lady-like way. "Medusa had nothing on you, my boy."

Darcy grinned.

"What shall I do when Georgiana marries?" she mused.

"You will always have a home at Pemberley," Darcy promptly assured her.

"Thank you," she said simply. "That relieves my mind of one worry."

"If you cannot like Miss Bennet, then I will increase the size of your apartments, or, if you prefer, I must have a cottage that you could have if you prefer more independence. Somewhere. We will have to find you a distant cousin to come and live with you to lend you countenance."

"Lend me countenance?" Aunt Sophia scoffed. "As though I needed it." She mused for a moment and then said, "I *do* like Miss Bennet," she said, tilting her head to one side. "That is one point in her favor. And her painting is exquisite. I like the Bingleys as well. I understand he is looking about for an estate to purchase. We must help him find one in Derbyshire. *If* you can convince Miss Bennet that she should marry your sorry self."

Darcy looked out over the lake. *Yes, if I can convince Miss Bennet to marry me.*

Chapter Twenty-Five

Netherfield Park, Hertfordshire...

Lizzy stood back, her thumbnail between her teeth, watching Jane and Charles' reaction to her painting. They had left Derbyshire seven days ago and she had been working on this landscape of Pemberley House for the last four days. She had decided to locate the house on a slight rise so that the viewer appeared to be looking up at it. The drive crossed the park from the right, through the magnificent trees that surrounded it. Because of that angle, the side of the ballroom could be seen at the back of the house, where it stuck out somewhat from the side plane of that wing, windows shining with candlelight.

The six Palladian columns shone with an inner glow, as though proud of their magnificence. The windows glinted. The stone walls displayed strength and endurance.

"You have painted it at night." Charles tipped his head to one side. "Interesting. I did not realize you meant to do that."

"I did not know, either," Lizzy admitted. His first observation had been unnecessary, but so like Charles that it did not annoy her.

"The twilight-blue is…compelling," Jane murmured, pointing at the profoundly deep-blue that marked the sky where a moon hung heavy, bright and full over the home wood tree tops. She shook her head. "Another marvel, dearest."

"It is remarkably atmospheric," Charles commented. "And

evocative, too. I feel as though I should be there. At the ball."

"At the ball?" Jane blinked at him and then stared back at the painting.

"Look at all the carriages," he said, waving to the vehicles lined up in the shadow of the great house. "And lights shine in the ballroom windows."

His wife nodded, smiling gently. "Of course. You are quite observant, husband." She reluctantly tore her gaze away from the image and addressed Lizzy. "How clever of you to use an event as the focus of your work, dearest."

"The fire pillars are a nice touch," Charles said, pointing to the half-dozen pillars supporting lit braziers. "Oh, dear," he murmured. "Did either of you see the flames move?"

"You are imagining things," Lizzy said sharply, pushing between them so she could focus all her attention on the flames. After several long moments where everyone held their breaths, Lizzy whispered. "No, thank heavens."

"The timing?" Charles suggested.

"Perhaps." She sighed. And the flames moved as though a wind had blown across them. Lizzy jumped back. "Dear Lord. Jane, you try."

Jane, her expression solemn, blew softly on the image.

Charles pointed. "There. Again. Just slightly, though. I am going to really blow hard, now."

Lizzy pressed her lips together. Occasionally, her brother-in-law took entirely too much delight in the vagaries of her art.

With cheeks expanded like the wolf in a fairy tale, Charles heaved a breath and blew onto the painting. The fires danced as though a gale had risen. As soon as he stopped blowing, the flames settled and did not move.

"As long as Mr. Darcy hangs this on the wall too high for anyone to blow on it, then I cannot see why you should not give it to him," Jane said, smiling with obvious relief.

"And, the glass should stop the influence of a draft." Lizzy felt annoyed that the painting she thought safe had been discovered to be just barely safe. Under the right conditions.

Charles shrugged. "Did he ever say where he meant to

hang a landscape of Pemberley House?"

Lizzy shook her head. "I am not certain he means to hang this painting. As a watercolor, he may choose to store it flat in a box, away from any light, with other watercolors in his collection. Then, if he shows it to someone, they will be very close to the picture, indeed. They might easily breathe on it."

"I would count it a shame if he does not hang your work, though," Charles said, frowning.

Jane pondered the painting for a moment and then said, "If Mr. Darcy chooses to hang it—and he is one who could afford to do so—Lizzy is right to surmise that it will be under glass."

"True," Charles said heartily. He touched Lizzy's arm. "I am so pleased that your painting will probably be viewed by more than an elect few."

Touched, Lizzy flushed. "Thank you."

"Is it dry enough to send?" Jane asked.

"I should like to leave it for a couple of days to cure," Lizzy replied. "And then I will use beeswax to seal it—in case he means to hang it."

"Excellent," Charles said, clapping his hands together once.

Lizzy frowned at him. *Why is he so pleased by that answer?*

∞

Pemberley House, Derbyshire…

Georgiana joined her brother on the front step. He tugged on his gloves and looked down at her. His haggard expression told her how well he had been sleeping. He would be better now that he had something to do. Inaction was anathema to him.

"I am uncertain of my reception," he admitted to her in a low voice. "And so I do not know how long I shall be away."

"Aunt Sophia explained that Mr. Kearn is to be our escort to London," Georgiana said, moving close enough to place a gentle hand on his arm. "I am certain you will be successful in wooing Miss Bennet, Fitz." She snorted in a light, teasing manner and reminded him, "But, *do not* tell her you wish to protect her. Every woman wishes to know that she is *loved*."

"I *do* love her," Fitz said in a soft, earnest voice. "I want to cherish and love her for the remainder of our lives. And for longer, if God wills it."

Georgiana hugged his arm. "Good luck, brother."

He hugged her, then, and whispered, "You are the best of sisters, Georgie."

"I am rather fond of you, too," she said with a tender laugh.

Hertfordshire…

Darcy stepped down from his chaise at the side entrance to The Golden Fleece in Meryton. He moved back to look up at the inn from the corner. Half-timbered in black and white, with a base of red brick, the building consisted of two floors, except for a wing with three floors. Bay windows stuck out invitingly from every storey along the front. A large hanging sign, decorated with a carving of Jason holding the golden fleece of Chrysomallos, creaked a little in the light breeze.

Booth approached. "I shall procure some rooms, sir."

Darcy nodded and followed him into the entrance hallway. A busy taproom to the right held a number of guests, some already enjoying their evening meal. The smell of lamb stew wafted to him and his stomach grumbled.

The portly landlord hurried out of the taproom, ready to welcome his new guests. As soon as Booth mentioned Darcy's name, the middle-aged innkeeper beamed at him and then bowed to Darcy.

"We've been waitin' for you, we have," he said. "Acer's the name. I've a nice private parlor set aside fer you, and two bedchambers. There are rooms in the stables for your groom and driver, too. Mr. Bingley will be that glad that you've arrived jist as he said you would. I'm to send Jem-the-ostler up to the Park to let Mr. Bingley know."

Darcy reached inside his coat, removed his case, opened it with a flick of his thumb, and removed an elegant card. "Have him give my card to Mr. Bingley's butler. I will not have Jem gossiping about my business in the stables at Netherfield."

"Yes, sir. Jem is not a gabbing man. He'll go and come straight back, he will." After that reassurance, the landlord led them up the stairs.

Before Darcy finished his evening repast, he had his reply. He unfolded the stiff note and moved over to the window to read it by the last rays of the setting sun.

"I have been expecting your arrival and am so pleased that you have followed my suggestion and waited. I am even more hopeful than I expressed in my missive of a week since. The ladies are visiting their good friend, Charlotte Collins, tomorrow morning. They mean to leave by ten of the clock and will stay at Longbourn for several hours at the very least. If you could make your way here in the morning, by half-ten, then I have something to show you that will be to your advantage. And to Lizzy's, I do not doubt. Pray, have a little more patience.

Yrs., etc., Bingley."

Darcy refolded the letter, feeling a mixture of emotions. Hope. Trepidation. Anxiousness. Impatience.

And humility.

Mostly humility.

He had assumed that his wealth and position would make any woman jump at the chance to marry him. That had certainly not been the case with his Miss Bennet. She had not cared a jot about anything he had offered. What would she have said if he had offered his heart, as well? *As I should have done.* He cringed at his stupid pride, having gradually realized that he had wanted her to admit that she loved him before he declared himself. *Foolishness.*

He tucked the letter back into his pocket and wondered at Bingley's secretiveness.

What will he show me?

The next morning, he hired a hack from the landlord and rode to Netherfield Park. From a discreet vantage point, he watched the barouche, carrying, he supposed, Mrs. Bingley and Miss Bennet away from the house. Darcy had to restrain himself from rushing after her and declaring his love to her that minute.

Once he could proceed without detection, he cantered up to Bingley's front steps. He must have been on the lookout for him, because Bingley hurried through the front door the moment Darcy dismounted.

"Welcome, welcome," Bingley said, smiling broadly and holding out his hand as he hastened down the stairs. Darcy shook it. "Come in." He glanced around, spied Renquist on the landing, and waved the butler forward. "Take Mr. Darcy's gloves and hat. Please."

"I hope you know that I was about to do that, sir," the man said with a bow to their guest.

Darcy climbed the steps and gave his gloves, hat, and crop to the tall man whom he recognised from his previous visit.

"Do you remember me?" he asked the servant.

Renquist bowed again. "Of course, sir. I see that you found my master."

"Indeed."

Bingley beamed. "And it is a good thing that you did, too. Come, do you require refreshments?"

Darcy shook his head.

To his butler, Bingley said, "Lay on tea and victuals in my study in an hour and a half. We should have worked up an appetite by then."

"Sir."

"Follow me," Bingley said, waving Darcy into the house. "Hurry. We may not have much time."

Frowning, Darcy obeyed him, following him up the stairs.

"I do not expect Jane or Lizzy any time soon, but I have much to show you before they return. Then, we shall partake of a hearty repast in order to gird our loins, so to speak."

"For battle?" Darcy asked, puzzled. "What is it that you have to show me?"

Bingley paused in his ascent, glanced around to be certain no one could overhear him, Darcy presumed, before he leaned closer and whispered, “Lizzy’s gallery.”

Darcy blinked at him. Bingley nodded.

“You shall see,” he promised, and then turned around and climbed the stairs two at a time as though he could not wait to arrive at the gallery.

His host led him down a long corridor, lined with paintings that Darcy had no trouble in assigning to artists other than Miss Bennet. No windows illuminated the space. Instead, candles in wall sconces provided their only light, making the passage appear oddly eerie. They stopped before a wide, unassuming door.

“Fortunately,” Bingley was saying as he fit a key to the lock, “this house had a double drawing room that faced north on this floor, which we turned into a gallery. Even so, we keep the shutters closed except when we enter to view Lizzy’s paintings. They are too precious to permit light to damage.”

He threw open the door and waved his guest forward. Darcy entered, gazing wonderingly about, glimpsing free-standing walls built in an orderly fashion throughout the large space. The shutters on the windows had been thrown open to light the gallery.

There were paintings on every wall. Small ones. Medium-sized ones. Large ones. Long ones. Narrow ones. And, they appeared to contain every subject.

Just as he was about to approach them for a better look, he heard the key turn in the lock behind him. Darcy glanced over his shoulder. Bingley approached Darcy, pocketing the key.

“To protect Lizzy, no one is allowed inside,” Bingley explained to his friend. “Not even servants. Jane and Lizzy dust in here.” He looked around, an amazed expression on his wide-eyed face. “No one except family, of course. Well, not Wickham—you know he cannot be trusted. No one, not even Lydia, has told him Lizzy’s secret. She can be exceedingly flighty, our Lydia, but not about this. If Wickham ever found out Lizzy’s secret, we would doubtless have to kill him. That duty would fall to us.”

“It would be my pleasure,” Darcy said grimly.

"I thought you might feel that way." Bingley indicated the nearest work of art. "Let us examine some of my favorites."

Darcy joined him, holding his breath in anticipation. Once standing before the work, he sighed in out-and-out delight.

The first painting they examined proved to be a night scene of a tall lighthouse on a promontory. The sea, dark blueish-green and storm-tossed, broke across the bottom of the white and red striped structure. The golden light produced by the lantern illuminated a sloop, just barely seen across the water. In the foreground, a path led to a separate stone house set back from the cliff edge.

"I am constantly dumbfounded by the skill and artistry of Miss Bennet's work," Darcy confessed in an awed voice. "I shall soon have a paucity of superlatives in which to describe them."

"I understand," Bingley said, pure delight in his voice. "When Lizzy finished this one and presented it to us for review, both Jane and I thought that all we had to do was wait and we would see the light rotate." He folded his arms and stared at the painting. "Or that the waves would move. Or that the sloop would crash. However, this painting is a perfect example of how the result of Lizzy's talent cannot be predicted."

Darcy looked away from the painting to Bingley's face and raised his eyebrows. "What happened?"

"Nothing happened, surprisingly. We sent for a frame, mounted the painting, and still nothing out of the ordinary occurred." Bingley sighed. "Lizzy was cautiously thrilled. Finally, she said, she had painted an image that was just an image."

"She was mistaken?"

Bingley nodded. He waved at the painting. "What can you smell?"

"Smell?" Darcy asked, frowning. He instinctively breathed deeper and then his eyes widened. "Oh, my. It is the sea. I *smell* the sea…"

His friend nodded. "It is quite remarkable. Once, I thought

I could feel the sea-spray on my face, but I may have been imagining it."

"But, surely, this painting could have been hung in another part of the house?" Darcy suggested. "No one would know from whence the smell came."

"Not our guests, no," Bingley agreed. "But the servants would have to dust it and sooner or later, they would notice."

Darcy shook his head and inwardly sighed on Miss Bennet's behalf. Bingley moved on and he followed.

"This one is charming," his friend said, indicating a wide, long canvas, painted in oils.

The scene was of a barnyard inhabited by various animals. A pink sow—a Welsh white, Darcy thought—and a group of her piglets played in a mud hole. Chickens pecked at the ground. A heavy brown horse, in harness, watched over the group, a calico cat perched on the rail beside him. White geese swam in the pond in the background. The image appeared to be the ideal, the quintessential farm scene that dwelt in the heart of city residents, who knew nothing about their country cousins.

"Ah, the sow has had her piglets," Bingley said, pointing at them. He counted under his breath. "…nine, ten. Ten this time."

"This time?" Darcy asked, hearing dazed emotions reflected in his voice.

"Yes. The number always varies. Lizzy painted a sow and a few months later, piglets arrived. When Lizzy paints pets, the images are stable. They do not move or make a noise or disappear. So, we think these animals are not considered pets because she painted them from her imagination. They do not exist anywhere but in this painting." Bingley pulled on his bottom lip and cast a fascinated look at Darcy. "At least, we do not *know* that they live anywhere else."

Darcy's frown deepened. "I do not take your meaning. How could they live elsewhere than in Miss Bennet's imagination?"

Bingley shrugged cryptically and moved on to another

work of art and wonder, and then to another, and another. Darcy's mind spun. This *talent* of Miss Bennet's went well beyond anything he had considered possible. The few examples he had seen before today did not even touch on the whole. The more he saw, the more Darcy understood Bingley's avowal that they could not predict what would happen with any of her paintings.

Another piece drew Darcy's attention. He stopped in front of a good-sized canvas and examined the image of a stone cottage, thatched, and nestled into the edge of a wood gowned in the bright leaves of spring. Cliffs towered above. Darcy had no trouble recognizing the Mendip Hills of Somerset spreading out behind the cliff. An old woman, slightly bent, dressed in black and brown like a mystic crone, stood next to a wooden, crank-type, butter churn, her hand on the crank. Nothing moved in the painting. A brass plaque, fastened to the bottom rail of the frame, displayed the title. He read it aloud.

"Mother Bernadine's Cottage."

Bingley, who had strayed ahead, came back to his side. "Yes, this is a particularly fascinating painting. Lizzy cannot recall ever meeting this woman, yet this picture came to her in a reverie following her tenth birthday."

Without looking away from the canvas, Darcy said, astounded, "Miss Bennet painted *this* when she was only *ten*?"

"No. She began painting in earnest after that, however. Lizzy finished this the summer of her fifteenth year."

Peering closely at the tableau, Darcy commented, "I cannot see any extraordinary change. The image is remarkably life-like and utterly beautiful, but how is Miss Bennet's curious talent manifested here? Is it like Bissell's painting? Does it alter only rarely?"

"Look at me for a moment," Bingley said.

Darcy straightened and focused on his friend. "What is amiss?"

Chapter Twenty-Six

"Nothing. You would think, would you not, that Mother Bernadine only churns butter?"

"Yes. Does she not?" A spark of awareness charged through him.

"Look again."

Darcy turned his attention to the painting. The churn had disappeared. Mother Bernadine, holding a broom with a crooked handle, now looked to be in the process of sweeping her stoop.

He sucked in his breath. "The seasons have changed. Summer has arrived."

"Yes," Bingley said. "The seasons change every time the viewer looks away." He pointed at the old woman. "And now she is sweeping. But, examine the edge of the thicket. What, or who, do you see there?"

Darcy spied two young women walking along a path. One had blonde hair and the other had brown hair. Their features could not be easily made out, but Darcy knew them at once.

"Your wife and Miss Bennet? Has Miss Bennet painted herself into other paintings?"

Bingley stirred and Darcy glanced at him. He was shaking his head. "Lizzy swears she did not paint herself, or Jane, into the image. When the painting changes to autumn, the girls disappear. They are only in the summer phase."

"Why is that?" Darcy wondered softly.

"We do not know." He chuckled. "Lydia was quite

annoyed. To her way of thinking, all the sisters should be in the painting."

Darcy looked back, searching for the girls once more. However, just as Bingley had said, the season had changed and the girls were gone. Golden leaves lay on the ground and the old woman—Mother Bernadine—now wore a homespun shawl wrapped around her shoulders. She held a sack from which she cast grain out to her chickens.

"Is she doing the same thing whenever each season comes around?" he asked.

"No," Bingley replied. "Everything is always different, always done outside, though. The painting never shifts to the inside of the cottage."

"I…I cannot find words to…I do not know what I am thinking. My mind is in a whirl," Darcy confessed.

"I know the feeling. One afternoon, when my Jane and Lizzy were visiting Mrs. Collins, I came in here to distract myself from my sister's importuning. Caroline had written, again, about her determination to marry a most unsuitable man—she has lived with my other sister and brother-in-law since my marriage. She was twenty-and-one and could marry without my consent but I had sworn to her that if she married the blaggard, I would not release her money to her until she turned twenty-and-five."

He took a deep breath before continuing. "She discovered his true character in time, thank the good Lord. Anyway, on the day another one of her letters arrived, I needed to be diverted from my frustration with her irrational requests.

"Oh, by-the-by, no one in *my* family knows about Lizzy' talent, either." Bingley snorted in kind disgust. "Regardless, that afternoon I spent an hour with this painting. I turned around every five minutes, examining each alteration of the image with every change of season. Never once did the altered images repeat themselves. Once, Mother Bernadine was right in the foreground, filling a quarter or more of the canvas, and she held her finger out as though she had been shaking it at me behind my back." Bingley cleared his throat before he continued. "That startled me, you may be sure. I have ever been grateful that I will never see that exact image again."

"Surely, she could not have known you were there?" Darcy demanded. He pressed his lips together and felt his jaw tighten. "What a question. How could she know? She is merely a painted figure."

Bingley chuckled. "I am not certain that *merely* describes Mother Bernadine."

Darcy blinked and raised an eyebrow.

Bingley's own eyebrow climbed as well, but his was accompanied by a mysterious smile. "Come, there is more to see before our tea is ready."

"Did looking at the painting help restore the tone of your mind?"

"Not at all," Bingley said with a laugh. "After she startled me, I quickly searched out other favorite pieces."

"And that helped?" Darcy pressed.

Bingley looked down at the floor, a smile playing over his lips. "Oh, yes. Lizzy's talent is a gift from God. I am convinced of it." He raised his gaze to meet Darcy's. "Can you not feel it?"

Darcy slowly nodded. "It is a shame that her art must be hidden away."

"Not all of it. The portraits of pets and children that she is commissioned to paint give moments of true joy to their owners."

Darcy had seen the result himself. "Yes."

∞

Lizzy raised her cup of tea and then paused with it only half-way to her lips. She had come this morning to Longbourn to distract herself from thoughts of Mr. Darcy and all she had lost by rejecting him. Even so, thoughts of him continued to intrude, as they had the entire time she had worked on the Pemberley House painting. The pleasure in his rare smiles and the sound of his voice had been such a delight.

However, something new was intruding. Something…wrong. But, what? She searched around the breakfast room, a small parlor that Charlotte had made her own personal domain, for something that might be out of place from the last time she visited.

Charlotte has been redecorating again. That must be it.

"What a lovely new carpet," Lizzy said, smiling. "I never liked the old one. Charlotte, this green one is charming. Where did you find it?"

Charlotte flushed pink with pleasure. "I hoped you would like it. It comes from Moorfield. Not one of Thomas Moore's, of course, or else we could never have afforded it. I chose it because of how cheerful I felt when I saw it. We went to London while you were both away."

"You have made cushions to match, and new curtains," Jane observed. "I hardly recognise the room from when we used to sit here in the mornings. Do you remember, Lizzy?"

"I do, indeed." Lizzy took a sip of her tea.

"How is our cousin?" Jane asked.

"He is very well, thank you, and keeps himself busy in the gardens and with the home farm. There is much more to do here than at the Hunsford parsonage. For both of us. Yet, I remember it fondly as being my first home as a married woman." She made a comical face. "What I do not miss is Lady Catherine's interference in our lives. She continues to write, you know."

They chuckled.

"I am looking forward to the time when we own our own home. Charles has begun to talk of searching for a small estate in Derbyshire," Jane revealed.

"Derbyshire!" Charlotte exclaimed. "So far away?"

"Nothing has been decided, yet," Jane promised. "We met some new friends who live there. The Darcys. Charles is excessively pleased with them. As am I. If we must move, I would like to know someone in our new neighborhood. However, there are many factors to consider. It is exceedingly far from London and Hertfordshire where all our family and friends live. Of course, you and our cousin will be invited to stay wherever we finally choose."

How will I bear to live so close to Pemberley and Mr. Darcy?

Lizzy subdued that thought and caught the swift, concerned look her sister sent her way. *She is worried about me.* A movement outside of the window drew her attention away from Jane's troubled regard.

A huge raven, of all things, black and glossy, hopped across the shorn grass. It cawed and Lizzy again experienced that quiver of awareness that something was not quite right. She could not dismiss it as the irrational superstition wrapped up in the viewing of this harbinger, though, for the feeling was so strong this time that it shoved her painful thoughts of Mr. Darcy out of her head.

She frowned and looked at Charlotte and Jane.

"Is aught amiss?" Charlotte asked, her pleasant features drawn with lines of concern.

"Lizzy?" Jane asked, tipping her head to one side. "What is it?"

"I have a feeling," Lizzy confessed. She took a sip of her tea in the hope that it would calm her nerves.

"What sort of feeling?" Charlotte asked, leaning forward in her chair. "Lizzy, you are not given to having odd *feelings*. Well, there was that time when you had a feeling about your parents." She paused and then added, "And, you have had peculiar feelings in regards to your art."

"*My art*," Lizzy whispered, her eyes widening. She stood up abruptly and handed her cup and saucer to Charlotte. "Jane, we must go."

"Now?" Charlotte asked, also rising. "You have only just arrived. Pray, stay."

"I cannot," Lizzy said, picking up her reticule. "I think someone is in my gallery. Someone other than Charles. What if Caroline has come for an unexpected visit and found a way inside the gallery? You know she has always been suspicious of my painting."

Jane rose. "In truth, Lizzy, she believes your talent only extends to children and animals. I am afraid that if she does want to know what is in the gallery, it is because she wishes to prove her point." Jane took a breath. "Oh, dear. I should not have said that," she said with a grimace. "It was not kind." Smiling again, she said, "Dear Charlotte, we will come again tomorrow, if we may?"

"Oh, yes. Please do." Still carrying the cup and saucer, Charlotte hastened to the door. "I will call for your carriage."

Lizzy hurried after her, almost careening into Mr. Collins, who now held the travelling cup and saucer, in the passageway. "I beg your pardon, Cousin," she said, dropping a hasty curtsy and rushing way, unwilling to become tangled in conversation with him.

"What is the matter?" he demanded of Jane. "Your sister is as white as a sheet. Did she see a mouse?"

"My sister is not afraid of mice, Cousin," Jane said, nodding and hurrying out the front door after her sister.

Upon their arrival at Netherfield, both sisters climbed the stairs with unseemly haste. Renquist called after them.

"Mr. Bingley is on the second floor, madam."

Jane and Lizzy paused on the landing. Lizzy called down to the butler.

"Is Miss Bingley come?"

"No, miss."

"Is someone else with him?"

"Yes, miss. A Mr. Darcy."

Lizzy froze. *Mr. Darcy.*

Jane took her arm. "Thank you, Renquist."

"Madam."

"Come, dearest," Jane said, forcing Lizzy to climb the stairs once more.

In a shocked whisper, Lizzy said, "Jane, what is *he* doing here? Did Charles invite him? Is Charles and Mr. Darcy in my gallery?"

"We shall soon see," Jane said in a soothing voice. "I have my key here in my reticule, as you know."

"As do I," Lizzy said. She nodded and increased her speed until she was pulling her sister along with her, urging, "Hurry,

Jane. Hurry."

Once they reached the second floor, they ran down the candlelit family gallery until they reached the door to her private gallery. They stood there for a little time, catching their breaths.

"I want to go in quietly," Lizzy said in a whisper, holding her hand out for the key Jane had fished out of her reticule. "I want to surprise them."

"You want to eavesdrop," Jane accused, narrowing her eyes. "Oh, I see. You want to discover what Mr. Darcy truly thinks about your paintings."

"Yes." She looked beseechingly at Jane. "Am I a fool? Should I charge in there, full of outrage?"

Jane observed her closely in the candlelight. "You do not look as if you are full of outrage. How do you feel?"

Lizzy thought about the emotions rushing through her. "So many things. Fear, surprise, hope, anxiety, and…and love. Shame, too, because I let prejudice color my opinion of him. And pride, too. Foolish pride. Oh, heavens, what if he hates them? What if—"

"Enough of *what ifs.* Let us go in quietly and discover Mr. Darcy's true opinion."

Lizzy gave a single nod. The hand she held out to the lock, however, was shaking too violently to be useful. She thrust the key back at Jane. "You do it."

Jane silently took the key and just as quietly let them into the private gallery. They tiptoed down the corridors between the display walls and only stopped when they could hear the men talking.

∞

Darcy and Bingley, by the windows now, stood looking at a still life where the pink roses and purple clematis were dying, drooping toward the table top, some of the leaves already dried and shrivelled as though no one had thought to change the water to keep the bouquet fresh.

"Ah," Bingley said with a sigh. "If you come back in another day or two, the flowers will have refreshed themselves."

"I do not catch your meaning," Darcy said. He leaned over and read the label on the frame. "The Phoenix Flowers." Recalling his mythology lessons, he said, "Do you mean to say that the flowers will die and be reborn, like a phoenix?"

"There, you have it," Bingley said in a cheerful, hearty voice. "I love this painting. It fills me with hope. No matter how final things seem to be, something beautiful can be recovered from the ashes," he explained. "Once all the petals, leaves, and vines are dry, they crumble to dust for a few hours and then back they come to life—if you can call it life, since the flowers are cut ones."

"And since they are painted," Darcy added dryly.

Bingley chuckled. "This is the first painting Jane and Lizzy showed me. I was dumbfounded, you may be sure. I viewed the painting in the morning, and I wondered, silently, why anyone would paint a dead flower arrangement. The detail was amazing, but not at all pleasant. They laid the painting, face-down, on a table and we played backgammon for an hour. No one entered the room and the painting was in clear sight the entire time.

"After the hour was up, Lizzy and Jane picked up the painting again. The dead flowers were gone. Now, the bowl was surrounded by piles of crumbled petals and leaves. Even the s talks were gone." Bingley shook his head and folded his arms. "I was thankful that I was already seated. They laid the painting down again and then explained about Lizzy's curious talent. Regardless of the evidence of my own eyes, I could hardly believe that such a talent existed." He perched on a window ledge. "Lizzy had moved in only the day before and she had brought crates and crates of her art. Both she and Jane were adamant that her art be out of Longbourn before Mr. Collins, their cousin, arrived to take possession of their home—he also does not know about Lizzy's unusual talent. I seem to be adding more and more to the list of those who are not permitted in this room."

"As their cousin, surely he had seen her work before?"

Darcy asked.

Bingley shook his head. "There had been an estrangement between the two halves of the family. Besides, Jane told me that every time one of Lizzy's paintings behaved oddly, Mrs. Bennet ordered them taken to the attic."

"I see. That could not have been easy on Miss Bennet," Darcy observed.

"I expect not. I am sorry for that. Mrs. Collins knows, though. She comes often to Netherfield to view any new works." Bingley scraped his hand over his face. "You know, Darcy, I had no quarrel with the volume of work Lizzy brought, for there is plenty of room here." He continued in a quieter, more somber voice. "The thing is, you see, I thought I would be hanging her work around the place. The paintings and sketches I had already seen were astonishingly lifelike and beautiful beyond description." Bingley sadly shook his head. "I did not realize that we would be hiding almost every piece away."

"We shall do the same at Pemberley House," Darcy promised, nodding decisively. "I have more than enough room for a dozen galleries. It shall be a private collection. Miss Bennet cannot be found out."

Bingley's mood picked up. He stood straight again and grinned. "I shall miss seeing them any time I wish to, of course, but if we find an estate in Derbyshire, we shall be over often."

"If she accepts me," Darcy qualified, frowning. The wonder of her art had distracted him from his main purpose in coming into Hertfordshire.

"She is only afraid," Bingley assured him.

"I will do my best to reassure her."

"Will you?" a feminine voice asked.

Lizzy blinked when Mr. Darcy and Charles swung around to face her.

Charles, his eyes wide with guilt, blurted out, "You are early. I thought you would be some time yet."

"Come away, dearest," Jane said to her husband.

He looked from his wife to Lizzy, guilt giving way to pleading. "I only meant to—"

"I think you have done enough, husband," Jane told him gently, joining him in front of the windows. "Let us leave them alone to discuss their future without our interference."

"Yes, dear."

Charles and Jane hurried off, wending their way through the maze of display walls. Lizzy and Mr. Darcy looked at each other, waiting for the sound of the closing door.

Before Lizzy could ask him what he was doing here, Mr. Darcy took a rolled-up paper from his pocket and held it out to her.

"Pray forgive me for taking your sketch of Georgiana and myself. I should not have done so." He added solemnly, "And, you look beautiful."

Lizzy felt even more color enter her cheeks. "What a thing to say, Mr. Darcy," she said in a scolding voice and taking the sketch. She did not open it. "I wondered if you had taken it. Thank you for returning it. But, here you are, in Hertfordshire, in my *private* gallery, where you do not belong, and, instead of apologizing for invading my home, you hand out empty compliments tacked onto the end of an apology for taking one of my sketches."

"I do not hand out empty compliments."

His deep voice reached into her chest and massaged her heart. She could not think what to say.

"You are beautiful to me," he said earnestly "Every part of you. Your mind. Your heart. Your person. Your character. And your art."

Lizzy swallowed hard. "My art?" She narrowed her eyes, "Do you not mean *even* my art? It is part of me. I will never, ever abandon it."

"I did not say *even* and I did not secretly mean *even*, either. That is your fear, is it not? You worry that I cannot love your talent even if I love you?"

Lizzy's heartbeat skipped. "Even *if*?" she asked boldly.

"Only *if*?"

Mr. Darcy cursed under his breath, took the two steps between them, and tugged her into his arms. She promptly forgot about the stolen sketch and dropped it to the floor.

"Even *though,*" he whispered hoarsely, just before his lips descended and captured hers.

Lizzy tried to gasp, but could not inhale air through her mouth. Instead, she breathed deeply through her nose while her senses scattered. No man had ever kissed her on the lips before. Mr. Darcy, her solitary serious suitor, had always treated her with respect and care. This passion, for what else could she call it, caught her by surprise. She liked it.

She tentatively moved her lips beneath his questing ones. He released her shoulders and held her with only his lips, making it possible for her to move away if she wanted. She did not want to move because his fingertips were caressing her cheeks in a highly inappropriate way and she liked that, too.

Mr. Darcy turned his head slightly to one side, breaking his hold on her so he could whisper, "Do you love me, Miss Bennet?"

"I…I…"

"And will you promise to marry me so that I might call you Lizzy, like your family does?"

Lizzy could hardly get a breath. His warm cheek pressed against her forehead and his strong and tender fingers had strayed to her nape, causing her to shiver. *What should I say? What will I say?*

She managed to whisper something. "But…do you…"

"I do. I do love you." He caught hold of her hands and pressed her palms to his lips, one at a time. He held them against his chest and she felt his racing heart beneath her palms. "Pray forgive me for making such a mull of my proposal at Pemberley. I have no excuse, except to admit that my pride kept me from revealing my feelings before you had admitted yours."

"Foolish pride," she murmured.

He chuckled and it sounded breathless to her. That quality

showed her he was not as confident as he seemed. She thought he had waited long enough.

"I do love you, Mr. Fitzwilliam Darcy," she admitted. He instantly pulled her into another hug, one strong enough to squeeze the air right out of her lungs. "I cannot breathe," she complained, hitting him on the shoulder.

Mr. Darcy eased off, laughing. Then he asked, "And may I call you Lizzy now?"

Lizzy leaned away, steadying herself by holding onto his shoulders. His expression was filled with wonder. He was so handsome in that moment that she could have cried. Her voice came out rough when she answered. "Would you mind calling me Elizabeth? No one calls me that. No one."

"Then I shall," he promised. He smoothed a stray curl back from her face. "What would you like to call me? My family calls me Fitzwilliam, as you know, but you may call me Darcy, if you wish."

Feeling suddenly extra shy, Lizzy ducked her head and asked, "May I call you darling? Does anyone else call you that?"

He raised her chin. "No one calls me that. I would be honored if you chose to call me that."

Lizzy hesitantly reached up and pressed her palm to his cheek. "But not, I think, until after we are married."

"I expect that would be best," he said softly. "And what will you call me when you are in company?"

Lizzy laughed, riding a surge of happiness. "Why, Mr. Darcy, of course!"

"I should have known." They separated and he clasped her hand, kissed it, and then released it. "Let us go down and tell Bingley and your sister. First, though, we need to close these shutters to protect your art."

Lizzy recognised in that minute that the love she had felt for him only a few seconds before had increased ten-fold. Why? Because she knew that the love he professed for her included acceptance as well.

"I have a painting for you," she told him, watching him

unfold the shutters. She stooped and picked up the fallen sketch. Opening it revealed her darling Mr. Darcy with a smile on his face that displayed all the joy of this moment. Tears pricked at the corner of her eyes. She blinked them away and rerolled the sketch.

"Do you?" Mr. Darcy asked.

"Oh, yes. A new one."

"And what is curious about it?"

"Let us see if you can guess," she said, smiling secretively.

"I cannot wait."

Epilogue

Pemberley House…ten months later…

Darcy found his wife in her studio, which they had moved out of the ballroom to another part of the house. The smell of oil paints permeated the space and he had come to associate the aroma with his wife, and so he loved it. She stood behind a huge canvas. He would always treasure the nighttime image she had given him before, but only oils could give them the lasting masterpiece he sought. There was the possibility that they would never be able to show the painting to anyone, though. Still, he could not wait to see the results of her efforts.

"Elizabeth, you have not started dressing," he accused, a laugh in his voice. "The wedding is in an hour and Georgiana is ready to go. I have never known her to be so punctual before an event."

She waved a hand in the air, a paintbrush at one end so he could see her. The paintbrush disappeared. "Just one more…yes…and another…and…there! I am finished."

Darcy's heart skipped in anticipation. "May I see it?"

"Come and look," she said, poking her head around the side of the canvas. "Or do you want to wait for Jane and Charles?"

"No more waiting," Darcy said firmly. "It has been weeks. I am claiming husband's prerogative."

Elizabeth laughed and he chuckled. He did not think he had ever laughed so much before his marriage to this dear woman. How he loved his wife.

Darcy joined her, keeping carefully away from her painting smock and paraphernalia. *He* had already dressed.

The painting, as he had thought, was magnificent. “Another evening ball?” he asked, frowning in surprise. “I thought it would be day.”

“Funny. That is what Charles said about the watercolor,” Elizabeth said, grinning. “I do not always know where a painting will take me. For some reason, Pemberley seems to like being painted at night.”

“Even the torches are the same.” Darcy leaned carefully closer and blew at the painted flames. Startled, he stood straight and exclaimed, “they do not flicker!”

“Nothing is ever the same, remember?” his wife asked. She moved away from him and stripped off her coveralls, revealing the dress she had chosen for the wedding. “As you see, I am already dressed for the wedding. I noticed something in the painting just after I finished the last stroke.”

“What?” Darcy asked, looking back at the painting. Then, he saw it. “Are the dancers moving inside the ballroom? They are! Hah!”

“You are very excited about this curiosity,” Elizabeth said, grinning.

“I am delighted by it. Hmm. We will need to hang this very high on the wall in the Great Hall. I do not think anyone will notice the dancers’ movements from the floor.”

“Do you still want to hang it in the Great Hall?”

“Of course,” he said, tearing his gaze away from the painting so he could smile at his wife. “Are you truly surprised?”

“No,” Lizzy said, smiling. “Darling, you had best get to the church with Mr. Kearn. Last time I saw him he looked about to faint.”

She raised her lips for a kiss. He kissed her, caressed her cheek, and said, “I love you. *And* the painting.”

“I love you, too, my darling. Now, go,” Lizzy said,

laughing. "Georgiana and I will be along shortly."

Once her husband had left, Lizzy covered the painting, cleaned her hands carefully, and left the studio, locking it behind her. Georgiana had not waited in her bedchamber. Instead, Lizzy found her walking beside the lake, the morning sun shining down on her pale seafoam silk dress, trimmed in white lace.

"Are you ready?" Lizzy asked, taking her arm. "Dear Georgiana, you look absolutely fabulous."

"I am so excited, Lizzy," Georgiana cried, her eyes sparkling. "Are Jane and Mr. Bingley bringing little William with them? I do so hope they will."

"William is only three months old. He will need to stay with his wet nurse."

"I am so thankful they have moved close to us. Their estate near Chesterfield is charming."

"Yes, indeed."

The two ladies silently stared at the swans gliding on the lake, their gray cygnets trailing behind them. Georgiana spoke first.

"Lizzy? Is being married to my brother as wonderful as you thought it would be?"

Lizzy squeezed her arm, understanding her secret question. "Your marriage to Mr. Kearn will be perfect, dearest. And, to answer your question…" She paused and blinked away sudden tears. Beaming, she whispered, "Oh, yes."

The End.

www.ingramcontent.com/pod-product-compliance
Lightning Source LLC
Chambersburg PA
CBHW070916260626
47162CB00007B/2686

* 9 7 8 1 9 2 6 4 6 7 2 5 2 *